Falling For Rome

Rome and Nakhti's Tale

Edwina Fort

Author Edwina Fort
P.O. Box 346
Keithville, LA 1047
www.authoredwinafort.com

Publisher's Note: This is a work of fiction. Names, characters, places, and incidents are a product of the author's imagination. Locales and public names are sometimes used for atmospheric purposes. Any resemblance to actual people, living or dead, or to businesses, companies, events, institutions, or locales is completely coincidental.

Falling For Rome/Edwina Fort. – 1ˢᵗ edition

ISBN

Works by Author

The Redemption Series
1. Redemption
2. Redemption : Earth's Cry

The Law Boys Series
1. Coming For What's Mine
2. Coming For What's Mine 2

The Law Boys Spin-off Series
Hitta's Tea Maker

Acknowledgements

As always, I'd like to thank the Heavenly Father for allowing me to be his vessel yet again. I'd also like to thank my family, my team, and my fans. Without y'all none of this would be possible. If these stories touch you in anyway, please pay it forward and try and make somebody's day. You'll be amazed at how far a simple smile can go, it could be just the thing to chase away a terrible woe. Something as simple as holding the door can make one feel as if they can bear it a little more...

Naw, I ain't never been much of a poet and expect by now that you all know it...LOL!

But seriously, the world is getting colder, y'all... we have to do all we can to shine as much love in it as we can... and that's real!

Peace

There is one who scatters, yet increases more. And one who withholds more than is right, But it comes to poverty. The generous being is enriched, And he who waters is also watered himself.

--Proverbs 11:24-25

Table of Contents

Chapter 1

Beautiful Surprise

Nakhti

I put the car in park and checked my GPS. This couldn't be the right address. The big grey building looked as if it had been one of those old industrial warehouses before it was turned into an apartment building. Several men and boys stood outside the building at the door, some looked like they were dealing and some looked like they were hanging out with the dealers. I raised my eyebrow at a group of young girls in short skirts and shorts that walked by laughing and posing trying to catch the eye of one of the men.

"Oh hell no." Reaching in my bag I took out my phone and pressed one.

"What's up, Nak?" The deep masculine voice came from the other end.

"What the hell, Jo? I'm in the hood." He chuckled.

"Yeah, I know. Did I forget to mention that?" I sat back in my seat leaning my head back against the head rest. I was too damn tired for this.

"Nak?"

I exhaled. "I'm here."

"Come on, darling, don't give me the silent treatment. It's not that bad. I just need you to find out what information he has about me and my family, and then erase it. I don't give a damn if you have to wipe his whole system clean. Somebody has been digging real deep and my gut is telling me it's him. We are at re-election time and we can't afford any slipups. This guy is buried in mystery, I need to know what he knows before he knows what he knows." I rolled my eyes.

"So, how am I supposed to get in there? This place is a fortress. Can you get me the blue prints to the building?"

"Already in your mailbox." Silence came from the other end for just a moment. "I wouldn't have asked you to do this on such short notice if it wasn't important. I know I pulled you from another assignment and you've had no recovery time. It's just that whatever system he's working with is impenetrable from the outside. I've had the best hackers on the agency's payroll trying to crack it. It's impossible. The only way in is through the front door." I exhaled, in no mood to put up with some ignorant thug, gangsta, wannabe playa.

"And you're sure this isn't a job that Miller or Terry could handle?"

"Neither Miller or Terry will be able to get through those doors. I need the best on this one. I told you he laid out Michaels and Baker. And get this… he was handcuffed at the time. Had I not come out the room when I did, he would have snapped Tom's neck. There's not a man around that can resist that pretty, innocent face of yours. It causes them to let down their guard and then like a black widow, you strike, which makes you perfect for this job. Just look at it this way, you get in, you get out. You'll be home wherever that is, in no time."

"So, if things get out of hand with this civilian, can I kill him?"

"You have no idea how much I want to say yes to that. But alas, he's my lady's brother and she loves him. She'll be crushed if anything happens to him and I can't stand seeing her hurt. But hey, the quicker you gather my information, the quicker you can be done with it."

I grunted, eyeing the man that was approaching my car with a spray bottle and a windshield squeegee that looked as if he'd *borrowed* it from the nearest gas station. Reaching in my briefcase, I pulled out a five-dollar bill before letting my window down.

"Wash your windows for you, beautiful lady?" He asked smiling, showing off his rotting teeth. The smell of alcohol and unwashed flesh singed my nose.

"I'll give you five dollars if you *don't*." He grinned as I handed him the money.

"Generous as well as beautiful. Have a blessed day." I rolled my window back up.

"Fine, but this is my last assignment," I said into the receiver. "I'm too old for this sh*t. I'm retiring." He chuckled again.

"Get out of here, you can't retire at thirty-four. I need you to have my back. I'll feel naked without you."

Dammit, Jo… he knew he had my loyalty for life. He knew that there was nothing I wouldn't do for him. The man had saved my life on more than one occasion. He and I went way back to the days of being two green eared Seaman recruits. All the way up through becoming the only two minorities in our SEAL unit.

It wasn't easy and several times I wanted to quit, but Jo never let me. He pushed me until I became the soldier that my father never was. My father who left home because I was just a stupid girl and not the boy he wanted, had tried several times to become a SEAL but could never make it through BUD school. Not only did I make it through, I became a decorated soldier in my own right.

When Jo left the military for the Bureau, he took me with him. Again, pushing me to be more than I thought I could. Yes, I was loyal to him unquestionably, but I was tired and he needed to know that.

"I can and I will. I'm thirty-four, but I feel sixty-four. You remember what happened last month in Libya?"

"Yeah."

"I still hear ringing in my ear from that sh*t. I don't think I will ever get my hearing back on my right side."

"You got too close to the fireworks."

"It's just the way it played out. Anyway, I said all that to say I quit after this, Jo, I'm serious. The agency already fired me, why won't you just leave me the hell alone?" He chuckled, the charming bastard.

"Because you're the best man I got in the field. I won't be able to run for office unless I know you have my back." He repeated for the second time, knowing what those words did to me. I bit down on my teeth determined to stand my ground.

"Yeah well, I'm done after this."

"Nak, on a serious note…" he said, brushing off my words.

Sh*t!

"Be careful with this one. I took this kid for granted and he surprised the hell out of me. He's smarter than you can imagine. He doesn't look it, but he is. And he's dangerous. My sources tell me he's responsible for many a stiff found floating belly up in Lake Michigan. You're on his turf, everybody within twenty city miles either way is loyal to him till the death. Keep your eyes open, and whatever you do, don't take this kid lightly."

I eyeballed the hustlers standing outside of the building and farther down on the corner. It was nothing about them that appeared spectacular, just your everyday average thugs. However, Jo was the most skilled soldier I knew, so if he told me not to let down my guard, then I won't.

"Roger that." Hanging up the phone I slid it back in my briefcase.

For just a moment, I sat enjoying the silence of my rental car. I had no time to rest from my last assignment for Jo, well, for his father really. The mission like most of my missions called for me to get close to a man and then kill him.

Pablo Consuela, an Argentinian drug lord had thought to blackmail the senator with some compromising photos to try and get him to vote to pass some legislation that would make it easier for him to move his product in The Gulf. I didn't know all the details, it wasn't my job to. My job was to retrieve the photos and erase them from any hard drive they may be on, and then put old Pablo out of his misery.

A job I had done flawlessly until I got too messy making my escape and ended up with a bullet wound in my side. I shook my head, this was just another sign signaling that it was time for me to walk away from this life. Jo didn't believe me, but I was going to show him, this was my last mission. When it was over and I was paid, I was ghost. I was disappearing in a way that even *he* couldn't find me.

I was going back home.

Nobody knew where my home was because I barely knew where it was. The only thing or shall I say the only person holding me there was my mom. I put her in the nursing home ten years ago under an alias. And the only way for the nursing home to contact me was through a message service that I checked from time to time, waiting for the call saying she's dead.

But I have yet to get it, so I guess she's still alive.

Maybe she was just waiting on me. Waiting to look me in the eye one more time and blame me for being the reason daddy left. Waiting to hit me one more time for not being the boy my father wanted more than he wanted either of us. Waiting to let me know just how much she hated me before she took her last breath.

After this job, she'll get her chance if she wasn't dead. Exhaling I pushed those thoughts from my mind. Those are the kinds of thoughts that can get you killed on a mission. Those were the thoughts I was thinking when the bullet penetrated my flesh the day before yesterday.

I reached in my suitcase for a pair of eyeglasses that would complete the look I was going for and slid them on my face. Then I popped two pain pills in my mouth because my side was killing me. I hadn't even had time to get it looked at. I had to remove the bullet and stitch it up myself, before lathering it with a tube of Neosporin, and slapping a damn bandage over it.

Perks of the job...

When I was prepared, I stepped out the rental car and after locking it, headed toward the building.

"Daaaammmmnnn!" Several of the men said as I approached, looking at me as if they had never seen a pretty woman in a two-piece fitted skirt suit carrying a briefcase.

Men...

Jo was right. For as long as I could remember, men have fallen over themselves for my face that *did* look very innocent, only to end up with their noses broken for thinking I could be taken advantage of. My face was one of the reasons the agency had hired me in the first place. They knew with my innocent looks, I would be able to slip under most people's radar.

"She look like a sexy school teacher. Hey yo, P, yo' teacher here, man!" One of the men that was holding a red cup in his hand said chuckling at his own joke. Judging by the redness of his eyes he wasn't drinking juice. I lifted my eyebrow at him checking my watch. Damn, it wasn't even ten o'clock. The smell of marijuana was also very strong in the air.

"Man, if she was my teacher, I would have stayed in school." A young guy, who I assume was *P* responded. He looked to be around fifteen or sixteen. I kept walking as if I didn't hear them. Blocking the door with both of his hands on the frame was another young man who could be no more that twenty-one or twenty- two.

He wasn't a bad looking guy. As I approached him, he passed the blunt he was smoking to another man that was much older than him sitting on the stoop. He slowly blew out the smoke as he took me in. When it was clear he wasn't going to move I stopped, but I bit down on my teeth to hold on to my temper.

Okay, so let me tell you guys why I got fired from the agency. Yes, I have an innocent face that most men consider beautiful and I look soft and approachable. Jo once described me as the girl next door. That being said…I don't have the constitution to match my looks.

I'm not friendly or soft and I could give a damn about beauty. I have a short fuse and I'm easily irritated. I may have used lethal force a time or two when pushed the wrong way. And I may have used excessive force when one of my directors thought it was alright to grab me and try to force me to kiss him one night while we were all at a bar celebrating the promotion of one of our colleagues. I was aware he was drunk, but it did little to assuage my irritation at his action.

I smashed his face into the bar, breaking it. Anyway, the agency said their hands were tied; I had too many complaints on my record to continue.

I told you guys that story to try and get you to understand what I was going through standing here in front of this civilian, allowing him to get away with his actions.

"How can I help you, sweetheart?" he asked.

"Is your name Romeo Reevers?" For a moment a look of surprise crossed his face before he shared glances with a few of the other men. Now that I had mentioned that name, none of them were smiling anymore. The air got really tense. Even the men farther down on the block had come to attention.

Jo had been right. Whoever this Romeo was, they were very loyal to him.

"Who's asking?"

"Brenda Bonita." The lie slid easily from my lips. I had studied Romeo's file on the plane ride home. What this situation called for was a case worker.

"That's all I'm at liberty to discuss with you unless your name is Romeo Reevers." I continued.

He chuckled. "You the law?"

I reached up and pushed the curly strands of hair that hung by my ear behind it, an act that made me appear soft.

"Excuse me?"

"Police," he said losing patience with me. "Are you the police?" I softened my eyes.

"Oh no! Nothing like that." He looked at me for a minute to determine if I was telling the truth. I blinked slowly, allowing my long lashes to sweep across my doe shaped eyes.

"Aight, follow me."

"Yo Rob, what you doing man?" The older guy that had joked about me being *P*'s teacher said as he lifted the blunt to his lips.

"Relax, Han. She cool." I looked back at the other men and they all wore a look of astonishment that he was taking me inside the building. As I followed him through the halls that were surprisingly very clean, he kept stealing glances at me.

"You look like some kind a case worker," he said, still fishing for my identity. I smiled at him. I liked the kid.

"Something like that," I told him.

He nodded. "Jo sent you, didn't he? To keep an eye on Rome?" I chuckled surprised by how astute he was.

"Something like that."

There were several children playing in the hall outside one of the apartments on the first floor. It looked as if the building had four levels. I could hear loud rap music playing from another apartment. We walked through a door that led to some stairs.

"I hope you don't mind taking the stairs. The elevator is broken and Rome's place is all the way up on the top floor." I smiled at him, yeah, I liked this kid.

"I don't mind."

When we got to the fourth level, there was a keypad on this door that wasn't on the others. Standing directly in front of it he keyed in a four-number code.

7,9,5,6…Got it.

I noted the fact that the fourth level was not open to the rest of the building. There seemed to be very little activity on this level. In fact, once we walked out of the stairwell, the door locked automatically when it closed behind us; there seemed to be only one other door that I could see. On this door was another keypad, he quickly keyed in the code.

3,2,9,7…Got it.

My eyes widened behind my glasses as we walked through the door. It was a loft, a very spacious loft, a nice very spacious loft. For the third time in a matter of minutes I was pleasantly surprised. The tall floor-to-ceiling windows ran along the east side of the loft, they looked to be at least twenty feet tall. They were also covered by beautiful golden drapes.

The loft itself had to run along the entire length of the building because like I said, it was roomy. One could play a game of futebol in its open space or what you Americans call soccer. There wasn't a lot of furniture, it didn't look as if Rome invested in that.

However, I now understood why I had been assigned this mission. I am an AIT specialist trained at Fort George to be able to handle missions were IT initial was needed. Along the entire length of the north wall was a state-of-the-art computer system. Secured to the lovely rust colored brick wall had to be at least twenty flat screened monitors. Although they were turned off, one couldn't help but wonder what appeared on them when they were turned on. In front of the elaborate system was a single plush leather chair on wheels.

It was a chair for a king.

A king whose throne was in front of several very impressive computer screens.

One thing was for certain, this beauty was something you wouldn't *ever* expect to find in the heart of the ghetto. My fingers twitched in anticipation of finding out what was stored on that massive hard drive. He spared no expense for it. There were million-dollar corporations that could not afford one such as it.

My guess was the owner of that beautiful system was lying in the bed that wasn't too far from it. Rob walked to a wall and hit a button, opening the curtains that were closer to the bed just a little. However, it was enough to shine a burst of sunlight into the loft. I came to a stop in front of the bed looking down at the occupants.

The man that I would assume was Rome lay sleeping on his stomach, my eyes traveled over his muscled back to the equally muscled arm that hung out the bed. He had on a pair of black jeans and expensive gym shoes. Asleep next to him completely naked was a very voluptuous young lady. Only the lower half of her body was covered with the sheet.

Rob wore a goofy smile on his face as he too stood looking down at the two. I could tell right off this kid was a rascal. His aim was to shock me with this. I looked at him and lifted an eyebrow, poor baby, it would take more than this to shock me.

"Yo Rome, you got a guest," he said hitting the man's shoe

"Beat it, chump," the sleeping giant grumbled turning over in the bed without opening his eyes. Rob chuckled hitting his shoe again.

"Get up, nigga."

"What I tell you about using that word?" Rome mumbled without opening his eyes. He had a very deep voice. The younger man didn't respond, instead he looked up at me with that devious grin still on his face. He nodded in a way to tell me to watch this.

Rome opened his eyes and turned to look at him, sitting up slightly. "You deaf, punk?! What I tell—" his words stalled as his light brown gaze came to rest on me.

Although I didn't show it, for the fourth time since coming to this place, I was completely taken off guard.

Rome was gorgeous.

He looked at me through a pair of amber eyes that missed nothing. He'd just woke up from a deep sleep and judging by the empty Hennessy bottles and cups, it had been a drunken sleep, yet his eyes were sharp. They took me in making me feel as if he was reading me like an open book. I shifted on my feet feeling uncomfortable with that. No one has ever looked at me that closely.

He ran his hand over his head. It looked as if he was fresh from the barber, his fade, beard and mustache was lined perfectly around a pair of lips that looked like they would work havoc on a woman's body.

Nossa, Nak! Where did your mind just go?

"What the f***, Rob?!" he growled. The grin on Rob's face grew wider as he blinked his eyes innocently.

"Bruh, you got a guest," he said gesturing towards me. Now that he mentioned it, I could see the resemblances between the two. Only difference being was that Rome was clearly older with more facial hair and his eyes were a lighter shade of brown than Rob's. He pointed at his little brother in a way that told him he will deal with him later.

"Hey," he said tapping the shoulder of the sleeping girl. She came awake with a smile on her face.

"Hey, daddy," she purred. I rolled my eyes, Rob chuckled.

"Get up, you gotta bounce," he told her. And for the first time she looked and saw us. With a squeak she snatched the sheet up to cover her breasts.

"Can you give us a minute?" Rome asked me, gesturing toward the other end of the loft where a living room area was. I lifted an eyebrow at his rude tone.

"Sure." I told him before turning to walk towards the sitting area.

As I did, I casually lifted my hand and slipped the bug from my watch, positioning it just right between my fingers. I used the same hand to ease down in the brown leather chair, securing the bug at the same time.

To the left of the chair I sat in was a huge brown leather couch, or what looked like a couch, but was really a modern rendition of a couch. It screamed contemporary bachelor pad. As if to confirm that, a ridiculously large flat screen TV was mounted to the brick wall to my right. In front of it on the floor were several gaming systems. There were quite a few game controllers sprawled on the floor around them.

When I looked back towards the sleeping area, it was to see Rome's amber gaze still on me. He was now sitting at the foot of the bed with his elbows resting against his knees. If I was the blushing type, I would be doing it right now seeing that he had watched me walk this whole distance. Finally, he turned to look up at his brother.

"Why you didn't take her downstairs to ma's place? Why the hell you bring her up here?" Rob, who had watched the whole exchange with that goofy grin on his face now wore a look of fake shock.

"Ma not home."

"Stop lying?!" Rome growled up at him, his face transformed in his anger.

Rob chuckled, not fazed a bit in only a way that a little brother could. "My bad, man. I just didn't think about it."

"You play too much," his brother responded standing up grabbing his t-shirt at the same time. When he brought it over his head, his muscled arms and chest flexed impressively. He was very tall as well.

"That's your damn problem," he continued admonishing his kid brother before he turned and noticed that the girl had not moved from the bed, she was in fact playing like she had just drifted back to sleep.

"Ay... Ay, shawty, you got to bounce. Get your sh*t," he called down to her. Amazingly she woke up and stretched, letting the cover fall from her ample breasts once again. Rob grinned shaking his head.

"Rome, you gon' call me?" she asked as she unashamedly slid out the bed reaching down to retrieve her dress from the floor.

I shook my head, women like her gave our whole species a bad name. If a man had talked to me the way he'd just talked to her, the only call I would be worried about is the anonymous one to the city morgue, telling them where to find his body.

"Rob, make sure Kiesha get to her car safe—"

"Toya!" she interrupted him, finally insulted. Rome chuckled as he scratched his head walking towards the bathroom.

"Who the f*** cares?" was his only response as he went into his bathroom shutting the door behind him.

"Okay, you can call me Kiesha, just call me...Please!"

"Come on, shawty. I'll walk you downstairs," Rob told her as she angrily slid her feet in her heels.

"It was nice meeting you, Brenda," he called to me as they headed toward the door.

"Nice meeting you too, Rob." It really was. I don't know why he chose to make my job easier, but he had. Had he not brought me up here, there was no way I would have gotten through that group at the door.

And had I by some miracle gotten through them, I would have never made it past the locked door on the steps.

Well... Not this easily anyway.

Rome took his time in the bathroom, I heard the shower start. I was not delusional to think it wasn't a test when it really was. Jo was right. This man was smart. He was trying to feel me out before talking to me. I was careful where I let my gaze roam. Although I couldn't see them, I was quite certain this whole building was wired with cameras.

Slowly, I got up and walked to the nearest window. The drapes were opened slightly, allowing a perfect view of the ghetto below. My eyes narrowed at the roof of the building across the street, there was a man standing on it leaning against the door smoking a cigarette. When he caught me looking at him, he winked.

My gaze went to the corner store at the end of the block, several men stood outside talking, but when one of them noticed me looking, he winked.

What the hell?

I looked towards the opposite corner, there was a man sitting on the porch of a building there, it looked as if he was smoking a blunt. When he noticed that I saw him, he winked.

"What are you looking for?" Rome's deep voice came from behind me causing me to nearly jump out of my heels as I whipped around, stopping myself from reaching for the piece strapped to the inside of my thigh. I looked up at him half startled and half surprised. How in the world did he walk up on me without me hearing him? He chuckled as he flopped down on his couch facing me.

He smelled good. Now dressed in a white t-shirt and a pair of blue jeans, he even looked good. I was surprised to see that I was capable of being attracted to the thug type. Who knew?

"Did I surprise you?" he asked. For a minute my mouth just hung open. Damn, can he hear my thoughts?

"Yes," I told him truthfully. He was continuing to do that.

"Sorry about that. How can I help you, Ms…"

"Bonita, Brenda Bonita." I said walking toward him to shake his hand. He didn't reach for my hand, instead he studied me with that unnerving gaze of his. I had to force myself not to look away.

Get a grip, Nak. You are not getting ready to let this young thug unravel you. Get it together!

I took a deep breath withdrawing my hand as I eased back down in my chair.

"It's common decency to shake your guest's hand in greeting," I admonished as I lifted my briefcase laying it gently on the granite table in front of me.

"It's common decency not to lie when your host asks you your name." My eyes rose to his.

"I told you my name. Why would I lie?"

He grinned then still studying me with that sharp gaze of his. "I don't know, but I'm sure I'll find out."

I removed several papers from my briefcase. One of them being a copy of the contract he signed with Jo.

"I've been sent here from Senator Warren's office. As you know, your sister a..." I looked at the name on the paper, although I knew it by heart. "Journey Reevers is romantically involved with Joseph Warren, Senator Warren's son. I've been hired to make sure the senator and his son's reputation remain on the up and up." I smiled warmly. He did not return my smile. In fact, the more I talked, the angrier he became. The little muscle in his jaw was working overtime.

"Of course you have nothing to worry about, I am a professional. Half the time you won't even know I'm here. I'm sure you are a responsible young man and would not be willing to do anything to jeopardize the senator's and future senator's office, what with all the work they do for communities like this." He sat up on the couch.

"Wait, let me get this straight. You come into my house to tell me, a grown ass man, that you're my what? Babysitter?" I smiled.

"Well, I wouldn't put it in those terms...but, yes." He narrowed his hypnotic eyes at me.

"Funny, you don't come across as a babysitter. Why do I feel as if it's a killer staring at me through your eyes?"

It took every bit of my training not to break my cover in that moment. Nobody has ever seen the real me.

Never!

I looked away, shuffling through the papers to cover my momentary lapse.

"I don't know what you're talking about, young man."

"You can kill all that young man, bullsh*t. It's not doing what you're hoping it would."

"And what is that?" I asked lifting my gaze back to his, daring him to say it. He didn't speak right away. He just let his eyes travel over my body in a way that made me feel warm all over.

"Discouraging me from imagining what those beautiful deceptive eyes of yours will look like rounded in pleasure as you come apart for me over and over again." I loudly cleared my throat. He smiled when he saw he had ruffled my feathers.

"Mr. Reevers—"

"Rome," he corrected.

"Romeo, let's go ahead and get a few things straight. I will not tolerate sexual harassment of any kind. If you sexually harass me again, I will call Joseph Warren and inform him that you've breached your contract. If you give me a hard time in anyway from this point on, I will call Mr. Warren and tell him you've breached your contract, in which point, the actions that Mr. Warren discussed with you will be taken." I looked at him giving him my no-nonsense look.

"Is that understood?"

Chapter 2

Three Fatal Mistakes

Rome

My brother had just sacrificed this fed's life. He knew better than anyone that no stranger was allowed past the third floor. Sometimes, I just didn't understand how his mind worked. He and I use completely different halves of our brains. Rob saw the world through the eyes of an artist. He clung to beauty, which was why he went against my rule. Not only had he brought a stranger up here, he brought a damn fed. Now I had to murk this chick.

At least… that was my first thought.

But then I watched her walk away in that tight skirt that clung to her nicely rounded a** that jiggled slightly as those red bottom heels sashayed across my floor as if she was walking a damn runway. And I had a change of heart.

This woman was good. When I stood, I had to adjust my pants because my body had reacted instantly to her.

That f***en' bastard sent in my Achilles' heel to spy on me. I balled up my fists. I was going to destroy him *and* his punk a** daddy. They messed with the wrong one. I had already discovered some things that could be the end of both their careers. I just had to gather all the information and see exactly what it was I was looking at.

It appears as if Daddy Warren has been telling a lie about Jo being his boy. Not only was he not his son, he bought him and paid a pretty penny for him. The information was very fragmented, somebody had tried to erase their trail. However, there was no such thing in cyber space.

Now that I caught the scent, the truth will not escape me for long. And once I had all my pieces in place, I will strike. My gaze went back to the woman Jo had sent. For now, I'll call her Ms. No Name 'cause it sure the hell wasn't Brenda Bonita.

Ms. No Name here made three fatal mistakes. One, she didn't do her research, she had no idea who she was f***ing with. Two, she let that chump Jo's name come from between her pretty lips, throwing it in my face like it's a protective cage that's going to keep her safe from the beast. It's not. Her fate is sealed. Now that she has seen my space, I can either kill her or make her mine.

And three…

She came up in this mutha***** looking like every boy's wet dream, dressed in a navy-blue suit that fit her sublime form as if the designer made it with just her in mind. The tight skirt stopped just above her knees. But damn, she had legs for days, long shapely legs. She coupled them beauties with a pair of black six-inch heels with the red bottoms.

She had her curly long hair pulled up in a messy bun, only letting a few strands escape. Then, she completed her look with a pair of glasses that I would bet my fortune she didn't need. I couldn't tell right off what her ethnicity was, but my guess would be something south of the border, Guatemalan, Brazilian. Yeah, definitely Afro-Brazilian, she had that look about her.

But all that I'd just described weren't her secret weapon. Although her body was banging and her beauty unparalleled, none of that was what she used to lure unsuspecting men into her trap.

It was her *eyes*.

If ever one needed a sloe-eyed model, she would be perfect for the gig. Her gaze was alluring and captivating, it made you think of heated nights of kissing and touching, teasing and tasting. Damn, I was getting another erection just thinking about it.

She kept referring to me as young man. Not for my sake, but hers. It's as if she had to remind herself of the fact that she was older than me in hopes that it would kill her attraction to me. And she was attracted. The way her eyes racked over my body as she stood looking down at me in my bed said it all.

Yeah, my brother sealed her fate by bringing her up here. And I guess I was looking at her through his eyes, because she was art in motion, and I was no savage…well, not *all* the time. I *too* can appreciate an exquisite piece of art.

No, I will not kill her. So, that only left one thing for me to do.

Make her mine.

"Aight, I hear what you saying. You want to play this thing by the rules," I told her and a look of genuine relief crossed her face.

She exhaled. "Yes."

"You want to keep things on the up and up, meaning you be straight with me and I'll be straight with you, no bullsh*t?" She was nodding before I finished speaking.

"Yes."

I smiled. "You have a deal, however—" I held up my finger. "Now pay attention, because me and you are getting ready to enter into a verbal contract. A contract that I will uphold by any means necessary. Do you understand?"

She didn't even bat her eye, she wasn't afraid of me. The grin that lurked right under the surface of her beautiful lips said she would agree to anything as long as it would get the job done.

I was counting on that.

"Sure," she purred.

Damn, when I got a hold of this woman, I was going to cause that devious look in her eyes to disappear and one of longing and raw uncut need to replace it. I was going to take great pleasure in ruining her for other men.

"As long as you continue to keep things on the up and up…meaning, what you say is what you do. Then I too will keep things on the up and up. I'll be on my best behavior. But…" I held up my finger again.

"If it comes to light that you're lying to me and you have an ulterior motive, then…" I paused for a moment, my eyes falling to her sexy legs she had crossed, working the hell out of those Red Bottoms. Very slowly my gaze raked up her body, taking in what was at stake before they connected with that droopy bedroom gaze of hers.

"You belong to me."

Nakhti

My mask slipped just a bit and for the life of me, I couldn't understand why. I had been here before. Men flirted with me often, they tried to pick me up, it was my job to engage in these kinds of conversations with them to get them to let down their guard and let me in just long enough to get my mission complete.

Yet, it was something about his threat that felt different. His amber gaze held so many mystery's and yes, so much wisdom. What did he know? Did it matter? He reminded me of a book I read once while I was on a mission in Ethiopia, I can't remember the name of it. But in it Queen Makeda, the Queen of Sheba describes what it was like meeting the great wise King Solomon.

She said his wisdom was like nothing she had ever encountered. And although he was extremely handsome, it was his wisdom that attracted her. I'd imagine that Rome was a descendant of the great king. He was seriously giving off those kinds of vibes. I couldn't shake the feeling that he was a couple of steps ahead of me. This was a feeling I was not used to; I was *always* ahead of my marks.

Get it together Nak, you cannot let this young man unravel you. You have been here before. He's no different than any other mark. Do your job and get out. The quicker you get it done the better. And then you'll be a ghost.

I cleared my throat.

"As absurd as your words are, Mr. Reevers, I'm going to agree, because I have nothing to hide. I've come to do exactly what I've stated. Nothing more, nothing less." The smile that came over his face sent chills down my spine.

"Wonderful, then it's sealed." He stood. "Come, let me give you a tour of the place."

****

Rome was taking me to meet his mom. He had given me a thorough tour of the building, explaining to me that he owned it and rented out apartments mostly to his *boys*, except for the apartment for his mom and little brother.

As we passed the said boys, they all spoke to him as if he was their king.

"Hey Rome, what up?" Or, "What up, Rome, everything good?" After which they would shake up in a fashion that showed they viewed each other as brothers. He was surrounded by his soldiers, men that were so loyal to him that if he told them to put a bullet in my head, they would with no hesitation.

When I asked him what it was he did, he chuckled.

"You know… a little bit of this, a little of that." I nodded.

"My report says you're a drug dealer."

"Oh yeah? And where did you get your report from?"

"Why, Mr. Warren of course."

"Hmm," was his only response.

"You seem like a pretty smart man. Why would you have drugs in your mother's apartment? It's common knowledge that drug dealers don't keep their product where they or their loved ones rest their heads. It almost seems as if you were using them to distract the FBI agents. Is that the case?"

He chuckled again. "Actually, they were my little brother's drugs, it was his room. I was simply trying to help him get rid of his product."

"Were you nervous or something? Because my report says you spilled quite a few of them, which kind of defeats the purpose of you getting rid of them."

"You asking an awful lot of questions, is this all a part of your job?" He held up air quotes when he said that.

"Quite naturally, I need to know what kind of behavior it is I have to keep you from." He came to a stop then and turned to face me so suddenly I gasped. We had just walked into the stairwell, so we were alone.

"Do you really believe you will be able to keep me from any of my behaviors?" he asked walking towards me. I took a few steps back, but was forced to stop when my back came up against the door. He cornered me in then, blocking off the rest of the view with his big body, putting his hand on the door by my head.

As his amber gaze raked over my face, I lifted an eyebrow. I could drop him right now. I won't, but I could. I smiled.

"Mr. Reevers, it seems you're quite good at deflecting."

"Rome," he corrected.

"Romeo," I insisted. He grinned as he ate me up with that gaze of his.

"What's your name?" he asked in a quiet voice.

"I told you my name, Brenda Bonita," I responded just as quietly.

His gaze lowered to my lips and the look in his eyes turned to one of want. He wanted to kiss me. Sometimes I allowed kissing to let a mark feel as if I was into him, but I didn't think I would with Romeo here. I had a feeling that if I let him kiss me, I will feel something too. And that was a no no while in the field.

He grinned as if he could read my mind. "The up and up. A deal is a deal. Come, let me introduce you to another woman that insists on calling me Romeo." He turned then and walked up the stairs. For a moment I just stood and took in his bow-legged swagger.

Goodness! I need to complete this assignment as soon as possible. This man was dangerous to my well-being.

"And who is this beautiful young lady?" Mrs. Reevers asked as I eased down on her couch. I sat my briefcase on her coffee table planting a bug as I did. At the same time, I looked around at her beautiful apartment amazed at all the healthy plants that were everywhere.

"This is…" Rome left off on saying my name leaving me to fill in the blank.

"Brenda Bonita," I told her. She smiled warmly at me. Rome's mother was beautiful. I see where he got his amber eyes.

"Nice to meet you, sweetheart."

"Nice to meet you too."

"Ms. Bonita was hired by Jo to be my babysitter." Rome told her as he leaned in to kiss her cheek.

"Ma, can you keep an eye on her for me? I have to make a run."

"Sure," she said.

Before I could say anything, he was gone out the front door. The bastard had just pawned me off on his mother. But this was good, my bugs were set, I didn't really need him anymore. I can take this time to get a little background information. Nothing mamas like to talk about more than their babies.

Well, everybody's mama, but mine. If mine said anything, it would be to speak about how I could never add up to the boy my father wanted. No matter how many awards I won or how many hurdles I jumped, it could never add up. It wasn't enough to keep him home with us.

"Can I get you anything to eat or drink? I put some black-eyed peas on earlier with a smoked turkey part. Will you have a bowl?"

Ahhh! So that's what smelled so good. Right then my stomach growled, the last meal I had was a MRE in transit to my next assignment. I couldn't remember the last time I had a home cooked meal. I think I may have been a small child in Brazil, before my avozinha passed away, while my mother chased after my father. It was my avô, my mother's mother that made sure I was fed properly and loved. But she died when I was eight, and the little love I received died with her.

"I would love some black-eyed peas," I told Mrs. Reevers getting up to follow her into the kitchen. "Your apartment is beautiful. The plants are magnificent."

"Thank you, I have my daughter Journey to thank for that. Once she started studying the science of plants, she took something as simple as having a few house plants to another level."

I sat on the stool at the counter as she slid a steaming bowl of smelling goodness in front of me. I had never eaten black-eyed peas before, but they smelled heavenly. Picking up the salt shaker I sprinkled a good amount on my food.

"Do you want to taste it first, I put a good amount of seasoning in my food." She asked frowning at the salt shaker that was still in my hands.

"Sorry about that, I like a lot of salt."

After blowing on my spoonful, I made to put it in my mouth, but Mrs. Reevers stopped me.

"Sweetheart, we thank the Heavenly Father for our food before we eat it." Feeling slightly embarrassed for getting caught being a savage, I lowered my spoon.

"Sorry, of course you're right." Bowing my head, I said a few words of thanks before my eyes opened and I went for my spoon, but Mrs. Reevers head was still bowed and her eyes still closed.

Ooookay... I closed my eyes again.

"Dear Heavenly Father," she began. "We come before you to say thank you for this meal. And thank you for bringing Ms. Bonita to us. We pray that you allow this meal to nourish her body and her heart."

As she continued, I thought about her words. Could a meal nourish my heart? Could black-eyed peas fill the hole that has always been there? If only her words were true and this simple bowl of peas could fix all that was wrong with me.

Surprisingly, I felt the burning of tears behind my eye lids.

"We also pray today that you allow your will to be done. And that you touch us all with your healing hands. We need you now Father more than any time before. Your people need you now. In the mighty name of Yahusha Ha Mashiach. Selah." She lifted her head and smiled at me. I returned her smile.

"You said the last of your prayer in Hebrew." I recognized the language from my time in the Middle East.

She blushed, pleased I had noticed her accomplishment. "I've been trying to learn a second language. Thank you for noticing."

All thoughts fled my mind as the heavenly taste of the peas exploded with flavor against my tongue. I take that back; this bowl of peas just may be food for my soul.

"This is very good," I told her. She smiled.

"Thank you, honey. You want some Kool-Aid? My son Rob makes it, and he put's way to much sugar in it, but it's still pretty good." I nodded. She had me at way too much sugar.

"It's the red kind," she said like I was supposed to understand the significance of that. I nodded in agreement having to bite the side of my cheek to keep from grinning. I think Mrs. Reevers thought that I was an African- American instead of an African-Brazilian. I wondered what she would do if I started speaking Portuguese to her.

"You know, I'm kind of glad Jo did what he did." I looked up from my bowl surprised. Wow! Didn't think the information was going to come this easily. I thought I was going to have to pry it out of her.

"What do you mean?" I asked.

"Well first, I'm glad he came back into Journey's life. Ayana need her daddy. And now he's forcing Romeo to clean up his act. My son is so strong willed. Once he makes up his mind that he's going to do something, there ain't much you can do to stop him." I nodded encouraging her to continue as I finished my bowl of peas and smoked turkey part.

"You see, my husband died when my children were younger, he was the breadwinner for the family." She looked at me hesitantly. "A progressive woman like yourself, probably think it was wrong of me to want to stay home with my children."

I shook my head. "Not at all. It's your right. There is nothing wrong with wanting to be a stay-at-home mom."

I wish my mother had invested even a quarter of the time in me that you had in your children. Maybe then I wouldn't be so worthless.

She patted my hand. "Mamas are only human, baby."

My eyes widened, startled at her statement. How did she—?

"Anyway, after my husband died. I had to go out there and get a job to support us." She continued. "But because I didn't have no education, the only thing I could do was go up north and clean a few rich folk houses. It was tough and I was barely making enough money to pay our mortgage and keep a little ration on the table." She patted her head.

"Child, them folks was coming to the house cutting the lights and the gas off nearly every other month. My baby Romeo who at the time I think was twelve or thirteen came in my room one night and saw me crying. He has a giving heart, just like his daddy. He hugged me and told me everything was going to be alright. Next morning, he was gone." She shook her head.

"You talk about nearly having a heart attack. I called the police and I bundled up my two youngest children and hit the street looking for him. I had just lost Romeo Sr. and I couldn't lose nobody else. We was all we had left." I drank my cup of Kool-Aid down in one pop; it was delicious.

"Would you like some more, honey?" Mrs. Reevers asked when she saw that I had tilted the cup up for the last drop. I smiled.

"Yes, please."

"Anyway, Romeo shows back up a week later with enough money to not only pay our mortgage and bills for that month, but the next one after that." She continued as she poured my drink.

"Wow! Where did he get the money?" She shook her head.

"I always thought he was dealing drugs, which broke my heart 'cause he dropped out of school. Do you know that them folks tested him and said he tested in at a genius level? He was getting all kinds of letters in the mail from schools around the world. I don't know how Sr. and I produced a genius, but we did. In fact, we produced three. Here, let me show you something." She disappeared in her room before she came back out holding a big sketched picture. When she turned it around and showed me, I gasped.

"It's amazing!" I told her. The picture was of a young beautiful girl with long locs, resting her chin against the back of her hands as she gazed out the window looking at a tree with falling leaves. The artist had managed to catch the girl's love for what she was seeing in her eyes.

"It's a picture of my daughter Journey. My youngest son Rob sketched it." She was right, he was a prodigy. This picture could be in any art gallery in the world and would bring in a hefty sum.

"And look." She went over to her plants. "All my life I've kept house plants. Journey's love for them came from me. But look at what she's done with them. She studies the soil and feed the little bugs in the soil certain things. Then the bugs poop and make the plant stronger or something like that…" She waved that away.

"Of course my daughter uses the scientific language for that process. When I asked her to make it simple for the simple, that's what she told me." I nodded as I finished off my Kool-Aid.

"Do you mind?" I asked her gesturing toward the pitcher that she left sitting on the counter.

She nodded. "No, go right ahead. Although I don't think drinking all that sugar is good for you."

Pouring another cup, I smiled at her. "Hey, got to die from something." I chuckled at my own joke, but when I saw that she didn't see the humor in it, I cleared my throat.

"You have truly been blessed to have three amazing children," I said to get her talking again.

She sighed. "That's what I thought too, but sometimes Romeo scares me."

"Oh?" I asked my ears perking up. "How so?"

"Folks around here treat him like he some kind of god. It seems like the whole neighborhood depend on him to function. Everybody from Laraine's Corner Store to Mr. Tommy's Hardware. They say it's 'cause of him this the only area in Chicago where the mom and pop stores have not gone under." She eased down on the couch looking sad.

Now good and full, I took my bowl and cup to the sink and after washing them, joined her on the couch.

"I just fear that all those responsibilities have forced him to do some bad things." I picked up her hand giving it a comforting squeeze. This day had taken a strange turn. First the black-eyed peas with the smoked turkey part, the prayer, the Kool-Aid, and now I found myself sitting here trying to comfort this stranger.

Whenever you are in the field, you need to be adaptable. It was no telling what kind of situation you would find yourself in, you needed to blend. But that was not why I was comforting this woman. I did it because she was good. In my line of work, I meet a bunch of sh*tty people, the scum of the planet earth. But not this woman, she was good.

"Mrs. Reevers, why are you telling me all this?" I asked, not being able to help being a little curious. She had just met me and she had given me a quick rundown on her family as if she needed to explain why things were the way they were. She blinked at me as if it was quite obvious.

"Well, because…Romeo has never brought a lady friend to meet me before. Never, not even once."

Chapter 3

The Educated Thug

Our experts warned us about the possibility of this phenomenon occurring, for they say that the slave's mind has a strong drive to correct and re-correct itself over a period of time if it can touch some substantial original historical base...

--Willie Lynch

Rome

I control everything that happens in my hood, from every loaf of bread sold to every bag of weed, from who buys a house in this area to who attends the neighborhood public school. Eighty-one blocks of the 24th Ward is mine. Inside my blocks are Four Corner Hustlers, GDs, BDs and Vice Lords.

People wondered at how I was able to keep the peace with four rival gangs all living and working in the same area. It was simple, all four of their chiefs answered to me. I did not deal with their men directly. If it was beef, their chiefs brought it to me and I solved it the way I saw fit.

It is my alderman representing in the city council and my mayor sitting in City Hall. The police officers that patrolled my streets were also on my payroll.

Now I know you say…

Damn Rome, how a hood nigga like you get a hold of so much power within the land of your captivity. And my answer is simple… I've discovered a few unpretentious truths. Truths that if my people discovered, would set them free.

One…

I am not nor have ever been a nigga. To simplify my existence in such a way is contemptuous. You see, me and my people are far more complex than that. The powers that be know exactly how much so, but they'll never tell you that.

Two…

The trick is to resist greed. By doing that, I'm allowed to work with certain amenities. Greed has been the downfall of many great sovereignties throughout history. In fact, in all my studies, I have never found one that didn't fall because of it.

Well…

All except the reign of the Most-High. A reign that is so complex in its simplicity it's mind boggling. But here amongst us flawed mortal men, greed reigned supreme and it has never failed to destroy. No, not ever…

I've discovered a delicate science to making this all work. I never try to go higher than my mayor. I am loyal to him to a certain extent and he is loyal to me. The governor has no idea I exist. I didn't demand control of the whole city from my mayor, just half of the 24th Ward. In return, I use my skills to make sure he stays comfortable in his position, and he uses his position to make sure I stay comfortable to practice my skills.

I guess you can call me the hidden hand. I don't suffer from vanity, so I don't have to be out front. I don't need everyone to know who I am. I am comfortable being behind the scenes. I don't need praise from others because I'd never met another who was as smart as I. Imagine me seeking praise from one whose brain does not have the aptitude to even begin to grasp mine.

And I know that statement in itself sounds quite vain indeed, but it's true. Remember, we are dealing with simple truths.

And third...

Now pay close attention because this is the most important truth I've discovered. Knowledge is power. He who holds the most of it will always hold the most power.

I've created a program for my piece of the 24th Ward, setting out to prove that ghetto youths with proper nutrition and brain stimulation can compete and even excel in the world market. My little sista's been screaming about genetically modified crops and how they're ruining the soil ever since she was a shawty.

So, I get to thinking one day while I'm sitting on my couch sipping Hen. If GMO's killing the soil and God made man from soil, then what the f*** is that sh*t doing to us? I started looking into the matter. That sh*t ain't just messing up the earth, that sh*t messing up the people that's eating it too.

I am now a silent partner in 21 restaurants and 42 corner stores inside my small slice of the Chicago pie. I've sat down with the other owners of each establishment and carefully chose the foods being sold in both restaurants and stores.

The affordable generic brand sold in my hood comes from organic farms that I use my particular set of skills to protect from the big-name GMO power houses that are moving through the land eating up the small men. I've instituted certain incentives to the shawtys in my hood for eating fruits and vegetables instead of junk food.

Have I hemorrhaged out a sh*t load of money?

Hell yeah!

But...

I make a sh*t load of money... you'll be amazed how much one would pay to make certain things appear and disappear from cyberspace. I just take what I make and put it back into my hood.

Am I a criminal?

Hmmm...

You may or may not think so...I guess that all depends on what side of the spectrum you find yourself standing.

Am I a hero?

The answer to that question is a resounding NO! What I am doing here in the 24th Ward is to prove a point to *myself*, because I really don't give a sh*t what anybody else think. I am always looking for things to challenge my own brain. My little brotha called me the Mad Scientist, because I shaped real life situations to entertain myself.

That may in fact be true, but what was also true was that thirty-two percent of the black educated ghetto youths who have come from Chicago and made waves in the world over the last five years have come from my streets.

I don't know about you, but that looks like some damn impressive numbers to me. Both Jo and his spy wondered why I would use dope as a cover to my operation. The truth is, if the powers that be got wind of what I was doing here in the black community, I would be dead before anybody even realized an assassination had taken place.

The dope boy isn't and has never been a threat to this great nation. Knowing the *Thug* is operating within the inner cities helps the powers that be sleep comfortably every night, because they know that their secret is still safely tucked away.

However, the *Educated Thug* strikes fear in their hearts. The *Educated Thug's* mind is more than likely to correct itself from the damage that hundreds of years of oppression has caused and stumble upon the truth, and what will the powers that be do then?

Yes, I am the Educated Thug. Now don't get me wrong, I started off being the stereotypical nigga, repeating what I saw on TV and what the OGs did before me, sh*t they also saw on TV. But the truth was, I got bored with that. There was no challenge in it for me. Being a nigga was just too easy.

So...

I set out to change the Nigga mind state and reinstate the diadem, first in my own mind and then in the mind of those around me...

Now that I've explained my strengths to you guys, allow me to explain the thug part of me. Many of you will get on me and say how could you not tolerate the word nigga, but be okay with the term *thug*?

And I have a simple truth for that as well. To deny one's nature is the very essence of stupidity, at least in my opinion.

Yes, I'm smart as hell, I know that. I'm also very uncouth at times. I have a temper that surprises even me. These sudden fits of rage come upon me and yes, sometimes they rule my actions. In a temper, I have laid many to rest, a fact that I'm neither proud of nor disappointed in. A cancer needs to be removed, no matter what form it comes in.

And finally, this is something that remains even a mystery to me, maybe they're putting something in the water. But I have that impenetrable sense of doom, a feeling that I need to make my impact now, because any day could be my last one.

Unfortunately, no matter how hard I try, I can't visualize myself as an old man. Frankly, I doubt if I'll live that long. So yes, like many ghetto youths, I live every day like it's my last.

The thug part of me is a product of my environment, but also a weakness, which is why I implement various self-control exercises in the training of myself and my crew. Yes, we easily lose control, but it's not a good thing…and it's not something we should just accept about ourselves.

We're not animals… no matter how the powers that be try to make it seem.

All in all, I'm quite satisfied with the little kingdom I've created for myself.

However…

There is one who have made it his mission to destroy all that I've built.

I brought my truck to a stop in front Ms. May's Soul Food Eatery, one of the restaurants I silently partnered. My financial backing enables Ms. May to cook with only good wholesome organic ingredients. Because of it, the restaurant attracts folks from all over the Chicago area, sometimes the line to get in wraps around the corner. It has been spotlighted in the Tribune four times already.

"Kado say that mutha f**** been in there for about fifteen minutes. Sitting down having lunch with some broad. He twenty-five deep." Hannibal, my right hand said as he pulled a Swisher Sweet out his inner jacket pocket and began to roll a blunt.

I didn't smoke because I couldn't stand the feel of my brain being hazy...but I didn't have a problem with those around me smoking, because I liked the smell of good weed.

Anyway, where was I? Oh yes...

Ever since the days of Cain and Abel, there has always been a hater sitting on the side plotting the death of the achiever. Basically, if I'm superman, this b**** made punk, Saw Buck, who got up enough balls to cross into my turf and eat at one of my restaurants is my Lex Luther. And what makes it so bad, he used to be one of my two best f***ing friends.

The other is Hitta, but I'll tell you more about him a little later.

It was Saw's father, G who had first put me on when I was twelve. I'd gone to him and asked if I could be his accountant in order to make money for my family. I was desperate...My mother was killing herself to take care of us. Working two jobs she barely slept. Just came in from one job, pieced together a meal for us, and then trudged right back out to go to another.

After getting my brother and sister in the bed at night I paced the floor worried about her. One night she told me how much it pained her to raise other folks' children while her own were growing without her.

I'd heard her crying so many times. Her tears tore me apart on the inside. I felt as if I was letting my father down. He'd laid on his death bed and made me promise to take care of the family. He told me that it was time for me to be a man, and that they were now *my* responsibility. And here I stood watching my mother killing herself to do the job that my father said was mine.

The night I left the house to find work, I swore my mother will never have to cry again. I'd already mapped out the perfect way to earn a lot of cash in a short amount of time.

At first, G and his whole crew had looked at me and laughed at my asking to be his accountant.

"Lil nigga, I sell dope, not real estate." He told me before he went into another fit of laughter.

I let him laugh, but when he was done, I showed him how he could triple his profits just from keeping books. I showed him where he was losing funds and where there was room for growth.

By the time I was done, he and his men were looking at me as if I was a freak of nature. That may have been the case, but after that day, I became the first twelve-year-old accountant in the history of accountancy, and for a drug emperor no less...

Because of me, G's small operation went from being a few blocks strong to all of the 24th Ward, but I was only biding my time. I didn't like the fact that he sold crack, I didn't like what it did to my people, which is why I don't allow it on my streets.

Saw Buck is the same age as me. I guess you can say G raised him, me, and Hitta, who is his nephew and also my age together. Back in those days, the three of us were inseparable. We made plans to grow and rule Chicago together.

But Hitta started knocking mutha f****s out early, back then, folks called him Hard Hitta. Instead of teaching him the dope game, G got him into boxing, forcing him to go to the gym every day. By the time he was seventeen, he was fighting professionally and had an impressive career that lasted nearly a decade.

An injury forced him to leave the sport and now he ran one of the biggest underground boxing arenas in Chicago. I use my particular set of skills to make sure he continued to operate without the law getting involved, trying to shut him down. I didn't need to use my skills to make sure he kept haters off him, 'cause Hitta is a goon in every sense of the word, and there ain't a mutha f**** around with enough balls to cross him, which left Saw and I to run these streets. At first, everything was good, till his and my views began to differ on how that should be done.

I tried to tell him it was a new day. Technology was becoming the force to be reckoned with. I studied my ass off and learned it without attending anybody's tech school. I told him this would be our key to taking over and doing it bigger than any of the OGs before us. But he wasn't trying to hear that. He couldn't see past the dope game. After his pops got gunned down, Saw wanted to continue where he left off and I just wasn't feeling it.

So, we split the 24 in half. My guys didn't crossover into his area, and his guys didn't crossover to mine. There was peace in our section of the Chicago map for a while. He chose to sell rock on his side, and I allowed the hustlas to sell bud on mine. But you know how I do…If I'm going to allow weed to be sold, then it got to be pure, non-GMO and not laced with no bullsh*t.

I found a crazy ass white boy in California who grew the best weed I ever smelled. He said his bud was all organic, said he used heirloom seeds that had been in his family for decades. When I met him, he was small time; I became a silent partner and now he supplied product for my whole area and was in a very good place for when Proposition 64 is voted in allowing legal usage of the herb by adults in California.

Folks came from all over Chicago to shop with us. It ain't no secret that we got the best weed in the land. That being said, Ol' Saw Buck's playa hating a** started noticing that my operation was outgrowing his... rapidly, and his jealousy set in. He thought we were balling like this because of that fiyah weed.

And I let him...I let everybody think that.

Only a small number of people knew what I actually did. Only a small number of people knew how invested in this neighborhood I am. Even my silent partners didn't know about each other. They all assumed I was in business with them only. Just like the mayor, they kept their lips sealed about our transactions. Upstanding citizens like themselves didn't want to be lumped in with a thug like me, it wasn't a good look, which was just the way I wanted it.

My model was simple...never let your left hand know what your right is doing. I am the specter.

A few years back, Saw Buck brought his clown a** to me asking about him setting up shop over here on my blocks. I laughed at him. I knew he was on some jealous sh*t and ready to start a war. It was foreseeable, I knew it would happen eventually.

I told him to bounce, 'cause he know damn well I don't allow crack on my streets. Not now, not mutha f***en ever. He tested me and sent in a few of his boys anyway. And we sent them mutha f***a's back in boxes.

That was when sh*t jumped off, small skirmishes began to happen here and there between his men and mine. Nothing so big that it would cause our two sides to go to war, but him being the b**** he is, snitched a few times and got some of my boys locked up. Because he didn't know that the mayor reported back to me, he had no idea I knew each time his lips went loose, my boys never spent longer than an hour in lock-up.

Through careful calculation and perpetration, I've managed not to lose any of my people. Like I said, we had to send a few of his crew back to him in boxes. My mother would call it a blessing. And maybe it was. But I also made sure my soldiers and future soldiers were trained in hand- to- hand combat and target practice. They didn't just talk a good game, they could back it up, whether throwing them thangs or busting that heat, all skills that were necessary to survive this concrete jungle.

The fact is, these streets would be a better place with Saw dead. If I didn't think it would start a war, I would walk into that restaurant and air his a** out right now without hesitation. The thing is, I'm responsible for every man, woman and child under my watch. And if I murk Saw, it would be an all-out blood bath by tomorrow. Lives would be lost on both sides, and I was not willing to sacrifice none of mine.

Nothing in life is easy. But that's alright with me. Just because Saw wasn't an easy kill didn't mean his days weren't numbered. There was more than one way to skin a cat. I took a page out of our government's playbook and carefully chose the man I felt would be a good replacement for him…Bobby. I've trained Bobby since he was a small boy and he was unquestionably loyal to me. Five years ago, I sent him in to get tight with Saw.

Ol' goofy ** punk opened up to him and took him right in. Now Bobby was his second in command. All his soldiers were ready to follow Bobby should something happen to him. And something will happen to him, I was just waiting for the perfect time to strike.

The problem was, Saw knew I wanted him dead and has become paranoid. Bobby said this fool slept with guards at his front door, bedroom, and back door. I'm surprised he got up enough balls to eat at one of my restaurants. He's really taking his life in his hands. Although he had come deep, there were several cars and trucks lined up behind and in front of his.

A few of his men sat in their vehicles while the others stood outside chopping it up with my soldiers, who were there to keep an eye on them. This area belonged to the Four Corner Hustlers, their chief is Kado, it was he that called Milo and alerted him to Saw and his men's presence.

I killed my engine when Kado spotted me and began to come my way.

"Yo, Rome this truck is sick, my ni--!" He caught himself. "Brotha!" His eye greedily took in my F-250 King Ranch Ford Pick-up.

"Is anything on this mutha f***a from the factory?" He asked clasping hands with me.

I chuckled. "You know better." was all I told him...and he did.

I didn't make it a habit of answering foolish questions and I didn't need to brag. One had only to look at the truck and see it was custom built. The executives at King Ranch had been nice enough to fly me in, and we sat down over lunch as they took down my vision for my vehicle.

"What up, Han?" he said to my passenger when he finally finished eye humping my ride.

Hannibal nodded without looking away from the blunt he was rolling. "Ay, what up, K."

I gestured toward the restaurant. "What you got for me?"

Kado leaned his back against my door folding his arms. "Like I told Milo, dude in there caking with some broad. You want us to ghost him?"

I didn't answer him right away. Everything inside me wanted to say yes as I pondered for the thousandth time on how I could murk him without starting a war. And for the thousandth time, the answer came back, *there was no way.*

I leaned back in my seat getting comfortable. "Naw, today ain't the day. Who is this broad he with?"

Kado shook his head. "I don't know, I ain't seen her around here before. She sexy as hell though."

"Here, hit this while I check it out." Hannibal told Kado, who wisely walked around the truck to get the blunt. Both of them knew if they'd rudely passed it in front of me, I would have hit the roof.

Han took his laptop out his book bag and pulled up the camera feed inside of Ms. May's place.

Yep! You guessed it! I got eyes on every place I invested in, including the farms. I'm a controlling mutha f****, I'm big enough to admit that.

"She is sexy." Hannibal said as Kado passed him back the weed.

The girl wasn't bad looking, but she couldn't hold a candle to that little spy who'd so foolishly decided to take me on. My phone dinged from where it sat in the cup holder. Lifting it I read the text message that had just come through. Speaking of my little spy...

Milo: The caseworker just left, she walking to her car.

"Yo, pull up the camera in front of the building." I told Hannibal who nodded and did as I asked.

He whistled. "Damn, who is that? She sexy as hell too!"

I leaned over to get a good look at my mystery woman. She had a hell of a walk on her. As she sashayed down the block in those red bottoms, all the brothas turned their heads to check her out.

Hmmm…

Lifting my hand, I rubbed my chest as a strange feeling filled it, a feeling I had never felt before… Surely, it wasn't jealousy. I shook my head, there was no way.

Me… Jealous?

Hell naw! Especially over no f***ing fed chick…

Han looked up at me and I realized he was waiting for my response.

"My caseworker." I grumbled, before I turned to look back at the restaurant, not wanting my boy to see the effect this woman was having on me.

He began choking on the weed. "Whaaat?! When the f*** that happen?" he responded when he got himself together before handing Kado the blunt.

"That p****a** dude my sista messing with sent her in to spy on me."

Kado looked inside the truck. "You want us to handle this?"

I shook my head not looking away from the door. "Naw, I got it."

Right then, Saw walked out the restaurant with the chick. When he saw me, he told her to get in the car before he began to head my way.

I eased my gun out its back holster and held it on my lap. I wish this punk would give me an excuse to waste his a**.

"Well, if it ain't the famous Romeo...tell me you didn't come all this way for little old me? You done got so big, you don't f*** with little niggas like me no more."

I didn't bother answering him. He always said corny sh*t like this in hopes of making me feel guilty for ending our friendship.

His gaze fell to my men. "Wat up, Han...Kado?" Neither spoke to him, they just nodded their heads.

"Cut the bullsh*t, Saw." I growled, fed up with the small talk. "What brings you to my neck of the woods?"

Chuckling, he threw up his hands. "Damn, man! Why can't I have come for the food? Ms. May got the best sweet potatoes on the Westside."

"Because you didn't. If you here, it's for a reason. Stop wasting my time and state your purpose!"

He put his hand on his chest and I exhaled. This was a clear sign that some garbage was getting ready to come out his mouth.

"Unlike you, I still love my brotha." He began. "I heard you had some trouble with the feds a few weeks ago, and I just came to make sure everything is alright. My sources tell me they kicked in yo' mama's door."

He got a fake look of concern on his face. "Is everything alright? I know we don't get along, but… I would really hate to see the feds get you."

I grunted. "Your sources, huh?"

He chuckled. "Well… you know how news like that spread."

"Indeed, I do."

"But let me put your mind at ease. If the feds do get you, I will gladly take care of that fine a** sista of yours." He smiled at me. "Sh*t…I may even make her the wife."

My hand twitched on the pistol that rested against my leg. Never had I ever wanted to end another's life like I did the man standing in front of me.

"Mutha f***a, you come anywhere near my sista and I will crack your f***ing skull!"

He threw his head back and laughed. "Rome, Rome, Rome! You still making idle threats! You see that's the difference between me and you. If I wanted a nigga dead as much as you want me gone, I wouldn't give a f*** about starting a war. I wouldn't give a f*** who had to die, mamas, grandmamas, great mutha f***en uncles, little nieces and nephews…they all can catch a bullet, just as long as the nigga I'm gunning fo' catch one too." I lifted an eyebrow surprised this b**** knew my reasons for not murking his a** yet.

I shouldn't be though, there wasn't a man alive outside of Hitta that knew me as well as him. That's what years of being best friends did.

He chuckled again. "What? You surprised I know why you ain't made your move." He stepped closer to my truck and both Hannibal and Kado drew their pistols, and although he didn't point it at Saw, Kado quickly made his way back to my side of the truck so that he was only feet away from him.

Knowing their chief well, a few of the fellas that had casually been standing in front of the liquor store made their way over, looking at Kado for word of their next move.

"Yo K, we got a problem?" His righthand man Poon asked. Kado looked at me…

"We got a problem, Rome?"

I studied Saw as he looked around taking in what he was dealing with. When his gaze came back to mine, I lifted one side of my mouth in a grin that didn't reach my eyes.

"Naw…not today." I told the chief of the Four Corner Hustlers without looking away from the clown.

"We cool!" Kado called to his crew, but they didn't retreat…in fact, more of them came to join the others. The air was tense, if Saw or his men made one wrong move, they were dead. Sensing this, the coward took a few steps back from my truck, but I could see the anger and the hate in his eyes, he'd just been punked in front of his crew.

"That's another difference between you and me!" He spat. "You always had to be the people's champion. And I can give a f*** about the people. Can you imagine how far you could fly if you wasn't trying to bring all these niggas with you? You need me!" He hissed jabbing his finger in his chest.

And just like that, he'd awakened the thug in me.

I NEED HIM!

That sh*t made me want to jump out my truck and bash his f***ing face into the cement until it was no longer recognizable as a face.

The only thing that kept me from it…was the many mamas, grandmamas, great mutha f***en uncles, little nieces and nephews that will get hurt if we go to war. He called me the people's champion, maybe I was, maybe I wasn't. But one thing I just could not do was be responsible for the lives of so many innocent ones.

"Look around you, playa!" I growled, fighting hard for self-control. "I don't need yo' bum a**! Never have, never will. You beneath me." I looked away from him, this conversation was over.

"Kado, won't you and yo' boys escort Saw and his crew *safely* off my blocks!" I turned the key in the ignition causing the diesel engine to awaken with a loud rumble that shook the ground before throwing it in first gear.

Saw Buck was good and angry that I'd dismissed him so casually in front of his boys. "Ay Rome, that's okay nig—"

Nobody could hear anything else he had to say, because right then, I stepped on the clutch and the gas at the same time, causing my wheels to spin and screech loudly as they filled the street with smoke…With a satisfied grin on his face, Kado stepped away from the truck awed at its power. I gave Saw's sorry a** one more look. He was standing there looking goofy and sh*t.

Chuckling, I shook my head before taking my foot off the clutch, causing my truck to peal out the parking spot so loud a few of the shawtys on the block had to cover their ears.

Hell yeah…it was ignorant.

And hell yeah…I was going to need four new tires in the morning…

But sh*t…the thug in me felt it was well worth it!

Chapter 4

You Should See Me in My Crown

Nakhti

As soon as I stepped through the door of the apartment that was mine for the next six months *if need be*, I placed the bowl of black-eyed peas Rome's mother had been nice enough to give me for later on the table and crossed the room to the stereo turning it on. When Bon Jovi's Dead Or Alive came through the speakers I cranked it up and began to strip out of the person I had become for this mission.

The first thing I did was kick off the shoes. I hated wearing heels…I preferred my trusty sturdy combat boots that I've had since my days with the SEALs any day.

Next, I unclasped the button on the back of my skirt and let it slide down my legs before sending it to join the shoes. I hate wearing skirts and dresses, so please **Desculpa a bagunça… Or rather, forgive the mess I was making.**

LOL, I have to remember I'm telling my tale to my mostly English-speaking family. I ask that you guys be patient with me. Although, thanks to my years in the military and on the bureau, I am able to hide my accent quite well, English is still my second language. So, if I say something in Portuguese, I

will try to remember to translate for you guys. But if I forget, please charge it to my head and not my heart.

Reaching up I unpinned my hair and let my wild curls fall to caress my shoulders and back. I really hated pinning up my hair…I loved the fact that it was wild and untamed. My hair in its natural state embodied me.

Finally, I took the glasses off and set them on the table next to the Tupperware bowl before removing the rest of the clothes that told the world I was civilized and approachable. And to make sure that I got all the pretend off me, I stepped under the hot water of the shower and let it wash away the rest of the make-believe.

What I absolutely hated most was pretending I was civil… I couldn't wait till this mission was over and I could disappear from society. I swear, once I'm out I'm never resurfacing again. I'm going to buy me a farm and try my hand at horse rearing.

And I know you say…Horses?

Really Nak, horses?

Yes horses… The freest I've ever been was racing bareback on a Mangalarga stallion across the *ravina* with my hair whipping around my face and shoulders. I'll never forget that day as the stallion's powerful legs ate up the earth, it was the closest I ever felt to God, I felt as if I was flying.

When I was a young girl, my mother had been the maid of a very wealthy Brazilian horse breeding family. People came from all over the world to purchase horses from them, but not just any people. Your average Jo could not afford a Winston horse, only the very rich. My mother said their customers were royalty, real princes and kings.

Anyway, sometimes when she would bring me to work with her, the stable master would let me help him tend to the horses. He said I had a natural gift with them and that they responded to me better than anyone he'd ever seen.

I don't know if I still have the gift, but I know I still have the love for them in my heart and I am damn sure going to try my hand at raising my own horses.

Believe it or not, the killing business wasn't paying like it used to; too many competitors in the game. Thankfully the Sarge a.k.a. Jo payed more than most, because he was my friend as well as my boss. Even old Albert thought so and he only worked light security detail for the Sarge.

I've been able to pay for my mother's stay at the nursing home and save up enough to be comfortable for a little while, at least until my horse farm starts bringing in a little revenue.

That is if I am reasonable and not try to go out and purchase Winston horses of course.

Although it would be a dream come true to get a Mangalarga stallion from there to sire my future prized beauties, the fact is, one stallion from Winston's would suck up a huge chunk of my savings, it just wasn't a smart move.

I will just have to try to find the best stallion and mare I can afford and pray that with my TLC, they'll produce something that resembles the majestic royal line of Winston's Mangalarga horses.

Once I was clean, I stood in the mirror for a moment and just exhaled. I've been on one mission after another since I got fired from the agency four years ago. Jo said it's the price I paid for being the best in the game. Maybe he was speaking the truth or maybe he was just speaking game. Like his father, half the words that came out his mouth could not be trusted. The man had a smooth tongue and was born to be a politician.

I however, believe I never got rest because these filthy politicians constantly had messes that needed to be cleaned up. And they sent nobodies like me with disposable lives inside to do the dirty work for them.

Picking up my tags from where I'd rested them earlier, I put them back around my neck, feeling instant relief at having them back on.

I hated taking off my tags… they remind me of what I really am.

A nobody…Disposable. That's why they came in two. A tag to identify the dead and the disposable, least we ever do something foolish like forget.

Speaking of reminding me of something, the pain in my side drew my attention to the wound that had just began to bleed through the bandage I'd slapped on earlier. I really should have gone to get it looked at by a professional.

However, this was not my first rodeo. In fact, this was my fourth time being shot. Each time had been in the field and each time I'd had to patch it up on the fly. Thank God they had all been flesh wounds and nothing too serious. Once I got the bullet removed, the rest was simple. And I survived to tell the story.

I frowned down at the wound as I cleaned it. It will be my luck that this one actually killed me. I shrugged throwing the rag in the sink.

Oh well…It's not like it's someone out there that will miss me.

After cleaning and dressing my wound, I slid my white wifebeater over my head, then stepped into a pair of military issue cargo pants, smiling at myself in the mirror.

That's more like it...

I made my way back to the living room to set up my equipment so that I could get to know my mark a little better, thanks to the bugs I'd left in his and his mother's place. I didn't know how long it will take me to get the Sarge's information. This apartment had been rented for me for six months, but I planned to be here no longer than six days.

After I got everything set up, I took the black-eyed peas and popped them in the microwave. When they were done, I sprinkled salt on them and then doused them in hot sauce. I know by now you guys may have noticed I have horrible eating habits. I like really sweet and really salty. I eat so much junk that whenever I eat an MRE, I feel that I am eating responsibly.

What did eating healthy mean to me with a high risk job like mine? Can you imagine me denying myself all the salty sweet goodness this world has to offer, so that I could live to a ripe old age only to be shot down by enemy fire? Hell...I'd kick myself all the way to the afterlife screaming, *why?* Oh why, didn't you eat that big juicy burger when you had the chance?

No thank you! I got mine while I lived. And if I so happen to die of a heart attack later...

Oh well...It's a far better death than I'd imagine I would have anyway.

If you're wondering how I stay in shape, it's simple...I go into beast mode about my workout. My job calls for me to be fit. I need to be able to run, climb, and jump on the fly. I've had to put every muscle in my body to the test doing what I did, so yea, I worked out. When I couldn't make it to the gym, I did pushups, sit-ups, and pull-ups... I kept all my muscles toned, anything else was not an option.

After settling down on the couch with my bowl of yummy beanie goodness, I turned on the television for visual stimulation before I put the headset on my ears to listen to what was going on in the world of the *thug*. Goodness, I can't believe Jo put me on this case. A thug? Are you kidding me?

I've taken down dictators, cartel drug lords...even a prince or two. And here I've been pulled to spy on a young...*thug?* I didn't know whether to laugh or be insulted.

Maybe it was for the better. Why shouldn't my last mission be an easy one?

Hopefully after a few days of listening in on him and learning his schedule, the opportunity will present itself where he slips out so that mama could slip in and play with his beautiful computer. How a *guy like him* got a hold of such equipment is mind boggling, a mystery I was determined to solve.

****

Would you guys believe the opportunity presented itself just a few hours later? The *thug* and his whole crew were getting ready to go to some club downtown called Exquisite, leaving his place lightly guarded. I listened in as they talked about the club they were all going to and who would be there.

Figures...

You see what I mean? Anyone of Jo's other men could have handled this mission. Hell, a uniformed officer could have handled this mission. I don't see why---

Hold on...

I frowned as I continued to listen. One of Rome's men asked him who should he leave to guard the building. And Rome told him nobody.

Nobody?

His man then asked him what if someone named Saw Buck rolls up and find all the guards gone.

Rome told him the guards will still be at the corners, so he will know as soon as Saw touches the block. But that all his personal guards deserved a break and that the party tonight will be just what everyone needed to unwind a little bit.

That crafty bastard knew about my bugs. He was feeding me information. It was a damn set up. Taking the headphones off, I sat back on the couch and thought about that. He was on to me...

The Sarge was right, this kid is a lot smarter than he looked. But he didn't know who he was dealing with. As far as I'm concerned, he'd just invited me in, and I've decided to take him up on his generous offer.

Let's see what you got, kid.

As I laced up my boots, I face-timed a message to Jo, letting him know that he was right about the kid, and that I will have to be caught in order to get his information. I didn't know how long it will take, but I told him I will be off the grid so if he tried to reach out to me with no response that was why.

What do you know! Mr. Romeo has decided to make my job easier. Like his little brother, he'd just invited me in. Well…let's not disappoint him.

I went to put my gun on my waist, but paused. The last time I was in Mr. Romeo's presence, he'd snuck up behind me and I'd almost shot him. I put my gun back in my briefcase. I could not trust my impulses, I'd better leave her here tonight.

Now, I don't want you guys to laugh at what I'm about to do, every soldier has a ritual they do before going into battle. Mine is standing still and listening to Lonesome Valley on full blast. I don't know what it is about the song, but the harmonious voices of the men helped me to come to terms with the fact that the mission may be my last, and that this may be the night I die. I don't have any fear. What must be done must be done.

But at the same time, if this is my last night, I pray that God see my heart and know that it's pure. I am what he created me to be, a warrior. My hands are covered in blood, the blood of *bad* people. I've never killed an innocent, only the very evil. So, if this is my last night, then I ask that he forgives me and washes me clean.

Of course I don't know if he will, but it helps to put me in the right frame of mind before a mission. I slid my hunter green bomber jacket that was the same color as my cargo pants on my arms over my wife beater, and then slid my skull cap that was the same color on my head.

Young Romeo might as well meet the woman he was getting ready to deal with, because there was no way in hell I was going to attempt to break into his place wearing those damn heels.

I left my car at my apartment, choosing to take the bus instead. It was clear Romeo had some kind of surveillance system set up where he knew who stepped foot on *his blocks* and when. And since I didn't know exactly where *his blocks* began or ended, I didn't take a chance.

You see, I didn't want him to see me coming. Yeah, I know he knows I'm coming, I just needed to do it on my own time as I studied exactly what I was getting myself into. The only way I will *allow* him to catch me is if I mapped a way out for when it was time to leave. There is no prison that can hold me; I always find a way out.

Before I left my apartment, I popped two more of the pain pills and placed the bottle in my jacket pocket. They are a Godsend because they did a great job of deadening the pain so I can do what needed to be done without my injury getting in the way.

An hour and a half later, I sat hunched down on the roof across the street from Romeo's place looking into his dark empty loft. A guard stood only feet away from me on the otherside of the roof's door. I wondered if it was the same man who'd winked at me earlier. My breath came through my lungs very gently. If I wanted, I could take his life before he even knew what hit him.

But that's not what I wanted. I'd come up here to get a better look into Romeo's empty loft and his roof. I'd already studied the building from the ground level as well as the neighborhood. And just like I figured, the men who'd been smoking and drinking on the steps earlier were now on the roof.

There was no one in front of the building. The street was very quiet…too quiet.

Silently, I sat back on my haunches to process all that I've seen. I'm not going to lie, I'm damned impressed. I've been on military bases whose defensive perimeters could not hold a flame to what the young Romeo has set up here.

Hell, I've seen *kings* protected by defensive perimeters that were far easier to penetrate than this kid's perimeter. I had to take to the sewers to get this close to the building without being noticed.

Jo was right, Romeo's influence stretched wide and as they say, the hood is always watching. What made what he has going on so clever is that one would never think the guys that were hanging out in front of the liquor stores or on the corners were as organized as they were.

On the outside, they looked like misguided youths, smoking and drinking their lives away. But if one just sat for a moment to study them, one would see that there is a method to their madness. There was an organization here that was damn impressive.

What the hell?

And I know you guys are saying. Well damn…they can't be that good if you're standing right next to a guard and across the street from the others, and not one of them have noticed.

For the record…You can't judge them by that fact. The deck is stacked against them. I've been trained by the best. And I'm not talking about the Sarge. I assume by now you guys have all met his alter, The Politician, Jo's dirty little secret.

He was my commanding officer for many years. A luxury I would not have been afforded had I not been able to keep up. Every soldier under his command had to become machines. Nothing less would do for that man…

Or…

Hell, I don't know what the Politician is. I don't think anybody does, not even Jo. However, I do know the thing is a war machine, and he trained all those under him to be war machines.

Quite frankly, I'm one of the best in the game. And that's not vanity speaking, it is just the truth.

Even still…

For the very first time in a long time, I felt out of my element. I'd been trained for many situations, but nothing like this. I'd never been trained on how to deal with a masterminded thug.

Who'd ever heard of such a thing? I love my brothers and sisters, I really do. But the fact is, the United States Government didn't look at the *Black Thug* as that big of a threat. They had never trained any of us for anything like this.

And I know some of you may think I'm putting on, but I'm not. Not only has Romeo somehow managed to organize a whole neighborhood of black and Hispanic youths…mind you, many of them are from rival gangs. I knew this because as I spied on various groups of them this evening, I heard them address each other by their affiliation. And from what I can tell, there are several affiliations in this area.

Okay, so the fact that he's somehow made that work is not the only miracle I've witnessed tonight. I'm pretty sure, that ugly grey building he lived in, that looks as if it was an old factory, is in fact a smart building.

Yep, you guys heard me…A freaking smart building.

What the hell?

Hmmm…

All of my good sense was telling me to retreat. It was telling me to take some more time and get to know young Romeo better. I'd taken him for granted, although the Sarge warned me not to. How could I have known the kid was a freaking genius? Who the hell hides a mind like that in the damn ghetto?!

Yeah, the best thing to do would be to retreat.

Except, I've never really been known for doing the best thing. I wanted to see for myself what he was actually capable of. He'd declared war, and I wanted to see if he could really handle me.

I know that's twisted...but I'm competitive that way.

Hell...who was I kidding? It's no need of lying to you guys, you're going to find out anyway that I suffer from a mental illness called Impulse Control Disorder, which basically means that I am prone to react on my first thought rather than taking the time to think things through.

This ailment made me one of Jo's best soldiers, but it also made me his worst. When out in the field, you had to think quickly and react even quicker, a split second too long and it could cost you your life. That being said, when not on duty I got in a lot of trouble for my quick reactions.

Anyway, I told you guys that so you'll know the reason I quickly ran towards the edge of the roof, disappearing over it as quietly as I'd come, landing silently on the fire escape. I could walk through the front door since he had been nice enough to clear the way for me, but where was the fun in that?

I climbed back into the sewer and resurfaced in the back courtyard of his building. Doing my best to avoid the cameras I could see, I quickly made my way up the back porches until I got to the top floor where I easily climbed the rest of the way to the roof.

Thanks to the blueprints of the building the Sarge had gotten for me, I pretty much knew the layout by heart.

The guys Romeo had watching from up here were looking over the ledge toward the front of the building, no doubt expecting this little lady to take the easy way and mosey right on through that front door that they cleared especially for me and into their trap. I shook my head as I silently walked right past them to the ventilation duct.

Men...

Gently lifting the metal grate just enough for my body, I slid in before carefully shutting it behind me. Taking my flashlight out of my pocket, I turned it on putting it in my mouth to hold it in my teeth as I crawled through the dusty duct.

Judging by the spiderwebs and the dust, this thing hadn't been used since the building was a functioning factory. The only reason I chose this way in is because it let out in what should be Romeo's bathroom.

Okay, so let me tell you guys a quick story. When I first joined the military, I was deathly afraid of spiders. It didn't matter what size they were. Those as small as the head of a pen, or those as big as my head, it didn't matter, I was afraid.

When I was fresh out of BUD school, I was asked what my biggest fear was. Foolishly, I told the truth and said spiders. The next thing I know, I'm being placed in a plastic box, and a bucket of Black Widows were poured over my head.

Had I panicked, they would have killed me. I had to move very slowly as not to startle any of the spiders to dislodge them and ease out the box. By the time I was free of them, I was no longer afraid of spiders. After that day, my brothers began to call me the Black Widow.

At least, I liked to believe that's why they call me that, and not because I've murdered more men under the guise of getting intimate with them than I can count.

Anyway, I told you all that story because this duct was full of the bastards. A weaker woman would have probably turned back, but not I, I trudged on.

When I made it to the grate that led to the dark bathroom, I carefully opened it and slid out, easing down on the sink. Although the bathroom was dark, there was enough light coming in from the street for me to see that it was very nice…and spacious.

It still had the old-world factory feel to it. But the all-white interior was state-of-the-art, including the huge claw foot tub over against the wall. I almost groaned when I saw it. That tub is every woman's dream come true. Come to think of it…When was the last time I took me some R&R time and just soaked in a hot soapy bath?

Damn, I can't even remember.

For the last fifteen years, my life has been on the go. I enlisted right after 9/11 and have been on one mission after another ever since. My retirement was long overdue, shame on Jo for not believing me. But I was going to show him. As soon as he paid me for this job, I am ghost. The first thing I was going to do when I finally made it home was soak in a nice long bath.

Home…

Would it still look the way I'd left it fifteen years ago? Will I still smell my mother's perfume in the air, or echoes of her disappointment in me for being born a girl? Will I ever feel worthy enough to exist?

I forced myself to focus on the task at hand. Now was not the time for self-doubt. It was thoughts like these that kept me from seeing that bullet coming yesterday while I was making my escape.

Focus, Nak!

Silently, I crossed the floor to the door and gently cracked it open. His place was dark, but the drapes were all opened and enough light spilled in from the streets for me to see clearly where I was going.

I exited the bathroom and waited for something to happen. Over in the sitting area, there was a GTA game paused on the big flat screen television. There was also a gentle light coming from his computer. Only one screen was on, it looked like the main screen.

Whiffs of his cologne lingered. He had expensive taste.

Slowly, I made my way farther into the loft, expecting him to jump out any minute. When nothing happened after a while, I began to wonder if I had been mistaken and he and his crew had actually gone to the club.

I mean don't get me wrong, sometimes I was off about these things…but not usually.

Carefully, I made my way to that beautiful computer and then I waited another few minutes. When still nothing happened, I shrugged and went to work. Just like I figured, he had a passcode to wake up this beauty. What good hacker wouldn't?

I pulled the decoder jump drive out my pocket and inserted it into the USB. Thirty seconds later I was in.

Wow!

This baby was powerful. I wish I had time to explore. But I didn't, it looked as if he and his men were actually somewhere watching, waiting for me to walk through that front door downstairs.

Chuckling, I shook my head.

"I guess you're not as smart as I thought you were, Romeo." I mumbled as I began to search for the information I needed…

However, my hands stalled on the keys when suddenly the overhead lights turned on as well as every screen in front of me, including the big one mounted on the wall. Rome's handsome face appeared on every one of them, but not individually, more like a puzzle that came together to make a whole.

"Well that all depends, sweetheart…How smart do you think I am?" Watching me with those light brown eyes that missed nothing, he licked his full beautiful lips before smiling down at me.

He was sitting on a couch leaning toward his laptop that must be on a coffee table or something. There was a scantily clad girl on either side of him pressing their bodies intimately into his. When I say scantily clad, I mean they were literally dressed in what looked like bathing suits. Bikinis… Each one was touching him trying to get his attention.

"Come back, Rome, we want you to play with us daddy…" One of the sex kittens purred...

I lifted an eyebrow. I swear I vomited a little in my mouth. It sounded as if they were at a party or something; there was a lot of noise in the background.

"Don't call me sweetheart…" I told him dryly.

"What should I call you then? Surely not Brenda Bonita the Caseworker…" He paused for a moment as his eyes took their time raking down my body.

"Maybe I should call you Sandy the Super Spy."

I grinned. "How about you call me unimpressed?"

A fake look of shock came over his face. "Come now, something I've done so far must be even a little impressive to you."

I tilted my head as if I was thinking about it. "No…can't think of a thing."

For just a moment, he stared at me through the screen and I swear, it felt as if his honey gaze could see straight through me to all my secrets. I began to fidget. I've never had anyone look at me so deeply, not even my parents. It was uncomfortable as hell…

Yet…

No, I was going to ignore the other feeling it caused me to feel. This was no place for those feelings.

"What happened to the sexy little caseworker I talked to earlier?"

I chuckled. "I killed her and replaced her with the unsexy, unimpressed woman you see before you."

He did this thing with those big kissable lips of his where he licked them right before they arched in a perfect grin that had me staring at his mouth in wonder. Clearly those honey colored, lady killing eyes of his isn't the only weapon in his arsenal. His mouth made you think of all the dirty things you would like to see him do with it.

It was a perfect mouth. Nice full lips that looked soft and so very kissable. Strong white straight teeth…beautiful pink healthy gums, and that wicked tongue that he kept flashing me with every time he licked his lips…

Nossa! No wonder the kittens were purring next to him. That mouth of his made one think of sex. Pure, animalistic sex.

"Unimpressed, you may be my dear, but unsexy you are not. Not by far. In fact…" He paused for just a moment. "I think I like the real you better, you're far prettier than that imposter that was here this morning."

Mmmm… Did I fail to mention his incredibly deep voice? His gaze traveled along my body again, lingering on my dog tags, or maybe my breasts. Either way, it irritated me that he looked at me like that while entertaining two other women…

What the hell?

Men like this really pissed me off. They felt that women were created to be their toys, to be used and abused and then tossed away. My father was a man like that. He used my mother and played with her head and when he was done, he tossed her away, telling her that it was because she'd given him a stupid girl and not a boy.

She'd believed him, instead of seeing that he just wasn't that into her in the first place. I hate women like my mother, women too blind to see what was really in front of them, like the two bimbos on each side of the lady killer.

Did they think he will really take them seriously? Did they think that they would put something on him that will make him magically look past the fact that they are loose and fall madly in love with them? Maybe they thought that he would buy them a tennis bracelet.

Suddenly a strong urge to defeat this man came over me. Just like the men that I've taken down before him. They are all like my father, wealthy and powerful, thinking they can do whatever the hell they like with no consequences.

I was going to allow myself to be caught...but now I don't think I will. I'll just have to find another way to get Jo's info.

I put my hands in my jacket pocket. "So, what is this...some kind of game?"

He lifted one side of that gorgeous mouth into a smirk. "Naw, no game. More like a test."

"Why you testing me?"

"I test everybody I don't trust."

It was my turn to smirk. "What? You didn't buy my social worker act?"

He laughed. Nossa! Even his laugh was sexy...

"Hell no!"

I shrugged. "Too bad...you and Ms. Bonita could have been good friends."

The laughter left his face as he focused that killer gaze on me. "Why should I settle for Ms. Bonita when I can have you instead?"

I shook my head slightly, giving him a pitying look. "Young man, you will never have me."

His eyes got really cold. "Shawty, I already got you. You belong to me. We had an agreement."

"Yeah, well sue me. I don't honor your agreement."

He chuckled again. "Too bad for you. Everybody honors their agreement with me."

"Oh yeah? Do you think you can make me?"

The knowing look that came over his face should have been enough to get me to step back and reevaluate my decision to challenge him. But then one of the girls leaned forward and rubbed her hand against his chest. The move must have irritated him because he knocked her hand away as if she was nothing.

And I knew then what I had to do...

I had to kick his punk ass for all of womankind. He was too arrogant. Somebody needed to knock him down a few pegs...And I guess the job was mine.

"I tell you what." he said as his gaze sharpened. "I'm a reasonable man. Clearly you were a bit hasty when you agreed to my terms earlier. I'm going to do something I never do...which is give you another chance. If you can make it out this building, then you're free. I'll give you the information you seek and let you walk away. However, if you can't make it out this building, then you're mine."

I lifted an eyebrow... "You sure you want to do this, junior?"

He grinned. "Oh, I'm quite sure."

He typed something into the computer in front of him and the door to his apartment swung open. I turned to look, expecting someone to be standing there.

"Tick Tock, Minha Anjo."

Startled, I looked back at the screen. He'd just called me My Angel in Portuguese. He grinned at my surprise and then tapped his watch.

Just then, bars began to lower outside the huge windows. I didn't waste any more time. Turning I ran back to the bathroom jumping up on the sink to lift the grate, I would go back the way I came.

"Damn!"

There were now bars blocking my entrance. Son of a b**** smart building. I ran back out the bathroom just in time to see bars lowering outside of the door. If that happened, I will be good and trapped. I took off for the door at full speed. There was no way I was going to make it in time...

Rome

I was prepared for her. I'd been watching her ever since she took to the tunnels on Sixteenth Street. If my suspicious are correct, she's a Navy SEAL like Jo, which meant she would come by water if she could.

I had eyes everywhere in my area, including the sewers. I'd set an alarm so that I was notified of anyone trespassing down there. And what do you know, a little over an hour ago, the alarm goes off and I see my sexy little spy dressed like the soldier she is attempting to sneak attack me.

As soon as she planted her little bugs in my place, I was alerted to their presence. She'd even planted three of them in my mom's apartment. Instead of removing them, I decided to feed her information.

Obviously, she didn't buy my going out to the club act. She's smart...I liked that. But then I sat enthralled and watched her scout out my hood. She moved like the shadow. Her steps were so light she could be a dancer if she wanted to.

There were times she'd stood right next to my men without them noticing. To say I'm impressed is an understatement. But then she went on to impress me even further. I watched her climb the building across the street like a f***ing spider. But what took the cake was when she casually walked past my men on the roof shaking her head at their stupidity. But they didn't notice because they were too damned busy watching the front of the building.

Tomorrow I will show them the footage. It will be an excellent lesson in the dangers of underestimating one's opponent. They assumed because she was a girl, she would take the easy way in.

Hell, if I was telling the truth, she surprised me too.

And once I got a good look at her standing in the hunter green cargo pants that hugged her hips and round a** in a way that made my hand twitch from wanting to squeeze it, I knew she was going to be full of surprises.

Her hunter green bomber jacket was opened just enough to reveal her dog tags and the fact that she wore a wife beater underneath with no bra. I prided myself in being something of a connoisseur when it came down to a woman's body, so I would guess those perky beauties of hers where a B cup, maybe C.

She wore combat boots on her little feet and a hunter green skull cap on her head, her thick long hair pulled in a loose ponytail that fell down her back.

Damn, this little soldier is sexy as hell.

I wanted her so bad I had to adjust myself in my pants. She looked at me with those big beautiful sloe eyes, startled when she heard me speak Portuguese. I swear I will make it my mission to break every preconceived notion she has of me.

But first I had to catch her. I activated the lock down code on my apartment thinking that was all it will take. In lock down mode no one can enter or exit my place. Every entrance was barred.

But then she surprised the hell out of me for the second time and ran full speed toward the lowering bars. She was fast, but there was no way—

"Will you look at that?!" I muttered to know one in particular.

She went down in a slide and slid under the bars just as they lowered and was back on her feet moving fast. Four of my men ran through the door she was heading for. She skidded to a halt as she took them in.

Milo told her to come with him and that his boss wanted to talk to her.

"Where is your boss?" She asked him.

"In the basement."

"Tell your boss he can kiss my ass!" I smiled… Gladly, Minha Anjo .

Milo opened his mouth to say something else, but I guess my angel was done with the conversation…moving at a speed that surprised my men, she hit Jermaine in the throat, when he reached up to grab at it, she kneed him in his jewels.

His cry of pain caused me and the other three men standing there to flinch. When they saw what she'd done they all went for her at the same time.

"Wow!" I sat back on the couch amazed as she proceeded to hand my men their a**es. And she didn't take long doing it either. She's good.

Milo got it the worse. He grabbed her from behind, she did some kind of maneuver where she came out her jacket, wrapped it around his head, climbed his body like a tree until her legs were around his neck, and then did a back flip, sending him flying away from her to crash into the wall.

There was no way in hell I will ever let him live that down. When her jacket came off, I received the third surprise of the evening. She had a full sleeve tattoo on her right arm that included the same tattoo Jo had.

My guess had been correct. She was a f***ing SEAL. No wonder she was whooping my men's a**es. Speaking of which, she ran into another group of them as she tried to go down the stairs. This time it was seven of them.

"Okay, okay!" she said breathing heavily. The way her chest rose and fell in that wifebeater was distracting. She had a light gleam of sweat on her caramel skin and it was sexy as hell.

"You got me, boys…" She cooed batting those beautiful eyes at them.

Oh! Come on!

That sh*t was low. There ain't a man alive who could stand up to those eyes.

"What are you going to do with me?" She asked, her voice sounding as if she wanted to be ravished.

I could warn my men who all wore earpieces, but I wanted to see what they will do. This is also a training exercise for them. Tomorrow they can all look at the footage and see where they went wrong.

"Our boss want to talk to you." One of them said. I could tell by the low rumble that was now in his voice, he was thinking with his dick and not his head. And he was getting ready to get his a** kicked for it.

They all came closer to her, their eyes drawn to her breasts that still rose up and down as she continued to breathe heavily. When they were within arm's length, the sexy smile left her face and a frown replaced it. The little savage even yelled like a f***ing war chief before she proceeded to hand them their a**es.

"Damn bruh, what are you watching? You staring at the sh*t like you watching the game." Rob said, flopping down on the couch that I was on with a blunt in his hand.

"Ay, give me a minute." I told the twins. They had been trying to get into one of my parties for nearly a year. Today they'd showed up in a bikini, and my boys let them in. They'd been glued to my side ever since.

"Yo, I'm in love!" I told Rob when the girls left.

For a moment he looked at me startled. And rightfully so…my little brother ain't never heard me say no sh*t like that before. But once the surprise wore off, he came closer to my computer screen to see who had caused me to utter such foreign words.

"What the f***! Who is that?"

I turned to look back at the screen. "The caseworker."

"What!!! Yo, she a gangsta!" Rob said, now just as enthralled as I was.

Hell yeah, she is…I know I should probably be helping my men, but this was sexier than a mutha f****. I typed in a code locking the lobby door…But surprisingly she didn't run to the lobby. She ran to the third floor and my mother's apartment.

Son-of-a-b****, my mom didn't let me do any enhancements on her apartment, not even a camera. That was ingenious of her to go to the one place I couldn't touch. She grabbed something out of her pants pocket and did quick work at silently opening the door and slipping in like a ghost.

My mother was probably in her room watching the news and did not even know she had company. I knew the SEAL wouldn't hurt her, but it may be a good idea to get her out of town until I tamed this girl.

Moments later the woman appeared out my mother's back door. She carefully pulled it up behind her and then grabbed the rail and leaped over the banister.

"Damn! She like f***ing Spider-Man!" Rob yelled, but I was up and moving.

Sh*t! I didn't expect her to make it look so damned easy. My men were ready for her. It was at least twenty of them between her and the street. Yeah, she had made quick work of the small numbers she had ran through, let me see her do the same with twenty.

By the time I made it downstairs, she had found a bat and was working my men over with the mutha f****. When she saw me, a huge smile came on her face as she swung the bat with all her might and nailed one of my men dead in the chest before she let it roll in her hand like a sword and take out the feet of another that charged her.

And I kid you not, she then proceeded to wield that bat like it was a pair of num-chuks and her name was Bruce f***ing Lee. She worked that bat like she was a super hero and it was her weapon of choice. By the time I made it to her, she'd disposed of the twenty men that were in place waiting for her. They were all on the ground holding their injuries moaning and groaning.

What the hell?

Several more men came around the side just as I reached her. She threw the bat at me before running toward the gate. When she reached it, she climbed it flawlessly and flipped over the top. Even I couldn't climb it that fast.

By the time I got over it, she was hauling a** down the street. Several of my men were chasing after her, but there was no way in hell they were going to catch her, she was too fast. I cut down the alley...I will cut her off on Fourteenth. Several of my men ran behind me. As soon as I hit the corner, I saw her running toward me looking behind her, when she finally turned around, her eyes widened to see that I'd outsmarted her.

But do y'all know this little savage a** girl cut to the right and ran towards a sewer opening that was only big enough for her little body to get through? Pumping my legs, I ran faster. I had to get to her before she got to it.

She turned back to see how close I was. When she saw I was closer than she thought, she didn't panic...

Oh no… She went down into a slide and slid the rest of the way into the f***ing hole. She had the nerve to look at me before she disappeared into it fully with a wicked smirk on her face, giving me the finger with both hands as she disappeared completely from my view and into the sewer.

"Son-of-a-b****!" I yelled.

Damn…

I'm in love…

Chapter 5

Just a Little Gentleness

Nakhti

When I was a girl my mom would go into these drunken rages where she would yell at me and tell me it was all my fault that my daddy left. I don't remember much about him, except for the fact he was twenty years younger than my mother, who'd given birth to me at forty-three, and he was African-American.

My mom often told me I looked just like him. She would say it right before she grabbed a fist full of my hair and smashed my head into the nearest thing. A wall, a bed...once the bathroom mirror. I picked shards of glass out of my head for nearly three days.

I promised myself when I left home for the military that I would never take another a** whooping again, which is why I've trained as hard as I have. And guess what. I've never taken another a** whooping...

Until today...

The *thug* just handed me my a** on a platter!

Let me tell you guys how this *travesty* went down.

So, I'd waited to resurface from the sewer till I was nearly a mile away from Romeo's place, thinking I was in the clear. I had a huge grin on my face because as it does each time, I completely wrecked shop, my endorphins were clashing with my adrenaline, making me high.

However when I turn around, it was to find the thug leaning against this bad a** shiny black pickup truck with chrome trim that was sitting on a crazy lift. I didn't know what surprised me more, the truck, it's monster tires, or the fact that the kid had come alone and was here waiting on me as casually as you please.

That perfect mouth of his was lifted in a grin. Of course, this made my grin disappear as irritation set in.

"How did you find me?"

"I've got eyes everywhere, Minha Anjo."

I balled up my fists wanting to scream at him. His arrogance was so freaking annoying.

"Yeah well, what do you want?!" I spat, not able to hide the fact that I wanted to scratch his eyes out for sh*tting on my victory.

I told you guys, I'm very competitive.

He lifted an eyebrow as his grin grew. "You seem...frazzled."

Ewww! I wanted to hurt him.

"I'm not! I'm just fine. It's your men that are frazzled." I put my hand to my chest as I pretended to be concerned.

"By the way, are they okay? I tried not to send anyone to the hospital...though they may be sporting a lump or two by morning." I blinked innocently at him.

That got under his skin. I could tell by the way that little muscle began to tick in his chin. My grin came back along with the blessed feeling of victory that unbeknownst to me was going to be short lived.

Very short lived.

However, I discovered something about my big friend here, judging by his response to my little jab, he was just as competitive as me.

He shrugged nonchalantly. "I mean, they may have a few lumps...I think the census when I left was that the situation was a bit... inconvenient if anything."

I threw my head back and laughed at that. "Inconvenient...is that what it was?"

Grinning at me he nodded.

"Well let this sink in...I conveniently spared all of their lives, something I don't normally do."

Ha! Think about that, Brainy Boy!

The grin left his face. "Get in the truck."

His tone said he was done playing games. I had to bite my lip to keep from laughing at him again.

I folded my arms. "Why?"

"I'm going to be having a little after party at my place for a real good friend of mine a little later, and I want to grab something to eat first, so...get in."

I shook my head. "I'll pass."

"I don't think you understand. That wasn't a question." He still leaned casually against that monster truck as if he didn't know he was in the presence of a goon. I took off my scully and shoved it in my pocket before twisting my hair up in a bun.

"Jo said you took down two of his agents while handcuffed. Is that true?"

"I took down three of Jo's punk a** agents while handcuffed," he shrugged. "But who's counting."

I nodded.

Three...

Hmmm...

You see, right then, I could have just turned and made a run for it. There were several things that warned against me engaging in a fight with him.

First of all, he was very big. If I had to guess at his height, I would guess 6'4"...maybe, and he was very muscular. He didn't have the big bulky muscles of a bodybuilder, no...his muscles were the lean type of a fighter.

First warning sign.

Second and by far the loudest, is the fact that he took out three FBI agents while handcuffed. That in itself was quite a feat.

But you guys just seen what I did. So you can understand why I still didn't budge to run or walk toward that truck. I felt that I could take him.

SMH...Vanity! Man's worst enemy.

"Now let's say I decide I'm not getting in your truck. What you plan on doing about it?"

He looked to the side and chuckled a bit, at that point he was still very relaxed.

"Then I guess…I will have to put you in my truck."

I looked amazed for just a moment. "Oh really?! Just you? You didn't think to bring any help?"

It was his turn to laugh. "I think I can handle it… Minha Anjo."

And that was the beginning of the end.

Instead of waiting for him to come to me, I charged him with a roundhouse kick, hoping the sneak attack would give me the advantage.

It didn't, he moved so swiftly that I nearly kicked his truck. The only reason I didn't was because he didn't just move out the way, but grabbed me around the waist and pulled me back. Now I could be a big person and admit he'd just saved me from possibly breaking my leg on his truck, or at the very least injuring it badly…

But I'd rather eat dog food than admit anything to this arrogant bastard.

I elbowed him in the neck…this was enough to break his hold on me. Then I went back on my right hand kicking up at him with both feet. Not only did he block it, he got a hold of my waist again lifting me into his arms.

I wrapped my legs around his waist in a Jui Jitsu hold that will squeeze the breath out of him while swinging at his head with both fists. He blocked both blows before bringing his elbow down on my thigh breaking my hold.

Damn…He's good!

But instead of letting go of his waist with my legs, I went back into a flip to try and throw his big body with them like I'd done his friend earlier. It was a move I did often when fighting with big men, using the strength of my legs to take them down.

But instead of resisting, which is what's needed to make this move work, he rolled with me reversing the hold.

Sh*t! He knew Brazilian Jui Jitsu!

That wasn't good…It was at that point I knew I was in trouble. We grappled on the ground for about another five minutes before I was spent…

This bastard was damn good at Brazilian Jui Jitsu!

And to add insult to injury, I couldn't shake the feeling that he was taking it easy on me. I'd thrown several blows, he…not one. If he was fighting someone he viewed as a threat, he would surely throw blows…

Great!

This bastard didn't even view me as a threat!

Right at the point, I thought I was going to have to tap out because he had my arm in a hold that felt like it was going to break any minute, he surprised me by suddenly releasing me.

He held up his hand that was covered in blood. "What the f***?"

Frowning he sat up, pushing me to lie flat on my back. I too stared at his bloody hand confused. Where the hell did all that blood come from?

It was then that I felt my shirt sticking to me. The blood was mine.

"Why are you bleeding?" As he asked his question, he was using his big hands to try to lift up my bloody tank top.

I slapped his hand. "What do you think you're doing?"

Lying on my back like this with my blood wetting up my tank, it was quite obvious I wasn't wearing a bra.

"Get over yourself, I'm trying to see why you're bleeding." He huffed before he shoved my hands out the way.

He lifted my top enough to expose my bandage. Very carefully he pulled the tape back.

"Oh sh*t! You've been shot!"

"Wow! You are a genius. The rumors are true."

He frowned at my sarcastic tone. "What the f*** happened to you?"

"I got shot." I told him dryly.

"Yeah, I can see that. When?"

I thought about not telling him, but he had a very determined look on his face, and I was just too tired to fight him. Hell, I think I've lost too much blood.

"Yesterday," I muttered.

He took his phone out his pocket and after scrolling for a second placed a call tucking the phone between his shoulder and his ear to scoop me up off the ground and into his arms.

"I can walk." I told him, but he ignored me.

"Yeah, I need you to meet me at my house." He spoke into the receiver. "Yeah now!" When he was finished, he held me with one arm and shoved his phone in his pocket with the other hand before bringing his arm back under my legs.

I looked at his profile as he carried me to his truck. He held me like a man would a woman he cared for, or a loving parent would a child. Nobody has ever carried me like this.

A few years after becoming a SEAL, my team and I were on a mission in an Iranian desert. On our way out, I took one to the leg. Rather than be slowed down by me, The Politician threw me over his shoulder and carried me the rest of the way back to our compound.

That didn't feel like this. I know it wasn't possible, but it actually felt like Romeo cared. Because I'd never been treated this way and was finding it quite fascinating, I let him put me in his truck and secure me in the seatbelt.

No one has ever cared for me, not even my mother. I wondered what he would do if he knew just how tough I was. Would he stop this gentle treatment?

Did I want him to stop this gentle treatment?

Maybe I could let it go on for a little while longer. What would that hurt?

"Are you alright?" He asked when he hopped up in the driver seat. With a real pathetic look on my face I nodded.

"I think so…"

Oh! Nak…you're really selling this, aren't you?

Shut up, killjoy!

When we got back to his building, he hurried around the truck lifting me out and back into his arms. I wanted to rest my head against his big shoulder, curious to see what that felt like, but didn't because that would be a bit too much.

"Yo! What you do to her?" Rob said as he rushed out the building towards us.

Romeo rudely pushed past his little brother. "I didn't do this, goofy! Move!"

Oh my goodness! He was really worried about me. I should put his mind at ease and tell him I was alright, I'd just busted a few of my hasty stitches… But when he looked down at me with those concerned honey gazers, I changed my mind.

What?!

Before y'all judge me, remember I've never had this. Can't a girl just have a moment of gentleness before my life goes back to the gruesome barbwire it's always been?

Now, where were we…?

Oh yes, he was laying me gently on his bed.

"You want me to get some warm water and towels?" Rob asked leaning over the bed just as concerned as his brother.

Wow!

Romeo looked up at him as if he was stupid. "Do I look like a f***ing doctor?"

Rob actually thought about it before he shook his head.

"Then why you gon' bring me warm water and towels?"

Rob shrugged. "I don't know, it just sounded like some sh*t I should ask."

Laughter bubbled up from inside me. Rob was the rascal to Romeo's seriousness, but the big brother did not find his little brother amusing. In fact, his frown grew.

"I told you, you need to stop smoking that sh*t, it's making you dumber."

Rob's grin didn't move an inch. "And I told you, you need to try that sh*t, maybe then you can manage to pull that stick from your a**."

That made me crack up. Rome's angry gaze came down to me, but whatever he was going to say was interrupted by a knock on the door.

"Yeah!" He called in that direction.

The man I'd thrown into the wall earlier with my legs, which so happened to be the same guy that Rob was smoking weed with on the steps earlier stuck his head in. "Doc's here."

"Let him up." Rome responded as he stood from the bed, but before he walked away, he slapped his little brother really hard in the back of the head.

Rob grabbed at his sore head. "Ouch! Man! What you do that for?"

"Pull that out your a**."

Rob rubbed at his head as he glared at his brother's retreating back.

"He better be lucky I'm over here worried about you, or I would have whooped his a**." he whispered to me.

"Say what!" Rome called from what I assumed was the closet area.

Rob's head jerked up. "Huh? Oh, nothing, I was asking her if she wanted me to prop up her foot."

I had to cover my laughter. Rob is a mess. And yes, he was higher than a Georgia Pine. There was absolutely nothing wrong with my foot. Rome came out the closet in a clean white t-shirt. The one he had on before was stained with my blood. When the doctor bustled through the door with a medical bag in his hand, Rome kicked his little brother out.

He was a young, attractive, dark skinned brotha and I couldn't help but feel a little proud to see him sporting that lab coat. I tried to hear what he and Rome were talking about by the door, but I couldn't. It's a very big loft and the door was way across the room.

It looked as if he was asking Rome for a favor. Whatever it was aggravated Rome who impatiently gestured to me, but the doctor didn't give up. He was younger than Rome and spoke to him like he was his little brother.

Finally, Rome gave in to whatever it was he was asking him.

"You only have one hour, and you need to fix her first!" He told him as he walked toward the kitchen area that wasn't far from the bedroom area. With a huge grin on his face the doctor got on his phone and made a call as he began to lay out his supplies on the kitchen table.

"What's going on?" I asked Rome confused at the doctor's behavior.

"Nothing…" He reached inside the fridge and came out with a bottle of water, then proceeded to drink half of it before he continued.

"He's been pestering me about letting him put his stupid machine on my head."

"What kind of machine?" He turned to me and smiled before he came down to one knee next to the bed. He moved with the grace of a trained fighter. Don't know why I looked past all this before.

"A machine that he claims can pick up thought patterns and determine what makes people tick." This he whispered to me, so that the doctor couldn't hear him.

"You don't believe him?" I whispered back.

He shook his head. "Hell no. There is no machine that can see the thoughts that live here." He touched my head with his finger.

"Sure, they may can see some electric reactions, but they are completely clueless to what that is. The kid thinks he's so smart because he can work the phrase space time continuum in every conversation."

That made me laugh. "Why are we whispering?"

He licked his lips and I nearly groaned out loud.

Damn! Maybe I did, because a knowing grin appeared on his face before he leaned closer. So close, those soft lips of his brushed my ear.

"I've invested too much into his education to tear down his confidence. If he thinks his machine can unscramble my thoughts, then who am I to tell him different."

After he said that he looked at me to see what I thought of that. And although I won't be telling him what I really thought, I will tell you guys.

One of the things that's a big part of training for the Federal Bureau of Investigation is profile analysis. Before you put on the suit, you're forced to study many different personalities, so that when you go into the field, no one catches you off guard.

This is a gift I excelled at even before I became an agent. When growing up with an abusive parent you learn how to read body language as if your life depended on it. Many times while out in the field, my brothers- in-arms waited for me to read a situation before entering it.

I have studied many profiles, but nothing like Rome. His mind didn't work like anything I've been trained to deal with. He's not my first genius…

Yet…

He is like none of the genius profiles we've studied. Maybe that was why the doctor wanted to put his machine on his head.

Rome watched me with those amber eyes of his for a minute and I wondered what he saw. Did he just now realize he'd shown care to the un-carable? Did he now understand that I was too rough for his gentleness?

Unnerved under his intense gaze I opened my mouth to ask him what he saw, but before I could, he winked at me and jumped back to his feet.

"One hour with your stupid machine, I mean it," he told the doctor before turning up his bottle of water and draining the rest.

"It's not a stupid machine," the younger man responded to him before he went back to his call.

"He said yes, come quickly, bring the equipment, we only have an hour…we won't get this chance again."

When he hung up the phone, he smiled down at me. "I don't know who you are, but I can kiss you!" He was excited like a kid in the candy store.

"You try it and it will be the last thing you do," Rome grumbled before he walked away toward the living room area to his paused GTO game.

The doctor looked up at his retreating back startled before his curious gaze came back to me.

"Wow! Never seen that before." He mumbled under his breath so that Rome couldn't hear.

"Seen what before?" I asked when he made it back to the bed from washing his hands in the kitchen sink.

"Him… territorial."

I started to tell him he was mistaken, but after he put on a pair of gloves, he took out a pair of shears and began cutting away my bloody shirt. I managed to get my hands up to cover my boobs before anyone could see them…

And yes, my boobs were so small they fit in my hands, but…

What I'm lacking up top, I made up for down below. I've always been told I have a nice butt. Many of men have gotten their hands broken trying to touch it.

When the doctor began to peel my bandage off, I turned to look at Rome and was startled to find him watching me. I'd thought he'd been playing his video game, but he wasn't. He was sitting on his couch facing me with his arms on the back of it unashamedly watching me.

"Ouch!" I cried when I felt a prick to my side. Panic shot through me when I saw that the doctor had given me a shot.

"What is that?!" I started to get up, but he put his hand on my shoulder gently pushing me back down.

"Calm down, ma'am, it's just a local anesthetic. After I check the wound and make sure it's clean, I'm going to have to re-stitch it."

I exhaled. A local anesthetic…

Okay, I can deal with that.

Damn it!

Rome was throwing me off my game. Ever since he's come into my life, I've been behaving unnaturally. I never let my guard down enough for someone to get a needle in me without me realizing it.

The doctor had used a local anesthetic, but it could have been so much worse. Like, he could have been trying to put me out.

"What kind of doctor are you?" I asked trying to feel the man out who was so eager to get inside Rome's head.

"I'm what is called a physician-scientist. I study the brain. I guess you can call me a Neurologist."

Well that explained his fascination with the brain. But what was it about Rome's brain that he was so eager to find out?

"Why are you so eager to see what's going on in his head?"

His hand paused in cleaning my womb and he looked at me as if I had suddenly gone lame.

"Are you kidding me?"

I shook my head. "No, I'm curious."

"He's a…" He searched his mind for the right word. "A phenomenon…"

"Oh, you mean a genius?"

He shook his head fervently. "No, I'm a genius, I think I may have found a way to separate space from time in the continuum." He tapped gestured toward his own head.

"Genius… He's a phenomenon…and I plan to be the one to crack the code to his brain."

The fact that he'd managed to say space time continuum just like Rome said made me chuckle. At least I attempted to chuckle, but my eyes were beginning to feel kind of heavy.

"I don't understand. What's the difference between the two?" Even my speech sounded slurred.

"Geniuses believe in what they can touch, taste, see, or smell. He…" He tilted his head in Rome's direction as he prepped my wound for stitching.

"He believes in things he can't see."

"Like what?" Nossa! I was getting really tired.

"Like God…" He leaned closer. "Do you know he claims to play chest with an angel every Tuesday in the park?"

"Do you believe him?"

That was the last thing I remember saying before everything went dark…

Chapter 6

My Captive

Nakhti

The first thing that assaulted my senses when I came awake was the overwhelming smell of marijuana smoke and bass from a near-by speaker that seemed to vibrate throughout my whole body. I tried to open my eyes, but they were so heavy and that sweet darkness was beckoning me to return to its embrace.

"How are you feeling, Minha Anjo?"

The sound of Rome's voice caused me to fight off the darkness. Although my body protested, I opened my eyes.

Rome stood at the foot of the big bed, but he wasn't alone. Rob grinned down at me from my right, the man I'd thrown into the wall earlier stood next to him, and two more men who I didn't recognize stood to my left.

I blinked to try and clear my vision. That bastard doctor had drugged me! Local anesthetic my a**--

The sound of metal hitting metal when I tried to lower my arms caused my thoughts to come to a halt.

What the hell?

My hands were handcuffed and fastened to something over my head. Instant panic shot through me at being vulnerable like this. Taking a few deep breaths to still my pounding heart, I quelled the fear. I've been in situations like this before.

Panic was not going to help me. I just had to try and clear the drug from my mind and think my way through this.

My first mission was to get my hands free…and then get the hell out of here.

"Wha—" I swallowed, my throat felt really dry. "What's going on?" I asked Rome.

The sound of a crowd of people clapping drew my attention. Turning my head towards the music I nearly cried out in alarm. Although there was no one close to the bed or really paying attention to me outside of the five men surrounding me, the loft was full of people.

It looked as if I'd been asleep in the midst of a full-blown party.

Ah…he did say he was having a little get together at his place later.

But this was a little bit more than a simple get together.

Over against the far wall was a band.

A band!

The music they played was a fusion of jazz and hip-hop. It didn't sound bad. In fact, it sounded really good. I narrowed my eyes at the man rapping on the mic. He looked so familiar. The song they were performing sounded familiar as well.

A woman dressed in a red mini dress strutted over to an area where a bar had been set up. She looked like a model. When she got to the bar she glanced over at Rome and smiled shyly before turning away.

Hmmmm…that was subtle.

When she got her drink, she strutted a little closer, as if the fact that she was clearly on the hunt wasn't evident.

"Rome, are you coming back to the party?" She cooed.

For the first time, he looked away from me and smiled at her. "Yeah, I'll be back over in a min."

"Okay…I've been trying to talk to you all night. I've got something I want to show you."

I rolled my eyes. It didn't take a rocket scientist to figure out what that was.

"For the safety of my guests, I had to cuff you to the bed."

I frowned at him. "What the hell did you think I was going to do? Go crazy and just start killing people?"

There was a little irritation in my voice. I refused to believe it was because I was jealous of the woman in the red dress who'd just given Rome a coochie coupon in front of all of us.

As if he could hear my thoughts he chuckled.

"Shawty, you just beat the hell out of my brother's whole squad." Rob said as if I'd asked a stupid question.

I drew a deep breath and killed my jealousy. I was tripping. Why in the hell did I care who Rome slept with? He was nothing to me…nothing! Just because he was gentle with me earlier didn't mean anything.

Get it together, Nak! You need to get out of here. Remember, stay focused.

I blinked up at Rome innocently. I was very aware of the power of my eyes and their ability to manipulate. They were one of my most powerful weapons. Many times they've gotten me out of jams.

"That's because they tried to hurt me. I don't just make a habit out of beating people up." This time when I spoke my voice was much kinder. It was the voice that matched my eyes perfectly.

"I was just protecting myself, Romeo…"

Of course that was all load of crap. I've beaten up a lot of people in my time, but they didn't need to know that, I was trying to get out of these cuffs.

Rob twisted his mouth to the side in a way that said he didn't believe me. "Yeah, right. You violent as hell." He poked my arm that was covered in art.

"Don't think we don't know that's a Navy SEAL tattoo. Yo' boy Jo got one just like it."

I looked up at Rome completely ignoring Rob. My tattoos were none of their business.

"Can I have some water? My throat is really dry." Subject change…

The grin that was on his handsome face as he studied me made me feel as if those honey gazers could see straight through my act. It was as if he knew as soon as he freed me, I was going to beat my way out of this joint.

"Now if I undo your hands, do you promise to behave yourself?" He asked.

Sucka!

Blinking innocently, I nodded. "I promise. I just want some water."

The man that I'd thrown into the wall earlier shook his head.

"Man, hell no! Don't fall for that. As soon as you let her go, she going to start busting up some sh*t. Leave her wild a** tied up for the safety of us all." He put his hand on the back of his head, probably feeling that egg-size knot I'd assisted him in obtaining.

"Knot true!" I cried. I couldn't resist. "I just want water."

The man narrowed his eyes at me, catching my pun and I nearly burst into laughter. I had to bite my tongue to keep from doing it and ruining what I had going.

Rome signaled for the men to leave him and me alone. Before he left, Rob leaned down until his handsome face was next to mine.

"A little word of advice. Don't try to lie to him. It won't work…it never does."

As he whispered those words to me, Rome walked to the fridge to get my water. After grabbing a glass from the cabinet, he poured half the water in it.

I watched him as he approached. Was what Rob said true? Is Rome a human lie detector? For a strange reason, I could feel that his words were true. Just a minute ago when I was putting on my little act to get out of these cuffs, he'd watched me with something akin to laughter in his eyes. It felt like he found me amusing.

He sat the cup of water on the table next to the bed before he completely took me by surprise by leaning over me as if he was doing a push up, with a hand on both sides of my head. His face was only inches from mine. Those honey gazers drew me in, causing me to forget we were in a room full of people. For just a moment I thought he was going to kiss me.

And the crazy thing about that…

There was no reflex anywhere inside of me to stop him.

Sh*t!

"I saw you use those eyes on my men earlier and I called them foolish for falling prey to them, only to fall prey myself. I don't think I could deny you anything when you look at me like that."

His hungry gaze lowered to my lips and I swear something strange happened to my breathing.

No…something strange happened to my body.

Men have always told me the effect my eyes had on them. But this was the first time it felt like a compliment.

"If I let you go, you have to promise to behave."

"What am I, your dog?"

"You're nobody's dog, my Queen. But there are a few things you should be aware of before you step foot out of this bed, a few things that could be very detrimental to your health."

Okay…

He had my attention now, and not because he'd just called me his Queen.

As if he knew it, he chuckled before sticking his hand in his pocket retrieving the key. Once he unlocked the cuffs, he helped me sit up. My limbs still felt a bit wobbly.

He sat on the bed facing me before handing me the glass of water. I hadn't lied about being thirsty. After I drained it, I handed the glass back to him so that he could pour the rest of the water in it.

Mid drink I remembered that before I went to sleep, the doctor had cut my shirt away. I nearly spit my water out trying to look down at myself. I exhaled, visibly relieved when I saw that someone had cleaned all the blood off my skin and put a brand-new white wife beater in my size on me.

What the hell?

My gaze flew up to his, but the words I was getting ready to say stalled in my throat. I caught him studying me with an unguarded look on his face. He watched me as if he was fascinated with me. I licked my dry lips and his russet gaze followed.

"Did you buy me a new shirt?"

He nodded. "That and few more items."

Before I could ask what items, he looked down at my feet. I followed his gaze. Someone had also taken off my boots and pulled the strings in both legs of my cargo pants to draw the material up around my ankles. There reflecting brilliantly in the dim lighting of Rome's loft were two beautiful golden bracelets, one around each ankle.

Spellbound, I leaned closer to get a better look at them. I'd never seen anything like them. They looked very expensive. The gold was soft and wide but not cumbersome. I flexed my feet and the cuffs molded around my ankles as if they were made from leather rather than metal.

In the center if each bracelet was a glass window. There was some kind of liquid in the glass and inside the liquid were little rotating golden gears.

They were amazing!

"There is a man who lives in the Dominican Republic named Enrique Almodóvar. He's the last alchemist of his line. The things the man can do with gold defy cognitive thought." Rome spoke low so that only I could hear him.

He lifted his hand to caress one of the bracelets. And I swear, as he spoke, it was like I'd fallen under a spell. The whole room seemed to disappear. It was just me drowning in that honey gaze.

How did he do that? How did he manage to draw me into himself like this?

"When I first saw these beauties, I knew I had to have them. I didn't know why. I just knew they were for me." He paused for a moment studying me again. "I thought to myself at the time, I'd just wasted a small fortune because there is no woman alive that I would ever want to cuff in gold."

He lifted a hand and brushed some of my hair that had escaped my ponytail back behind my ear. "But then I met you, little savage, and I knew I will do whatever it takes to keep you. Even imprison you in golden shackles."

I frowned, the hazy love bubble he was building around me popped. "Golden shackles?"

My gaze went back to the beautiful bracelets. Why would he call them shackles?

"Why do you call them shackles?"

He smiled at me then, but it didn't reach his eyes. His honey gaze had gone cold.

"Because Minha Anjo, if you step one pretty foot off this bed, the gears in that bracelet are going to go in reverse. And if they go in reverse, they are going to create a spark that is going to ignite the accelerant the gears are resting in and separate that little foot from your body."

"Say what?" I knew I heard him wrong. Did this bastard just say—?

"You are wearing bombs around your ankles."

He's lying. "How is that possible?"

"There is a very tiny microchip inside the bracelets that controls the gears. The chip has been programmed to reverse the gears if you step out of this bed. I can program it to allow you free rein of the loft…"

He paused for just a moment as his intense gaze fell to my lips. And for the first time I realized how close his head was to mine. And that he'd been starring at my lips this whole time. My breath stalled somewhere in my throat when I saw his head lowering even closer.

Nossa! He was going to kiss me.

When his lips touched mine for the first time, it was like his caress earlier… So very gentle. He didn't kiss my lips full on but rather just the corner.

As if he there was nothing else in the world he'd rather be doing, his lips lowered to my chin, just below the corner of my mouth. My eyes closed when his lips lowered to my neck.

I know I should be stopping him. I know I shouldn't allow him to take such liberties. But his lips were softer than I'd imagined. When I felt his warm breath on my lobe right before his tongue a shiver went through me and I had to ball my hands into fist to keep from grabbing him.

Why was he teasing me like this?

It was the slightest of touches, but it was enough to awaken my lust like a roaring lion.

"Yeah, I can see myself giving you free reign of a lot of things…But we haven't reached that point yet." He whispered in my ear, causing another shiver to go through my body.

And then he stood, throwing a cup of cold water on the fire he'd just started. "The chip has also been programmed to reverse the gears if someone tries to remove the bracelets without the key…So tread with caution, little wild one."

Would yall believe he turned and walked away. Leaving me all hot and bothered.

"You're bullsh*tting me, right!" I called after him. I didn't know if I was talking about the bombs around my ankles or the fact that he'd just toyed with me so effortlessly.

He turned to look at me with a grin on his face. This time it reached his eyes…

"Am I?"

Completely flabbergasted, I watched him cross the floor and rejoin the party. If you can really call what he did rejoining. He took a seat on a couch that was empty, which was amazing seeing as to how the room was so crowded.

Yet...no one sat on that couch. When I saw him lean forward and open his laptop on the coffee table in front, I saw why.

The bartender came from behind the bar with a single glass of brown liquid on the rocks. I knew the drink was for Rome. Everybody else was drinking out of red plastic cups...Only the King got a glass.

And well...he'd given me a glass as well, but I will not read more into that than happenstance.

Once the bartender got near Rome's couch, he waited for the signal for him to come closer to hand him his drink.

Rome had everyone here trained not to disturb him when he was on his computer. What good hacker would be comfortable with someone looking over their shoulder? But I had a feeling Rome was often alone in a crowd.

My gaze went back to the golden cuffs around my ankles. I exhaled...

Damn, bombs...I'd like to say that this is the worst situation I'd ever been in, but then I would be lying. In fact, this is quite breezy to some of the scraps I've found myself in. Remember me telling you guys I got shot while fleeing an assassination that got kind of messy?

Well what I didn't tell you was that I was fleeing out of an eighty-four-story window and had to fight with my chute that had a hole in it because the bullet had pierced it before my flesh and didn't get it to work until I was halfway down.

Miraculously, the thing opened enough for me to land unscathed to make my escape. That parachute saved my life in two ways. Had the bullet not gone through it first, my wound would have been a lot worse than just the flesh wound I ended up with.

I turned my ankle so that I could see the other side of the bracelet, and sure enough, there was a little opening in it where a key would go.

No, this wasn't traumatic, but it sure the hell was problematic. It had thrown a monkey wrench in my second mission, which was to get the hell out of here.

Oh well!

Being here was my original plan anyway, so there was no big loss there. He said he can program the bracelets to allow me the run of the loft. If I could convince him to do that, then I could find the key. It had to be here somewhere.

Once I found the key, I can get the Sarge's information and get the hell out.

"Would you like something to eat?"

A very soft voice came from the kitchen area pulling me from my thoughts. A beautiful pregnant young woman stood at the dishwasher loading it with dishes smiled kindly at me.

Oh my God! Was she Rome's woman? That bastard!

"Are you Rome's girlfriend?"

She chuckled shaking her head. "No, I'm Derrick's girl." She gestured to a man that stood off to the side talking to one of the men who'd stood by my bed earlier.

Instantly my gut tensed up. Derrick was a bad man. I could smell his stench from across the room. I've always been able to spot evil. Turning, I took in the beautiful young lady, now studying her closer.

My instinct that me and my whole team have always trusted, coupled with my training, screamed that this girl was being abused.

I nodded. "Yes, I am very hungry. What do you have?"

She went to a side table where a buffet had been set up. There was a man in a chef jacket standing behind it. When she came back the plate was laden down with goodies.

"Here, sit with me while I eat. I don't know anybody here and I feel kind of lonely." It was a lie. I just wanted to get a closer look at her.

She had long braids that she let hide her face. When I invited her to sit with me, she blushed as if I'd just bestowed a great honor on her, before easing down on the corner of the bed.

All of her movements spoke of her abuse. The way she'd have yet to look me in the eye. The way she eased down on the bed as if she was used to stepping lightly as not to upset someone. When she pushed her braids behind her left ear, I saw it.

She was covering a bruise on the side of her face with make-up. To those with untrained eyes she looked normal...just a shy young lady.

But I knew the signs...

I knew them really well.

"Why are you cleaning up behind Rome's guests?" I asked as I spooned potato salad in my mouth.

She looked up, startled that I cared, but quickly looked away before chuckling nervously.

Nossa! She was being abused badly.

"Rome pays me to clean up his place."

"What?!" That bastard...this beautiful girl was nobody's maid!

"No, please!" She held up her hands to calm my anger and I instantly felt bad for getting worked up around her.

"It's a good thing. He pays me more than some nurses make. God knows with the baby coming we need the money."

"What about your man, doesn't he work?" I could not hide the contempt in my voice.

"He was working, but he got into an accident on the premises and they laid him off. He's looking for a job though."

Let me translate this for all of you at home who's never seen this before. Her man was high and messed something up at the company he worked for and they fired him.

"But look at you." She said turning the attention from her and her f***ed up man.

"Rome has you here laying on his bed like his Queen." She chuckled. "He put gold ankle bracelets on you while you slept." Longing came into her eyes.

"He honored you. You're his ghetto Queen."

Wow, this one's head is way in the clouds...

"What's your name?" I asked her, bringing her back down to earth.

"Happy."

For a moment I thought I heard her wrong. "Did you say, Happy?"

She nodded and then smiled at me, and I realized why she had that name. Her smile brightened the room. Happy was also a dreamer. Maybe a poet…She was optimistic and genuinely happy for me and the honor she perceived Rome had given me by decking me in gold while I slept.

She was happy for me although she was going home to hell.

If only she knew that he'd put golden bombs around my ankles…But I didn't want to destroy the image she had created for herself. She's the type that experienced happiness through other people, because she didn't know she could have it herself. If only she'd be brave enough to walk away from her tormenter.

"My name's Brenda." The lie slipped easily from my lips…

"Please to meet—"

"Happy! Come here!" Derrick said, snapping his fingers at her.

She jumped when she heard his voice, before looking at me, trying to cover her action with a chuckle.

"I have to go, Brenda. It was nice meeting you."

I watched her go, nearly snapping the plastic fork in my hand from wanting to follow her and beat the shit out of Derrick. Maybe Rome had been right in having the foresight to prevent me from leaving this bed.

As God is my witness, I would be whopping that bastard right now. My hand twitched under the plate of food I was holding. Every cell in my body signaled for me to toss it at the bastard.

"Nak, what the hell is wrong with you?! Your impulsive reactions are going to get you killed! You're my best soldier, but I will ground your a** if you don't learn to control that."

Those were The Politician's words to me my first year under his command. And do y'all know the crazy thing? I think those were his last words to me the last time he and I went on a mission together.

The moral of the story, I have yet to learn to control my impulsive reactions. Here I was getting ready to send this plate sailing across the room to smash Derrick's woman beating a** in the face.

My muscles tensed, ready to carry out the action, but I don't know what made me look up just at the moment. I made eye contact with those honey gazers and stalled. He looked at me from across the room and still managed to make everything and everyone else fade...

How in the world did he do that?

As if he could read my thoughts, he shook his head.

What the hell? There is no way he could read my thoughts.

I lifted my hands as if to say, what?"

He chuckled, shaking his head at me again, but his attention was drawn away by the lady in the red dress, who was stepping in front of him to ease on the couch next to him. He looked up at her as she passed, because she was practically shoving her big fake boobs in his face.

At the same time he let her slide past him, he closed his laptop, sitting back on the couch so that she could get by. My hand twitched under my plate again.

Oh wow! This has never happened to me. I have never been jealous of another woman for the attention of a man…

Not ever.

What was happening to me?

"That's a damn shame to have something as sexy as you in his bed and still find a way to play with the trash."

I had been focusing so hard on Rome and the tramp that was practically throwing herself at him that I didn't notice the man standing by the bar watching me.

I took him in. He was a handsome enough man, but he was not good. He was treacherous and full of envy for Rome. I'd seen his profile a million times. If we were going to infiltrate Rome's organization, this would be the man we would put the wire on.

The traitor…

Still, he was a man, and a useful tool to help me ground myself and get over whatever jealousy I was feeling.

Two can play at this…

I smiled at him. And his mouth fell open a bit in surprise.

Yeah, I was putting it on a bit strong, but I was emotional. It was my first time feeling jealousy, and at the moment, I just wanted not to feel that.

"The trash is his only option…I'm not on his menu." I practically made love to the man with my gaze.

And just like most men do in my hands, he turned to putty and actually came closer to the bed.

"Wait! You and Rome ain't together?"

I shook my head. "Nope...Why?"

"I mean, if you not with nobody then—"

"Then what?" I asked cutting him off, smiling shyly at him.

"Then maybe I can take you out some time. You don't want to f*** with Rome anyway, a nigga like that can't be true to you. He got b****es fighting to be with him...every night he got a different ho in his bed..."

See what I mean? Although he hangs in Rome's shadow, he does it with a heart full of hate...praying for his downfall.

However, that wasn't my problem. My problem was getting rid of this feeling of jealousy in my heart. So, I threw my head back and laughed like what he'd just said was the funniest thing in the world to me.

Yeah, I know it was petty...and a bit childish, but my feelings were hurt, and remember I told you guys about my impulsive reflexes...so please, don't judge me.

Pray for me...

Meanwhile, the hater took another step closer to me, falling easily under my charm.

"Come sit by me for a moment." I told him patting the bed next to me...and would you guys believe he actually took a step my way?

"You think I'm a b****, Ray?" Rome's deep voice caused old Ray to nearly jump out of his boots.

I leaned over looking behind the now frightened man to see Rome handing the bartender his glass, telling him to refill it... Then he walked over to stand between Ray and me.

"Rome...I—"

"What's the matter? You had a lot of sh*t to say just a minute ago. Please...don't let me interrupt."

Ray looked at me and I widened my eyes in fake surprise.

Rob, the man that is knot my biggest fan, and a few more guys came to stand around us, sensing the tension in their leader. Rome turned up the glass and drank the double shot of Hennessy straight down. When he lowered it, he laughed. And for the first time, I realized he may be a bit intoxicated.

Uh-oh!

"Ray, how long have you been trying to roll with us?" He asked rotating the glass in his hand so that the ice clinked together.

Ray shrugged. "I mean, I've been trying to roll for a minute...Why?"

Nossa! This guy was trying to save face instead of bowing out. Maybe because our little scene had attracted a good amount of attention and he didn't want to look like a coward.

"I finally let you roll, and you come in my house and disrespect me?"

Ray shook his head. "She said she wasn't yo' girl."

"I'm not!" I volunteered trying to lend a hand to old Ray, he looked like he could use it.

Rome turned his angry gaze on me...

Yikes...He was really mad. The muscle was twitching like crazy in his chin.

But ask me if I care. I had to bite my lip to hold onto my laughter. He could tell and it made him angrier. He turned to face Ray.

"Because she playing games, I'm going to let this one slide. But don't bring yo' busta a** back to my crib. Bounce!" He spat those words through clenched teeth.

Ray looked back at me as if to say he'd get up with me later, and then turned toward the door...

Because there is something so seriously wrong with me, I held my hand out and called...

"Take me with you!"

I didn't expect what happened next to happen, not in a million years.

Ray turned back for me and actually held his hand up for mine...Nossa!

Rome moved so quickly he caught us all off guard...one minute Ray was standing on his feet, and the next he wasn't. Rome kicked the back of his legs...hard, sending him slamming to the ground...and then he was over him punching him in the face with the glass...The second hit caused the glass to shatter!

But he didn't stop, he started going in with his fists.

So, that's what it looks like when he hits somebody.

I looked up at his little brother, who watched the beatdown with amused horror. I really liked Rob, he and I had a kindred spirit.

"Now maybe a good time to help that poor fella." I told him.

As if snapping out of a daze, they all moved at once to pull Rome off the man. He was mad that they did, even turning his rage on them causing them to scurry back out his way.

Nossa! I may have taken it a bit far. The man was so angry he was red in the face…

By this time, the music had come to a halt and everybody was staring at Rome… He stood for a minute fuming, battling with himself to get control…

I loved it!

When he had it, he smoothed his clothes out and stretched his neck in a way that said he was barely controlling it…

"I'm sorry you all had to witness this." He spoke to the room. "But most importantly, do we all understand why this happened?"

All the men nodded their heads. Rome exhaled… "Good…that's good. Get this mutha f**** off my floor." Several of his men hurried forward to drag the unconscious man out of the loft.

Rome's eyes came to me and I saw the anger still there, very much alive.

I loved it!

He pointed at me. "Don't do that sh*t again!"

For a moment I held his gaze, trying to hold on to my laughter, but then I thought why should I? And collapsed back in the bed, my laughter filling the now quiet loft…

Romeo…my dear, Romeo. You have no idea of the tempest I bring…

Chapter 7

I Don't Want to Fall in Love...With You

Nakhti

The sound of someone running on a treadmill woke me. I opened my eyes and was surprised to see the sun spilling into the big windows to lighten the loft beautifully. In the center of the loft Rome ran on a treadmill facing the windows.

For a moment, I just lay there enjoying the sight of him in only a pair of basketball shorts and gym shoes. His beautifully defined tanned muscles glistened tantalizingly from sweat as he turned the treadmill up to a light sprint.

Many of my missions have called for me to get close to my target. How close is purely at my discretion. Because I'm good at my job, I've never had to go all the way with any of them.

Sure, I've gotten really close, but I've always managed to finish the job before actual intercourse takes place. Trust me, if I'm close enough for penetration, I'm close enough to make the kill.

In that moment, the kill is always easy because by that time, my skin is crawling at the feel of their hands and mouths touching my skin. I have never had a target I wanted to sleep with, they have all disgusted me.

My gaze traveled down Rome's beautifully sculpted body, taking in each intricate detail. And I think for the very first time in my whole career, my thoughts may have changed.

Because I've been so busy, I can't remember the last time I had sex…I mean, until this very moment, I hadn't even thought about sex.

Nossa!

I think it's been over seven years and before that, even longer. I had a boyfriend in high school who took my virginity on prom night. After that, he and I had a regular sexual relationship until I left for the military a few months later.

I can count on one hand the number of times I've had sex from that point on. And it's not that I haven't wanted or needed sexual gratification, it's just that I've been too damn busy.

If I'm being honest with myself, my need of late has become a little more pressing. I think I may have reached the age where it's said women experience a hormonal shift that makes them, how shall I say…? *Super horny.*

Or damn, maybe it's just the effect this kid was having on me. Hell, he had the effect on many women. Last night I sat here and watched them preen and strut for him. I watched several women completely make a fool of themselves to get his attention.

After he beat down the hater, the lady in the red dress left in a huff because he angrily returned to his computer and told his men he didn't want to be bothered, they in turn refused to let anyone get close to him.

There were many women shooting evil looks at me for being the one responsible for putting him in such a mood.

Now…

Ask me if I care…

LOL! I'd spent the rest of the evening talking to Rob, who is a whole nut. That boy doesn't have a serious bone in his body. And he is a chain blunt smoker. How somebody could get so high and still be as sharp as the kid is beyond me.

At some point he disappeared with one of the girls at the party, leaving me alone. I wanted to talk to Happy some more, but it looked as if her boyfriend got mad at her about something and sent her home. She stopped only long enough to tell me she would be back sometime today to clean up.

By the time the party was over and the band cleared out—

Oh! I knew what I wanted to tell you guys. So, do you remember me saying last night that the band looked familiar?

Turns out, they looked familiar to me because they're freaking famous. It was THE SEEDS…they're a famous group from Chicago, whose ability to smoothly blend jazz and hip hop has set them apart.

According to Rob, Rome was the one to pull some strings a few years ago to get the band noticed. So anytime they were in Chicago, they came and did a private set for Rome and his crew.

Wow! Imagine that.

Anyway, what was I saying?

Oh yes…so, by the time THE SEEDS cleared out I had nodded back off, feeling a little drowsy from the anesthetic that was taking its time clearing from my system and slept like a log till now.

Sitting up in bed I groaned from the pain in my side. It was safe to say the anesthetic was completely worn off, I felt like I'd been shot.

"Your pain pills are on the table next to you." Rome said without slowing down on the treadmill

Groggily I turned to look and sure enough, the bottle of pills that was in my coat pocket, sat on the nearby table with a bottle of water. Next to it was a blessed cup of steaming hot coffee. I nearly skipped the pills and the water for the coffee, but thought better of it and took the pills.

My gaze fell on the golden cuffs on my ankles. The sun shining through the window made the gold light up in a way that was breathtaking. These bracelets were absolutely amazing.

Too bad they were instruments of torture. When it was time for me to leave, I was going to try my best and preserve them, they will be a nice little trinket to always remind me of the gorgeous, educated thug that changed the way I will forever view his species.

"How did you sleep?" He asked as he brought his treadmill to a cool down.

I lifted my cup of coffee and bought it to my lips, watching him over its rim as he stepped off the treadmill.

"Not too bad. How about you?"

He shrugged as he dried himself off with his towel. "I don't sleep."

I wasn't surprised by that information. Most people with brains like his had trouble shutting them off enough to actually sleep. When his body forced him to shut down, it was probably just for an hour or two in front of his computer.

"You were sleeping when I first met you."

He chuckled as he sauntered my way, looking like a thug model. *Nossa!*

"It took two bottles of Hennessy and a good fu—"

I lifted an eyebrow and a smirk came to my face when he cut his words off. "What were you going to say?"

He shook his head as he reached into the fridge for a bottle of water.

"I forgot."

"I just bet you did." I told him chuckling.

He brought one of the kitchen chairs, placing it in front of me and then sat. For a moment he didn't say anything, he just studied me.

I continued to drink my coffee, studying him back.

Let me tell y'all something...Rome's amber gaze is intense. It made me want to squirm like a little girl under its power. I had to force myself not to reach up and try to tame my hair that I knew was all over my head. I cannot let my last target be the one that breaks me.

"What's your name?"

I didn't answer, instead, I took another sip of coffee.

"You know, I can find out everything about you if I put my mind to it."

I took another sip of my coffee.

He leaned forward resting his elbows on his knees. "Are you going to always be this difficult?"

"Probably…you should spare yourself the grief and let me go."

He chuckled sitting back in his chair. "Why would I do that when you've presented me the biggest challenge I've faced in a long time? Didn't you know, Minha Anjo, challenges to me are like catnip to cats…? I've never met one I can walk away from."

"Wow…that is something you and I have in common."

"If my suspicions are correct, you and I have a lot more in common than that." He stood from his chair and walked toward me. "I need to leave town for a couple days."

That was surprising. Was he taking me with him? Surely, he wasn't going to leave me in his place without him.

Wait…

Was he going to try and leave me chained to this bed by these devices around my ankles? I would go nuts!

I sat my coffee cup down on the table and looked straight up at him where he stood directly in front of me.

"What's going to happen to me?"

"You're going to be my guest while I'm away…Now, give me a hug so I can jump in the shower."

"Eww! Gross! You're covered in sweat!" And he was, his muscled chest and stomach was drenched in it.

When he suddenly reached down for me, I tried to scramble out of his way, but my sore side kept me from moving fast enough to escape him. I screeched in laughter when he lifted me into his wet arms burying his sweaty face in my breasts.

"Oh my God! Stop, Rome!" I yelled as he began to use my body like a towel.

He stopped but didn't put me down, he just watched me with those honey gazers that wreaked havoc on my nervous system.

"I'll stop if you kiss me."

Mmmmm… The muscles in my stomach clenched at his words like I was on a roller-coaster. What is this power he held over me?

Every alarm inside of me was blaring loudly…

Rome , don't do this to me! I don't want to fall in love… with you

Biting my bottom lip, I shook my head.

He shrugged. "Suit yourself."

He lifted me higher burying his sweaty face into my breasts again. I held my head back and laughed because his beard and mustache was tickling me.

"Okay!" I yelled. "Okay, I'll kiss you!"

He stopped instantly and stood patiently waiting for me to gather my courage to initiate the kiss.

I couldn't believe I was this nervous. I couldn't believe this man made me this nervous. I've never felt this way. No one has ever caused my stomach to feel as if butterflies danced inside of it…

Please God, don't let me fall in love with this man…

Slowly, I wrapped my arms around his neck and leaned in to gently touch my lips to his. Just a brief kiss was what I was aiming for, but when I went to draw my lips back, his mouth followed mine and took my lips in a hungry kiss that made my toes curl.

Like him, his kiss was different from anything I'd ever experienced. It was not forceful or dominating. Well, not really... Instead, it coaxed. It forced you to crave more.

I tightened my arms around his neck, needing to get closer to him. A moan escaped my throat when I felt his tongue enter my mouth. When I broke the kiss off to draw desperately needed air into my lungs, his hungry mouth continued to my neck.

I could feel the muscles in his arms flexing as he lifted me higher so that he could get better access to the flesh he sought. Closing my eyes, I gave myself up to him.

There was no use of me pretending I didn't want him. Everything about him called to me. I wanted to experience his intensity.

However, the sound of his phone ringing from his pocket brought me back to reality. When he felt me stiffen in his arms, he tried to kiss my lips again, but I turned my head. I couldn't do this!

Everything inside me warned that if I allowed Rome to make love to me, I will be lost. I will start to second guess things. And that was dangerous. I needed to be able to pull this mission off without second guessing anything.

He leaned his forehead against mine for just a moment as he got himself together. The kiss had affected him just as much as it had me; the evidence of that was pressing against my leg.

"Damn, shorty, what am I going to do with you?"

"You can let me go." I whispered.

Please let me go...

He gently placed me down on the bed, his amber gaze had grown cold. "Naw, that ain't an option. We're going to have to find another way." And then he turned and headed toward the bathroom.

Damn that...I will get out!

"What about the bracelets? Are you going to force me to stay in this bed?" I called after him.

He paused for just a moment, when he turned to look at me, his golden gaze was so intense it stole my breath.

"You don't know how much I would love to force you to stay in my bed. Then I can do all the freaky sh*t to you I'd imagine doing this morning as I watched you sleep. I would keep you there for days and f*** you till I got you out of my system, and I no longer hungered for your taste." He grabbed the bulge in the front of his shorts adjusting himself, not even trying to hide his erection from me.

Oh...

Damn!

"But as much as I would love it, now is not the time. I've programmed the cuffs to allow you the run of the loft. If you set one foot outside this door, or window, or that duct in the bathroom you came in, you will lose it."

I lifted an eyebrow at him. "That's a bit much, don't you think?"

This made him laugh. "Are you kidding me? This coming from the same woman who single handedly beat up thirty plus men." He threw his towel over his shoulder as he headed into the bathroom.

When he got to the door, he turned to look back at me. "I don't think so." And then he was gone, a few minutes later, I heard the shower turn on.

I had to sit there for a minute and process all that had just transpired. The doctor had been right about Rome. He is an enigma. Inside one man is a genius, a thug, a rascal that liked to rub his sweat on a screeching girl, a freaky nasty person that didn't mind sharing his thoughts in a form of dirty talk that had the ability to cause extreme wetness.

How can a human woman not fall for someone like that? I never imagined that I would meet somebody like him. For my own safety, I had to complete my mission and get as far away from here as I can.

The good news is he was leaving town for a few days. By the time he got back, I will be in the wind.

Very carefully I put my foot over the side of the bed, bracing myself for an explosion. I know Rome is a genius and all, but even geniuses made mistakes. Maybe he thinks he's programmed the bracelets to allow me to move out the bed, but he really hasn't.

Sweat puddled on my head as I put one toe on the ground. Holding my breath, I waited to hear a bang and feel the pain of my foot blowing off my body.

When nothing happened after a few seconds, I eased the other foot out the bed. By the time I made it to a standing position, Rome was coming out the bathroom with only a towel around his waist.

Nossa!

When he saw me taking each step with caution, he held his head back and laughed as he headed into his closet.

"It's not funny!" I called. "Can you remove these so that I can shower?" I held my breath hoping that he would.

"No worries, they're waterproof!" He called back.

Damn! There goes that hope.

Eventually I made my way to the bathroom. There was a new toothbrush and a few essentials waiting for me when I got there.

Another thing I'm learning about Rome, he moves several steps ahead of normal people. I'll tell you what I mean. This morning when I woke up, there were pain meds, water and hot coffee waiting for me.

Hot coffee…

Waiting…

Which means he timed my waking up perfectly. And he knew I was going to wake up in pain and had the meds waiting and water to take them with.

I know you say, what's the big deal?

Well believe it or not, most people in this day and age are too self-centered to think that far in advance for the well-being of another person. If you who's reading this are one of those people that does…then take a bow, you're a rarity.

I eyeballed that tub, wanting badly to run a bath. I know he said the cuffs are waterproof, but I was too afraid to take the chance, so I turned on the shower instead. Inside the shower was a new bottle of women's shampoo, conditioner and body wash.

I opened the bottle of shampoo and was surprised at how amazing it smelt and even more surprised at how good it made my hair feel. After I finished in the shower, I opened a brand-new bottle of women's body lotion and moisturized my skin. Like the body wash and shampoo, it smelt delicious.

I wondered when he had time to acquire these things. Knowing him, he'd probably gotten them when he first made up his mind to set me up and feed information to my bugs.

After I finished, I combed the kinks out of my hair and just let it fall down my back to air dry. Standing with the towel around me I stared helplessly down at my dirty clothes.

I didn't have anything clean to put on.

Nossa…I was going to have to go out there and ask him for clothes with nothing but a towel wrapped around me.

My heartbeat increased to a dangerous level…And I honestly didn't know if it was from fear or anticipation.

I put my hand on the door knob and had to build up my courage to open it. When I came out, Rome stood shirtless at the stove cooking something. The designer jeans he wore hung low on his tapered hips, showing the top of designer black boxer briefs. On his feet were what looked like a brand-new pair of designer gym shoes.

He glanced my way before turning back to the stove. It must have taken him a second to process that I stood here in only a towel, because his head whipped back around and his eyes devoured me.

Now because I was beginning to understand him a little better, I knew that it was always his plan for me to walk out like this. Someone that was always several steps ahead of the next man would have left me something to wear in the bathroom.

I clutched the towel closed at my breasts so tightly my knuckles turned white.

"I don't have anything to wear."

He had now turned to face me fully. Whatever he was cooking that was smelling really good by the way, was forgotten as he unashamedly took me in.

He grabbed the front of his jeans, once again adjusting himself. "Damn, shorty, you so f***ing sexy!"

I had to bite my lip to keep from cheesing. That thing that he does where he grabs himself is so vulgar…

Yet…

It never failed to cause an answering reaction in my center. I had to avert my eyes from his manhood and squeeze my thighs together to quiet my womanhood.

When I got myself together, I nodded toward the smoke rising out the skillet behind him.

"Sh*t!" He said turning to remove the skillet from the fire. "You got me f***ing sh*t up!"

I held my head back and laughed at him. "That's your own lust getting the better of you."

When he got the burning skillet under control, he grinned at me as he slowly approached me. "Let me help you find something to wear."

Every cell in my body screamed for me to run, they were telling me that if I let him get too close, it was over.

"Do you know how surprised I was to find out you had a sleeve of ink underneath that prim and proper suit you wore here yesterday morning?"

Nossa! He wasn't walking toward his closet, he was coming towards me. I took a step back and then another. Oh God, give me strength. I can't sleep with this man.

"You had that proper a** bun in your hair...and the only thing I could imagine is what it would look like after hours of lovemaking."

I took another step back...trying to ignore how good he looked without a shirt.

"Where are you going? You said you were going to help me find something to wear. Your closet is that way." My voice sounded desperate.

I felt like a doe being stalked by a golden-eyed lion. When my back came up against the wall, my breath sucked in sharply.

"Relax, Minha Anjo..." he said taking my free hand into his bigger one, bringing it to his mouth where he kissed it gently before he began to lead me towards his closet.

I exhaled a breath that I wasn't even aware I was holding. I wish I can describe to you guys just how it felt to have that gorgeous specimen stalking me. He is so unapologetically a thug...

It was something that was so much a part of him, it was in his swagger. In the way that he grabbed his manhood. In the way that he grinned. In the way that he dressed. In the way that he drank a bottle of water.

Yet, he was built like a UFC fighter... And although he had a thug swagger, there was also a lightness in his step that spoke of his skill level. Anybody that was a true fighter would recognize it instantly, and if they're smart, proceed with caution.

His eyes were sharp and missed nothing. There was so much wisdom in his gaze. His mind was brilliant, and it showed in everything that he did and said. His brother told me that Rome was a human lie detector, and I believed it. The doctor said he was a phenomenon, and you know what? I believe him.

However, none of those things I just mentioned to you is what frighten me the most about him. It was that side of him that had me clutching this towel in front of me for dear life.

It was the look he got in his eyes when he licked those beautiful lips. It was those unguarded looks of his, where I would catch him staring at me as if I am truly a wonder to him. How can I be a wonder to someone like him?

It was the hunger that came into his amber eyes as he studied me. I know that I am an attractive woman. Men have checked me out before I was old enough to understand why.

But when I tell you I have never had a man look at me like Romeo, I'm not lying. And not only that, I have never had a man to make me feel the things he makes me feel. He makes me feel...special.

Like to him, I'm somebody. Like to him, I'm worth more than my ability to kill. Nobody has ever looked past that. Nobody has ever wanted to see past that and look at the real me. I've never meant that much to anybody.

And although I know it's impossible and just the devil playing tricks on my mind because it's my last mission and I'm almost free..., it feels as if Rome can see the real me, and he likes what he sees.

My thoughts came to a halt when he flicked on the light in his closet.

It was huge and very well organized. So organized I think it was safe to say Romeo may have a slight case of OCD, which would explain so much.

I took my time and explored it, you can learn a lot about a person by studying their closet.

Everything was sectioned off. His jeans were all pressed, color coded and hanging together. Next to them were his t-shirts, that too were pressed, color coded and all together.

Would you guys believe that even his wifebeaters were on hangers, pressed, color coded...blacks on one side, whites the other, and greys in the middle?

However, what did surprise me was the number of suits hanging in the closet. He didn't take me for a suit wearer.

I looked back at him over my shoulder. He had silently followed me, watching me take in his clothes. He knew that I was profiling him, and he waited to hear my thoughts.

Instead I took down one of his expensive white button up shirts that had been pressed perfectly. And while keeping my back to him, slid my arms into it. The shirt was so big it nearly fell to my knees.

I could feel him standing right behind me. Slowly, I let the towel slide to the floor and then stepped away from it. Just like I figured he would, he bent down and picked it up tossing it into the dirty clothes hamper.

I went to his drawers and searched through them until I found his underwear. I took out a pair of red boxers that were covered in smiley faces. Turning to face him I held them up with a questioning look in my eye.

He grinned. "On everything, I ain't never wore em'."

"Why not?" I asked as I slid them on. "I think they're sexy."

"They are…on you." He muttered as his gaze took its time raking over my body.

"If you don't like them, why did you buy them?"

"I didn't buy them. They were a gift."

I raised an eyebrow. "A gift from who?"

"Why? Are you jealous?"

"Not at all, just wanted to know whose gift I'm wearing."

He reached out wrapping one of his arms around my waist pulling me close.

Nossa! My breath sucked in sharply at the feel of his big hard chest pressed against my soft breasts.

"When I get back, we can go shopping for you some clothes."

Nodding, I licked my lips nervously. He groaned, looking down at my mouth with hungry eyes.

"Of course, you can always give Milo the keys to your place and he can pick something up for you."

Ha! Nice try…

"Is Milo the guy I—"

"Threw across the room with your legs…" He nodded. "Yeah, that's him."

I patted his chest…mmmmm, what a nice chest.

"I think I'll just wait till you get back." I muttered, sounding breathy to even my own ears.

He chuckled. "I figured you were going to say that."

He leaned in pressing his face gently against my neck. "You smell so good, Minha Anjo."

Be strong, Nak…You can fight this. Just push him away.

He lifted his head and looked into my eyes. "My plane leaves in a few hours. Are you going to miss me?"

I bit my lip to keep from grinning. Rascal Rome was back.

"Why would I miss you? You're holding me prisoner."

"In a golden cage, baby." His words were quiet.

Oh y'all, I was drowning in his gaze. Lifting my hand, I gently buried my fingers in his full beard; I wanted to see if it was as soft as it looked.

It was softer… "A golden cage is still a cage, Mue Rei."

His body stiffened and my eyes widened in horror.

Oh God! Please let him not have understood what I just called him.

I couldn't believe I'd let those words slip from between my lips.

He grinned at me. "Is that how you really feel?"

I shook my head frowning, in full damage control. "I don't understand what you mean."

I tried to step out of his arms, but he only pulled me closer, this time wrapping both of his arms around my waist.

"You called me your King. Is that how you feel?"

Chapter 8

I'm Broken

Nakhti

"You speak Portuguese?" I shouldn't be surprised. With a mind like his, he probably learned it one day when he was bored.

"And you're deflecting."

I tried to push out of his arms again, but he wouldn't let me go. My eyes came back to his.

"Romeo, you have to let me go."

The grin left his face and a frown replaced it. "Why?"

I looked away from him, not able to take the intensity of his gaze. "Because, I—I…"

I'm no good for somebody like you. You're looking at my pretty face but don't know I'm ugly on the inside. I will damage someone as beautiful as you. I am not good enough…

I'm broken…

He shook me causing my eyes to come back to his. The frown that was now on his face was chilling.

"Tell me why." He hissed through clenched teeth.

I shook my head. "I'm not what you think I am."

Why was I telling him that? I was blowing my mission. I never blew my mission.

Oh God! I had to get away from this man!

"Then tell me who you are."

I tried to push out of his arms again, this time by trying an evasive maneuver. But he was waiting for me and braced himself solidifying his hold. I ended up with my back against the wall and his big body holding me there.

"Romeo, let me go!" I yelled in his face, now good and angry. He was forcing me to feel things I could not afford to feel at this point in my life.

"Not till you tell me why."

"Because, I'm not good for you! I'm broken!" I yelled.

The shock that came over his face was real. "What?"

"You heard me. I was not born for love." I hardened my heart and my gaze. I was not the type to feel sorry for myself. It is what it is…

"That's bullsh*t!"

I shook my head. "You don't know everything. And you don't know me…So just let it drop. I know men like you. You want sex, right? I can give you sex, but then you must let me go. Promise you won't try and hold me. I will only hurt you. I'm so f*** up on the inside, it's not even funny."

He let me go so suddenly that I almost fell.

"That's bullsh*t! It's easier for you to tell yourself that rather than face yourself. And I'm going to prove it to you. Come, eat...your breakfast is getting cold."

I stared at his retreating back for a moment. What the hell did he mean he was going to prove it to me? Eventually I followed him out the closet to the table. He was still very angry with me and didn't even look at me as we sat.

I shrugged. I didn't come here to please him anyway.

However, I was starving. I looked down at my plate and frowned.

"What the hell is this?"

Sitting on my plate looking like something foreign was a white omelet that was stuffed full of something green topped with sliced sautéed tomatoes. I lifted the plate looking under it for the meat and potatoes.

The grin came back to his handsome face as he picked up his fork and dug in. "The doctor said you have prehypertension."

Prehypertension? What the hell kind of nonsense...?

"What?" My voice was laced with my disgust.

His honey gaze came up to mine and there was real joy in his eyes. The bastard was enjoying my pain.

"You have to watch the way you eat, you have prehypertension."

"I heard you spew that nonsense the first time. What the hell is prehypertension? Is that like hypertension?"

He chuckled. "No, it's prehypertension." His calm patient tone was really getting on my nerves.

"Maaaaannnn, where is the meat?"

"You know, too much meat isn't good for you. Try your omelet; I stuffed it with organic heirloom spinach and low fat, low oil mozzarella cheese. Those tomatoes were grown in Mrs. Kimble's community garden."

I looked at him with pity as I shook my head, this poor bastard. "Are you trying to poison me?"

He choked on the bite of food in his mouth from the sudden burst of laughter that came from him. Once he had his passage way cleared, he put his hand on his chest and roared with laughter. He laughed so hard he had to wipe tears from his eyes.

"Oh damn!" he cried when he regained control of himself. "I ain't laughed like that in years."

His watery gaze settled on me. "Baby, just taste it."

I frowned down at and poked it with my finger. "Why is it white?"

"Because I used egg whites. The yolks are not good for you. Taste it, it's good."

I exhaled. "Fine, do you have some hot sauce?"

He shook his head. "You have to let go of the hot sauce, it's not good for your prehypertension."

"Prehypertension is not a real thing!" I screamed before I got up and shoved his plate of garbage to the center of the table. "I'll make my own breakfast!"

He gestured to the fridge settling back in his chair. "Be my guest…"

I narrowed my eyes at him. The glee in his gaze told me I was amusing him.

"You find me amusing?"

"Very…"

I marched to the fridge. "Whatever… when I make my good breakfast you can't have any. So, don't even try to ask."

What the hell was wrong with this man? Prehypertension! Either you got the hypertension or you don't. What the hell?!

I snatched open the fridge and stared into it wide eyed.

Oh my God! This was a nightmare…

It was packed full of greens, yellows and reds…there were even a few purples. Rabbit food! What I didn't see was any meat. Nothing prepackaged and ready to go. No buffalo wings or burgers…

I whipped around to look at him…This was not going to work. He sat there as if he was waiting anxiously to see my expression, when he did, he erupted in another fit of laughter, only angering me more. I didn't play about my food. It was my only joy in life.

"Where is the meat?"

"Sorry, Minha Anjo, I'm a vegetarian." He couldn't have slapped me and shocked me more.

"What the hell kind of thug are you?" I folded my arms pissed. "You're no real thug, you're a disgrace to the homies on the street!"

This made him erupt in another fit of laughter and I swear I was going to throw something at his head.

He must have realized I wasn't joking because he stood forcing himself to stop laughing at me, although he couldn't quite wipe the grin off his face.

"Come here, baby." He took my hand and led me back to the table before gently pushing me back in my chair. Then he reached over and grabbed the plate of trash pulling it back in front of me.

Squatting down next to me he took my fork and cut a piece of the omelet. "I want you to be a big girl and at least try it." He said holding the fork full of omelet to my mouth.

I folded my arms again, turning my head away. "I'm not going to like it."

"How do you know unless you try it?"

"I know because I know myself. I'm not going to like it."

He gently touched my lip with the omelet. "Come on...open up. You can do this."

I had to bite my lip to keep from laughing. He was talking to me like I was a small child. What kind of thug did that?

When I saw that he wasn't going to give up I opened my mouth for the food. As soon as the unsalted product hit my tongue I gagged, but then tried to chew it quickly to get it over with and ended up gagging two more times before I could get it down.

He smiled. "See? It wasn't that bad."

I clutched his arm. "Rome, you can't leave me here without any food."

His honey gaze brightened with amusement. "What do you mean? The fridge is packed."

"With rabbit food."

He stood. "You have to change your diet, sweetheart, it's killing you. Don't worry, I'll help. Finish your breakfast. I need to get ready to head out, my flight leaves in two hours."

I sat there and stubbornly refused to touch that plate as he finished getting dressed. I'd rather starve.

He told me he had a chef that came three times a week and that I would like his food better. He said he was going to send Rob and Happy to check on me and for me to not try and bribe them into giving me anything unhealthy, because he'd already talked to them and they knew better.

Right before he headed out the door, he came to stand in front of me, pulling me out the chair and into his arms.

"There are a few things you're going to have to face. You belong to me now, and you're not going to get hypertension, because I won't let you. Now stop pouting and give me a kiss."

Over my dead body!

I turned my head to face the cabinets, but he chuckled and put his finger under my chin turning my head back.

"Come on, Minha Anjo. I know you're mad at me, but anything can happen. My plane could crash and I die…then you'll regret you didn't give me those luscious lips of yours so that I can at least die happy."

I shook my head. "I will not…"

But that wasn't true. If he died in a plane crash, I would be hurt. So, because of that, I didn't stop him when he lowered his lips to mine.

And I didn't stop him when his tongue sought entrance to my mouth. It was only because of the fact that he could die that I wrapped my arms around his neck bringing myself closer to him.

The moan that escaped my throat when he deepened the kiss was a simple farewell…have a safe journey. And he when he lifted me off my feet, bringing me as close as he and I could possibly get, I wrapped my legs around his waist—

Aww! Who was I kidding? I wrapped my legs around his waist because I needed to feel his hardness pressed against me. Our kiss got so heated I ended up with my back against the fridge and him grinding his hardness into my heat needing to fill me completely.

"Bruh, Ma heading downstairs…you ready?" Rob said from somewhere behind us, pouring cold water on our flame.

Rome rested his head against mine as we both tried to catch our breaths. "We'll finish this discussion when I get back."

I nodded… "You promise?"

He lifted his hand and gently rubbed my bottom lip with his thumb. "Hell yeah…are you going to be good while I'm gone?"

Grinning I shook my head. "Probably not."

He chuckled as he let my feet slide to the floor and then after placing one last brief kiss on my lips, followed his brother towards the door.

"If you need me…call me."

I frowned at his retreating back. "But I don't have your number."

"You don't need my number…Just call out my name,"

And then he was gone…

I stood in the window and watched as he opened his truck door for his mother while Rob loaded her luggage in the back seat. She was not happy. It looked like she didn't like riding in the truck, probably because it was such a high climb to get in it. She was chewing him out pretty good about it.

He said something back to her and tried to take her arm to help her up. She smacked his hand away and said something like she could do it herself, and then she grabbed onto the door and put her leg way up on the foot pedestal. But he must have lost patience because he put his hands around her waist and lifted her the rest of the way.

I laughed because I could hear her screech way up here and the whole time he was lifting her in the truck she was slapping him in the face and on the head telling him to put her down. Several of his men stood waiting for him to get his mom loaded in.

Once he shut the door he spoke to them for a minute and then pointed at Rob, clearly warning him about something. His little brother waved him away, telling him to relax and that he'll take care of everything. But there was doubt in Rome's eyes.

Eventually he walked around to the driver side and climbed up behind the wheel. But before he dipped his head in, his amber gaze came to me, and he pointed at me and mouthed, behave.

I threw my head back and laughed…Yeah right, buddy!

Romeo

"Don't think I don't know what you're about, Romeo Reevers." My mother said from the passenger seat of the rental.

I continued to type on my laptop trying to decode my sister's front gate security box. This is a redeeming factor for Jo's punk a**. At least he was truly trying to keep her and my niece safe.

"I don't know what you mean, Mom. I'm simply trying to find the email Journey sent me with her gate code in it."

She huffed. "You think I'm so stupid. I may not know how to speak computer language, but I know you're up to no good. I heard that boy call you a hacker. Rob told me you're like Neo from the Matrix."

"Don't listen to Rob, you know he lies." I was almost in… "Got it…"

The gate opened and I drove through.

"Wow, it's beautiful! I know Journey is loving this."

I grunted. "It's alright, nothing really to write home about."

"Romeo, you do realize you're going to have to get over whatever beef you have with Jo. Your sister loves him."

"Stockholm Syndrome."

"You know what? Sometimes you can be just as stubborn as your father."

"Well, he was my father."

She hit my arm. "Watch your mouth, Romeo!"

I exhaled. "Sorry, Ma…"

"I can't wait to see my grandbaby." she continued as I helped her out of the car.

"Ma, can you see if I dropped my phone in the trunk, I can't find it."

As she dug in the trunk, I picked the locks. By the time her head popped up to tell me she didn't see it the door was open.

I held up my phone. "I got it…it was in my pocket the whole time."

She eyeballed me as she walked past. But then she stopped right in front of me, pointing her finger in my face.

"Don't think I don't know you pawning me off on your sister so that you can misbehave with that pretty caseworker."

I grinned. Oh yes! I planned on misbehaving with that pretty caseworker all right. I planned on misbehaving a lot. Had Rob not walked in when he did, I was going to get some quick misbehaving in before I left.

Now I'm standing here a tortured man, counting the seconds till I can get back and finish misbehaving. But I didn't tell my mother none of that. I got her inside and told her to look around while I went to pull the rental around to the side of the house. I didn't want to alert that bastard to my coming.

I had already taken over his camera feed and put it on a loop so that he won't see us here. He had cameras all over and from what

I was finding out about him, it was for good reason. I still haven't decided if my little sister and niece were safe with him.

He was definitely into some sh*t. And whatever it was, someone was going through a lot of trouble to hide it. But just like I told my little spy, I loved a challenge. I was going to find out what Jo and his punk a** daddy was into, and then I was going to use that information to destroy them.

I don't know who the f*** he thought he was dealing with. Coming up in my sh*t making demands on me and my family like he run some sh*t! When I was done with that b**** the only thing he gon' be running is from big Bubba's a** in the lock up yard.

Every time I think of his p***y a** contracts telling me what I can and cannot do…where I can and cannot go, and who the f*** I can and cannot talk to…I wanted to murk his a**.

My word, if he wasn't my niece's father, I would have the same day he handed me my first a** whooping in my mother's kitchen.

It was something up with that as well. The way he moved was on some next level type sh*t, almost robotic. And I ain't just saying that 'cause he kicked my a**. The bastard was strong as hell. It felt like he was hitting me with a sledge hammer.

Yeah, it was something up with that sh*t. I wouldn't be surprised to find out that the government been pumping him with some kind of crazy a** steroids or some sh*t. He probably was some kind of super soldier.

"Oh, my goodness! How did y'all get in here? I have a high-tech security system at the gate!"

My beautiful little sister cried coming through her door looking surprised as hell to see us. For just a moment I studied

Journey to see with my own eyes that she was okay. Our mother keeps telling me not to worry so much about her and that she was a big girl now, saying that I needed to let her fly.

Maybe she was right, my little sister was practically glowing. The truth of the matter is, I was having a hard time seeing her as an adult. I think she will always be the little pain in my a** with the dreads sticking straight up on her head, who always tried her best to get me in trouble with Ma.

The first thing our mother did was take Ayana out of Journey's arms and hoard her all to herself.

Just selfish…

"I see y'all have made yourselves comfortable." Journey huffed, a little steamed that my mother didn't even acknowledge her.

I chuckled. "Aww, don't worry 'bout that, lil sis, you know we had to come check you out, make sure everything was okay."

She gave me a look that said she wasn't buying my crap. My little sister knew me well. I went on and filled her in on the real reason I was here. I'd come to pawn Ma off on her.

However, dropping my mother off was to serve two purposes. Yeah, I wanted to get her out of my business for a while, at least till I tamed that wild a** girl back at the house. But also, so that she could keep an eye on Joey boy and make sure he's behaving like a gentleman should.

That being said…my trip here was to serve two purposes, yes, to drop my mother off, but most importantly to get into Jo's private computer. His fed tech geeks had done their jobs well, because I was having the hardest time getting in from the outside.

I'd been trying for a while now. I knew I was going to have to make the trip eventually, but thanks to my beautiful little spy showing up yesterday, it became top priority.

She wouldn't tell me her name...

That was a cool, I will soon know all there is to know about her. In fact, my need to know her had me cutting my trip with Journey short.

But before I left, my mother said something that resonated down to my very soul. I think she may have given me the key to cracking through the thick shell my house guest has built around herself.

"Ms. Bonita is a beautiful woman, not just on the outside but on the inside as well, she just doesn't know it. Maybe my son can show her."

"How?" I asked, desperate for any advice she could give me. My mom was good at this kind of stuff.

"Tenderness..."

Tenderness?

Tenderness?

My house guest was a savage. Just this morning I'd had to hem her up in my closet. I'd made her breakfast and she yelled at me because there were no meat and potatoes.

Tenderness?

I kissed my OG's forehead goodbye. I think she was losing her touch.

My house guest needed a lot of things. Hell, this morning when she looked at me and practically said she wasn't good enough for me, I thought about putting her over my lap, pulling down those ridiculous boxers that some chicken head whose name I couldn't even remember gave me, and spanking her a**.

Then afterward I would have used my hands and mouth to sooth her before making love to her, showing her that she's a queen.

My Queen…

Mmmm…Damn.

I had to push such thoughts away, or else I was going to be on the first thing smoking back to Chicago. I wanted to be inside her so bad I could barely focus on anything else.

Needless to say, she needed a lot of things…tenderness was not one of them.

I was still thinking about my mom's words when I made it to Jo's office. My burrowing bot only needed 8 minutes to do its thing, which meant I had to entertain this prick for 8 whole minutes.

I followed his secretary back to his office. She kept sneaking glances back at me as if she expected me to rob her. I chuckled shaking my head as she moved to the side to let me in.

"Wow, look at you. I see you're being a good little boy and following in your daddy's shoes just like you've been trained to do. I'm sure he's so proud." I told the a**hole as I took in his lavish office.

God, I hated this punk.

He sat back in his chair and hit me with his fake a** politician smile. The cocky bastard…everything in life has come way too easy to him. He's the kind of prick you just want to hit in the mouth with a hammer as soon as he opened his mouth to speak.

"And I see you finally grew a pair and ventured out of your hood. Didn't think the ganstas ever did that."

See what I mean?

"How have you been enjoying my sista, chump?"

"Just fine, thanks for asking."

I balled up my fists. It took everything I had in me not to jump over that desk on his big RoboCop a**. And here I was without my pistol. Yeah, he was some kind of super soldier, but I bet his a** can't dodge bullets.

I told him that I was aware he sent a mole in to spy on me just to see his response. The chump put on a poker face. So I upped the ante and thanked him for giving her to me. While at the same time letting him know just like he'd f***ing taken my sista out of my house, I've taken his little spy.

And the mutha ****** wasn't getting her back.

By that point, my little burrower bot was inside his system laying eggs everywhere. If his tech team was any good, they will find the bot before the week's out. But the eggs they will never find. They are encoded to clone themselves to resemble other programs already in his system.

His tech team will look right past them, although they'll assure him everything is okay and that they've safeguarded everything with impenetrable firewalls. I chuckled to myself. Got to love those tech guys.

Before I left, I decided to see how much Jo knew about what I'd found. I was curious to see if he knew the senator was not his real father.

"You have bigger issues to deal with…Like James Bennet Law." I'd told him when he got to asking questions about my house guest.

He frowned. "Never heard of him."

Wow! He wasn't lying, which meant Jo had no idea he was adopted. Or at least I think he was adopted.

That was the grey area. I couldn't find any adoption records for him anywhere. Birth records either for that matter.

Hmmmm…

The old senator had some serious skeletons in his closet. Skeletons that I had a feeling were going to do a lot of damage when they surfaced.

If my sister wasn't involved with this dude and fancied herself in love with him, I would walk away from this sh*t. This well went deeper than I wanted to go, but I couldn't walk away from this.

My mom thinks Jo was going to try and marry Journey. I needed to get to the bottom of this sh*t before that happens. The problem was, this information was constantly on the move, and I could use a little help.

"It appears as if you, my not so good friend have a homework assignment. Let's see if those imbeciles the FBI call their tech team can figure it out." While me and my bots come along for the ride.

As soon as I got in my rental, I opened my laptop and began my tour of Jo's system. By the time I made it to the airport, I'd found my house guest's file. And oh, what a file it was.

Her name is Nakhti Thomas. She'd enlisted in the Navy in '01 after 911. Two years later, she'd graduated from BUD school and became one of two female SEALs that year. She had quite a few medals…but even more disciplinary reports.

Jo became her sergeant in '05, and it was his signature on most of the reports. On several of them, he wrote that she was and I quote, Bat sh*t crazy.

After I settled down in first class and was handed a Hennessy on the rocks, I put in my ear piece and clicked play on the first of many videos in her file.

The video opened up with a clearly angry Nakhti being roughly shoved down on a stool in front of the camera. She was dressed in a tan tank top and black cargo pants similar to the ones she wore yesterday.

Her curly hair framed her face from where it had escaped her pony tail. She was sweaty and there were smudges of dirt on her beautiful face. It looked like they were in some kind of cave or something.

She rolled her eyes at the camera. Jo, dressed in similar gear paced behind her. There were others in the cave, but they weren't standing where their faces could be seen.

"Speak, soldier!" Jo demanded.

"My name is Nakhti Thomas and I'm bat sh*t—" She stopped talking and turned to look at him.

"I don't see how this is helping anything, sarge!"

He glared at her and I frowned. There was something off about him. I paused the footage to see if I could put my finger on it, but the picture was too grainy for me to get a good look at him. I pressed play.

"In the famous words of Judge Mathis," He told her. "Sometimes, you have to call a crackhead a crackhead, now confess to the damn camera."

What the hell was this corny bastard talking about?

Nak's thoughts must have been identical to mine because she looked straight at the camera and said underneath her voice. "He's quoting Judge Mathis."

She exhaled like she'd done at the breakfast table earlier and spoke louder. "My name is Nakhti Thomas and I'm bat sh*t crazy. My actions today almost got my whole team killed, although it was my actions that saved—"

"Nak!" Jo warned from behind her.

She glared back at the camera. "My actions today almost got my whole team killed. It was wrong of me to run over the suspect with the Humvee. I should have followed my sarge's instructions and waited for the sniper to eliminate the threat."

The footage went off. I clicked on the next one.

Several men ran into a tent where it looked like a meeting was going on. "Sarge, come quick, Nak has lost her f***ing mind."

The camera was a bit choppy as everyone rushed out the tent, when it cleared again, it was to show Nak on the back of a big giant of a man punching him in the head, screaming like she was crazy.

Someone went to grab her off his back, but she hauled off and kicked the sh*t out of them before going after the giant that was now running from her. There was real fear on his face. When she caught up with him, she picked up a chair and smashed it across his back, he went down and she went down on top of him, continuing to pummel him.

Jo crossed the yard with angry strides and snatched the wild cat off the man. He threw her to the ground, hard.

I balled up my fists. That mutha f****!

The screen went blank for a moment before it showed an angry Nak back sitting on her confession stool.

"My name is Nakhti Thomas and I'm bat sh*t crazy. It was not alright to beat the sh*t out of Bear because he's dumb. He can't help the fact that his brain is not as swift as others and he thought it was okay to dispose of a live grenade just feet away from me. Next time I will show patience and gently explain to Bear's dumb a** the right way to dispose of a live grenade."

The next footage was of Jo. He was being questioned by a small group of men who were higher ranking than him about his decision to keep Nakhti on as a part of his team.

"I know she's a bit wild, but she suffers from Impulse Control Disorder."

One of the older men frowned at him. "Is that even a real thing?" He asked in a deep southern drawl.

"Yes sir, she's met with the Department of Psychology who has noted improvement in her behavior, sir." He paused for just a moment.

"I can't afford to get rid of her. She's one of the best soldiers we have in the field." Then he began to list off all the things that she's accomplished. After he testified, the other soldiers on their team came behind him one at a time with a different story about how Nakhti had saved their lives.

The end result was them all agreeing not to discharge her, but for Jo to make sure she continued to meet with the psychologist.

The next footage was of Jo yelling at Nak. He was so angry the veins were bulging in his throat and head. She stood at attention with her arms by her side looking straight ahead. Her clothes were dripping wet. The other men on their team all stood around watching him berate her.

"Why are you so f***ing crazy?!" He yelled. "Who the f*** jumps out of a plane without a chute?!"

"Sir, there was no other choice, sir!" She yelled back.

"There is always a choice! Only someone who is bat sh*t crazy would make the choice you made."

"Permission to speak freely, sir!"

He waved as he turned away. "Yeah, go ahead." He muttered sounding tired. Poor bastard, Nak was wearing him out.

What she did next had me hollering with laughter on the plane. She drew a deep breath and then yelled…

"Call me crazy one more mutha f***** time! I dare you!"

Jo whipped back around and there was death in his eyes. He walked back to her until their noses were nearly touching. The men that were standing around watched with surprised eyes.

Even Nak's eyes widened…And it was then I saw that she truly did have Impulse Control Disorder. She was now very clearly regretting her outburst.

I ain't gon' lie. Jo is a big mutha f****, and he looked pissed.

"Crazy!" He growled. "What you gon' do about it?"

She grinned and threw her arms around his shoulders. Not in a hug way, but more in a holding-his-arms-down-so-that-he-doesn't-swing kind of way.

"Nothing, boss, violence never solves anything!" she yelled before she stepped back to attention.

But before she turned, she shared a look with one of the other men that clearly said…Damn! I almost died!

The screen went blank for a minute before it came back up with Nak sitting on her confession stool.

"My name is Nakhti Thomas and I'm bat sh*t crazy. It is not alright to yell at my commanding officer and dare him to say anything to me. Also, it is not alright to jump out of a plane without a chute, even if someone was threatening to shoot you and the ocean was there to break your fall.

By the time my plane landed in California for my meeting with Chadwick the crazy a** white boy, the other passengers in first class were staring at me as if something was wrong with me. Nak had me laughing so hard there were tears in my eyes.

I don't know how God knew, but he sent me the perfect woman. She was just my type. It had been so long sense I noticed anything about a woman outside of her body.

Apparently, I liked bat sh*t crazy!

I liked it a whole lot…

Chapter 9

Falling...

Nakhti

To my credit, I didn't go searching for the key to these ankle cuffs right away. I waited for at least an hour. I know that he was probably watching me, but I didn't care. I planned on being long gone before he got back.

I started in the closet, carefully looking in the places I would stash a key. He was so organized that even his jewelry was placed on his dresser in order of size. Everything was gold. He had a few golden chains and a few watches.

I picked up one of the watches and looked closely at it, like my ankle bracelets, it had a very complex design. I couldn't tell what each golden gadget did, but there was no doubt in my mind that it was very expensive. Carefully, I laid it back on the cloth it rested on.

Next, I searched the antique bureau that seemed a little out of place it the state-of-the-art closet. I was pleasantly surprised to find my jacket hanging neatly on a hanger and my boots stacked perfectly underneath it. I looked inside my jacket pocket for my jump drive and was *not surprised* to find it missing.

Closing the bureau, I continued my search until there was nowhere else to look.

Damn it! I hope he didn't have the key on him.

As I made my way out the closet I ran into Happy. She nearly jumped out her skin. Instantly she tilted her head so that her hair fell to cover the right side of her face before she gave a nervous smile.

"There you are. I thought you'd left."

"No, just finishing up in the bathroom. How are you?"

She sighed. "I'm here, so a guess I'm doing better than most."

Her answer spoke volumes… I wanted to come right out and ask her did he hit her last night, but I know she would stiffen up at such a direct question, so I settled into going the around about way.

"Was everything alright last night? It looked like your boyfriend was angry with you."

She shook her head as she grabbed a garbage bag and began to pick up all the things the caterer missed.

"He just got on me for bugging you. He said Rome's lady didn't have time to talk to nobody like me."

"That's not true though. After you left, I missed you."

She looked up at me surprised. "Really?"

"Yeah." I told her grabbing another garbage bag to help her. "It got really lonely and I didn't have anybody to talk to."

When she saw me grab the garbage bag she began to fret. "No, that's alright. I don't need any help. Please girl, I need this job."

"Relax, Happy…I don't have anything else to do. Romeo left me here to just stare at these walls."

"You sure you don't mind?"

"Not at all…so, why would your boyfriend tell you I didn't have time for you?"

She exhaled as she went back to throwing red cups in the bag. "He does stuff like that all the time. He don't really like me having friends."

I just bet he doesn't. Don't want nobody in her ear telling her to leave his sorry butt. She stopped and looked at me.

"But I really want to be your friend."

"Why?" I asked smiling kindly at her. I didn't want her to think I didn't want to be her friend, but I was curious as to her reasoning.

"Because you're brave and you don't take nothing from no one. Everybody in the neighborhood is talking about you. They're calling you and Rome King and Queen of the ghetto."

"You know…You can be brave too."

She turned around laughing. "Naw…not like you. I'm scared of everything."

I was going to ask her to explain, but right then Rob walked in holding a brown bag in his arm that had grease stains on the outside and my stomach immediately started to growl.

"What's that, little bro?" I asked walking toward him. It smelt delicious. I could smell something fried smothered in barbeque sauce.

He grinned at me, his bloodshot eyes sparkling in the sunlight that was streaming through the window. This kid was full of mischief. But he was quickly becoming one of my favorite people!

"Naw, sis! Get away from me. My brother told me you had to eat carrots and sh*t."

Happy hit him with her trash bag. "Why would you even come up here with that if you knew she's on a diet?"

"Wait! What? I'm not on a diet. I don't know what your brother said, but he was mistaken." I continued to stalk him. There was no way he was leaving with that bag. If I had to result to violence I was partaking one way or the other.

Sensing my desperation, he laughed as he walked a large circle around me to the kitchen table. "I just came up here to have a little lunch. Don't mind me, carry on. Pretend I'm not even here."

He put the bag on the table and carefully tore it open with flourish. And I swear the heavens opened and the birds began to sing a new song.

"Wow! Rob, it's so beautiful." I whispered close to tears. Nestled in a red and white paper basket were beautifully fried golden chicken wings...

"I know..." He whispered back.

"What is that wonderfully smelling sauce on them?"

He looked down at the chicken as if he was a proud father. "That, my wild sista is mild sauce."

"*Mild Sauce,*" I repeated, loving the way the words rolled of my tongue. "And where did you get these beauties clothed in *mild sauce* from?"

"Uncle Remo's…the King of fried chicken."

Happy burst out laughing. "Oh my goodness! You should see the two of you. Y'all both staring at that chicken like it's a gift from God."

"Rob?" I said completely ignoring Happy. I still hadn't looked away from the prettiest sight I've seen in days…

"Mmmhhhmmm…" He didn't look away from it either. Knowing him, he probably had the munchies.

"Brotha?"

"Mmmmhhhmmm…"

"Can I break bread with you?"

"Mmmmhhhmmm…"

And that was all she wrote. The three of us sat down and devoured that chicken. *Nossa!* Rob is the man. He had the foresight to order extra. The wings sat on a bed of fries that were also drenched in this blessed *mild sauce.*

I ain't never tasted nothing so good. When we were done we all sat around the table stuffed like fat cats. But I had to know something.

"Why did you bring me food?" I asked him.

He sat up in his chair and shook his head a bit. "Because I feel sorry for you, sis."

"What do you mean?"

"Rome eats like a f***ing gerbil. And now he's going to make you eat like it too." He frowned his face as if he smelled something rotten. "When the man is in the mood to eat dangerous, he eats chicken fried cauliflower."

I put my hand on my chest horrified. "Is that even chicken?"

His frown grew as he shook his head. "Naw maaan…It's cauliflower made to look like chicken strips."

"How the hell is that eating dangerous?"

"It's fried."

Dear God! This situation was worse than I thought.

He nodded… "I'll do what I can for you sis. But I can't make no promises. My mama say you like Kool-Aid."

"I *love* Kool-Aid! The red kind!" I told him getting excited.

"I'll make you a picture for dinner. You better get it in while Rome's gone, 'cause he hate Kool-Aid with a passion. He say it was created by the devil to kill black people."

"What?!"

Rob nodded. "He always saying crazy sh*t like that. Just wait, you'll see."

Unbeknownst to me, this would be the beginning of a very long relationship between Rob and I, because at the time, I still thought I was going to find that key and be gone by the time Rome came back. I didn't know that Rob was going to become my pusherman.

And the product he was pushing was junk food and Kool-Aid...the red kind.

After we finished eating, we both helped Happy clean up the loft. And then she hurried back home, saying she had been gone too long.

"Derrick gon' beat that head in when she get home." Rob said plopping down on the couch with a game controller in his hand.

"So, he is beating her?" I asked curling up in the plush chair kitty corner from him.

He nodded as he began the game. "It's crazy too, because she like seven months pregnant."

"Why don't somebody do something about it?"

"Man, we've tried. She just end up going right back to dude. Because Derrick is loyal as f*** to my brotha, Rome tried to talk to him and her. But she just cry and tell everybody to stay out her business. She love dude. She say sh*t like, it ain't his fault, and she could have done better."

"She was going to school to be a nurse, but he shut it down. Didn't want her doing better than him. My brother felt bad for her and offered her the job cleaning his pad. Hell, he pay her more than what she would have made at the hospital anyway. Of course Derrick don't have no problem with that 'cause he think her working for Rome will somehow get him in. He been trying to be down with Rome's crew for the longest time."

Nossa! Rob was a wealth of information.

"Her mama came up her from Louisiana a few years ago and tried to take her back home where she could try and help her get on her feet, but she wouldn't go. Derrick begged her to stay with him. Now dude don't even let her see her mama no mo'."

Pausing the game, he looked over at me. "The moral of that long a** story is, you can't help nobody that don't want yo' help." Un-pausing the game he went back to playing.

Well…

Although his words were kind of crass, he had a very valid point. Many times people have risked their lives to help someone out of an abusive relationship only for the person to turn around and go right back to their abusers. Look at me…It took me eighteen years to finally work up enough courage to leave home.

My mother took her anger out on me every time she had more than two glasses of wine, which was practically every day. There were a few rare occasions where she'd smile at me and tell me how pretty I was.

Those occasions be the reason you stay. Hoping that today will be the day your abuser decides to smile at you rather than hit you.

I shook my head. Even though I knew Rob's words were true, that you can't help anybody that don't want your help, it still didn't quell the rage in me. It still didn't make me not want to bash Derrick's head in.

I swear y'all, if I didn't have these explosive devices around my ankle, that's where I would be right now. Happy would just have to cry, 'cause I'd be kicking the sh*t out of his a**!

Rob ended up staying for a little while before he left promising to come back with some more goodies for dinner. I picked up my search for the key after that.

However, after about an hour or so when I still didn't find it, I ended up doing something I hadn't done in a while.

I laid in Rome's big bed and took a nap.

And it felt wonderful.

True to his word, Rob came back high as a kite with something called Gyro Cheeseburgers and a huge picture of red Kool-Aid. He and I sat at the table and ate and laughed. He had me in tears telling me about the fight between Rome and Jo.

I would have given anything to have seen it. Until I meet Rome, the Sarge was the only person I knew that could defeat me in hand-to-hand combat. Well…maybe old Albert too…

Maybe…

I can only imagine how shocked Rome was to be so easily defeated. If only he knew, there was nothing normal about Jo. Up underneath all that smooth talking and politician smiling was a natural born killer. I've seen the Sarge… Or rather the Politician do some things that defy nature.

He's faster, stronger, and more vicious then any human I'd ever met. My brothers-in-arms and I used to make fun of him, calling him the real-life superman. And we all knew that although we shared a few laughs about it, didn't make it any less true.

Poor Rome, somebody should have warned him…

After dinner Rob helped me clean up so there wouldn't be a huge mess waiting for Happy when she got here in the morning. She said she came for about an hour every day. Because I think it was something of an escape for her, I didn't want to step on her toes. But at the same time, I didn't want her to think I was some pampered princess, because that was the furthest thing from the truth.

When Rob left, I kind of roamed aimlessly around the loft for a bit before I found myself sitting in that King-sized chair in front of that beautiful computer. Very carefully I booted it up...

Instead of starting an immediate search of the hard drive, I searched the web for some mundane things and casually found myself looking through some files. An envelope popped up in the corner of the screen that said, *click me.*

Even though I had a bad feeling about it, my curiosity won.

I clicked it.

A few seconds later I was sitting back in my chair surprised when all the screens in front of me woke up, and videos I thought was long gone showed up on them. Each screen was playing a different one of my confessionals.

My name is Nahkti Thomas, My name is Nahkti Thomas, My name is Nahkti Thomas... played on each screen at different times making a rhythm.

What the he---?

The big screen went black before Rome's handsome face appeared on it.

"Good evening, *Minha Anjo.* You've been a very naughty girl."

I looked up as the lights overhead dimmed and nearly jumped out my seat when the heavy drapes began to close. When it was done the loft looked like it was lit with a hundred candles. Next, the sound of smooth Neo Soul came out of speakers that were overhead somewhere.

I sat back in the chair astonished as each screen began to flash the last sixteen years of my life on them. On one screen was my medical history from the time I enlisted in the military till my last check up a few months ago.

On another screen was footage of me in the field. There was footage of me dressed in a little black cocktail dress wearing a hot pink wig flirting outrageously with my mark. Footage of me wearing a black wig dressed in another mini dress sitting at a bar waiting for my mark to approach me because I was just his type.

There was even footage of me slipping out of a black Cadillac truck, my mark dead in the front seat.

What the f***! That happened in Moscow. How in the world did he get a hold of that video?

Another screen showed me sitting in the psychologist office nodding off while he tried to get me to talk about my father.

Another screen showed me with a huge grin on my face being chased down the streets of Siberia by several Siberian officers.

Another screen showed me dancing at a bar before it fast forwarded a little and showed me swinging on some fool that couldn't take no for an answer. The footage fast forwarded a little more and showed me running through the crowded bar that had erupted in a huge brawl and jumping over the bar to take down the bartender who was on the phone with the cops blaming me for the whole thing. The footage fast forwarded a little more to show me being led out in handcuffs…fast forward a little more to show Old Albert bailing me out of jail.

My shocked gaze rose to connect with Rome's amber one on the big screen. I had never been made before. And to be made at such an extent.

I opened my mouth to speak, but no words came out. I have never felt so exposed. It felt as if he could see my soul.

Instead I distracted myself by studying his background. It looked as if he was sitting in front of a very nice glass house. Reflecting in the glass was the beach. I could hear the waves and the seagulls in the background. The sun was setting behind his head.

It was a very beautiful scene.

He lifted a snifter of amber liquid that matched his eyes and took a sip, seeming to be in no hurry at all, just patiently waiting for me to take in the flood of information before me.

Nossa!

There was no way he should have been able to get a hold of these files. What the hell?

"What's the matter, Nahkti Thomas? You look as if you're sitting in the room with a ghost."

I was sitting in the room with a phantom or rather looking at one on the screen. This guy was more advanced than Jo thought. Now I understood the look on the doctor's face when I asked why he wanted to study Rome's mind.

How in the world had he gone unnoticed all this time? How could one with these capabilities not be on every government watch list in the world?

And then it hit me…

"By pretending to be a drug dealer." I said out loud.

Now it all made sense. He'd fed the world a stereotype and they'd believed him. They never thought to look past the white t's, baggy jeans and designer gym shoes. Just assuming because he was black, young, and a thug, he was dumb.

He took another sip of his drink. "What have you figured out, *Minha Anjo?*"

"You." I told him looking at him with brand new eyes. "How—?"

I was so astonished I couldn't even finish my question. My gaze took in the other computer screens that still had the last sixteen years of my life flashing across them.

He was brilliant!

For the first time in a long time I felt exposed. I felt open. The Navy's psychologist had been trying to make me feel this way for the last ten years with no luck. And here all Rome did was flash my life before my eyes in a sequence that made me see me.

And most importantly, let me know that he saw me...

"Why have you shown me this?"

He didn't answer right away, just continued to study me with that intense gaze of his. Now more than ever it intimidated me. Now I understood that he saw way more than I could imagine. Now I understood what the doctor meant when he said Rome was not a genius, but a phenomenon.

What was going on with him felt spiritual. It felt as if his power came from somewhere else.

"I need you to know that I see you. And..." He paused for a moment and for the first-time since I've known him, looked vulnerable. "I think you're perfect."

His words were low. He spoke them in a way that let me know he'd never said them before. Just like me, this was new territory for him. I settled back in his chair drawing my feet up hugging my legs close.

He'd dimmed the lights and made it so intimate it almost felt as if he was right here with me instead of sitting on a beach somewhere.

"Did you decide to go on vacation?" I muttered. Now that my cover was blown, I felt like this was his and my first real conversation. If felt strange…

He chuckled. "Believe it or not, I'm here on business."

I nodded…

"I have a question for you…" His deep voice came from the speaker. "What's with the confessionals?"

Chuckling, I shook my head… "Jo went from being our brother-in-arms to our sergeant almost overnight and it freaked him out. So, he started reading all these self-help books on how to command your friends basically."

I laughed a little remembering how bad he sucked at it at first.

"He really had a hard time dealing with me, he and I were practically raised together. We're like sister and brother. His book told him to set up video documentaries so that his friends could confess to the camera what they can't necessarily confess to their commanding officer."

"But none of us wanted to do it, so he would have to force us. Of course, I was always in trouble, so my video time became confessionals. He made me go through the same steps as an alcoholic by first telling my name and then admitting my problem."

Rome shook his head frowning. "What an idiot..."

I held my head back and laughed really good... "I thought so too."

"No, I mean he was wrong."

I frowned up at him. "Wrong about what?"

"He was wrong about you being bat sh*t crazy."

Hmmm...I could tell him Jo wasn't wrong and that I was a little crazy. Sometimes I felt a little crazy. But I was curious to see what a person with a phenomenal mind thought about me.

"Explain."

He nodded sitting up in his lounge chair a bit. "At first I too thought you were crazy as hell. But then I studied your file a bit and went back to match some of your therapy sessions with your outbursts. Take a look at the screen to your left."

My medical records changed to show footage of me sitting in therapy while the doctor asked me questions about my father, and I answered them to the best of my knowledge.

"In this session the doctor probed you about your father. Take a look at the screen next to it."

On the screen next to it, it showed me and a few of my brothers singing karaoke at this little dinky watering hole in the dessert.

"This is the same night after your session. As you can see, no violent outburst, no fits of rage. Now, look back to the screen on your left."

The screen now showed me in a therapy session, but this time the doctor was asking me questions about my mother. I didn't want to talk about my mother, I closed my eyes and pretended to be tired.

"Now this is what happened that night after the session."

The screen next to it showed me pistol whipping one of the informants that was trying to feed me bad information.

"When I went back and studied all of your outburst videos, the common denominator was you being in therapy earlier that day or the day before discussing your mother."

He typed something in his lap top and the painful footage of me trying to tell the doctor I didn't want to talk about my mother went away.

"So, as you can see, Jo is an idiot. You're not bat sh*t crazy at all. You're angry. You're angry because you have mommy issues."

Dear God!

I don't know if you guys ever had someone read your soul, but this was a first time for me, and the only thing I could do was stare at him and try my best not to cry. I'd been told my whole life I was crazy.

By first my mother, then my teacher, my friends in high school, my brothers-in-arms…even old Albert told me I had a few screws missing in my tool shed.

Could what Rome said be true?

After all these years, could I have been lashing out in anger? I've convinced myself that I didn't need my mother's love. I didn't need anybody. So why would I be angry?

I wasn't angry…

Was I?

And if I am angry, how do I fix it?

Even though I didn't want him to know how vulnerable I was right now, I wanted to know the answer to my question more…so I asked him.

"How do I fix being angry?" My words were barely over a whisper. I couldn't look him in his eyes, instead I stared at the reflection of the setting sun in the huge glass windows behind him.

"Tenderness…"

My gaze flew to his. Did he just say tenderness?

Tenderness???

What the hell am I supposed to do, gently beat the hell out of my enemy? Maybe I should massage their backs before I plant my foot in the center of it.

I shook my head. "Naw, I don't think that's it."

He chuckled. "You sound like me earlier. But upon further examination, that is exactly what you need…Someone to teach you tenderness."

"Whoa, wait… you mean I need tenderness?"

With a grin still on his handsome face he nodded before pointing at me through the screen. "You need tenderness, and I'm the man who's going to teach you."

I stared at him for a moment to see if he was joking. When he didn't say anything else, I threw back my head and laughed.

Do y'all hear this? The thug that put explosive devices around my ankles says he's going to be the one to teach me tenderness.

Ha! That was hilarious.

He took a sip of his drink. "You know, *Minha Anjo,* the last time you challenged me, I'd asked you your name, and you wouldn't tell me. I warned you that I could get all of your information if I put my mind to it, and you still didn't tell me. Back then I only wanted your name, but know I feel as if I know all there is to know about you."

His statement brought my laughter to a dead stop.

Damn it!

He's right…He'd asked me my name and I didn't give it to him. And what did he do? He ended up dissecting my whole life. He'd not only dug up my name, but my medical records, my therapy sessions, he even found footage of me out in the field.

Note to self: *Stop challenging this man!*

"By the way, where is your mother now?"

His question took me off guard and before I knew what was happening, I opened my mouth and this came out:

"Dead…she died a few years after I enlisted."

"Oh, okay…I was wondering why I couldn't find anything about her in your files."

"She was not a U.S. citizen…apparently it was the one thing my father did for me before disappearing out the picture. It's his last name that I have."

Sensing that the topic made me uncomfortable, he thankfully changed the subject, and would you guys believe he and I ended up chatting all through the night until the first rays of the sun touched the sky? Me sitting in his king size chair and he in his lounge chair at the really nice glass beach house. At some point he'd gotten up and walked into his room for the evening.

He said the house belonged to his associate who he'd flown to California to meet with. He'd agreed to stay overnight because they had to meet again in the morning and it didn't make sense to go to a hotel, when his associate's house was way nicer.

Once he made it back to his room he'd settled down in the bed and proceeded to talk to me about everything. And guess what. He was right earlier when he said he and I had a lot in common. For one thing, the both of us hated Star Wars, but loved Lord of the Rings. He told me the earth was really like that before Noah's flood.

"How do you know?" I'd asked him.

"It says it in the Bible. Genesis 6 talks about the time giants walked the earth."

My mouth dropped. "You've read the Bible?"

He chuckled. "Several times. Although we didn't go to church much, my mother brought us up to acknowledge the Most High in all we do. Granted, I am a bit of a heathen these days, my goal is eventually to get my life together and start living right."

I couldn't believe he was telling me this. I know he had an image to uphold and being a man that walks with God may not fit into that image.

"Why are you telling me this?" I asked him for the second time that night.

"I know you felt vulnerable with me knowing so many of your secrets. I figure if I let you in my head and share a few of mine with you the score will be even."

Oh my goodness! That is so sweet. And yeah, it did make me feel better.

"So, you were telling me about the Bible."

He smiled. "It's a great piece of work. I've never seen writing like it. Many people believe the book has several different authors, but the truth is, there is only one."

I frowned, I didn't know much about the Bible, but even I knew there was books named after the men who wrote them.

"Isn't like the book of Ezekiel and—"

Hmmm…this is a terrible shame. I couldn't name another book.

"Yeah, there are different names to the books. But when I say one author, I mean that everybody who contributed to the book was possessed by the Rauch Ha Kodesh, which would make the Rauch the author."

"The Rah—"

"Rauch…it's Hebrew for Set Apart Spirit or what many refer to as the Holy Spirit."

I nodded, I had heard of that.

"It explains why the Scriptures are so layered. And don't get me wrong, I have read the works of those the world considers to be literary geniuses, and yet, I have yet to find one that can write in layers like scriptural writing."

And then he proceeded to blow my mind by explaining to me the layers he's noticed. "The MessiYah speaks in these parables. Parables that he says only those who are meant to hear will understand. But get this…Those who are meant to understand take from them only what they can handle at the time they read it…"

"They go away and then come back a few years later. Life has shown them a few more things, molded them a little more…and they read the parable again, but this time they see something on a completely different level than what they saw before. Now keep in mind, it's the same parable, the same words…yet, because where they are in life, they are able to see it from a different angle."

He smiled, getting a little excited. "Isn't that amazing? How can one passage shift to reflect where you are in life? It's the only book I've ever read that makes me feel grounded. It makes me feel lowly, dumb even."

I chuckled. "How is that possible, it's safe to say you're the smartest man I know. How can any book may you feel dumb?"

"There was a man named Enoch, he lived before the flood. He mapped the heavens. He studied the course of the sun and the moon. He studied the portals they come in at the different times of the year. I too study it but compared to Enoch and the things that he knew, my knowledge is not even grade school level."

My eyes widened. "Seriously?"

He nodded…

At some point the topic of conversation shifted to children and rather or not we wanted to someday have a family.

Although I didn't tell him, this topic made me sad, because I'll never be able to bear children. When I was eleven my mom threw me down the basement stairs. I began to bleed and when the bleeding did not stop, she took me to the local clinic where the doctor told me I'd suffered damage to my uterus and would never be able to have children.

Before tonight I'd thought I was fine with what had happened. But after listening to Rome speak about the children he wanted to have and how he had feelings about his younger sister starting a family before him, I silently mourned for the fact that I will never be a mother.

And then he rocked my world by looking down at me from the screen and saying…

"I had this unexplainable feeling of doom. For the life of me, no matter what was going on, I could never see far into the future. Like I'd never seen myself starting a family, becoming a father and maybe even a grandfather." He paused for just a moment as his amber gaze traveled across space and time to meet mine.

"That was until I met you. For the first time in my life I see myself starting a family. I see myself growing old…with you. That's not something that happens every day. For me never before. I know we just met. And this may seem a bit fast, but I don't have to ponder on things like others…I know that me and you were supposed to meet. You my rib, shawty, I can feel it, like I can feel God's love."

He licked those perfect lips. "When I get home tomorrow night, I want to make love to you. And I want to do it without anything between us. I've seen your doctor records, I know you're clean. I had a doctor meet me hear to check me out earlier…you'll have the records tomorrow."

"What are saying, Rome?" My voice quivered, I was on the verge I tears. He studied me for a moment before I spoke, reading my soul in only the way that he could.

"I don't want anything between us, ever. Whatever happens…happens."

Chapter 10

She's Mine, I'll Spoil Her If I Want To

"Love makes your soul crawl out from its hiding place."

— Zora Neale Hurston

Nakhti

The first round of gifts came before I got out of bed. After staying up all night talking to Rome, I was not ready to get up just yet. However, the knocking didn't stop, so I grudgingly dragged myself up, checking my watch as I did.

Damn! It was 12:30 in the afternoon…

"I'm coming!" I called to the knocker.

When I opened the door, I stepped back dumbfounded as Rob, Milo, Hannibal, and several other men I didn't know shuffled through the door with their arms laden down with bags and shoe boxes.

"*Nossa!* What's all this?"

"A brand-new wardrobe for the lady." Rob called back to me as he sat his load on the floor by the closet, the other men followed suit.

Milo was still not my biggest fan and barely spoke to me before he left back out the door.

"You're going to have to forgive him, he a little salty. Rome made you tossing Lo across the room into a meme and sent it to all our phones this morning, the fellas been roasting him ever since." Hannibal, one of Rome's closest friends, who I met last night said after he put down his load next to Rob's.

"I am so glad my girl was tripping and wanted me to stay with her the other day, or I might have been with them other gumps who got they a** kicked by a little slip of a girl."

I put my hand on my hip and eyeballed Hannibal. "Little slip of a girl?!"

He held his hands up. "Oh no! I don't want no trouble, Ms. Lady. I just meant you're not very tall or big…that's all."

He chuckled. "Let me get my a** out of here before you change your mind and decide to do me like you did that fool Lo…" And then he threw his head back and laughed as he walked out the door.

The other guys followed, all except Rob. He reached into his jacket and pulled out what looked and smelled like a breakfast sandwich as well as an envelope.

"You better enjoy this now, 'cause your man on his way back. And after he get here, it's going to be celery sticks and tofurky for you."

I almost threw up just listening to that as I opened the envelope. It was Rome's test results of the blood work and the exam he'd gotten yesterday. He'd gotten tested for all STDs and received an N for negative straight down the line.

I folded the paper and placed it back in the envelope before addressing Rob. "Your brother is not my man." I told him as I poured myself a glass of water to take my pain pills.

He pulled up a chair to the kitchen table and opened his sandwich. "Naw, shawty, you wrong. You belong to Rome. Once he gets his sights set on something, he won't stop until he get it. You might as well make both of y'all jobs easier and just give in."

After I took my pills, I sat down with him and dug in. "You think I'm stupid, I see all the women your brother has chasing after him. I'm not interested in joining his harem."

I didn't feel strange admitting this to Rob. Over the last couple of days, I've developed a relationship of honesty with him. Plus, he was really easy to talk to, which was surprising for one so young. His mother called him a genius as well, but in the way of an artist. He saw the world different from the rest of us. I think it's what makes him so relatable to everyone he comes in contact with.

"On everything I love, I ain't never seen him act the way he acting toward you to no other girl. Never!" He held one hand up and put the other over his heart. "This dude was on the phone waking niggas up at 5am, sending us to meet with some chick who dragged us from store to store getting clothes for you."

He shook his head as he took a huge bite out of his sandwich. "And this sh*t ain't cheap!"

I took a bite of my sandwich trying to pretend that his words were not affecting me. Last night after Rome told me he wanted to have unprotected sex with me, I was surprised at the pleasure that went through me.

However, I scolded myself and him, telling him that it was impossible for him to have such strong feelings for me only after knowing me for a couple of days.

"Why is that impossible?" He'd asked. "Tell me you don't feel that force pulling us together. As a matter of fact, you don't have to tell me...I know you feel it."

I lifted an eyebrow. "That's pretty presumptuous of you. How do you know that I feel it?"

"Because I'm not dead."

I frowned confused. "Excuse me?"

"If you didn't feel it, I would be dead by now."

I shook my head. "That makes no sense. We fought and you beat me fair and square."

He gave me a sad look. "Nak, Nak, Nak...tell me you're not one of those people who lie to yourself. Yeah, I beat you in the fight, but you're the kind of person that don't give up. If you wasn't feeling me, you would have did some sh*t like stab me in my neck with a rock when I went to pick you up off the ground."

I opened my mouth insulted at what he was insinuating. "Damn it, Romeo, I am not a savage, no matter what you think."

That made him roar with laughter. "Baby, I ain't making this sh*t up, you stabbed a man in the neck with a rock in Berlin, I saw the footage."

Nossa! He was right...Crap!

I held my head up high, not willing to admit to defeat. "None of what you're saying has anything to do with why it's impossible for you to feel so strongly about me in such a short time."

His laughter disappeared. "And you still haven't told me why it's impossible."

"That's easy, we don't know each other. I'm telling you I'm dama—"

"I swear to God, Nak, if you say you're damaged to me one more time, I'm going to pull you across my lap and spank your a** till those succulent cheeks of yours turn red!"

Well...

Damn...

Can you guys tell me why his words had me squeezing my thighs together when I should have been enraged?

What the hell was happening to me?

So yeah, it took me a minute to get my thoughts together after that, but as I lay in bed, I thought about that force he spoke of. I'd been feeling it ever since I met him. I thought it was only me.

He told me last night after I insisted his feelings were premature that he would prove it to me. I asked him how.

"When a man is digging a woman, he shows her how much he values her to the best of his ability. A poor man may write a poem. A carpenter may build her a house. A gardener may bring her his prize roses. A rich man... will give her heart's desire." He paused for a moment as that russet gaze studied me, dissecting me more than anyone has ever done.

"It hurts my heart that no one ever showed you your worth, but I'll be lying if I say that I'm not thrilled that the honor is all mine."

I don't know why all his words seemed to have such a strong effect on me. When he's talking dirty or wisdom…it doesn't matter, his words pull at my soul. Yes, there was something between us, I wasn't just imagining it, although I tried to convince myself that I was.

It was the real reason I was in no rush to leave his place. Had he been any other man, I would have found a way out of these cuffs. Let's just be real about it.

Had he been any other man, I would have destroyed this loft that had become my prison. And he was right, had he been any other man, he would have been dead, make no mistake about it.

"For the first time in my brother's life, he's in love. I have never seen him want anybody the way he wants you." Rob said bringing me back to the present.

I chuckled. "How do you know that?"

"Well first of all, he's my brother and I know my brother, but also by the look in his eyes when he watches you. The other night he stared at you in wonder. He ain't never met a girl like you. Apparently yo' savage a** do it for him. He like everything about you."

He wore a little smile on his face. "He needs this, shawty."

"Why?" I asked taking another bite out of my sandwich, just sucking up all of Rob's words. They had me feeling like a young girl falling in love for the first time.

"He don't want to be looked at as a hero, but he is. He's the heartbeat of this community. I ain't never seen nobody that give back like him. All he do is give…" He shook his head. "And ain't nobody giving to him. Look, I don't know how long you're going to be here, but if you can just…"

He searched his mind for the right words. "Love him while you're here, that will be good, 'cause he need it."

He spent the rest of the morning telling me about all the things Rome was doing for the community. By the time he was finished I was in tears. He was the reason so many of the children here in the community were going to college.

And get this… Not only had he paid and is still paying for the doctor who'd re-stitched my wound to go to med school, he actually studied with him to help him pass his exams, which would explain why he talked to Rome as if he was his big brother and not a patient.

Rob said Rome has an open-door policy with any of the youth who need help with their assignments, from grade school level to graduate school; they all came to him if they needed help understanding something.

It didn't matter what he was doing. If one of the kids came by and said they needed help he let them up and helped them.

He was not only involved academically, he also pushed them to be physically fit by promoting exercise and healthy eating habits. He met with several of the youths once a week to practice Capoeira and met with his men once a week to practice Brazilian Jui-Jitsu, which would explain why he'd so easily defeated me.

What kind of person does that? Who gives so much of themselves in such a way?

Now more than ever the doctor's words made so much sense.

Rome is a phenomenon.

But what puzzled me was how somebody like that could want somebody like me.

I am nothing like him. I didn't preserve life, I took it. I'm selfish at best and had a hell of temper. And if I'm being honest with myself, I am a bit of a savage. I have mommy issues. Impulse Control Disorder, which no doubt stems from my mommy issues. And tons of other problems. Why would he waste his time with me?

I don't know…

And this is going to sound strange to some of you, but for some reason the thought of it was working havoc on my libido. Not only was the kid younger than me. He was smarter than me…hell, I thought Jo was a superman.

No, Rome is the *real* superman.

And he wanted me. He even wanted me to bear his little genius children. The fact that I couldn't sadden me more than I'd like to admit. I've always been alright with the knowledge that I'll never be a mom, until now.

I shook away those thoughts. Those were dangerous thoughts. Instead, I focused back on the lust that was strumming through my loins. If I could never have the pleasure of bearing his children, at the very least I could enjoy his body while I'm here.

My life after I left here will be one of solitude. I wanted to enjoy myself just a little while before that. I wanted to enjoy Rome's gorgeous, young, strong body.

Was that so wrong?

The thought got me so hot and bothered I had to kick Rob out so that I could run myself a bath in that beautiful claw foot tub in hopes that a nice soaking would take my mind off my body's demands. The doctor had left me some waterproof bandages for my wound which was perfect, because I wasn't waiting another minute to experience this tub.

It was during my soaking that I discovered that if I call out Rome's name his smart house dialed his phone. I thought about his parting words, when he told me if I needed him just call him, and I told him that I didn't have his number and he'd answered back, "Just call out my name."

So I was sitting in the tub with bubbles up to my ears and the hot water was doing nothing to quiet my libido. I think it was only making it worse. And it didn't help that I couldn't get Rome's words or the look of his heated gaze as he told me he wanted to feel my heat surrounding him with no barriers between us out my head.

I wanted him…

I wanted him so bad…My Impulse Control Disorder kicked in and I held back my head and called his name.

A few seconds later his deep, capable voice came over the loud speaker overhead. "*Minha Anjo,* how are you, baby?"

I closed my eyes wishing he was here to take me and soothe the fire that was building in me.

"How am I talking to you right now?" I asked instead of coming right out and telling him I needed him to come quick because I was super turned on by him and wanted to have sex right now.

Wheew!!! *Control yourself, Nak! Nossa! You're going to wear the young man out!*

He chuckled and for a minute, I had to wonder if he could read minds. With all the things that he was capable of I wouldn't be surprised. He was truly a gem hidden in the heart of the ghetto.

"When you say my name, the house dials my phone."

"Wow! That is so cool..." I cooed, praying my voice wasn't laden with my lust.

"What are you doing? Is that water I hear?"

"Mmmmhhhmmm...I'm taking a bath."

"Whaaaat? You thought about a brotha in your bath. Oh sh*t..."

I held back my head and laughed at his silliness. "And here I thought you could see me as well."

Oh my God! Why did I just say that?

There was a long pause on the other end before he spoke. "Do you want me to see you, Nak?"

I bit my lip. "I think I do..."

"Gentlemen, will you excuse me for a moment, I have to take this call in the other room."

Oh Damn! He was in the middle of a meeting. I slid down in the tub submerging my head embarrassed. Great! I am now officially a cougar, purring for a man that was nearly five years younger than me.

"Where are you, baby?" I heard him call.

"Here." I gasped, coming back up out the water.

He chuckled again. "Why are you hiding from me?"

The lighting in the bathroom suddenly dimmed in a way that made it feel like a spa, then the sound of smooth jazz came from the speakers overhead, the combination made me feel more relaxed. It's amazing how he can adjust the settings in his loft from where ever he is.

"Can you really see me?" I asked looking around for the camera. I didn't see one anywhere. Didn't even see where one could be hiding.

"Turn your head and look out the bathroom door."

I did as he said and sure enough, there was a small camera directly across from the bathroom above the huge windows. I was a little relieved it was not in the bathroom. That would be a little creepy.

I waved at the camera.

"Hello, beautiful." His soothing voice came from the loud speakers.

I bit my lip again to try and control my grin. This man was breaking me down. Since knowing him, I've blushed more than I ever did in my whole life.

"How is your meeting?"

He exhaled. "Long, I'm ready to be home with you."

Home? With me? That felt way too good.

Dear God!

I was *falling for Rome…*

I cleared my throat. "Thank you for the clothes and things you sent this morning, although you didn't have to send so much."

"You're mine, I'll spoil you if I want." He paused for a moment and let me absorb that. I chose to ignore how good it made me feel, just like I did when he said he wanted to be home with me.

"How do you like them?"

"Surprisingly… I love them. How did you know my style?"

It's true, when I went through the items of clothing, I was surprised to see that they were my style. More cargo pants, shorts…tanks, a few pairs of jeans and t's. A brand-new pair of combat boots…a few pairs of name brand gym shoes.

When I took them into the closet, I was secretly thrilled to see that Rome and I had a couple of pairs that were alike. Rob had teased me holding up one of Rome's baby blue Jordan's and a smaller version of them that belonged to me.

"I figured you were a bit of a tomboy." Rome's deep voice came from the speaker seeming to vibrate through the bathwater to my heat. "Although I do have you a few dresses coming, knowing you, you probably hate wearing them, but you look too sexy in them not to own at least one."

Laughing, I told him he figured right. He and I chatted for a little while longer before he had to get back to his meeting. But before he got off the phone, he said something that nearly made me come apart in the tub.

"I can see your need in your eyes. It's driving me mad with want. I'm hard as a f***ing rock. I swear when I get a hold of you,

I'm going to make you come so many times you're going to beg me to let you rest."

Well…

Damn…

****

When I got out of the bath, I took my time and moisturized my skin. I wanted my brown to glow perfectly. I left some of the conditioner in my hair so that it curled tightly, and then rolled it up in a messy bun, letting a few tendrils hang down my neck and face. This style made me look soft and feminine.

There was a box of perfume, I couldn't tell what it was because it was wrapped in golden paper. I unwrapped it and nearly dropped it.

Nossa! Channel No. 5 Grand Extract

I looooooovve this fragrance. But never bought it because I couldn't freaking afford to spend $5,000 on a bottle of perfume.

The first time I'd smelt it had been when Jo's mom had sailed past me in all of her pomp-ass glory. When I'd asked her what she was wearing she did that phony little chuckle the very rich do when they are talking to common folk.

"Oh dear, this is *Channel No. 5 Grand Extract*. I assure you they don't sell it at Walmart." And then she turned and glided off.

Old Albert had to hold me back, I was literally going to stick my foot out and trip her.

Anyway, she was right. When I finally found a bottle, my eyes bugged out my head at the price. The sales lady in the fancy French boutique wouldn't even give me a little squirt of it on sample paper, telling me that a squirt of it was worth a hundred dollars.

My hands shook with excitement as I gently sprayed a few puffs on my skin.

"Awww, this smells so good."

How in the world did he know this was my favorite? I shook my head as I headed into the closet to choose an outfit, knowing Rome, there was no telling. He'd probably got a hold of the store footage of me begging the woman for a sample.

The underwear Rome's shopper had gotten me ranged from mildly sexy to very sexy, and then there was a purple panty and bra set that was extremely sexy. I chose it. Needless to say, there will be no panty lines in my outfit today.

It took me a while to choose said outfit, because I had a lot to choose from. I don't think I've ever had so many clothes. I ended up settling on a cute pair of jean shorts that were kind of short, but not ridiculously so and a light pink loose-fitting tank top that will complement my bra that will show a little under the arm perfectly.

To finish off my look, I slid my feet in my brand-new combat boots. I didn't bother to tie them, opting to wear them in a loose fit.

When I was done, I stood looking in the mirror very satisfied with my reflection.

It wasn't too long after that Happy knocked on the door. She surprised me when I opened it by throwing her arms around my neck and hugging me. I stiffened, not knowing what to do, but after I realized she wasn't attacking me managed to hug her back.

You see what I mean? Damaged!

"Mmm, you smell good." She muttered as she bustled in and got busy.

Like yesterday I helped her clean up, although she didn't have much to clean. And just like yesterday Rob joined us, but this time he brought drinks. I don't know if I've told you guys, but Rob was the man. I grabbed us two cups while he opened the brand-new bottle of Hennessey.

He told me that a few of Rome's buddies were probably going to come through and have a drink with him, which is something they always did when he came back into town after being gone a couple of days.

When Happy was finished and was about to go home, I talked her into staying for a little while, not wanting her to go home to that bastard just yet.

"Girl, sit down and chat with me for a minute. Here, I think Rome has apple juice in the fridge."

A look of doubt and yearning crossed her beautiful face. "Maybe I can stay for just a little while longer."

"Yeah, just a little while." I told her as I took a sip from the rocks glass.

She was having such a good time, the little while turned into seven hours later. Rob on weed and liquor was too much. He had both Happy and I dying laughing. And when poor Milo and Hannibal joined us, he really turned into a nut, asking Milo about the knot in the back of his head.

I had to apologize to the man just so that he could stop moping. And surprisingly when I did, his spirits picked right up. It was either that or the Hennessy he was drinking. He and Hannibal brought another bottle with them.

Milo didn't smoke weed, but Hannibal did and in the space of a few hours, he and Rob must have smoked four blunts.

Nossa! I didn't know how they did it. Rob offered me a pull several times and I told him no. The last time I'd smoked I ended up smashing all the car windows out of a man's car who thought it was funny to speed through a school zone while little kids were present, nearly hitting a child and the crossing guard.

Yeah, I got arrested, and yeah, Old Albert had to come and bail me out. When Jo found out I'd smoked weed with my condition he hit the roof and threatened to fire me for the hundredth time. Apparently, it was not a very good idea for someone with Impulse Control Disorder to do drugs.

Anyway, enough about that, several more people showed up, including a big giant of a man named Hitter.

Now let me pause for just a moment and tell y'all a few things about Hitter. He made me regret the fact that I didn't have my piece on me.

No, he didn't do anything to threaten me physically. His presence was threatening enough. Everything about him screamed violence, and that coming from me said a lot. He was at least 6'5… and was all muscle. There wasn't an inch of fat on him.

He had big massive hands that had so many scars on the knuckles that it didn't take a rocket scientist to tell you what he's done with them.

And as if to confirm my thoughts, Rob told me that Hitter used to be a professional boxer, but had to retire due to terrible migraines that the doctors told him came from his chosen profession. So now he ran the biggest underground boxing arena in Chicago. Apparently, he is Rome's best friends. He didn't speak much, in fact, he wasn't very sociable at all.

But it seemed as if everybody was used to him, because they went on drinking and laughing as if a very violent man was not in the room. The only one he talked to was Rob, who he treated like a little brother, grabbing him and roughing him up a bit. I think that was the only time something that resembled a smile appeared on his face.

Even the few women that had shown up with some more of Rome's men gave him his space, although they shot fishing glances his way. Out of the men here at the moment, he was clearly the alpha male, but he wasn't taking any of their bait.

He wasn't a bad looking man, in fact, he was quite handsome, but his fierce scowl made him feel very unapproachable. I asked Rob if he was angry or something and he told me that was his permanent look. He said I didn't want to see an angry Hitter. And I believed him. He was the kind of brotha you had to shoot. Damn trying to fight him.

Happy told me he wasn't paying any of these women any attention because he was obsessed with the Tea Maker.

"Tea maker?" I'd asked. She nodded sipping on her apple juice.

"Yeah, she's a cute little thing that just opened a Tea Shop in Oak Park. Her and her brother stay in an apartment not too far from Hitter's gym. Rome say Hitter is obsessed with her, but she won't give him the time of day. She ain't into brutish men or thugs, and Hitter is both."

I was going to ask her another question, but right then Rome walked through the door holding a golden bag flanked by two more of his men.

I don't know if it was the Hennessy or the fact that I'd been purring for him all day. But everything else seemed to fade to black. Happy was saying something to me, but I couldn't tell you what. I placed my hand on the sink behind me to brace myself as I took him in.

I'm going to try and describe how good he looked, but I know I'm not going to do him any justice. He wore a pair of dark blue jeans that fell perfectly on his bow legs. He'd partnered the jeans with a dark blue t-shirt and a pair of brown Timberlands.

Around his neck was a gold chain and charm that wasn't too blingy, but did have enough ice to catch the soft lighting in the loft. That coupled with his gold watch and the diamond stud in his ear was just enough jewelry to not to appear as if he was trying too hard. He topped it all off with a New York Yankees baseball cap.

His beard game was killing it. It looked as if he was fresh from the barbershop, the lining so tight it looked as if it had been drawn on.

Damn! This brotha looked good in dark blue. His clothes fit on his tall, lean, muscled, bow legged body like he'd been paid to model the outfit.

Several of his men came to him to do that hand clasp slash one arm hug that men do, but his hungry gaze never left me. The whole time I was taking him in, he was doing the same to me.

My breath got caught somewhere in my throat and my stomach when I realized he was walking straight for me. He never stopped, if someone managed to get a hand clasp in, they were good. It was clear to all watching that Rome had tunnel vision.

When he got to the kitchen where I was, he gently put the bag in his hand on the table and turned his hat to the back without stopping his trek to me.

I opened my mouth to say something… I don't know, maybe hi. But never got a chance because he was there in front of me, blocking the rest of the loft from my few with his big body, taking my lips in a kiss that caused my knees to buckle.

I kid you not, he had to wrap one of his arms around me to hold me up.

He kissed me like a man starved. I had never been kissed this way, I felt it all the way down to my core. Forgetting we wasn't alone I wrapped my arms around his neck when he deepened the kiss.

Good God!

The smell of his expensive cologne, the feel of his strong arms wrapped around me, and his hungry perfect mouth pulling from mine, it was too much. He lifted me bringing my mouth closer to his and I wrapped my legs around his waist.

"Damn, Bo! If you put yo' tongue any further down her throat you gon' choke the po' girl!"

Rome lips lifted in a smile before he turned his head to take in his friend.

"Hitta!" He let my feet slide to the floor, but took my hand as he used his other to embrace his friend.

"If you come around that must mean you have a fight set up for me."

Hitter chuckled. If that could even be considered a chuckle. "Come on, man, I don't just come and see you when I need you to fight."

Rome gave him a skeptical look. Hitter hit his shoulder. "Aight! Maybe I do…But you my champion. Everybody want to fight the champion. And that do'work two ways, Bo. The only reason you come around the gym these days is to blow off steam."

Hitter's English was so broken he almost sounded like he was from the islands. I was having a hard time understanding him. This must have been why he didn't speak much.

"You still stalking the Tea Maker?" Rome asked.

Hitter chuckled shaking his head a bit. "Y'all laughing…But I'm gon' get her a**. Watch, she gon' be mine."

I shivered. I don't know who this mystery woman was, but I almost felt sorry for her. Hitter was the very definition of a brute… thug edition. I didn't follow boxing, but Happy said he used to be really famous before his injury. She said he was the reigning champion for several years.

Rome excused himself from his friend, telling him he'll be back to talk to him about the fight. With my hand still in his he took the big gold bag off the table and guided me to the other side of the loft that was fairly empty.

"I have a gift for you." He said pulling me over by the huge window that looked out over the ghetto.

I threw my head back and whined…"Oh no, Romeo! You've already given me so much. I don't need anything else."

"I'll be the judge of that." He said pushing the gold bag in my hand. I sat it on the windowsill and reached down inside the tissue paper. My hands closed on what felt like a big bag. But it was a lot heavier than a bag should be. I pulled it out and my gaze flew to Rome's.

"Is this real?"

He gave me a look that told me not to insult him. "Of course it's real."

"Rome, Louis Vuitton only made 24 of these."

He nodded. "And you are now the owner of one of them."

I didn't think I could close my mouth if I tried. I was not a big purse person, but I loved this bag. I loved it because it was so different from all the bags that were being designed. It's from their patchwork line. Some people thought the bags were too big and ugly, but I loved them. They only made 24 and they are deathly expensive. I saw Beyoncé with this bag in a magazine once and thought, now that is a bag I would carry.

But how in the world did Rome know that? And even more importantly, how in the world did he get a hold of one of the bags?

Something suddenly moved inside it, I screeched dropping it. Chuckling Rome reached out and caught it before it hit the floor.

"What the hell?" I asked.

Grinning he handed it back to me. "Look inside."

I opened the bag and this time when I screeched, it drew everybody's attention in the loft, but I didn't care. Throwing my arms around Rome's neck I planted about a hundred kisses on his handsome face, and the whole time he was trying to catch my lips with his.

Out of all the gifts he got me, this was by far the best one, because it was something I always wanted since I was a little girl. It was a Miniature Poodle inside looking up at me with the most beautiful puppy dog eyes. As I lifted him out, he yelped wagging his little tail excitedly.

"He's so tiny!" I cried bringing him close to my chest.

"He won't get much bigger than that." Rome said using his index finger to rub his little head.

Oh my goodness, guys, I was in love with Rome and the puppy. He was so tiny I could hold him in the palm of my hands.

"I'm going to call you Giant."

Rome frowned. "Giant?"

I nodded. "Mmmmhhhmmm, 'cause I bet you have a giant personality." I told the little fella hugging him close.

I was in love…Dear God help me, *I had fallen for Rome.*

Chapter 11

Strung Out on that Thug Love

Rome

I lifted my drink and took a sip as I relaxed back on the couch watching Nakhti through lowered lids. Because she'd been secluded here the last couple of days, she moved around my loft like the Queen she is as she and Happy chased the little puppy around.

When she squatted down to secure him in his pen in the kitchen, my gaze traveled up her long, muscled yet softly curved legs that I couldn't wait to feel wrapped around my waist while I slid into her moist heat, up to her a** that has kept me in a constant state of semi-erection and anger all night watching it jiggle in those little shorts as she walked.

More than once I'd had to make eye contact with one of my men who'd dared to look too long. It was important that they all understood…

Something strange has happened to me.

I'm not the same man they knew before she moseyed her a** into my life. I've become obsessed, and it took all the control I barely held onto not to lash out and destroy them when they looked at what is mine.

Mine…

Mine, mutha f***a!

I bit down on my teeth as I lifted the glass and took another sip.

Hitta sat down on the coffee table in front of me, blocking my view of Nak. Only he or my little brother would dare approach me when I'm in this mood.

"You see that look in yo' eye, Bo?" He said pointing at my face. "That's the look of a man that see his tomorrows. Now you can finally understand my feelings for Angel. Now you can understand why I can't stop until she mine, until it's my arms she sleeping in every night." He shook his head. "I'm gon' get on out of here. I'll see you the day after tomorrow, try to get some rest."

I shook up with him. "Aight, man, I'll holla at you later."

I don't know how long I'd laughed at Hitta for pining over the Tea Maker. This dude did sh*t like sit outside her crib in his truck and watch her get on and off the bus. Hitta could have any other girl he wanted, it just so happened he wanted the one girl that didn't want him.

He was stronger than I though. Now that I had Nak, I couldn't really see giving her up.

When I walked through the door today, she'd looked at me as if I was her hero. No doubt my little brother has been filling her in on all the good things I do for the community and what not.

But she had no idea how sick I was capable of being. She had no idea I'd imagined chaining her to my bed where no one else could ever see her, stripping away her clothes and consuming all the flesh on her bones. I wanted to taste her so bad, I've been able to think of little else.

I took another sip of my drink as my gaze followed her across the loft.

She had no idea I'd become obsessed with her, and how much strength it was taking to sit here across the loft and just watch instead of acting on my hunger and kicking everybody the f*** out so that I could get my taste.

Over the last twenty-four hours I've studied all there is to know about my little prisoner.

Of course, what I'd shown her yesterday was only the tip of the iceberg. If she knew how much I truly knew about her she would freak the f*** out. Once I found out her name and social security number the rest was history.

Between the FBI and the CIA databases, there was nothing about her I didn't know, including the fact that she was horribly abused by her mother in Brazil and abandoned by her American father.

She thought she was barren because of what some rinky-dink a** doctor told her in a little poorly founded Brazilian clinic. She had no idea that a department of the CIA has been tracking her movements ever since she left the Bureau to work solely for Jo.

Whenever she has a few days off, she rents a hotel room in Queens, New York very near her father's family and visits a dog shelter, her favorite dog was a Miniature Poodle named Crumble, who was too mean and ornery to get adopted. But Nak couldn't adopt him although she wanted too, because she worked too much.

The owner of the shelter name is George Newman, he uses it as a tax right off. Because he secretly lusted after Nak, he recorded her coming to visit the dog that she related to, because she too felt unwanted and unloved. He used his camera and invasively zoomed in on her breasts and a** every time she bent over or reached for something. He stored the recording in his computer under the tab, The Sexy Puerto Rican B****, along with thousands of other videos, mainly child porn.

He liked Nak because she looked young and innocent. He'd been brought up on several counts of rape and harassment, but because he came from money, had managed to not serve any time.

I took another sip of my drink.

I could not delay my trip home another day to fly to New York to clean up a little trash, but I called in a favor on a Sicilian business man who stays there that reaches out to me quite often to make his illicit deeds disappear from cyberspace.

George Newman was pronounced dead three hours and twenty-six minutes ago.

Nak turned to look at me after she secured Giant in his home for the night. The look in her eyes said she was tired of waiting, she was ready to mate!

My sentiments exactly.

As she crossed the floor heading toward me, I swear she worked them f***ing combat boots like those red bottoms. With a slight wave of my hand I gave the signal that the party was over.

Nakhti

I was noticing the different sides to Rome. I'd met the genius and the giver…I'd even met the cynic…it wasn't till tonight that I'd officially met the thug. And it was something about the thug side of him that made me feel reckless.

I'd done something to upset him. For the last couple of hours, he's sat alone over on his couch watching me with the eyes of a predator. There was anger in his gaze, but there was also hunger. And even that made me feel reckless.

The lighting over his head was dimmed more than the rest of the loft seeming to cast him in shadow. The only thing that stood out was his golden gaze. As I crossed the floor to him, I wondered what I'd done to upset him.

And then I wondered what I could do to change his mood. When the thought came to me, I just acted on it. And as if the forces of nature were working with me, the next song to come on the speaker overhead was Rihanna's *Needed Me*.

This was the same song I danced to in the private room of a high-end strip club in Vegas minutes before I'd slit the throat of my mark.

Although I hated every minute of it, I'd had to train with a professional stripper for weeks preparing for that assignment. It was that training I used now as I walked toward Rome. The thug in him was an unstable creature. It was not like the genius or the giver. It was unbalanced and it called to the impish side of me.

When Rome's men started clearing everybody out of the loft, I smiled.

Perfect…

I didn't stop walking until I was standing on the coffee table in front of him, then I squatted down facing him with my legs spread and as I slowly stood, I rolled my stomach to the beat. Many people don't know the muscle that it took to do this kind of dancing.

You needed to be in top shape to be the best. Something my trainer had drilled into my head as she taught me how to seduce with the movements of my body.

Still slouched back against the couch he watched me, letting his honey gaze drink me in. I bit my lip to hold in a moan when the tent in his pants grew big…

He didn't even try to hide it. He wanted me to see what I was doing to him. I closed my eyes as I let the music take over me. It was as if Rihanna lived in my shoes and wrote this song especially for me.

Bet you never could imagine
Never told you you could have it

You needed me
Ooh
You needed me

Her words reminded me what my job was. I make men need me. But they can never have me.

Never!

They just need me…and then—

An angry growl came from the couch before Rome moved so suddenly, he took me by surprise, grabbing me off the table bringing me to straddle his lap.

"You damn right I needed you! So I took you! I didn't f***ing ask. And when I'm done with yo' a** tonight, you gon' know fo' sho' who you belong to!" He growled before his big hands palmed the sides of my face as his mouth devoured mine.

That moan did escape when the impact of his hungry kiss made its way down to my core. I rubbed my softness against his hardness, eager to feel him fully.

"I swear if you wear these f***ing short a** shorts around other men again, I will rip them in two." He muttered before his hungry mouth made its way down to my neck.

Hmmm…It was hard to think of anything with that mouth and his strong hands washing over me, taking control of my body.

But eventually the reason for his anger penetrated through the haze he'd created around me. He was jealous of the other men looking at me in these shorts. His jealousy only heightened my arousal. And it was my arousal that I blame that for not being able to control the impulse to rile him up even further.

"Stop tripping, you ain't gon' to do nothing to my shorts…" I muttered with a devious grin on my face, loving the thug side of him.

That growl of anger emitted from his throat before he once again moved so suddenly the only thing I could do was squeak. One minute I was straddling his lap and the next he'd flipped me under him on the couch. His big hands grabbed my shorts at the waist, the sound of the fabric ripping only turned me on more. As he ripped them from my body his angry amber gaze met mine.

Damn! That was *hot*!

I reached for him, pulling him down so that I could kiss those perfect lips, but he had a different destination in mind.

"No, I can't wait any longer to taste you. I've been hungry for this nectar all night."

When his mouth began to work on me, he had to palm my belly with his big hand to hold me down on the couch when my world shattered. His mouth made me a savage. In that moment, I felt like I was dying a very agonizing, pleasurable death. I clutched his head to me, wanting him to stop, but needing him to continue.

He took his anger out on my tender flesh, and it felt like my whole body was on fire, I was being consumed by all things Rome...

What was happening to me? I had never shattered this way. I did not recognize my own voice when I screamed out his name.

The orgasm that hit me was so strong that when his slurping kiss began to bring me down gently to the ground, the only thing I could do was moan his name, over and over again as aftershocks shook my body.

"Romeo..."

"Mmmm...Romeo"

I just wanted to curl up in a child's pose and sleep. But little did I know that was just the beginning.

He gently lifted me off the couch and carried me to his bed. I lay there and watched through lowered lids as he removed his clothes.

Nossa! His body was a work of art. It was the body of an athlete.

"I want to kiss your pretty nipples." He told me as he helped me take off my shirt and the sexy bra.

Gently he pushed me back before taking my lips in one of those drugging kisses of his. He was in no rush, *taking* his time to work my body back into a fever with only a kiss. By the time his mouth made it to the peak of my breast, my back arched off the bed as intense pleasure made its way down my spine.

He drew from my breast hungrily while using his hand to drive me wild.

"Romeo...Please." I was so close.

"What do you want, Minha Anjo?" He whispered against my breast.

"I—I need..."

Right then his mouth drew strongly from me and my world shattered again, this time causing a scream to rip from my throat as he used his big fingers to heighten it. But this time, he didn't bring me gently to the ground.

In fact, he didn't let me come down at all...In the next breath he was over me, looking in my eyes with the honey storm brewing in his...

And then he was filling me...

And filling me...

Oh God!!!!

****

"Where are you going with that?" Rome asked eyeballing the juice in my hand as if it was a pile of crap.

"I'm putting it in the cart."

"No, you're not."

"Yes, I am." I told him going to put the juice in my hand in the cart. But the bastard moved it out the way and my hand met air.

"Romeo! Stop playing!"

He chuckled, "I'm not playing."

I put my hand on my mud encrusted hip. I'll tell you guys how he and I got covered in mud in a minute, right now, we were getting ready to have a huge fight in the middle of the grocery store.

"Why can't I put my juice in the cart? I thought we agreed to go grocery shopping and get some food that we both liked."

"We agreed to go grocery shopping and get some *real* food that we both liked." He pointed to the juice in my hand. "That's not real food."

"Duh, it's juice." I went to put it in the cart, but once again he pulled the cart out the way.

"Romeo!" I growled stomping my foot, causing clumps of mud to fall to the floor.

By this time, we had gained a little audience. In fact, as soon as we stepped out of Rome's mud-covered truck in the grocery store parking lot, we had an audience.

"Nakhti!" He said, mocking my tone as he continued to push the grocery cart down the aisle like nothing was wrong.

Side note: Another thing I was learning about my honey-eyed lover, he was stubborn as a mule.

"Why can't I put my juice in the cart?" He stopped and gave me that placating look I was beginning to hate.

"Because, it's not real juice."

"Yes, it is." I angrily pointed to the bottle. "It say's fruit punch. Everybody knows that's juice."

He took the bottle out my hand turning it around to read the ingredients. "Show me where this says juice anywhere."

I stood next to him to read. It said a lot of things, but nowhere did it say juice.

"It doesn't have to say juice!" I snapped snatching it away from him. "You know it's juice because it says fruit punch. Dammit, Romeo! It's not pop!"

He exhaled. "Nak, you eat like sh*t. Don't think I don't know my little brother has been smuggling you trash." Pointing at me he took a step closer. "I hope you enjoyed all that sh*t, 'cause now that daddy's home, we gon' get yo' a** healthy. If you want juice, get juice. Fruit punch ain't sh*t but high fructose corn syrup and red dye. Bury me and smother me in sh*t before I ever buy that!" He folded his arms clearly ready to go to war.

I held up my arm and made a muscle. "Look at that." I said pointing at it. "I am healthy! You seen my record. And I owe it all… to this!" I told him holding the fruit punch in the air like it was the answer to all life's questions.

He snatched the bottle from me tossing it to the side. Then he reached back and grabbed a bottle of orange juice putting it in the cart.

"You have pre-hypertension. It's the silent killer, you won't see it coming."

I held back my head and exhaled loud and ignorant. "What the hell is pre-hypertension?" I yelled to the ceiling before looking back at him.

"Is that like pre-broken leg or pre-headache? You driving me nuts with this crap. Either I have hypertension or I don't! Ain't no such thing as pre-hypertension."

"Yes, there is. And you have it. You might as well give up. You're not going to win this." And then he continued on down the aisle clearly done with the conversation. I stared after him for a moment seething in anger.

He was a sexy, mud covered, stubborn peacock. And although he angered me like nobody's business, I couldn't help but feel cherished that he would go through such lengths to keep me healthy.

Nobody has ever cared before him.

Not ever…

Okay, so let me tell you guys how he and I ended up covered in mud.

When Rome finally let me rest last night, I collapsed in his arms and slept like the dead till morning. He had kept his word. My world had shattered so many times I was in tears the last time, begging him to let me be.

It was sweet torture. After I'd come the fourth time, I tried to run from him, telling him I couldn't take anymore. I thought if I could just make it to the bathroom, I could lock myself in and not come out until I knew he was fast asleep.

But because my legs were like rubber, I couldn't run as fast as I would have liked, and he had caught me, scooping me up in his arms and carrying me begging for mercy to the shower. With one hand he turned on the water, with the other he'd held me still so he could fill me from behind.

I swear I didn't think I would be able to get into it again. But I was so wrong. Not only did I get into it, I found myself clawing the walls begging him to go faster, harder. That time when my world shattered, I had nothing left in me. I just lay there in his arms lifeless as he washed us both off and then carried me to the bed.

I was fast asleep before my body even touched the sheets. This morning when I woke up, my body was deliciously sore all over.

The first thing I noticed upon coming awake was that I was in the bed alone. I cracked my eyes and what I saw caused me to suck in my breath sharply.

Rome sat at least fifteen feet in the air on a step ladder that had been pulled in front of a floor-to-ceiling bookshelf.

Nossa!

Who could have guessed that the whole south wall slid back like that? It was breathtaking! There had to be over a million books there. And not only that, he sat on the ladder reading a book with a pair of black reading glasses on.

I grinned. *He looked so cute in his glasses.*

Do you guys see what I mean? Here I've discovered another side to this wonderful man, the side of him that was a bookworm.

With his nose still in the book, he climbed down and walked back to his computer. There were a few gadgets on the desk in front of him. He was building some kind of software. Leaning close with a soldering iron he touched it to something that emitted a little pop.

"Mutha f***a!" He hissed snatching his hand back. In a fit of rage, he picked up the book and tossed it across the room. "Damn idiot!"

I sat up in the bed chuckling. "Do you ever sleep?"

He removed his glasses rubbing his nose, clearly irritated. Exhaling he looked up at me with those honey gazers, but when his eyes dropped to my exposed breasts the irritation slowly left his face.

I should cover myself, but what for? He'd seen every part of me last night. And I do mean *every part*.

Rome is a freak. The things he'd done to me in this bed last night will forever damage me for other men. There was no way another can live up to his performance.

"What do you mean? I slept really good last night." He told me.

I chuckled again shaking my head. The smell of coffee drew my attention to the table next to the bed. Just like the other morning, a glass of water sat on it next to my pain pills and a cup of steaming hot coffee.

Goodness!

While I sipped my delicious beverage, he went back to working on his little device. I thought about the girl that had been in his bed when we first met. She too had been completely naked, no doubt having had a night like the one I'd just had.

Which would explain why she didn't care if he called her by another name, just as long as he called her. Poor girl...

Because he was so focused on what he was doing and wasn't talking to me, I wondered if he was ready for me to leave too. That was something I did know about thugs and men in general. A lot of them looked at women as being disposable. Once they got what they wanted they were done.

I sat there and wrestled with my emotions. Surely, I wasn't feeling pain by that thought. I mean, didn't I want him to let me go?

Giant started yelping at me from his little pen. With a smile on my face, I stood wrapping the sheet around me and went to scoop him up in my arms. He was so excited to see me he was like a ball of energy in my arms.

I reached down to pull his potty-training mat out, but stopped when I saw it had already been changed and replaced with a new one.

"I had Rob take him out for a walk earlier." Rome told me without looking up from what he was doing. He'd put his glasses back on.

Nuzzing, Giant's little head, I took in Rome's body language, completely in my feelings that he'd already tuned me out for his little device.

And come on y'all, don't get me wrong. I was not an attention hog...It's just that last night was our first night sleeping together and I was feeling a little self-conscious.

I didn't know if like the girl before me, he really wanted me to leave and just didn't know how to tell me or what.

"Do you want me to go home?" I asked. Unlike that poor girl, he didn't have to kick me out. I will gladly leave. I am not my mother. I will never chase after a man.

Never!

I don't care how good the sex was.

His lifted his head and looked at me, studying me. Chuckling, he took off his glasses sitting them on the desk.

"Are you still sore?" He'd asked as he began to stalk me.

I bit my lip and took a few steps back, and although it was a huge lie, I shook my head no. The way he was looking at me was doing a hell of a job stirring up my libido. The only thing I could think about was the kinky stuff he'd done to me before dawn.

And yeah...I wanted more.

He took an unhappy Giant out my hands and sat him back in his pen, and then he charged me. Laughing, I turned to run, he reached out and grabbed the sheet snatching it away from my body. I opened my mouth in feigned surprise, but he just dipped, swooping me up in his arms being careful of my wound and carried me to the bed.

"I see you forgot how much I need you." He said as he gently laid me down. "That's okay, I don't mind showing you again." And then he was kissing me, using his mouth and hands to soothe away my soreness.

By the time my world shattered the first time, I was sore no more. And when he gently filled me, taking his time and loving me thoroughly, I no longer doubted his feelings.

"So, I guess you don't want me to go home, huh?" I asked after he and I showered. He leaned down and gently kissed my lips.

"No, I want you to get dressed so that we can take the truck for a spin in the mud."

He didn't have to ask me twice, that sounded amazing. Thirty minutes later, he and I were both dressed in boots, cargo pants, and t-shirts. I scooped Giant up and followed Rome to the door.

"Wait..." I said when I didn't see him go to his computer and deactivate the ankle cuffs.

"What about the bracelets."

"What about them?" He asked grabbing his car keys.

"Are you going to deactivate them?"

He looked at me for a moment and I could see the amusement in his gaze, his bottom lip moved in a way that said he was trying to suppress a smile.

"I can't believe you bought that."

My mouth dropped.

What did this bastard just say to me?

When he saw the look of surprise on my face, he could no longer hold onto his laughter. And what made it so bad, he was laughing so hard he had to clutch his sides as he walked out the door.

"Are you kidding me?" I yelled after him.

Guys, I was so mad at him that I didn't speak to him the whole way to the mud park.

"Aww, come on Nak, don't be mad at me, baby. I needed to tell you something to get you to stay put till I got back."

I sat with my arms folded staring out the passenger side window, Giant lay asleep in my lap. I couldn't believe I fell for that crap.

Damn! Explosive golden ankle bracelets...I should have known that was a bunch of bullsh*t! I was angrier at myself for falling for the okey-doke than at him for pulling one over on me.

Oh, my goodness! If Albert or Jo ever hears about this, they will never let me live it down.

Never!

"You could have told me the truth. You had me believing all this time that if I made the wrong move, I would lose my feet."

I huffed and stared back out the window when he started laughing at me again.

"Okay..." He said trying to get control of his amusement. "Tell me this, if I had told you the truth, would you have waited there for me till I got back?"

Hell no!

But because I couldn't tell him that, I just continued to stare out the window ignoring him.

"Nak?" He reached for my hand. I snatched it away from him.

"Come on, baby, say something."

"I'm not talking to you." I told him.

And I wasn't. In fact, I had planned on not ever talking to him. That was a real low-down thing to do.

However...

Ten minutes later, I was screeching in excitement as he drifted his truck through the mud, those big monster tires skidding up clumps of it to cover the windows. By the time he looked at me and asked me if I wanted to drive, I was practically percolating with adrenaline.

"Hell yeah!" I told him jumping down out the truck to quickly change places with him.

I couldn't remember the last time I had so much fun. If ever...

I don't think I've ever had so much fun!

We played in the mud all morning and afternoon, till we managed to get the truck stuck in a ravine.

"Look what you did." Rome said shoving me, causing me to tip over in ankle-deep mud. I was back on my feet in a heartbeat.

"What I did?! I told you not to make that left back there!" I yelled as I ran and jumped on his back tackling the peacock to the ground. I tried to smash his perfect face into the mud. But he quickly turned the table and had me fighting to keep my face from getting smashed.

By the time another one of the mud riders with a bigger truck pulled Rome's out the ravine, he and I were covered from head to toe.

Chapter 12

The Nak Effect

A Wise Woman Knows the Importance of Speaking Life into Her Man. If You Love Him: Believe in Him, Encourage Him and Be His Peace...

--Denzel Washington

Rome

"Hell naw, Saw, don't even try to bring this bullsh*t in my gym!" Hitta growled as he and his men charged the door.

I could hear the commotion from the ring where I was shadow boxing to warm up for my fight that was taking place in a few hours. Nak was helping me run my drills. She was a tough trainer. I think she was trying to get me back for not allowing her to buy *red* Kool-Aid from the grocery store yesterday.

However, when we saw Hitta and his crew rush the door, it drew our attention that way. And sure enough, Saw, with about thirty of his shady men surrounding him was trying to get through mine and Hitta's crew that sat at the door.

"Stay here." I told Nak before I leaped over the ropes to stand with Hitta, more of my guys fell in behind me. But it was my girl I felt at my back.

I smiled to myself...

See? This is what I'm talking about. This is why she makes the perfect Rib for me. She ain't defenseless... I love that about her.

Sh*t...I let her loose, she'll whoop Saw and his whole crew's a** up in this joint tonight.

By herself...

She'll start a war, but she'd whoop that a**.

She's the kind of queen that while you sleep, she at the window with that heat watching your back, daring a mutha f**** to come for her man.

How many fellas out there can say they got a girl like her? She's drop dead gorgeous and sexy as hell, every boy's wet dream. I'm addicted to her taste. Although I've made love to her nonstop since the day before last, it was not nearly enough.

The more I loved her, the more I wanted her...

Generally, after I take a woman once, I'm bored and ready to move on. Not Nak...

I couldn't get enough of her. The feel of her heat surrounding me has become my dependency. And when it gets really good to her, she moans in Portuguese, saying sh*t like:

Yes, Mue Rei ...*right there*.

And

Don't stop, Romeo, you make me feel so good.

Her voice soothes me. It quiets the anger that's always there simmering under the surface. She's one of a kind. My mother would call her a blessing…a gift from God.

I ain't never letting this girl go.

No! Not ever.

Anyway…

Back to this b**** made punk standing in front of me.

"Come on, Hitta." Saw said throwing his hands up. "What's with all the hostility? I'm yo' family or have you forgotten?" He gestured toward me. "This nigga putting that much dough in yo' pocket that you'll turn on family like that?"

"Nigga, please!" Hitta bit out. "I don't give a f*** who you is, you ain't coming in my gym on no bullsh*t."

Saw smiled. "I know that, cuz…and I ain't come here empty-handed. I came to put a hundred grand on my fighter."

"What fighter?"

"Oh, you didn't know? It's my fighter going up against yo' champion tonight." He and his men stepped to the side and a Nephilim walked through the door.

For you out there who don't know what a Nephilim is…google it. They're real…

Do y'all here me out there? They're real…

Dude had to be at least seven feet, three-hundred and fifty pounds easily. Big muscle head, Deebo looking mutha f***a.

But neither Hitta nor I was worried about it, those be the ones that fall the hardest. And when they do, they bounce, which make great footage for resale later.

However, judging by the look of glee on Saw's face, he felt like his fighter had already won. I wonder how long he had to search in order to find somebody he felt could take me out in the ring. No doubt he'd paid his fighter to try and kill me tonight.

I shook my head, this dude never learned.

"Let me see that dough." Hitta said with far less hostility now.

Saw signaled for one of his boys that held a duffel bag to come forth and open it. We both looked down in the bag. When Hitta looked up, there was a smile on his face…or the closest thing he could get to a smile.

"Yeah, that's what I'm talking about, cuzo. Yo' fighter and his team can get ready in the locker room to the left. He can use the ring to warm up when my fighter done. He and Rome are the main event. It's going to be three fights before them. Have him ready when they knock on the door."

We all stood and watched them head toward the locker room. Saw was the last to go, several of his men lingered with him. He stood there and stared at me with that grin that I really hated on his face.

"Yo' Rome, when my fighter break yo' neck, I just want to reassure you that I'm going to do my very best as your former best friend to take care of yo' mama and yo' sister, and now…" His eyes fell on Nak and I wanted to rip them from their sockets.

"Since I'm in a giving mood, I'll even add the pretty little *Boricua* to my list."

I balled up my fists. There was no way a war could be avoided now. He'd crossed the line. I knew this day would eventually come, I was getting ready to choke the sh*t out this nigga. Hitta turned to me and grabbed my arm, at the same time Nak slid her hand in mine.

But it was her bored sounding voice that helped me gain control over my rage.

"You clearly weren't the brains of this outfit, I'm not Puerto Rican... genius."

Her tone was so dry that Hitta's head fell back as he tried his best to stifle his laughter. I didn't stifle mine and neither did my crew. We had a good laugh on Saw's dumb a**.

Nak just prevented a war. For a moment I had lost focus.

Damn, what was happening to me? I never let Saw's a** bait me into war. That's what he wanted. He didn't care if he died, he just wanted to take down everything I've built with him. He knows what I feel about the people I look over. He will make it his sole duty to take out as many innocent folks as he can, knowing that will hurt me the most.

He took a step towards Nak and I sobered instantly, sending my fist slamming into his jaw and him falling back into the arms of the guys that had stayed behind with him. When his other men saw what happened to their boss, they came running back toward the front, but my men upped that metal, bringing their charge to a halt.

"Reach for it and you dead, mutha f***a." Hannibal told one of Saw's boys that tried to lower his hands to his waist.

When Saw made it back to his feet he reached up and wiped the blood off his mouth before looking at me. Although there was rage in his eyes he grinned.

"Calm down, young Romeo, it don't need to come to this. My cousin don't want no bullsh*t in his gym. Although I don't see him saying nothing about yo' boys pointing guns at mine. But that's alright, I see how the game is played."

He spit out a wad of blood on the floor. "Before you got violent, I was just going to say...when word got to me, that somebody had finally caught my best friend's heart, I didn't believe them. But now that I've met her...and see how *spicy* she is. Now..." He said wagging his finger.

"Now, I'm a believer." His gaze settled on Nak again and Hitta's hand fell on my right arm this time with all his strength, holding it in place.

"Don't let him take you there, Bo..." He muttered to me.

"You see our young Romeo here loves challenges." The nigga continued. "He can't fall for a simple girl like the rest of us...no, he'd get bored with her very quickly. I can see you going to be good for him...You look like the challenging type." He turned to walk away, but stopped as if he'd just thought of something else.

"Oh, and I may not be a genius, but I can tell you this. Romeo has trust issues, and a woman like yourself will probably feel cheated if you knew your man didn't trust you. So, when he run you off..." he gave me puppy dog eyes and I wanted to punch his a** again.

"And he will, because that's what he does to the people that are closest to him. Come on the other side of the twenty-four and I'll treat you like you need to be treated."

"B****, I'll f***ing kill you!" I growled, Hitta jerked me back violently. "My word, you come anywhere near her, Saw, and I will f***ing bury you!"

He held his head back and laughed as his punk a** hurried away knowing damn well Hitta ain't going to be able to hold me for long.

"Rome, don't let that dude get in yo' head…he just trying to throw you off yo' game." Hitta hissed in my ear.

I snatched my arm from him. I was so sick and tired of being the bigger man when it came down to this nigga. If he was anybody else, he would be dead f***ing with me!

I clutched my head, telling myself not to run after him and just snap his neck. All my troubles will be over if with one simple twist of the neck.

I hated this nigga!

I tried to think of all the babies that play on my streets. They play worry free because they count on me to keep them safe. I tried to think of all the mamas including my own that walk through my neighborhood. I tried to think about my little brotha that was out there somewhere right now. I tried to think about my little sista…my niece.

When war came to the streets it showed no partiality. Many innocent people die… casualties of war. I tried to think of all that. But the only thing I could see was that nigga looking at my woman. Telling my f***ing woman to come to him!

Hell, mutha f***en naw…that was crossing the…line!

I felt her arms come around me burying my head in her soft sweet-smelling breasts. Her arms felt like cool silk wrapping around me. Instantly my rage abated. It was like her touch was causing it to flee.

That has never happened to me before.

"You want me to kill him?"

She said that sh*t so matter of fact in my ear, it caused me to look up at her. I kid y'all not, she was dead serious. How could something that smelled, tasted, felt and looked so sweet be so deadly? The fact that she was such an antilogy brought a smile to my face. I absolutely loved that about her.

Wrapping my arm around her neck I pulled her close. "No, with yo' wild a**."

She hugged me back tightly and it felt good. I think *Minha Anjo* was developing some feelings for me.

****

Nakhti

I sat at a table in the fancy Downtown Chicago night club having a celebratory dinner with the reigning champ, Hitter, and one of their good friend's, Kaleb...who I was pretty sure was some kind of mob boss, judging by the three men who'd accompanied him; they stood off to the side chatting it up with Milo and Hannibal.

One of his bodyguards, whose name so happened to be Tiny was bigger than that monster Rome knocked out earlier. Speaking of that monster, Kaleb and Hitter was having a damn good time filling Rome in on how I'd lost it on the side of the ring while he was fighting the bastard.

"But what took the cake was when she threw her little leg over the ropes, ready to come in the ring and knock ol' boy out for you." Kaleb told him around his laughter. "I ain't never seen Hitta move as fast as he did, plucking her off those ropes." By this point, he was laughing so good we could barely understand him.

"Hitta was pulling and she was clinging to the ropes. She even wrapped her arms around them while trying to kick back at him. But wait—" He said trying to catch his breath. "When he did manage to get her untangled from the ropes, she went wild on him. Man...I was like, damn, has Hard Hitta finally met his match?" There were tears coming from his eyes as he laughed, pounding on the table.

He pointed at me. "My wife Monica would love you. Seriously!"

"I'm glad you find that funny. I think she threatened to cut my balls off." Hitter grumbled before taking a sip of his drink.

I threatened to do more than that.

Okay, so let me give y'all the run down on what really happened. Apparently Hitter and Rome had something of a hustle going on.

Rome, who had been trained personally by Hitter was his champion that folks paid a lot of money to come watch knock people out. Before they'd perfected their hustle, Rome would do the Mike Tyson and the fight would be over shortly after it started.

Obviously folks felt cheated at paying so much money for a fight that was over in seconds. So, they'd come up with an idea to drag the fights out a bit, thus maximizing on their profits.

Now I didn't know that. The only thing I knew was that man Saw Buck was a bad man. Every one of my spidey senses was ringing when he and Rome had their confrontation by the front door. I know evil when I see it…And the one they call Saw is pure evil.

So when his fighter started cheating in the ring and Rome looked as if he was struggling with the giant of a man, I'd lost it…

And yeah, I tried to get in the ring to help him down the bastard. However, when Hitter wrapped his arm around my waist pulling me from the ropes, I'd assume he was in on it, and he and Saw was trying to do Rome in…

So yeah, I really lost it.

Now you guys remember me telling y'all that Hitter is the kind of guy that one would need a gun to down. The thing was, I didn't have a gun, lucky for him. All I had was my words…

I threatened to come back and slit his throat. I told him I'd have a bullet in his head before he knew what hit him…and yeah, I'd threatened to cut off his balls.

But all of it had been in Portuguese, because my emotions at that point were raging out of control. Not to mention at the same time, I was trying to buck out his arms that felt like iron around my waist. He carried me to a back room and put me in there, ordering three of his men to make sure I stayed put.

Ha! That was classic…

Hitter was built like a mountain…a mountain of muscle, his men were not. I had them all sleeping peacefully in a matter of minutes and was back running towards the ring to help Romeo, who I'd thought at the time was being set up.

Needless to say, it was not a set up. As I was running toward the ring, he hit the giant with an upper cut that took him off his feet.

I knew instantly he was out. When his body hit the floor, time seemed to slow down as it bounced like three times.

I was so amazed. I let out a happy screech and slid underneath the ropes and into Rome's waiting arms. My adrenaline was flowing deliciously through my veins as I grabbed his face and kissed those perfect lips.

When it was all said and done and all the cheering was over, Hitter had looked at me with a surprised look on his face, I guess in all the excitement, he'd forgotten he locked me in a room with those poor saps.

The look on his face spoke volumes. His first thought was that his men had disobeyed him and let me out. When he asked how I'd gotten past his men, a look of pride came on Rome's face as he chuckled holding me close.

"Brotha, you better go and check on yo' boys, make sure them mutha f***as still breathing."

Hitter's stunned gaze fell on me and I shrugged. "I was gentle."

He let out a curse before he jumped out the ring and ran to go and check on his men. Rome and I had a good laugh about it on the way to Exquisite, which I found out is the club of another one of their friends, who hosted a celebratory party for Rome after all his fights.

"Yo, that uppercut you did. That was a different technique. Where you learn that?" Hitter asked Rome after Kaleb's laughter died down.

Rome picked up his drink and took a sip. It was clear he didn't want to answer that question. But now that Hitter mentioned it, I've seen that uppercut before. Right upon impact, a twist of the wrist is applied, thus shifting the momentum, making it easier for one's opponent to fly backward.

Not only have I seen that uppercut before, I've tried and failed to duplicate it.

You guys are not going to believe this…But that was Jo's uppercut. The same one Rob said the Sarge had used on Rome.

"Ummm…" Rome cleared his throat. There was no way this peacock was going to admit that he'd learned it from the man who'd laid him low with the same blow.

"Just something I picked up in passing." He shrugged.

And that was it, I burst with laughter. He knew it too…he knew why I was laughing. With a slightly embarrassed look, he took another sip of his drink.

Rather than sit there and laugh in his face, I excused myself to go to the washroom. Oh my goodness! Wait till I tell Jo…This is gold!

By the time I had made it to the little girl's room I'd laughed so good my mascara had smeared a bit. It was while I was fixing it in the mirror that a loud group of females walked in. I scooted over a bit to give them space.

"Jackie, what's wrong with you, girl?" One of the girls asked another young lady that was standing washing her hands in the sink next to me.

She stood and faced me, making me pause in wiping my face.

"I had to watch this ho throw herself at my man all night!" As she spoke, she pointed at me, bringing her finger really close to my face.

"I think you made a mist—" I began to tell her, but she came at me and I reacted automatically, snatching the arm she'd swung, pulling it down and her with it. Then I followed with a blow to the back of her shoulder, dislocating it.

I could have broken it...but come on guys, she didn't know any better.

When she howled in pain two more of her friends charged me swinging wildly. I kicked the first one sending her crashing back into the stall. Before lifting the girl's head I still held and slamming it on the sink...she dropped. Then I used the momentum of the third charger to slam her head first into the wall. The fourth friend stood there looking at her downed comrades with wide, shocked eyes.

I turned stepping over the unconscious woman by the sink to continue to fix my mascara.

"Run along, sugar bug, your friends are going to need medical attention."

When I walked past her, she tripped over her feet trying to get away from me. I just held back my head and laughed.

Great, now I'm going to have to fix my mascara again.

When I made it back to the table the guys were discussing Saw Buck and how angry he was when Rome knocked his fighter out. They all feared he was going to do something in retaliation.

However, our food had made it and I couldn't concentrate on anything else. For the last few days Romeo has been torturing me. His fancy chef came by and cooked for us and I didn't know who I wanted to strangle more, him or Rome.

I've eaten more vegetables since I've known him than I've eaten in my entire life and it was killing me, but not tonight. Rome was in such a good mood he didn't blink an eye when I ordered a burger.

Tonight, y'all...I was having a burger.

The first bite was heaven.

"That bastard offed Treyone's little brother." Kaleb said as he dipped his fries in ketchup. "I heard the kid was only like fourteen. Saw said he stole a bag of weed from him." He shook his head.

"That shawty's life gone over a bag of weed."

"Hey, man, I never got a chance to reach out to you after your little brother—" Rome began, but he didn't finish. He didn't have to. Kaleb nodded his head cutting him off.

"Don't worry about it, ahk it's cool. It ain't been easy, but my wife and daughter really helping me get through."

Rome and Hitter both nodded their heads, the mood at the table becoming very somber. I wondered what happened to his little brother to make them all suddenly seem so sad...

However, neither of us got to ponder on it much longer, because just then several bouncers ran through the club towards the women's washroom. Everybody had stopped eating to look towards that direction trying to see what was going on.

Not me...I kept on eating because I knew what was going on, and there was no telling if Rome would snap out of his victory high and realize I was stuffing down a half pound of juicy charcoal grilled beef with yummy melted cheese, extra mayo and ketchup.

I moaned when I took my next bite. Plus, who knew when I would get a chance to eat this good again?

"What the hell?" Rome hissed when the bouncers came back out of the restroom carrying the unconscious women on stretchers.

The three men at the table slowly turned to look at me, their faces all resembling Hitter's in the ring earlier.

"What?" I said around a mouth full of juicy, yummy, goodness. "I was gentle."

Chapter 13

Every Superhero Needs A Weapon

'Do not forget to show hospitality to strangers, for by so doing some have unwittingly entertained angels.'

--Hebrews 13:2

Nahkti

"Sometimes it gets so overwhelming until I just stop and think, what am I doing? I can't do this. The problem is too big. The black community is so damaged, and no sane man would try to fix it on the level in which I've done. So then I think...F*** Rome, you're f***ing nuts to try to attempt what you're attempting."

I reached up and rubbed the frown away from his brow with one hand, my other lay on his chest and my chin rested against it. I've been here for a little over a month and in that time, I've found the secret to getting Rome to sleep at night.

At the end of the day, after making love, he needed to be able to vent. He needed someone to listen as he sorted out all the things that were swimming around in that brilliant brain of his. If not, he'll be up all night on his computer.

"Sometimes I feel like giving up. We are suffering from 400 years of damage. What the hell, Nak? Why in the f*** did I think I could even begin to fix it?" He chuckled without any humor. "On the grand scale of things, I haven't even made a dent."

"But that's not true," I told him. "You've made more than a dent. When you're with those kids, they get a look in their eyes that many of us didn't have growing up. Belief…"

I lifted my head a bit so that I could look him directly in the eyes. "Don't you see…You have helped to start a ball rolling that nobody can stop. Maybe you won't be the one to lead them out, but you have sparked the fire in the one. Who knows what young mind you are molding? Who knows what you've given birth to…?"

He grunted… I leaned down and gently kissed his lips.

"Even now, there is some child lying in their bed with dreams of continuing where you left off. You created a legacy…you should be proud."

"Proud of what? I'm a damn criminal."

"You're a hero."

He began to shift restlessly underneath me. He hated when I called him that.

"Come on, Nak…I told you about that." He muttered, sounding like a big kid.

I gently rubbed my finger across those beautiful lips that had just kissed my body so tenderly.

"You know…you don't have to feel guilty."

He stiffened underneath me. "What you talking about?"

I moved to the side as he sat up, throwing his legs over the side, giving me his back. Chewing on my bottom lip, I thought that maybe I should have kept that to myself. Sometimes men didn't like admitting to their weaknesses.

I sat up on my knees behind him, the loft was dark, but he'd left the drapes open, so the street lights cast a warm glow inside. I could hear Rob out front talking mad crap to somebody. But that was nothing new…that's what he did best.

"I think you feel guilty because you're smarter than everybody else around you." I spoke quietly to his muscled back. I was already out here now, might as well see it through.

"I believe it is why you over extend yourself, even to the point of exhaustion."

Slowly I moved closer to him, lifting my hands to his big shoulders where I began to rub the stiffness out.

"And that's alright, because although you don't see it, that's your real gift. The Creator made you for the people. You're doing exactly what you are supposed to do…and that makes you a hero."

"Nak—" He began, but I gently put my hand around his mouth.

"It's alright to be hero, Romeo…You don't have to feel guilty because the Most High has blessed you with a beautiful brain. You read the Bible; you know he did the same for King Solomon."

He chuckled. "I am no King Solomon, baby."

"Yeah, but you're probably a descendant of his. And how do you know what God did with King Solomon he hasn't done with you?"

"Well…because I don't do the right thing all the time. I'm not perfect."

I shrugged. "Neither was King Solomon. I'm not claiming to be learned in the Scriptures, but even I know that the great king messed up pretty bad a few times. Because, baby…Like you, he was only human. Granted, like you, he was a very smart human, but still…human."

I increased the pressure on his shoulders, forcing the tension out. "You don't have to feel guilty for being smart, Mue Rei. And you don't have to work yourself into the grave. What the Most High has begun through you, no man can stop. You are helping to awaken brains that have been asleep for a very long time and that baby, makes you a hero."

He reached behind him wrapping one arm around my waist…I giggled when he suddenly lifted me so that I was straddling his lap.

At first he didn't speak, he just looked up at me with eyes that saw way too much. I bit my lip, trying not squirm under his stare. It was something different about this night.

"I love you."

I sucked in my breath, completely taken aback by his words. "What?"

He grinned at the squeak in my voice. "You heard me."

Yeah, I did. But I think I was going to have a heart attack.

Love?

Did I love Rome?

Was I brave enough to admit that to myself?

"Do you love me?"

God, how did I know he was going to ask that?

I chewed on my bottom lip, terrified. I can't open myself up like this. It was dangerous. The last time I opened myself up for love, I'd received nothing but hate and pain. It damned near killed me.

And it was somebody whose love should have come easily. My mother...

She hated me. She took my love and shoved it back in my face. I swore I would never love again.

"Nak?"

"I can't..."

"Why?" He whispered. I tried to get off his lap, but he just tightened his arms around my waist.

"Talk to me, baby."

Tears came to my eyes. "Rome, my mom...she—" I cleared my throat when it felt too thick for me to talk. "She messed me up, you know?"

He reached up and wiped away my tears with his finger. "I know...but she's dead now. And can't hurt you anymore."

For a moment, I'd forgotten I told him my mother was dead.

"Where is that brave girl who jumped out of an airplane without a parachute?"

"Terrified of love apparently." I whispered.

Thankfully, he let the love topic drop that night. But because we are talking about Rome, you know I'd only presented a challenge by me not saying the words back to him.

Nossa!

The man wasn't lying. Challenges are like catnip to him. A week later, he had those words out of me.

I'll tell you how he did it.

So, I pretty much spent most of my days talking to Happy when she came by to clean and Rob, whenever he made his way upstairs to visit me and sneak me a piece of candy or a cup of Kool-Aid. Rome was busy all the time, the only time I had him to myself was at night.

When he came in, we sat down to eat whatever vegetarian meal his fancy chef put together for us.

Oh…and FYI…even that was growing on me. I know longer needed my food drenched in hot sauce and salt to eat it. Vegetarian food wasn't that bad once you got over the fact that it will never be as good as meat, although I still very much treasured the treats that Rob snuck my way.

Anyway, where was I? Yeah… Rome. He was always on the move, and the phone of his…rang constantly.

But as for me, the majority of the time I was either working out to build my strength back up from my injury, playing with Giant, watching TV, playing Call of Duty or just outright napping. For the first time in my life, I felt like a pampered princess.

Sometimes Rome would come home during the day to help some little one out with their homework; he didn't turn anyone away. The other day, a little lady that had to be about seven, showed up with huge frustrated tears in her eyes because she couldn't get divisions down.

He'd patiently sat at his kitchen table and helped her until she got it. He never raised his voice or degraded her. In fact, twenty minutes after she arrived, he had her beaming with pride because he constantly told her how smart she was.

The day after that, a law student showed up, and Rome helped him put together a mock case that was a part of an assignment of his.

Just amazing…The man is amazing.

He was also an amazing criminal.

One night he came in with a beautiful dress for me and told me to get ready because he and I were having dinner with the mayor and his wife. At first, I didn't believe him. But sure enough, we attended a private dinner at the mayor's house.

While his wife showed me her prized gardenia bushes, the mayor seemed to be discussing something very grave with Rome, who sat there and quietly listened, only nodding here and there to acknowledge that he was taking in the information.

I wanted to be a little closer so that I could hear what they were saying, but Mrs. Wheatly kept me so far away that all I could do was try and read their body language. The mayor was good and worked up; whatever was going on had him very distraught, but Rome didn't seem that worried about it.

As we were leaving, he told the mayor to breathe easy, he would handle the situation.

Later that night, I sat on the bed and watched enthralled as Rome worked. Overhead, Beethoven's Symphony No.5 in C minor blared through the speakers. He stood in front of his computer, on one screen he was involved in a chess game that he'd been playing over the last week.

Get this…he was playing the game with the world champion who he'd already beaten five times, but their games were lowkey. Rome didn't play him in front of the world, because he didn't want anyone to know about him.

However, the champion knew and kept challenging Rome because he couldn't accept the fact that although nobody else in the world knew it…he was really second best. Rome said that if the guy knew that he was a thug from the ghetto, he would probably go insane.

Anyway…Rome is standing in front of the computer playing the game, Beethoven blasting overhead, while at the same time directing two of his men through the earpiece he wore to move through what looked like a closed office building.

Their movements were up on the big screen. I wanted to ask him what they were doing, but didn't want to break his concentration.

He guided them to the buildings server room and walked them through planting his little bug.

"Good job, fellas…get on out there." He told them, going back to his chess game.

His opponent typed in tons of questions, asking him to explain how he'd come up with a certain move, and where did he learn to play like that. But all his questions went unanswered. Rome said the little geek was always trying to get in his head.

As he and I lay in each other's arms that night, he explained to me that the mayor was being black-balled by someone that is trying to move in and push him out. Rome said he can't let that happen because the mayor made sure he pretty much operated with immunity in Chicago.

"So, what did you do about it?" I asked, curious as to what it is he actually did.

"You'll see..." was his only response as his hand lazily rubbed up and down my back, lulling me to sleep.

The next day, he came home early with a long box in his hand. I had been sitting on the couch trying to teach Giant to fetch. Rome picked up the controller and turned on the television.

Breaking news flashed across the screen. "This just in," A beautiful news anchor said seeming to still be receiving the information.

"A certain Chicago lawmaker's house is being raided by the FBI after reports of collusion with a dangerous Italian Mob family have come to the surface." She touched the device in her ear listening to whatever was being said to her.

"Oh God! Although I-News is still receiving information, it appears as if documents may have been found tying Paul Graebel in with the death of porn star Pussy Willow who until now, cause of death had been labeled a suicide. Oh—Okay, the mayor is giving a press conference now, let's see what he has to say about this."

The screen cut to the mayor that we'd just had dinner with standing in front of a podium. He looked very stressed, but I was able to see he was only acting. Last night he'd really been distraught. He held up his hands to try and calm down the barrage of questions that was being thrown his way.

"My office just received the reports. We need to allow the FBI to do their job. But you don't have to worry, I do not tolerate this kind of filth in my city. Fear not, if there needs to be cleaning in the house, then I will sweep it clean. Please…no further questions."

I turned to look at Rome, who winked at me as he sat on the couch next to me.

"There are always skeletons in the closet. My job is either to expose them or if the dough is right, bury them a little deeper."

"Is that what you're doing with Jo? Are you trying to expose him?"

Just like he always does when I brought up my boss, he changed the subject.

"I have a gift for you." He said bringing the long box from behind his back.

Giant instantly started to nibble on the ribbon, pulling it with his little head.

"You know, you don't have to keep buying me stuff."

He lifted his hand and gently pushed a loc of my hair back behind my ear. "If a man wants to deck his queen out in diamonds and gold, that's his prerogative. Have you ever met a shabby queen?"

I grinned. "No, I have not. But I'm not a queen either."

"Sure you are. You're *my* queen. Open the box."

Feeling like a young girl, I tore into the box.

"Oh my God, Romeo! Is this—"

"Real?" He asked. "Yes, it is."

I lifted the beautiful bat out of the box. It was made of pure gold. Written on the side of it was, *Minha Anjo*. I was holding a small fortune in my hands.

"I'd never seen anything as amazing as you beating the sh*t out of my men with that bat. It was poetry in motion. You call me a hero..." He shook his head.

"You're the real hero. F*** that, you're a *super*hero. And every superhero has to have a powerful weapon. This one is yours."

I stared at him through tears. I could see it in his eyes that he truly believed I was a superhero. Gently, I placed the bat back in the box. And then I threw myself at him, wrapping my arms tightly around his neck, hugging him as if I feared he would disappear if I didn't.

"I love you..." I told him...

And it was true...I loved him with my whole heart and my whole soul. And I wasn't scared to admit it anymore.

He was amazing. But most importantly, he made me feel amazing. He made me feel like I was somebody. For the first time in my life, I had a name and a purpose.

For the first time in my life, I felt loved.

"I love you too, baby." He told me, beaming that he'd gotten those words out of me. "I want you to try your best to stay out of trouble. Just because I've given you a superhero weapon doesn't mean you should actually use it..."

I chuckled, giving him the...*Really* look.

"You know I have to tell you that. You're prone to violence."

"You don't have to worry about me. I won't get into any trouble at all…"

He looked as if he doubted that, but then I straddled his lap and kissed him. The toughest thing about being away from him all day is having to wait to make love to him. Now that he's awakened the inner sex kitten in me, nothing can quiet it, and only he will do.

I reached down and grabbed the hem of his t-shirt pulling it up and over his head and tossing it on the couch next to us. Poor Giant let out a little bark in protest, because I'd mistakenly tossed it on him.

"I missed you today." I told him as I kissed his strong neck. He always smelled so good. "Did you miss me?"

"Mmmmhhhhmmm…" He responded settling back on the couch as my kisses trailed down to his muscled chest. I could feel his heartbeat increasing under my touch.

Nossa! He always tasted so good.

Slowly I slid off his lap and unto my knees between his legs. "I promise to be a very good girl." I purred as I undid his belt.

"Sh*t Nak! I don't care, just…stop torturing me!"

And I did…I put him out of his misery. However, the next day, he had to bail me out of jail.

But before I tell you guys what happened, I just want to first say it wasn't my fault.

The day started off like any other. Rome had left shortly after breakfast and I had gotten a quick work out in while waiting for Happy to show up, so she can fill me in on the day's gossip.

But strangely she never showed. Rob came instead.

"Ay, you want to see Rome's angel?" He asked sticking his head inside the loft door.

I sat at the kitchen table polishing my superhero bat, testing its weight in my hands and balancing it on my palms. Rome's goldsmith must have created it. It's perfect, and it felt as if it had been made just for my hands… I absolutely loooovvveed this thing.

"What?! Is that real?" I asked him about Rome's angel.

Now that he mentioned it, I vaguely remember the doctor telling me something about an angel or something that Rome meets with to play chess.

Rob threw up his hands. "I don't know…but he thinks it is."

I stood sliding the bat in the shoulder sling Rome got designed for it.

"Isn't this cool?" I asked Rob.

He chuckled. "You and my brother make a good couple. Y'all into the corniest sh*t."

"Whatever!" I told him bending down to pick Giant up in my arms. "Let's see this angel."

Rob's car was pretty cool too. It was a black Dodge Charger and just like his brother, he'd gotten it souped-up underneath it so that it rumbled really loud. We drove for about twenty minutes before he pulled into a park, bringing his car to a stop in back of Rome's truck.

"There they are." He said killing the engine.

I looked to where he was pointing and frowned at what I saw. Rome sat at a bench table with his fists pressed to his head as he stared down at the chessboard. It didn't look as if he was winning. And it didn't look as if he was handling not winning very well.

But what caused me to frown was the fact that he was playing chess with a homeless man. At least he looked homeless. And he wasn't wearing any shoes. While Rome looked very stressed out, the homeless man didn't look bothered at all.

In fact, it looked as if he was reading a newspaper. Rome put his hand on a piece, but then pulled it back before putting his hand on it, moving the piece. The man didn't even look away from his newspaper as he reached over and moved a piece...

"Checkmate..." I saw his lips move to say.

Rome studied the board as if he couldn't believe it.

Rome

"You can at least make me feel as if I gave you some kind of competition." I growled.

I hated losing!

I really hated losing!

The fact that I was forced to sit here and suffer through this week after week is what I hated the most.

The man with no shoes...

I've known him most of my life. He started visiting me and beating me in chess when I was seven years old. It was through losing to him that I learned how to play. It was also through losing to him that I've done all that I've done in life.

He rarely talks during our visits. We just sit down and he defeats me in the game. It's later, while I'm thinking about what move I could have made to have a different outcome that I know what it is I need to do.

For example, the week Nak showed up, he beat me in three moves, and two of the moves were just using his queen. Later, when I went over the play, I realized that if I'd captured his queen with my second move, I would have prevented the loss, which is how I knew when I saw Nak, that I had to capture her.

The week Jo showed up to get Journey, he'd checkmated me in a double move using his knight. Later, when I thought of how I could have prevented that, I realized a simple castling would have prevented it, which is why all that week I hung close to my mom's place, avoiding my own.

I know this sounds strange, but this is his and my relationship. I guess you can say in a way, he's guided me through life. I was fourteen when I realized he wasn't a man at all. And yeah, I know that sounds *really* strange.

The thing is, we've been trained to believe in only what we can see, smell, taste, and touch, but that is looking at a multi-dimensional place through a one-dimensional lens. I remember this Scripture that my mom would always read to us.

'Do not forget to show hospitality to strangers, for by so doing some have unwittingly entertained angels.' A Scripture she would always read before she took the little money we had and bought stuff to prepare bag lunches for the homeless.

You see, she believed that although we didn't have much, we had more than most, and it was our responsibility to share what we had. It didn't matter if it was only two pieces of bread, we shared it.

It was during one of these trips when I was seven years old, that I met the man with no shoes. I'd handed him a bag lunch and I'll never forget what he said.

"What do you call a man that gives when he doesn't have much to give?"

I'd shrugged. *"I don't know."*

"Blessed...come back and visit with me Tuesday."

And I did, and every Tuesday following that.

"Why would I pretend you are competition, when you're not?" He spoke suddenly, surprising the hell out of me.

I couldn't remember the last time he did.

"To preserve my feelings." I told him sarcastically.

"You mean to preserve your vanity." All this he said without looking away from his paper.

"I'm not vain."

He chuckled. "Sure you are."

"What's so important in that paper anyway?" I asked changing the subject.

"The warnings have begun to go forth, but mankind won't see them, because the enemy is working overtime to keep them distracted. And because of it...mankind shall not repent. Tell me, young prince…have you seen it? Have you seen the shift in the times?"

Yeah, I saw it, but I've been doing my best to ignore it. What I told Nak was true. I didn't plan to be a heathen forever. It's not my fate. There was something else out there calling me, I've heard it my whole life.

"The world is growing colder." He continued. "Can you see it?"

I nodded. He continued to read his paper. "Woman cooks baby in the oven after getting into an argument with husband." He read before turning the page.

"Man shoots and kills child for playing music too loud in the car next to him." He turned the page.

"Man found eating the face of another man, shot to death." He turned the page.

"Twenty-six people shot dead in night club." He turned the page.

"In a fit of rage, woman drives car into a crowd of protesters, killing five. Teenage boy found in a garage eating husband and wife, feared to have been high on bath salts. However, when tested, no bath salts were found in his system. Woman sacrifices baby in ritual to Baal. Father stuffs cross down daughter's throat, killing her. When asked why he did it, he responded, because she was possessed by the devil. Prisoner beats cellmate to death. When questioned about his actions, he stated that he had awakened to cellmate sitting on the toilet. He complained about a foul stench that was unlike anything he'd ever smelt. He claimed the man's who sat on the toilet face had disappeared and a demon had taken his place. He proceeded to beat the man, fearing for his life. He claims the whole time he was hitting him, the demon laughed at him. When the guards finally made it to his cell, the man who sat on the toilet was dead and his cellmate's hands were covered in his blood."

He turned to the front of the newspaper... "Meanwhile, Booty Black slapped Chocolate Blondie at Fashion Week in Paris, because Chocolate Blondie accused her of stealing the lyrics to her song..." He paused for a moment as if even he couldn't believe what he was about to read.

"King Shlung Dong..." His gaze came to mine. "That made the front page."

Carefully he folded his paper. "Do you think all of these people are crazy?"

I opened my mouth to ask him, if he meant Booty Black and Chocolate Blondie, but before I could he spoke.

"No, I don't mean the distractions."

I shook my head. "No, I don't think they're crazy."

"Man is dying faster than they are being born. That makes man an endangered species."

I exhaled, turning my head to look into the crowd of children that played in the park.

"But as you know, this has to happen. The Father has taken peace from the earth, son. The days are only going to get worse. You need to prepare yourself."

"Prepare for what?"

"You're going to be taken away from the place you've always known as home. Away from the men you have come to see as family. You will be guided to new family."

I shook my head. "I don't like the way that sounds."

"It doesn't matter. You and your new family have a job to do. One day soon, it will be made abundantly clear what it is. In one hour, life as man knows it is going to change. And you and your new family will find yourselves on a journey. It is during that journey that you will grow into the man you were meant to be."

"The warrior woman has been given to you as a gift. But because you are so stiff-necked, you are going to lose her."

I shook my head. Who said angel knew everything? "Nope…I'm not."

"Yes…you are."

I shook my head again. "Nope."

"See what I mean? Stiff-necked."

He went back to reading his paper. "This is our last time meeting for a while, son. The next time I see you, the world will be on fire."

I didn't know how I felt about that. Yeah, it's true, I didn't necessarily enjoy our meetings. But like I said, we've been meeting every Tuesday since I was a kid, I've come to depend on his guidance.

"Don't be afraid, Romeo. The warriors you will find yourself with need you, and you are going to need them. They have been created for one purpose."

"What is that?"

He turned to look at me again, his eyes more piercing than daggers. "To destroy…They are demon slayers, son."

I frowned. "Is it Joseph, punk---?" I stopped myself from cursing. My friend here didn't care for foul language.

Please don't let it be Joseph...Please don't let it be that bastard.

"It is..." He continued to read his paper.

"Yeah, but I don't really like him."

"So...?" He turned the page.

"So, I don't really want to work with him."

"It doesn't matter. Your paths were destined to cross. Not only him, your woman, and Joseph's siblings, natural born demon slayers. They have all been called to be warriors for The Ancient of Days."

I was a little confused. If they are the demon slayers, why the hell did they need me?

"You...you, are going to be the brains of the outfit." He chuckled at his own joke.

I shook my head...that was really corny. But then he turned to look at me, piercing me with his gaze, all humor gone.

"You need to find out what really happened to Joseph and his siblings. They are going to need you to help them defeat the toughest demons they will ever battle." He paused for a moment. "Their own."

"In order to become one with The Ancient of Days, they will have to let go..."

Nahkti

"What do you think they're talking about?" I asked Rob.

I've never seen Rome appear to be learning from someone. It seemed strange. But I knew deep down in my gut, he was learning.

"I don't know. I think that cat is really smart. My brother meets with him every Tuesday without fail. And after he beats Rome in chess, my brother just sits quietly." He shrugged. "It's like he be playing their game over and over again in his head or something."

I nodded…and for a minute, Rob and I just sat and watched Rome talk to his angel. But then I was reminded of something.

"Have you seen Happy? She didn't show up for work today."

"Ohhhh!!" He sat up straighter in his seat looking over at me. "You ain't heard?"

"Heard what?" The look on his face was beginning to give me a bad feeling.

"Dude put her in the hospital last night."

"What?!"

He shook his head. "Sis, he beat her so bad they had to take her to the hospital."

My heart turned cold. "Take me to her…now!"

He didn't ask any questions, he started his car and wisely began to drive.

"I'm sorry, sis, I thought you knew." I held up my hand stopping him.

I needed him to stop talking. I was battling with myself not to kill a man. Happy would be crushed if I did that, but I was hanging on by a very thin string.

He needed to die!

I was going to—

No! I couldn't kill Happy's child's father.

But he needed to die! Every cell in my body thought so.

By the time we got to the hospital, I was barely holding on. But it wasn't until I walked into her room that I knew without a shadow of a doubt that I wasn't going to be able to control myself.

She lay with her back to us. I could tell right off that something was seriously wrong with her. I was almost afraid to walk around the bed. I didn't want to see what I knew I was about to.

She lay staring out the widow, her face covered in bruises with huge tears in her eyes.

"Happy?" I whispered. Rob stood by the door as if he wasn't sure if he should come in or stay out...he looked extremely uncomfortable.

"Happy?" I gently touched her shoulder.

"She's dead..."

I leaned closer, because she spoke so low, I didn't hear her. "She's dead...my baby is dead."

Oh dear God, no!

I sat down in the chair next to me. Happy was so excited to be a mommy. It's all she talked about; what clothes she was going to buy the baby. Just the other day, she and I were looking at baby cribs in a magazine. She saw so many she liked, but the one she really wanted was too expensive, so me and Rome had already decided we were going to gift her with it.

I'd even started thinking about putting her together a little baby shower.

Oh my God! Her baby is dead.

I can't—I just… can't.

Before I knew what was happening, I'd jumped to my feet, my adrenaline was shooting through my body at an alarming rate. My soul was going into battle mode whether I wanted it to or not. My mind had begun to plan a killing. Her hand shot out grabbing me when I turned to head for the door.

"I know the truth about you. I know you kill people for a living." Her angry gaze came up to mine. "You know how you're always going on about how sometimes you be gentle with people?"

I nodded.

"Well don't…Don't be gentle with him! I…hate…him!"

"Say no more…" I leaned down and kissed her gently on the forehead. "Say no more."

Rob held the door for me as I stormed past him.

"I know where that mutha f***a at too!" He told me before I could even ask the question.

Fifteen minutes later we were pulling up in front of a house that had several men sitting on the porch smoking and drinking. The bastard was one of them. I jumped out the car.

"Wow! Look at this coward! Did you know your woman is at the hospital mourning the loss of the baby you beat out of her, alone?"

I had lost it, I was screaming at the top of my lungs. My screaming drew the attention of others. The men who sat on the porch with him gave him that look that said…Daaammmnnn!

He stood. "B**** who you talking to?"

"I'm talking to you, you sorry bastard." I didn't stop walking until I stood in his face. I wanted him to hit me.

I wanted him to hit me so bad.

"You better go on by yo' business. I ain't Rome, I ain't going to put up with yo' lip."

"Oh yeah?" I said making a doppy face. "You ain't going to put up with my lip?"

Rob and the men on the porch started laughing at him. "What you going to do about it, coward?" I shoved him. "Only a coward hit a woman!" I shoved him again.

"Hit me! I'm a woman!" He bit down on his lip, balling up his fists.

"Ay, I dare you to hit her…" Rob muttered as he pulled a blunt out. "She gon' beat his dumb a**…"

"Man, I ain't got time for this." He went to turn around, but I stuck out my foot tripping him. Rob and the other guys laughed really good at him.

That was all it took, he whipped around and punched me...hard. The blow caused me to spin around. I was now facing Rob. For a moment he looked worried. I lifted my hand and wiped the blood off my lip, allowing it to fuel my rage. Lifting my gaze to Rob's concerned one, I winked at him before spinning back to face the coward.

As I turned, I pulled that golden bat from its handy dandy shoulder sheath. What better time to test out my superhero weapon? Let's see how well it handles.

Did I fail to mention to you guys that I'd damn near went to college on a baseball scholarship? My batting average was damned near .300.

The first blow was to his right knee. He yelled out falling to the ground as the sound of it cracking filled the street.

"Damn!!!!" I yelled, holding the bat up to get a good look at it. I can tell y'all this...Gold hits way better than wood any day. I'd just shattered this bastard's leg.

My stunned gaze went back to Rob... "Did you see the power in this thing?"

He shook his head blowing out weed smoke. "Naw, sis, I missed it. Do it again."

I grinned. "Yeah, that's probably a good idea. Maybe I misunderstood what I just saw." I spun the bat over my head to gather extra momentum before bringing it down with all my might on his left leg.

He screamed out like a girl as that leg shattered.

I whipped back around to look at Rob. "What you think, bro?"

He nodded. "That mutha f***a make quite an impact!"

"Yes, it does!" I yelled before I turned back around swinging the bat as it did, bringing it down across his spine.

"You beat women because they're weaker than you, and it's the only way you can win at anything in life. Do you know why that is?"

I brought the bat back down across his spine, smiling when I heard the satisfying crunch over his scream.

"It's because you are weak." I told him leaning down so that my lips were close to his ear. "You are so f***ing weak!" I yelled in his ear.

I swung the bat over my head one more time and then I let loose my full fury on him. Swinging over and over, getting high on the resounding crunch that followed each blow.

It got so good to me that I didn't hear Rob tell me we had to go because the police were coming. I could kill this coward, but I wanted to make him suffer. I wanted to break as many bones as I could in his body before ending him...

However, I never got the chance. I was tackled from the back and handcuffed before I'd realized what happened. The next thing I knew, I was standing in front of a booking officer giving them one of the aliases Jo had set up for me and my temper that was always getting me in trouble.

They led me to a cell...with the grin still on my face I sat down on the little cot. But then something happened after my adrenaline died down.

Something strange happened. For the first time in a long time, I felt...

I felt depressed.

I thought about the look in Happy's eyes, a look that should have never been in the gaze of one so beautiful. Somehow, she'd managed to still bring joy in other's lives although she suffered tremendously at home. Somehow, she still managed to be happy.

But now... Now, I doubted if she would ever be happy again. She'd become the mother of a dead child.

No...She would never be happy again.

And that made me so sad, the only thing I could do was ball up on that little cot and fight the tears that wanted to escape my eyes.

Life wasn't fair. Happy is a beautiful soul. Why does she have to suffer so? Why did life abuse the good people?

It was this world. This place we live is so dark...Everybody is so evil!

I hated this place!

I hated it so much...

Rome

"You have to go now." He began to chuckle a bit. "The wild one is in trouble, yet again."

As soon as he said those words my phone rang. Frowning I looked at it and saw that it was my brother's number and instantly I got a bad feeling.

Damn, I knew I shouldn't have given her that bat.

"Yeah," I said into the phone standing from the bench.

"Bro, Nak got arrested!"

I gave the man with no shoes one last glance before I headed for my truck. He just smiled at me, giving me a nod that said 'go on'.

I wanted to ask him if this really was going to be my last time seeing him for a while, but never got to do it, because my feet were now running for my truck.

"What happened?" I barked into the phone as I hopped in.

As Rob told me what happened I clutched the steering wheel as anger ripped through me.

"That mutha f***a hit Nak?!"

Really, I didn't hear much else after that. His fate was sealed.

But first I had to get my girl out of jail. And take that f***ing bat from her.

It was Lieutenant Miller herself that took me to Nak's cell. The whole way back she apologized for the misunderstanding, claiming they didn't know Ms. García was with me. Thanks to me, Lieutenant Miller's daughter was attending her second year at Stanford University.

Not only was I sporting a good percentage of the bill, I had put in a lot of hours preparing her for her S.A.T's that she scored a 1560 on.

Quite naturally, Lieutenant Miller was a bit worried. However, I was too angry to deal with her right now. There will be repercussions for this, for all parties involved.

"What the f*** did y'all do to her?" I growled as soon as I saw Nak balled up on the cot like a small child.

The lieutenant turned red as she began to stutter, trying to assure me that they never touched her.

"Open the bars." I hissed, cutting her off, in no mood to hear her excuses.

"Nak? Baby, are you okay?"

When Minha Anjo heard my voice, she sat up and reached for me as if she was a small girl. I sat on the cot next to her lifting her into my arms.

"Baby, why are you shaking?" I swear, Derrick's a** was dead.

She wrapped her arms around my neck tightly, burying her face in my beard.

"Happy's baby died!" She whispered before she erupted in tears. I held her tightly as she cried. I'd never seen my fierce warrior princess cry like this.

I mean she was really balling.

"It's going to be okay...baby."

She shook her head. "No, it's not, Romeo. Nothing is going to be alright in this dark place. Can't you see? It's so dark...the darkness is everywhere."

The fact that she'd just pretty much said the same thing the man with no shoes had told me was verification enough for me.

I held her tighter. The tides were shifting, his words were true, my life was getting ready to change.

"And they took away my superhero bat." She muttered into my beard.

That made me smile. "No worries, Minha Anjo, we're going to get it back for you." I went to kiss her lips and saw that her bottom one had been busted. And I saw red.

"What happened, baby?" I asked, gently touching her lip.

"Derrick hit me…" She said pouting like a little a** girl.

"He hit you?"

With big sad eyes she nodded. "Yeah…"

It took me damn near a week to get her to smile again. The whole time, Derrick's a** lay up in the hospital recuperating from damn near having every bone in his body broken.

I smiled…My girl did that.

Damn, she made me so proud.

Anyway, the day he was released, the nurse wheeled him out in a full body cast. Hitta and I showed up to pick him up and give him a lift home.

"Derrick my man, how you feelin'?" I asked taking the wheelchair from the nurse before sliding her an envelope.

She nodded, quickly sliding it inside her pocket. I'd already doctored up the hospital camera feed so that none of this would show up.

Seeing my gloved hands caused Derrick to panic, he tried to turn his head and beg her not to leave him with us, but she'd already disappeared back into the building and his dumb a** could only make muttering sounds because his voice box had been shattered.

"Relax, D man, I figured since it was my girl that did this to you, the least I can do is make sure you make it home safely." I wheeled him to the bed of my truck.

"Hey Hitta, help me get this man gently in the back…careful now, most of his bones are broken."

"Sure thang…I'll be real careful." Hitta, who also wore gloves muttered as he helped me lift the mutha f***a out his chair and throw his b**** a** into the truck bed. By this point, he was yelling in pain, but it only came out as little grunts. I slid the bed cover in place, hiding him from view.

We then drove him down to this little spot by the river. Hitta helped me take him out and wrap him in a piece of thick plastic. The whole time he squirmed trying to beg for his life through his f***ed up throat.

Once he was covered in a few layers of the plastic, we wrapped a big chain around him that was connected to a five-hundred-pound weight. Then I doused his a** in gasoline and lit a match. We stood and watched him burn till he stopped moving. The plastic had melted around his body and the chain to form a big hard lump. Then together Hitta and I pushed the weight into the river.

The next day, I sent for Happy's mother and sent them back to Louisiana with enough money to start over.

As her and my girl gave each other tearful farewells, I stood to the side praying she made better decisions.

Chapter 14

Storm Warning

Such a sense of loss tonight
Nought to do but ride it out

Can't stop a river when it's burst its banks
I wonder how long it's gonna take
To get over this heartbreak
Storm warning, feels like a heavy rain
Winds on the coast tonight
We may get tossed tonight

--Bonnie Raitt

Nakhti

"Nak, baby, can you run back to the loft for me and get that little box I left on my desk?" Rome asked handing me his truck keys.

I'd just gotten a daisy painted on my face and was trying to hurry and stuff cotton candy down my throat before he took it from me. I think I was enjoying the block party more than the children.

"Sure…" I told him with a mouth full of the sugary treat.

Smiling, he leaned down and kissed me and my treat nearly fell from my fingers. Cotton candy tasted good, but Rome tasted better.

"Alright, break that up. There are shawtys present." Rob said from his little stool where he sat painting a little girl's face to resemble a bunny.

Oh y'all, did I tell you guys how wonderfully amazing my man is?

He was so generous and giving. As we speak, I am standing here at an end of the school year block party that he's put on for the last five years for the kids in the neighborhood. There were free food and games, carnival rides and live entertainment from local artists.

But what was super amazing were the grade booths.

There was a booth for C's, one for B's, and a booth for A's. The kids stood in the lines holding their report cards and baskets to hold all their goodies. For each C, they received little small gifts like balls, jump ropes, paper and pens, back packs and stuff like that.

For B's, the prizes got a little better, brand name gym shoes, sports hats, bikes…

The A booth offered even better gifts…Play stations, laptops, I-pads…

Nossa!

If someone had done this for me when I was a kid, I would have gotten better grades than I did. You can see the excitement on their little faces as they collected their end of the year treasures, rewarding them for all of their hard work.

But it was the straight A booth that took the cake. Rome manned this booth himself. He looked over each report card and talked to each child individually about their goals and how they felt about their accomplishments. You can tell he really cares about them. And their little faces while they talk to him are priceless.

He's really making a difference in their lives.

When he's done talking to them, he hands them an envelope. From what I've seen, the envelopes have different things in them. For example, he gave the seniors vouchers for scholarships funded by him and a few of his clients (his words) for the college of their choice.

And for some of the younger children, vouchers to attend whatever summer programs they were interested in that will help them continue to head towards their goals.

Amazing!!!

He is a real hero.

Just imagine what could happen to the world if more people had hearts like his. If more people had the pay it forward mentality.

He made me look at myself. I was thinking about changing some things about me.

First, I think it may be a good idea for me to read the Bible. I just wanted to start at the beginning and work my way through to the end. I'd found his and was amazed at all the notes and marks I saw in it. He wasn't lying about studying it thoroughly.

For the last few years, I've been having this feeling that something else is calling me. It's this feeling that there is a shift in the air. Times are changing. I can't really explain it. But when I read some of Rome's scriptural notes, I felt...

I felt that the answer as to who I am, what my purpose is, and even why my life has gone the way it has is there in that book. And I want to know the truth.

I need to know the truth…

Next, I was going to try and find a way to pay it forward. I don't know what purpose God has for me, but I feel that he has something he wants me to do, and I'm going to search for it.

Rome is inspiring. Just like he does all these children, he makes me want to be a better person. He makes me want to search out my true potential and live up to it.

I turned to head toward the truck, but Rob stopped me.

"Hey sis, I have something for you." He reached down next to him and pulled out a brown parcel.

"Don't open until you leave." He muttered, clearly embarrassed at having given me a gift. Smiling, I leaned down and kissed his cheek. One day, like his big brother, he was going to make someone a very good man.

I gave Rome, whose straight A booth was in the same area as his brother's another kiss.

"I'll be right back." He grabbed my hand…more like clutched it to him.

"Promise?"

Something about his tone and the way he was clutching my hand caused the smile to disappear from my face a little.

"Of course…" I told him, confused at his sudden clingy behavior. I rubbed away the frown that was on his brow. "What's the matter, crazy man?"

"I just…" He paused for a minute searching for the words. "I just want you to know that no matter what happens, I will never give you up. I can't let you go, Nak."

Smiling I leaned down and kissed him again. "No worries, Mue Rei. If we truly belong together, nothing can separate us."

****

[Fifteen minutes later…]

When I was a little girl, my mother would play Bonnie Raitt's Storm Warning on repeat, mourning for my father. I could never understand why she couldn't let him go. At the time, my mother was the prettiest woman I'd ever seen. Men would go out of their way to get her attention.

But her heart belonged to another. It belonged to someone who could never appreciate it, someone who didn't deserve it.

I hated my mother for not seeing that. I hated her for not being strong enough to survive without his love.

I hated her… because I was not good enough.

I was never good enough, just a constant reminder of a love she'll never have, but that her soul craved.

I chuckled without any humor. It was so easy for me to sit on my high horse and judge my mom, because before now, I'd never allowed myself to love...

Before now... I'd never gotten my heart broken.

As I stood in front of Rome's computer staring at a file that said Joseph Law, I acknowledged the fact that this was my fault. I knew better. It didn't matter what he told me with his mouth, I knew better.

Hadn't my father told my mother he loved her? Hadn't he made her feel special?

Lies!!!

All Lies!!!

With hands that shook, I clicked on the file that Rome had so obviously left here for me to see and tons of information flooded the screen, all the information the Sarge had sent me here to get, but I couldn't see it. The only thing I could see through tears that I refused to let fall was that Rome had decided to test me.

"I test everybody I don't trust."

My heart hardened as I eased down in his chair.

I had been such a fool!

How could I have allowed myself to believe in a f***ing fairy tale?

I knew better! I f***ing knew better!!!

I will not be weak like my mother...I will not!

*I am not my f***ing mother!!!!*

Ha! There my hypocritical a** go judging her again.

I'll tell you what I mean.

Over the last couple of weeks, Rome hasn't been sleeping. He's been looking into gene manipulation. Because I knew he won't sleep if he can't talk out his thoughts, I've tried to talk to him about it, asking him what he had discovered that had him so enthralled to the point that he was fervently going back and forward between his massive wall library and his computer.

But he would only give me vague answers before distracting me with his drugging kisses that would eventually turn into his drugging love making that always left my body deliciously depleted.

It was easy for me to look past the fact that I'd been here over two months on my own accord, intentionally not doing anything that will make me look suspicious, because I wanted him to know that I really cared for him and would never betray him, not even for Jo, who I'd known most of my life. Yet he still refused to discuss certain things with me.

Hmmmm... I guess I'm my mother's daughter after all, because I'd just let that slide off of me, convincing myself that it didn't matter. Convincing myself that he wasn't talking to me about what was going on in his head was because he was still trying to work it out, and not because he didn't trust me.

I balled up my fists as the tears fell. He'd told me he loved me, and I believed him. Even though everything within warned against it, I allowed myself to love him back.

I clutched my stomach feeling sick. I am so damn stupid?

He'd set me up…He'd set it up so that I would be here in the loft in front of his cameras with the information he'd found about Jo.

He was testing me to see if my words were true. He was testing me to see if I meant it when I told him I loved him, which means all this time, he'd not believed me.

Didn't he know what it took to confess my love to him? Didn't he know how I'd had to break myself to change enough to love him?

What hurt so much is that it never crossed my mind to test him…because I trusted him. He told me he loved me and I believed him.

I am my mother's daughter!

Rage built up in me to a blinding point, but I didn't let it show. My escape defenses had been triggered. You see, I was at a point where a lot of women find themselves; it's the first real time their lover hurts them.

Now I could ignore this, like I'd done him shutting me out. But then, where does it end? I'm sure Happy asked herself that question before her baby died, but she chose to ignore it until it was too late.

I'm sure my mom asked herself that question and she too chose to ignore it…

Not me…Once was enough!

He showed me how he felt about me and now I was getting ready to show him what I felt about his feelings.

I will never forgive him for hurting me…And I will never give him a chance to hurt me again.

Period!

In a way I'm glad this happened. Before I met him, I knew what needed to be done. I had my future all mapped out. I had everything in place. But then, I did something dumb like falling in love and had been more than willing to flush years of planning down the toilet.

I continued to search through the files, because not to would look suspicious, and I wasn't quite ready to alert him to my plans yet.

Although, I wasn't looking at Jo's information; I wouldn't do what Rome is expecting me to do, which is betray him, no matter what he thinks of me. His words before I left the block party came back to me.

"I will never let you go…"

I grinned; no doubt he really thought he could keep me when I didn't want to be kept.

"What do we have here?" I muttered when I came upon some much needed information. Although my ankle bracelets were not explosives, he was tracking me through them, which is why he felt confident sending me back here by myself. There was also a tracking device in Giant's collar.

But now that I'd found this information, my window for escape had narrowed. He can see what I'm looking at on his computer. I set my watch for three minutes…It will take him at least seven to make it to me…

All I needed was three…

Romeo, my dear Romeo…Chess champion of the world you may be. But even champions play the wrong move sometimes.

Rome

I watched her as she stood in front of the computer looking at the information I'd left for her. I had to know for sure if she was down for me. I was ready to put my ring on her finger… But I needed to know that she will not betray me for Joseph's punk a**.

She is the only person to ever see my guilt. Nobody, not even my mother knew I suffered from it. The fact that she can see the real me was a miracle. And I knew I will never find somebody like her again. For the first time in my life I felt whole, and I knew it was because of her. She was my other half, I hate to sound corny, but…

She completed me… I need to make her mine.

I was on some selfish sh*t too, because I wanted all of her. Not just her beautiful body, I wanted her mind, her soul…

Her loyalty.

I needed her to say f*** Jo and roll with me.

I needed to own *all* of her…

She eased down in the chair clicking through the file. I changed my phone to a split screen pulling up my computer monitor so that I could see what she was looking at.

Over the last couple of weeks, the intell on what's going on with Jo has really been spilling in. I'm afraid I may have opened Pandora's Box.

This thing was huge…Jo thought he was the only child, but he wasn't. He had four other siblings. He and all his siblings had been a part of some kind of government experiment. Y'all remember when I told you that cat was a super soldier?

Little did I know when I said that, that he really *is* a super soldier, he and all his siblings. It's wild, this well goes very deep, and I'm still trudging through it to see just how deep.

I think my sister and my niece may be in danger, but I didn't know for sure and I wasn't going to make a move until I did. But what was the crazy part about all this is that I had no idea of how I was going to tell Jo, who had no idea he was a f***ing government experiment.

Over the last few days, Nak had been trying to talk to me about it, and I didn't know if she was doing it trying to get intell or if she really cared. I wanted to talk to her, because she understands me like nobody else...but it's been hard.

After today, I will know for sure. I've given her all the tools she needs to betray me, the information Jo originally sought. An empty building, so that she won't feel pressured to do the right thing because my men are there...even the keys to my truck.

I was honest with her that I will never let her go. Even if she does betray me, I will get her back. I don't care if I can't trust her, I just need her next to me. I'm addicted to the feel of her in my space. To have it different is not an option.

I had tracking devices in the truck, her ankle bracelets, and Giant's collar. There was no where she can go that I will not come for her...

Nowhere...

I frowned down at the screen, she wasn't looking through Jo's information. In fact, she was going somewhere she shouldn't be.

"F***!" I hissed when I saw that she was looking at her tracking devices. "Rob! Let me get the keys to your car."

"Is everything alright?" He asked tossing me his keys. But I didn't answer, I was already half way across the parking lot.

"Nak, what you doing, baby?" I asked, speaking into my phone that was now coming through the speaker inside my house.

She didn't answer, she just continued to quickly throw a few items into the bag that I'd bought her, looking down at her watch as she went.

"Baby, talk to me!" I tried again as I jumped in Rob's car starting it.

"Mutha F***A!" I yelled hitting the steering wheel.

The parking lot was jammed with touch and go traffic.

"Nak, wait for me, I can explain." I told her as she removed the golden charm bracelet I'd given her from her wrist. One of the charms on the bracelet was the key to the golden ankle cuffs with my tracking device in them. Squatting down she quickly used it to remove the cuffs from her ankles.

She was moving like she was on a mission, quickly and meticulously.

"Baby, please!!!" I cried when she bent down and scooped up Giant, removing the collar from around his neck...seconds later, she was out the door.

I tried to think of who I could call who was not at the block party. Whose a** she wouldn't kick. The only person I could think of was Hitta, but there was no telling where he was.

"Mutha f***A!!!!" I yelled hitting the steering wheel again and again.

I can't believe this was happening. I can't believe I had miscalculated like this.

By the time I got out the parking lot, my truck was moving fast. I sent the truck's location to Rob and Hannibal's phone, telling them to follow us.

She had about a seven-minute head start on me and was moving fast. But she didn't know the city like I did. She was heading toward the e-way.

I cut down a few alleys to avoid some of the traffic…I would catch her before she got to the expressway.

However, the dot on my truck stopped moving and I frowned, trying to figure out why. When I made it to the location where it stopped, the only thing I could do was sit there and stare in shock.

My truck sat still running with the door open, but it was surrounded on all sides by people. Instead of going to the express way like I'd thought, she brought the truck to a stop and exited at the busiest f***ing train station on the Westside of Chicago.

It had to be at least a thousand people getting on and off the trains that were pulling in and out of the station. I got out of the car and tried my best to spot her in the crowd.

But even I knew that was a waste of my f***ing time. Nak was a f***ing spy, she could blend into a crowd like a f***ing shadow blending in with the night.

Needing to let out my rage, I turned to my truck and kicked the door closed.

"Mutha F***a!!!!"

Chapter 15

Should Have Bet on the Queen

True Love is Like Playing Chess. The Boy Plays and is Always Afraid of Losing His Queen. The Girl Plays and Risks Everything to Protect Her King…

--Unknown

Nahkti

"Rise and shine…sunshine," I said to the slumbering man, careful to keep my voice low so that the guard who slumbered right outside his door didn't hear me.

When Saw Buck realized I was straddling his chest his eyes widened. But when he realized that all of his muscles were paralyzed and he couldn't move anything but his eyelids, panic set in. His lips twitched as he tried without success to cry out.

I held up the little brown canister of the gas I'd used to paralyze him, showing it to him.

"Believe it or not, this nerve gas was created to be a pesticide in 1938 Germany. But Adolf Hitler made a decree that anything that can be used as a weapon for the military had to be reported. So the creator of this silent but very deadly chemical brought it in to be inspected and the Hitler regime picked it up instantly. But it didn't become magic in a bottle until our government got a hold of the recipe and perfected it. You see, it can't be detected in the system four minutes after ingestion." I smiled down at him. "Isn't that awesome?"

The smile disappeared off my face. "However...there is a downside to it. Unfortunately, it's going to cause you to have a massive heart attack in about ten minutes. By the time your men find your body in the morning, they will simply assume that all those years of sucking down rib tips and T-bone steaks have finally caught up with you. I did a little searching into your medical records and it looks like you've had a few scares over the last few years. Doctor's been telling you for a while you have to change your diet."

I put my hand on my chest shaking my head sympathetically. "Hey man, I feel your pain. Apparently, I have pre-hypertension. Looks like I'm going to have to make a few changes before I end up like you...who believe it or not, is having a pre-heart attack."

When his eyes opened wider, I held up my hands. "I know...I know! Pre-anything is really silly, isn't it? But in your case, it is a reality. You, my not so good friend, is Pre-dead."

I couldn't help the giggle that escaped my lips. That was just damn hilarious.

"Anyway, I woke you because I wanted to tell you a few things before you go and meet your maker. First, you were right about Rome, he does have trust issues. And I have mommy issues... I think we were doomed from the beginning." As I spoke a fresh wave of pain resurfaced and a tear escaped my eye to run down my cheek.

As I wiped it away, I gave him a pathetic smile before shaking my head. "It's a shame too...Because I love him."

It had been nearly a week since I left Rome, a week in which I've laid low. Believe it or not, his reach was pretty far, he had the whole city looking for me. The airports were a no go. The bastard had hacked the system and had an APB put out on me that couldn't wait. He'd put images in the system of how I would look in various disguises, including wearing a beard and mustache… it was crazy.

Chicago had a lot of cameras and I didn't doubt he had access to every one of them. But none of that mattered because I'd found my way out…I just needed to clean up this little mess here before I left. Rome, the chess mastermind, had studied my file until he knew me better than I knew myself… He was aware of what I could do and yet still never thought to play his Queen.

"So, I bet you're wondering, why I'm doing this to you when you were right about Rome all along."

I could see in his gaze that he was. I leaned closer so that my lips were very close to his.

"I'm doing this because you are a bad man. You are a cancer on the planet, and if not stopped, you will only spread to destroy as much life as you possibly can. I'm doing this because I am the vengeance of God and your time has come to an end. I'm doing this because although Rome may make a horrible boyfriend, he is a blessing to this earth, and he gives life and plants seeds that will grow into great trees that will bear beautiful fruit one day. I'm doing this because I will destroy anything that tries to stand in the way of that." I sat up smiling brightly.

"K?" I told him patting his cheek again before I stood. His frightened eyes followed me, but I could already see the life leaving them.

For his sake, I sure hope he made some kind of peace with the man upstairs. Judgment was going to be a monster for him.

Careful not to disturb anything, I made my way back to the window I'd come in, and as quietly as I came, I left, gently closing the window behind me.

Rome

I picked up the burger and took a huge bite as I continued to scan the screens in front of me just like I have been doing for nearly two weeks. Jo's office had purchased her an open ticket for a flight to D.C. for when she'd completed her mission.

And although I knew she was too smart to use that ticket, I had rotating footage of O'Hare airport up on one screen. There wasn't an entrance or exit to the building that didn't rotate across the screen every four seconds. On the other screens, I had Midway Airport, the train station and rotating footage of every Greyhound bus station in the city.

I'd also hacked into the city's streetlight cameras that the public didn't know was face recognition software and programmed them to search for Nakhti's face, alerting me if they picked her up. There was nowhere she could go in this city where I could not find her.

And yet…It had been nearly two weeks and my arms were still empty. I couldn't sleep in my bed because it felt foreign without her. I couldn't eat normal food because it felt strange not forcing her to try something or watching her flinch from the taste of vegetables.

Damn, I even missed watching her pretend to gag from anything that said low fat or low sugar.

"Yo…Bro? It's some sh*t going on in these streets that you need to know about." My brother's timid voice came from behind me.

He and my men have been tiptoeing around me because I'd threatened to kill them if they spoke to me without the whereabouts of Nak. I didn't want to hear anything else. And yet here he was trying to tell me some other sh*t.

He carefully approached me.

"Is that a burg—" he gasped when he saw the burger in my hand. "Oh, hell naw! I'm calling ma…" He turned to hurry toward the door.

I shook my head…I was surrounded by idiots. "Rob…" I growled, not wanting to talk to anybody.

He stopped. "Yeah?"

I exhaled. "You said it was something going on I needed to know about."

"Oh yeah! Saw Buck dead." And then he turned to head back toward the door.

"What?"

His steps halted again and the chump turned around with that grin on his face that said…*I knew that would get your attention.*

"Who killed him?"

He shook his head. "Nobody, dude had a heart attack."

I narrowed my eyes as I watched him go.

Heart attack?

My phone dinged on the desk. I snatched it up as excitement shot through me. *Please let be Nak!*

When I saw it was Jo I squeezed the phone in my hand to keep from throwing and smashing it.

Bastard Fed: Need to talk to you on a secure line...

I knew this was coming, even though it was hard for me to stop searching for Nak for even a moment. The fillers I had put out there about Jo was finally bringing me information I could use and I ain't going to lie, this sh*t was wilder than I could ever imagine. Jo was a victim. He had no idea of the sh*t that was done to him, he nor his siblings. The man with no shoes had been right, Jo was a triplet, he had two identical brothers.

One was a DEA Beast. He was feared in the field by dope dealers and cops alike. His record was full of lawsuits, complaints of unnecessary roughness and unnecessary kills. Sh*t, dude had hardcore drug dealers wanting to go into witness protection to be protected from him. No question, like Jo, he was a goon. But unlike Jo, he was a bully... And according to his record, kept testing positive for weed in his piss.

His other brother was retired and considered extremely dangerous. He'd worked for a branch of the government I'd never heard of before. But that was nothing unusual, branches were created on a regular. If there is a problem, the American government got together a group of people whose job it was to study the problem, infiltrate the problem...and then destroy the problem.

Jo's brother was the latter part of that equation. He cleaned up situations before anybody ever knew there was a situation. He was considered a ghost in the field. Only those that knew him knew about him.

While in the field, he'd almost lost his left eye, suffering complete blindness in said eye. He was no good to our government in that condition, so they'd let him go, although they are keeping a close eye on him.

Now he was a civilian living pay check to pay check doing security work. I shook my head, all those years he'd served his government, and in the end, he still had to struggle to survive.

Jo had two more siblings, but their whereabouts are a little grainy. He has a sister named Debra, she disappeared in the system after receiving a juvenile life sentence for killing her mom's boyfriend. When I pulled up the last remaining files on her case, and when I say last remaining, I mean someone went out of their way to make them disappear.

But now that my bait is catching fish, I'd managed to entice that information to the surface. Anyway, in her file, she told the police that the man had used his finger to hurt her before he stabbed her mother, who'd tried to stop him from raping her child in the chest. Only then did Debra grab the knife and stab him in the neck.

The fact that she received a juvenile life sentence for that let me know that there was foul play involved.

Jo's oldest brother is by far the most mysterious. There is hardly anything found on him, except that he's wanted dead or alive by damn near every government on this planet, including ours.

But like I said, the dam had just broken, and I really haven't had time to look over everything I had. So I didn't have a full breakdown for Jo yet.

Me: Where are you?

Bastard Fed: Home office.

A few clicks on my computer and I'd successfully hacked into his. The surprise on his face was amusing.

"You hacked a system I was told was un-hackable."

That was funny…

"Oh yeah, is that what the brochure told you?"

"That's what the man who cleaned out your little bug told me."

The fact that his man had only found one bug let me know that his man was an idiot.

"Yeah, well, he lied to you. Once I'm in there is no getting rid of me."

After finding out this new information about Jo, my feelings for him had changed. He still irritated me greatly, because he was a cocky bastard and he had absolutely nothing to be cocky for. However, these folks had done a real number on him and his siblings.

I'd found footage of how they were tortured as children in order to break their minds. They went through sh*t that I wouldn't wish on my enemy…

Speaking of my enemy, something about Saw Buck suddenly having a heart attack wasn't sitting well with me. As I spoke with Jo, I pulled up Saw Buck's autopsy report and sure enough, it stated that the cause of death was a massive heart attack.

A massive f***ing heart attack?

I texted Hannibal and asked him when the funeral was. I had to see it with my own eyes. Something was telling me that Nak was behind this.

Damn it! She would do this sh*t! As if her leaving me wasn't f***ing tearing me apart. She would take out my enemy before she went, searing the fact that I am the dumbest mutha f***a in the world in the center of my forehead.

Hannibal hit me right back letting me know the funeral was today. It was happening now.

Although I didn't think he did, I asked Jo if he knew where Nak was. It didn't hurt to cover all my bases. But once he told me he didn't, I got extremely irritated and needed to stop talking to him. But before I let him go, I warned him to protect my sister and niece.

Although I really didn't know how dangerous this situation was, judging by the trouble that was gone through to hide the information I'd found, it could be quite dangerous.

Once I disconnected with him, I grabbed my truck keys.

"Where the hell you going?" Rob asked as I walked past him and a few more of the fellas on my way to the truck.

"To Saw's funeral..." I growled. I had to see for myself. I had to see if she left me with this burden to carry. She wasn't satisfied to just rip out my heart.

No...

She had to throw the mutha f***a to the ground and then stomp on it.

"I told y'all this nigga done gone crazy..." Rob said as he and my men hurried to their cars to follow me.

Yeah, it was crazy as hell to go to this funeral. But I didn't care if they killed me. I had to see if this was Nak's work.

As soon as we entered the funeral, everything came to a stop.

Sh*t, I was going to try and slip in and slip out. But since they had made a show of it, I might as well walk it out.

I strolled down the center aisle, my men looking just as confused as Saw Buck's followed.

When I got to the casket, two of Saw Buck's generals stepped in my way.

"What you come for...to gloat?" One of them sneered.

Bobby who had been comforting Saw's main girlfriend stood and put his hand on the general's shoulder stopping him.

"Naw...it's cool. They was boys once. If this was him in the casket, I'm sure Saw would have paid his same respect."

He wouldn't have. But folks needed to believe all kinds of lies about the dead. The general nodded without asking any questions. It was clear Bobby was now chief.

My gaze went to his. "You chief now?" I asked because I ain't supposed to know that.

Playing his role well, Bobby folded his arms in a very hostile way. "I am..."

I was too miserable to congratulate myself. Instead, I turned to look down at Saw's dead body...and I knew.

It hit me like a ton of bricks. This was Nak. Nak had destroyed my enemy in a way that looked completely natural. She had done something I hadn't been able to do. Not only did I feel like the biggest f***ing loser in the world for losing her, I also felt like a fool for underestimating her.

What the f*** had I thought?!

I don't know if my knees gave out or if I just lost the will to stand, but the next thing I knew, I was clutching the casket staring at this dumb mutha f***a, who had finally broken me down. And not because he was dead…But because it was his death that made me see how dumb of a mutha f***a I really was.

I'd f***ed up!

I f***ed up so bad!

"Come on, Rome, it's gon' be okay." My brother said as he and Hannibal tried to pull me back to my feet.

When that didn't work, Rob's dumb a** started humming some old negro spiritual and rubbing my back. "Let it out…let it out, it's okay. Saw in a better place now, bro." Then his dumb a** went back to humming.

What… the… f***?!

I looked up at him to see if he was serious. Would y'all believe that he was? His red hazy eyes had watered up and everything. And that's when I realized that Rob smokes entirely too much weed. His f***ing brain cells were fried!

I couldn't take it…I stood to my feet and stormed out of the funeral home. I needed to find her. Dear God, if you help me find her one more time, I promise I'll never lose her again. And I'll never underestimate her.

The man with no shoes was right. I am a stiff neck. I had been so vain and stupid…thought I had everything and everybody figured out. How could I be so careless with love?

When I got back to my loft I sat down at my computer and refused to move till I found her. Minutes turned into hours and hours into days.

My mother came back and I vaguely remember talking to her. A fever had come over me and I was determined to find Nak. There was no other option. And because I wasn't born with the giving up gene, I would keep looking...I will never stop.

I don't know how many days passed, but outside of showering and my mom forcing me downstairs so that I could eat, I didn't leave my computer. I'd searched everywhere. I had several private investigators in New York and Brazil watching her father's family and because there was no known address for the house Nak grew up in, I had them searching the area around the clinic she'd gone to when she was younger.

So far, nothing.

My mom and my brother were worried about me. Even my men tried to lure me out of my den. But I wasn't trying to hear anything that didn't have to do with Nak's whereabouts. Eventually, my punk a** brother brought in the big guns.

"Ay Bo, let's go, I need to chat with you."

I exhaled as I continued to stare at my computer screen. In between searching for Nak, I'd been looking into Jo's case and I think I had it just about figured out.

"Bo, I know you hear me," Hitta said from behind me.

Damn, I was not in the mood to deal with this big mutha f***a. But I could hear in his voice that he wasn't going to leave till he got what he wanted.

"Not today, Hitta, I'm in the middle of somethi—" The last of my sentence came out a squeak because the big bastard snatched me right up out of my chair.

"Damn mutha f***a! What part of I'm busy didn't you comprehend?" I growled when he put me back down on my feet. "If you wasn't so big, I'll knock yo' a** out right now!"

He stood grinning at me, not in the least worried about my threat, as his eyes took me in. "You look a mess, Bo. When the last time you been to the barbershop? If that wild a** girl do come back to you, she gon' take one look and run back out the door."

I reached up and touched my head and then my beard that had gotten out of hand.

Sh*t! It had been a while...

He jerked his head toward the door. "Come on, man, I got some sh*t to run by you. I need to get a cut too."

When you Hard Hitta, the barber comes to you. He and I sat in two barber chairs in the basement of the gym, where believe it or not was a small barbershop. He had two barbers come out so that neither of us had to wait.

"You know what you did with ol' girl? You know how you got her to yo' crib?"

Because he was my best friend and I spoke Hitta fluently, I knew he was being invasive because of the barbers, so the *ol' girl* he was speaking of was Nak. And how I got her to my crib meant me practically kidnapping her.

"Yeah, what about it?"

He exhaled, "I've been thinking about doing some sh*t like that with Angel."

I chuckled, my boy had finally gotten desperate. He and I were two peas of a pod. We both had women throwing themselves at us on a daily basis, and here the two we wanted didn't want to have anything to do with us.

Suddenly I had renewed energy, I was going to help my boy get his girl because it was time out for these f***ing women trashing our hearts... My man here had been letting the f***ing Tea Maker know how he felt about her, and she was still walking around like his feelings don't mean sh*t!

"Okay, this is what you have to do... First, you need to study yo' girl. Find out what she likes, what she don't like, where she like to go, the kind of sh*t she like to see. Find out what she's lacking and the stuff she dreams of one day having."

I sat up in my chair as a second wave of hope entered my body. "Then you need to come up with some bait, some sh*t you know she can't resist...that's what you're going to use to lure her in. Now once she takes the bait, she's yours." I held up my finger.

"But you need to make sure you create an environment that's a hundred times better than her present environment. You need to create a world for her that she will never want to leave." I didn't have to go into more detail.

Many people didn't know it, but Hard Hitta was a very smart man. His speech threw a lot of people off and most folks just assumed he was uneducated because of it. But that was the furthest thing from the truth.

Growing up, he learned with me.

A lot of the sh*t I was into, Saw wanted to have nothing to do with. He'd say something like... *"Come on, don't start this nerd sh*t!"*

But Hitta...Hitta was always interested. He would sit and learn with me for hours. Neither of us finished school, but that didn't stop us. After I finished reading a book, I gave it to Hitta…and vice versa.

However, there was something neither of us knew much about…

Love…

"Whatever you do, man…Learn from my mistake, never take her for granted, because then you may lose her when you've only just found her…"

Hitta reached over and put his hand on my shoulder giving it a reassuring squeeze. "Don't let it break you, Bo…If you and her meant to be, then y'all will be."

I turned to look at him…those were the last words Nak had said to me.

As soon as I pulled my truck back up to the house, my mother and Rob came running out the building toward me. I could tell by the look on their faces that I was getting ready to be upset.

"Journey's been shot!" My mother cried clutching for my t-shirt. "I don't know if she's okay…" By this time she was crying so hard, I could barely understand her.

"Ma, calm down and tell me what happened!"

Damn it! Damn it!

I should have brought her and my niece home weeks ago. I've been so damn distracted that although the warnings were clear as day, I'd ignored them because my mind had been on finding Nak.

"I was on the phone with Journey's driver—"

"Who, Albert?"

She nodded…

Thank God! I'd found out some things about Albert as well. The fact that Jo assigned Journey to him proved his love for her.

Albert is a beast…

"What happened then?"

"I heard gunshots and then I heard Albert telling Journey to hold on and that he was going to get her to the hospital. I could hear Ayana screaming and crying in the background…Oh, God! Romeo!"

"Rob, get Ma in the truck, I'll be right back!" I was on the phone dialing the mayor as I ran in the house for my computer bag.

We needed to get there quickly and the only way we could avoid the lines at the airport is to use the mayor's private plane.

Dear God, please let my sister and niece be okay… I knew who was behind this. Them mutha f***as was going to pay for this.

I'd already prepared a little treat for them. I had a feeling they were going to do something to piss me off.

But first I needed to get to the hospital…

Please God, let Journey be okay…

Chapter 16

A Reason, A Season, and A Day...

There are two kinds of people that come in our lives...They are temporary and permanent. Temporary people come to teach lessons like hurt, pain, selfishness, dishonesty, and disloyalty. Permanent people come to live in our hearts, they are the ones that give us strength, confidence, loyalties. Real love is found here.

The truth is, you need the two of them because one teaches values over the other...

--Unknown

Nakhti

I sat at the bistro across the street from my father's house that he shared with his wife and three children, eating a grilled chicken salad.

I have two sisters and a brother, whose ages are, 19, 15, and 12.

I bet you guys are wondering why I'm sitting across the street watching the house rather than walking up to the door and ringing the bell right?

Well…The are two reasons.

Before I became a SEAL, I'd come home on a short leave and decided I would push my fear to the side and go and talk to my dad. He and his family were all at my brother's little league game, apparently, my batting average came from dad and ran in the family.

Anyway, I'm standing there in my uniform, praying that once he sees it, he will be so proud that he'll pull me in and give me a great big hug, telling me it didn't matter that I wasn't born a boy. And although my mom drilled that into my head, it wasn't the real reason he'd left. Then he'll bring me and introduce me to my little siblings.

I've watched them from afar a long time, and I knew all three of them look just like me because we all look like him. So…I squared my shoulders and marched forward.

He looked up from where he had been squatting next to my brother giving him some pointers in his ear to see me walking toward him. There is a big nervous smile on my face, but it slowly disappears when he stands giving me such a hostile look it freezes my blood.

I know he recognizes me instantly because his look says he's angry that I still exist. He wishes I would just disappear. I'm the mistake he's ran from in hopes of never, ever seeing it again. He's convinced himself that it was a mistake he'd never made… But seeing me reminds him that he had, in fact, made the huge mistake of getting a foreign woman pregnant while on tour, and now his mistake had found him.

And then…

And then…

Wheww!!! Lol!! It's still a little rough on the second telling, but I want you guys to know, so here goes.

He takes my brother and turns him around so that he can't see me…and then just walks away, leaving me standing there in my freshly clean and pressed uniform, and he never looks back. Not once…

Anyway, it hurt…but hey, what can you do about it? Ever since then, I came from time to time to watch them from a distance, because I'm pathetic. However, I think I understand why he did it.

For the most part, they look happy. He goes to work, comes home every night, helps the kids with their homework…kisses his little wife on the cheek.

I remind him of the chaos in his life. With me comes too many unanswered questions. To retain the happiness of his house, sacrifices had to be made…And the sacrifice was me.

I'm already damaged…he can save his other children. And we all know the best way to do that is to keep them away from me.

Well…After today he'll never have to worry because I've come to say goodbye, from a distance of course…but still goodbye. This will be my last time spying on my perfect family…made perfect because they don't know me.

I won't be coming back to New York, there is nothing that draws me back here. Even my favorite pet store has closed. I wondered if my little buddy Crumble was okay. I'd come back to adopt him because Giant could use a friend and since I was officially retired, I was free to take him home, only to find a for sale sign on the pet shop's door.

I exhaled…

Life sucks…

The second reason I was sitting here at the bistro across the street from my father's house instead of someplace closer is because Rome had three private investigators watching the house. One sat four tables to my left, watching a car race on his phone. Every few minutes he'll look up and glance across the street to see if anything new had happened.

Chuckling, I shook my head.

Men…

"Moving on is hard to do, isn't it?"

That deep voice came from my right, I turned and gasped when I saw the big man sitting at the table next to mine with a cup of tea in his hand.

That was not what startled me. First of all, I didn't hear him sit down. A man that big should have made a sound. And second, he looked like a bonified black cowboy. The smell of his leather duster engrained its authenticity.

My gaze traveled down his powerful frame to his feet that were covered in a pair of black cowboy boots, with spurs…

Nossa!

Chills went through my body. It felt like I was sitting next to a ball of powerful energy that was barely being contained by the flesh of the man.

I cleared my throat. "Yeah, it is pretty hard."

He nodded his head as he lifted his tea to his lips. "A reason, a season, and a day."

"Excuse me?" I asked, not understanding his meaning.

"There are some people who come into our lives for a reason, there are some who come for a season, and then there are some who come for only a day." As he spoke, he stared out the window seeming to be lost in his own memories.

I couldn't help but wonder who it was in his life that had come and gone, and who was still there. It was frightening how close his words hit towards home. I narrowed my eyes as I stared at the fella.

There was something else about this guy… It felt as if I knew him, he felt familiar, like a father, or a grandfather, which was strange because he didn't look old enough to be my father, or my grandfather. He looked to be my age, maybe slightly older.

"I thought the saying was a season, a reason and a *lifetime*?" I told him, toying with my fork.

He chuckled… "I assure you that everybody that says hello will eventually say goodbye…We only have a season to get it right. Assuming a lifetime is vanity."

I nodded, I guess I can see that. He turned and looked at me then and I inhaled sharply. His dark eyes were ancient.

Nossa!

The things he must have seen to make them that way. Suddenly, I knew that it wasn't a coincidence he was sitting here next to me. This is going to sound strange, but I felt like I wanted to cling to him and never let him go.

He chuckled again looking away from me. "You are stronger than you believe, child."

"Who are you?"

And why does it feel like my soul is connected to yours?

He shook his head a bit. "I'm nobody...most folks call me The Preacher."

I frowned. "Are you a preacher?" He didn't look like no preacher I ever seen.

"Not in the way you're thinking. I'm a convener in the true sense of the word. What I do is not for show, I don't have a huge following, and I only make myself known to those who need to hear what I have to say."

"Why did you make yourself known to me?"

He turned to look at me then with those unsettling eyes. "Really soon you're going to be forced to stop running. Like the rest of us, you must pick up your stake and carry it." His gaze went back to my father's house.

"A reason, a season and a day, child. Some of us weren't meant to live normal lives. Although we can't see it...Sometimes the Ancient of Days removes obstacles that if remained, would become stumbling blocks in our path. And unfortunately, we've reached a critical hour and there is no longer time for certain... distractions." As he spoke, my father, looking so very handsome in his suit, came out of his brownstone and walked to his car.

The private investigator that was sitting a few tables away from me got up and hurried out the restaurant to follow him.

"But that's okay because The Great One rewards his servants significantly. And although it seems as if you're drowning in your sorrow, this too shall pass. The young prince will find you and for a moment, you and he will have normal. Cherish those days, because they won't last. Perilous times are coming, and everything we once knew will be destroyed in one hour."

His gaze came to me one last time… "The moment will come where you will have to choose to take a chance at love again." He nodded. "Be brave and choose love. You two are destined to inherit the Kingdom together. Enjoy the little time you have left."

And then he stood and pulled a hundred dollar bill out his pocket… "Lunch is on me."

He placed the bill on the table and walked out of the bistro without looking back. When he opened the door, the wind blew his coat open slightly, and it was then when I saw the impressive sword there on his hip.

I looked around to see if anybody else had noticed. Nobody had…

Hmmm…

I wasn't big on the supernatural, not like Rome, who believed with his whole heart and soul. But I'm pretty sure there was more to the Preacher than what he presented.

My gaze went back to my dad's house. A reason, a season, and a day… The Preacher was right, to assume a lifetime is vanity. I'd assumed Jo would be in my life forever, but that had been vain. After what had gone on with Rome, I didn't even try to contact him.

As far as he is concerned, I'm dead. This was all his fault. He sent me into a situation that I was doomed to fail. He'd used me to get to Rome, and Rome had used me to get back at Jo. The Preacher said to give love another chance, but I don't think I will.

If Rome was the prince he spoke about, he was wrong in his thoughts that he will find me. Once I left the United States, nobody will be able to find me.

I stood gathering my things, leaving the hundred-dollar bill on the table. My salad was about ten dollars, and the Preacher's tea couldn't have been any more than two.

This blessing I will pay forward…

It was time for me to move on with my life and begin anew…

****

"Nossa, we weren't aware Mrs. Garcia had any remaining family left here in Ribeirão da Ilha." The nun dressed in the all-white habit said to me in Portuguese as she led me back to the area where they took the residence for afternoon games and entertainment.

I smiled at her, but my mind was a million miles away. When I first got back here to Brazil, I had contemplated not making this trip. I wanted to begin anew, but I knew it could not be done without the closure of this part of my life.

Watching my father and his family go on about their daily business, not knowing I existed was breezy compared to this. My father was a stranger…the pain of his rejection will never add up to the pain of my mom's…Not even close.

"Your mom hasn't made much of an improvement. She has her good days, but of late, they are pretty far and few in between. I am glad you came to visit when you did…"

She left off right there, but I knew what she meant. My mom didn't have much time left. I nodded... "I'm glad I came too." The lie slipped easily from my lips.

As I followed the sister back, I took in the serenity of this place. As a child, my mom and I had passed this monastery many times. The sisters here did all they could to make sure their patients were comfortable in their last days.

It's why I chose this place... Well, that and it was completely off grid. They did everything here old school. I knew for a fact there were no computers and if there were phones, they were the good old fashion landlines.

I had set up a direct deposit directly to their bank. But the good sisters here at Mary Catherine's would continue to take care of my mom even if they didn't receive payment. They served the community. The residents of Ribeirão da Ilha were the only ones in the world that even knew the beautiful monastery existed.

She led me to a heavily gardened area. Beautiful rose vines grew up the wall everywhere. In some areas of the garden, art easels had been set up for those that wanted to paint. At the far end of the garden, it looked as if some kind of elderly aerobics class was taking place.

My gaze landed on a small figure that sat bundled in several blankets in a wheelchair in front of a small fountain. Someone had put her salt-and-pepper thinning hair in two braids that fell over the back of the wheelchair. Her head leaned to the side as if it was too heavy for her to hold it straight up.

It had been nearly ten years since I last saw her, and the nun nurse was right, time had not been kind to her.

"Ms. Garcia…You have a visitor. Your daughter is here to see you."

My mother didn't bat an eye. Had it not have been for her fist that she balled up tighter in her lap, I would have doubted she'd heard the nurse at all.

"This is not one of her good days. She's refused to eat and won't talk to anyone. I'll leave you with her, maybe you can get her to eat a little something."

She smiled kindly and eased past me. I stood for just a moment, not sure what to do or to say. This was the woman who had damaged me so badly that I've never been able to have a successful relationship with another human being.

She was the reason I could not trust love.

She was the reason why love didn't live here anymore…

I eased down in the chair in front of her…as soon as her eyes touched me, they widened a bit as she took in all the changes that had happened to me. However, a moment later she rolled them before turning to look away from me.

Disgusted…

"Hey, mama." My voice quivered a bit as I fought the pain I felt at her rejection.

She huffed balling up her fist tighter in her lap.

I laughed without any humor. "How have you be—"

My words trailed off. What was I doing?

Why was I even here?

After all these years of having to be tough, I felt tired. Being with Rome for that short time had made me forget my tiredness, but it was back…with a vengeance.

I exhaled. "You know, mama, after all these years, I've finally figured out why you hate me. You hate me because I'm just like you."

Her little fist balled up tighter in her lap. So tight her tan knuckles had turned white.

"I fell in love, mama. I fell in love with a great man. A far better man than my papa." I chuckled again without any humor. "Although, I don't know what he saw in me."

She turned then and looked at me. And for a moment her gaze felt normal, like a caring mother listening to her daughter tell her about the time her heart got broken. Tears welled up in my eyes.

"I'll never be good enough for him," I muttered as I wiped the tears away with my hand that slightly shook.

I took a deep breath, trying to get a hold of my emotions. Although I've felt like it, I haven't allowed myself to have a good cry about Rome. I guess I didn't have it in me to show that kind of weakness. But that cry was always there, threatening to explode from me like a dam.

"I'm moving back to the house, mama." I continued, changing the subject. "I haven't been there yet. I came here straight from the airport. I know it needs tons of work."

I'd been battling with myself about whether or not I was going to try and buy a new house or fix up the one we already have. And I'd decided to save money and just fix up the one that we already had. The land had been in our family since just before slavery officially ended in Brazil in 1888.

My great, great grandfather's master had given it to him in 1885 when they passed the Sexagenarian Law here freeing all the slaves over sixty-five. It was said that his master was also his brother and there was actual love between the two. So he'd given my grandfather twenty-two acres located at the base of Morro do Ribeirão or the Hill of Ribeirão, for his family.

When I was a little girl I would climb to the very top of the hill and look out across the bay and just imagine what the United States was like. I knew my father was there, and that he'd brought my mom there for a short time to give birth to me so that I could be a citizen. But then something had happened and I and my mom ended up back on the Brazilian Island of Santa Catarina.

Most of the land had long since been abandoned. Before I left to go to the military my mom and her aunt were the only two remaining relatives still living here. My mom's aunt died some years ago, which meant nobody had lived here in a long time and I had my work cut out ahead of me.

But that wasn't bad, I welcomed the distraction. I planned on throwing myself into fixing up the farm until I became too busy to think about Rome or anything else for that matter.

My gaze settled back on my mom and suddenly I felt like I was suffocating. One visit was enough to take me back to those days of feeling completely worthless. I stood from my chair needing to be free from this place.

I leaned over and gently kissed her forehead… "I just want to let you know that I forgive you for hurting me, mama."

****

I dropped my bags on the floor just inside the front door and a cloud of dust flew up causing me to sneeze. I took my shades off and looked around amazed to see that everything was still how I'd left it. When I came to put my mom in the nursing home over ten years ago, I'd covered the furniture that had all belonged to my *avozinha* in white sheets.

At the time I didn't think I would ever come back here. Before my avozinha died I had good memories of this place, but after she died, my memories became haunted by a mother, who'd at one time been a raving beauty, only to be rejected by her lover and become a bitter shell of the woman she used to be.

No...I didn't think I'd ever be back.

Yet here I am. I turned to walk back out to the porch, which will need all new wood and just looked out over the space. There was an old farmhouse that sat between our place and my great aunt's place.

I will begin my work there so that I can get it ready for my future prized babies. I'm sure I can hire on a few hands to help me. I'll use this week to get the house in a livable condition and then take a trip inland to the Winston stables.

I wonder if Juan the old stable master was still around. I wondered if he still remembered me.

I wondered if I could make it through this day without giving in to the tears that were choking me.

Needing a quick distraction, I decided to go down to the river and wash the road off me since the water and electricity weren't on in the house yet. I squatted down in front of my bags to remove a fresh tank top and a pair of shorts when my hand fell on the package Rob had given me before I'd left the block party.

In all the excitement of getting out of Chicago and then New York without Rome seeing me, I'd forgotten to open it.

My hands shook a bit as I untied the twine and then gently peeled back the cloth to see that it was a painting.

But do you guys remember those tears I told you I was fighting to hold back? Well let me tell you, they were flowing now.

He'd painted a very detailed picture, displaying his genius, of Rome and I asleep in the bed. It looked as if we had just made love because neither of us was wearing any clothes. He'd managed to capture the contentment we felt for each other even in our sleep, on our faces. There was a sheet draped over our lower half and Rome's muscled arm was draped over my breasts, holding me to him as if he was afraid to let me go…

Nossa! Rome's arms had become my favorite place to sleep…

I put my hand to my mouth to stifle my cry… Why had Rob done this?

Why?

I turned the small canvas painting to the back and written at the bottom so light I barely saw it was the words… *Rome's Blessing*.

And that was it… The dam burst.

I wanted to throw the beautiful painting away from me, but ended up clutching it to my chest as I wept for all the things possible that I will never experience because I was damaged…

Like love…

How did I ever think a man would love me when my own parents couldn't stand the sight of me?

Why had God been so cruel to deny me love?

Everybody needs love, right?

I mean…didn't everybody want to be loved?

A reason, a season, and a day… words I'll never forget.

Chapter 17

Civilian Life...

Nakhti

2 Months Later...

Let me tell you guys something, civilian life sucks!

"Put your hand on my breasts again and I will slit your throat, pig!" I hissed in Portuguese to the cop that was guiding me out of the cell I'd spent the last three days in.

"Too bad your bail was posted. I was looking forward to having some more fun with you and those beautiful boobies of yours."

He had no clue he was a dead man for the *fun* he decided to have with me. As God is my witness, I was coming back for this pig and I was going to slit his throat.

I jerked my arm from him when he reached up under the pretense of grabbing it to grab my breasts for the hundredth time since I'd been thrown into this cesspool of a jail.

Nossa! Never thought I'd miss the jails in the U.S. These cops in Brazil got away with murder. This pig that was leading me out had made me lift my shirt and show him my breasts for everything, to go to the bathroom, to get food and water...

If I didn't think it would have put me on the radar, I would have slit his throat days ago. However, now that I'm free, breast man's days were limited.

I was so angry it took a minute for his words to register…I was free…

Someone had posted my bail?

What the hell? How can that be when no one knew I was here?

I knew it wasn't my mother, she didn't even know who I was these da—

Huh?

What was that?

You guys are wondering how I ended up in jail?

First, let me start by saying that it wasn't my fault. I've been on my absolute best behavior since I came back to Brazil.

I've been working on my place, preparing the farmhouse to be able to house a few horses. I even hired me two helpers that came during the day to lend a hand.

I'd found a way to give back. When we were done working at the farm for the day, Giant and I went to the nursing home to help the nuns with my mom and the other patients.

And guess what. It hasn't been that bad. The days that the nurses called my mom's bad days have actually turned out to be good days… at least for me and my mom. On her bad days, she forgets who I am and is actually very kind to me.

I greedily suck those times up because she has never been kind to me. There were times when I was younger that she would smile at me and tell me I was pretty, but even during those times, there was resentment in her eyes.

When she forgets who I am, she allows me to comb her hair and feed her apple sauce. Sometimes she even tells me about the times she was so beautiful men would follow behind her like puppies… Her words.

But then her memory would filter back and she would instantly clinch up and refuse to look at me or talk to me. And each time that happened, no matter what I told myself, it hurt like hell.

When she'd get in those moods I'd go and help out with the other patients, like Mr. Olivera, the little old man in the room next to hers. He was always kind to me and had asked me to read to him. When I asked what it was he wanted me to read, he handed me a little black Bible written in Portuguese.

And thus began my journey. Because he'd already read it several times, I decided to start from the beginning…The book of Genesis.

After our first session, he told me I could keep the Bible. He said it will keep me safe just like it kept him and his mom before him. Now that he'd reached the end of his journey, he didn't want it to end up in someone's hands that will not understand its value. The only thing he requested was that I bring it to him to read to him when I came and visited.

I loved it!

Outside of my superhero bat, it was the best gift I had ever been given. It was the perfect size to slide down into my cargo pants pocket. I took it with me everywhere I went. And yeah, I began to feel as if it kept me safe.

I don't believe in coincidences, I knew for sure that it was a reason I ended up with this book and I don't care how long it took me, I was going to read it from the beginning to the end. Like Ro—

No!

We didn't think of him…

I'd finally began to feel like I can move on and that I didn't make the biggest mistake of my life walking away from my thug. I will not be thinking about him so that my doubts can resurface. It was bad enough he and his freaky ways invaded my dreams at night. Several times I had to get out of bed and take a cold shower because my skin felt like it was on fire, needing to feel him filling me again.

Anyway, …that's not what we are talking about, you guys wanted to know how I ended up in jail for three days.

Everything was going well, I was very proud of the way my life was headed.

But then something happened. A restlessness came over me that frightened me. It had been a long time since I'd killed anyone and I was beginning to feel ill. Not ill as in a sore throat or upset stomach, but ill as in mentally.

I began to feel depleted…

So I decided to go to the bar Friday night to blow off a little steam. I may have had a bit much to drink…a bar fight may have kicked off…

And I may or may not have been the reason it happened.

The only thing I remembered was a pool game, a bet that didn't get paid…and me cracking someone across the head with the pool stick before all hell broke loose.

The next thing I know, I'm waking up in Ribeirão da Ilha little dinky jail with a perverted freak demanding to see my breasts so that I could relieve my bladder, which at the time felt like it was going to burst. He'd made the mistake of touching my breasts the first time while I wasn't handcuffed and almost got his hand broken for it. I had to constantly remind myself that I had to remain low-key.

Killing a police officer at a police station would surely put me on every radar in Brazil. And if Rome was still looking for me, which I doubt very seriously, he would surely find me that way.

However, when I rounded the corner to see who'd bailed me out my thoughts quieted as a very uneasy feeling settled over me.

"Sister Sousa? What are you doing here?"

Seeing the head nurse from my mom's nursing home standing in the jail's booking room cannot be good.

"I have bad news, sweetheart." She spoke confirming my thoughts. My gaze lowered to her hand that she used to clench her skirt so hard her knuckles had turned white.

Nossa! *Please don't rock my world, sister.*

"Your mama died last night in her sleep."

I sat in the chair nearest to me as I studied her face. Was she serious? Sister Sousa wouldn't joke about anything like that.

No, she wouldn't…

I put my hand on my chest as pain shot through it leaving me confused. I didn't understand the hurt that I felt. Didn't I know my mother was going to die?

Sister Sousa rushed toward me and began to rub my back. I looked up at her with a smile that didn't reach my eyes...shaking my head, trying to tell her she didn't have to comfort me, because I was alright.

Only...

When I tried to push her arms away, I ended up clutching them instead.

I was alright...

There was no love lost between me and my mom...

Only...

There was a lot of pressure in my chest and I didn't know why.

The perverted jailer came from the back with my things and all I saw was red. Needing to lash out I jumped up from my chair to kill...

But as if she had some kind of radar the sister slid between us reaching for my things...

"Muito obrigado, ofical..." She said thanking the bastard as she took my items from him. For just a moment when he looked at me, there was real fear in his eyes.

I wanted him to be afraid...I wanted him to understand that although the sister had just saved his life, he was a dead man walking. I was going to kill him.

With a forced smile on her face that begged me not to cause any more trouble, she turned and handed me my things, which wasn't anything but the small Portuguese Bible Mr. Olivera had given me, a tactical pocket knife, and a crumbled up twenty-dollar bill.

I clutched the Bible sliding it down into my cargo pants pocket where it belonged and just like that, the lump that was choking me in my throat loosened a bit.

I looked at Sister Sousa with eyes that were blurred with tears that refused to fall.

"What happened?"

****

As I stood and watched my mom's casket being lowered in the ground, I felt numb all over. I could not come to terms with the pain I felt over her death. In one breath I felt like a fool for grieving for someone who hated my guts in her right mind and in another, cold-hearted for feeling like a fool for grieving my dead mother.

They say God doesn't put on you more than you are able to bear, but I don't know if that is true, because I think I've reached my limit a while ago.

After the two graveyard workers got the casket lowered half-mast, they took off their hats and came to join me. Apparently, they were not only graveyard workers, but also fill-ins for empty funerals like this one.

Because death was a very real thing for the nuns at the monastery, they tried not to attend any of their former patient's funerals to preserve their own sanity, which left only me standing in a black veil and dress that belong to my avozinha and the two graveyard workers to send her on her way.

It was pathetic...

But what was even more pathetic was the realization that my funeral will probably look very similar, only with one less person...Me.

My tragic life played before my eyes.

Everything from being a young child just wanting her mama's love to being a young child forced to take her mama's hate. Every time she hurt me and tried to destroy my face because it looked like my fathers. Every time I needed to feel her arms around me, only to feel her fist.

I was a damn fool...

I snatched the veil off my head and tossed it in the grave, then I turned and walked away, leaving the poor graveyard workers confused.

My life was a tragedy. Like my mother, I was a hot mess. I didn't stop walking until I got to my truck. Once I got behind the wheel I just started driving. I had no idea where I was going. I just needed to drive...

I needed to fly...

I needed to feel close to God...

Rome

As soon as the Ribeirão da Ilha police station ran her fingerprints she was mine. I'd been in Brazil for the last month searching every nursing home I could find for Nak's mom. Jo's parting information had been gold. It would have been easy for Nak to disappear by herself, but there was no way she could hide an ailing mother.

A hunch told me to search the cities around the clinic Nak had gone to all those years back. I'd just made my way to the city of Florianópolis when the hit came on her fingerprints. Seconds later I'd hacked the camera feed on the little dinky jail.

They didn't have the best technology, but it didn't have to be the best for me to hack it. As I made my way this way, I'd been forced to sit and watch that jailer force her to lift her shirt for everything…water, food, to go to the bathroom.

What kind of jail didn't have toilets in the cells?

Naw, scratch that. I'm glad there were no toilets, that little pervert would have probably stood at the bars and watched her use it.

I was so angry that he would dare take liberties with what was mine that I'd gone to see him first. Needless to say, I'd lost precious time, because it took longer than I'd expected to find a place to bury the body, while manipulating the federal database to appear as if *Officer Friendly,* who couldn't keep his hands to his f***ing self, feared for his life due to threats he'd been receiving from the cartel.

Edwina Fort

In this part of the world, death by the cartel was everyday life... No one would even question it. Either way, I will keep a close eye on the investigation and make sure to steer them in the way that I want.

By the time I'd gotten to the graveyard after finding out Nak's mom had passed, she'd just taken the black veil of her beautiful head and tossed it into the grave. For a moment I was struck dumb at the sight of her.

I'd missed her so much my f***ing stomach felt as if I'd just taken a blow from Hitta to it. She was so beautiful she held me mystified. The black dress she wore looked old, but it molded to her sexy body in a way that had me adjusting myself in my linen slacks from suddenly needing her with a hunger that frightened me.

Her beautiful curly hair that was as wild as her soul blew around her face as she turned and headed toward a truck that looked like it had been taken right from the set of Sanford and Son. All the men she passed turned to watch her go, her beauty grabbing them the way it did me.

I clutched the steering wheel, realizing I didn't know what the f*** to say to her. The only thing I'd worried about to this point was finding her. And now that I've done that, I have no clue what to do now.

Her mom had just died...should I go and get flowers?

Sh*t!

I didn't think about this...

What will she say when she finds out that I found her? Will she try and run from me again?

I balled up my fists...No f***ing way I was allowing that sh*t to happen ever again. I don't give a damn how she feels about it. She was never getting away from me again.

At a safe distance, I followed her, careful not to arouse her suspicion. However, she looked so distraught when she walked away from her mom's grave, I doubted if she was paying attention to anything that was going on around her.

Damn...I wanted to hold her so badly. I needed to let her know that everything was going to be okay. The look on her face as she walked away ripped at my heart. She needed me and I had not been there for her, because I was too busy killing a man and then manipulating a crime scene.

F***ing bastard! I wish he was alive so I could kill his punk a** again.

She turned off on a road that led to a huge commercial ranch. There was no way I could follow her down that road without her noticing, so I kept driving down a little further to the main entrance that said Winston Stables. There were a lot of cars going and coming, I was glad I'd upgraded my rental to a Benz truck because there were no shabby cars amongst them.

It looked as if I was in the market for a horse today. I kept my gaze on Nak's red truck as she brought it to a stop at a big stadium that was located on the west side of the property. After parking in the guest parking lot, I reached into the passenger seat for the cream Dobb that I'd bought to match the cream linen suit I wore.

When in Brazil, one needs to dress like the locals.

This was not my first trip here, in fact, I'd been here many times, I studied Jiu-Jitsu at the Gracie Institute in Rio. I knew well how to blend in.

Even though I wanted to run across the acres separating me from Nak, I forced myself to take my time and appear to be shopping like the other guests. The security guards that patrolled the grounds were trained to spot those that did not belong here.

As two of them passed me, I saw their eyes go to my soft Italian leather shoes. They took in the quality of the linen my suit was made of. No blends…When in Rio, I frequented a tailor who did only superior work. He was my first stop when I touched down in Brazil.

I can't be showing up to my girl's door looking like a scrub. Their eyes landed on my watch that cost more then they'll see in a lifetime. I lifted my hand and tipped my hat to them so that they could get a better look.

"Good day, senhor." They both said as they passed me by.

"Good day, gentleman."

Shortly after that, I was approached by a waiter, who asked me if I would care for a cool lemonade or perhaps something a bit stronger in Portuguese.

"Something a bit stronger…" I responded in Portuguese and told him to bring me a double Hennessy on the rocks with a splash of water.

When he returned with my drink, I tipped him a hundred dollars. Now…he will make sure my glass stays full.

Nak had gone to an area of the property that was for employees, but there were a few guests who wondered in this area as well…those who wanted to see how the employees handled the horses behind the scene.

I pulled my hat lower on my face so that if she looked up, she wouldn't see me. Without seeing my face, she wouldn't recognize me dressed like this. She'd only seen me dressed for the block.

I made my way next to where she stood talking to an older man, just out of her line of sight, but still close enough to where I could hear their conversation. The two of them watched a beautiful tan stallion that looked as if it had not been broken. I rested my back against the fence, lifting my drink that was getting low.

Right then I looked up and sure enough, the waiter I'd tipped was coming my way with another double Hennessy on the rocks with a splash of water on his tray.

Nakhti

"He's beautiful, Juan."

"I thought about you when he came in. Like you, his soul is restless...Winston got him at a discount because it's said he's untamable."

I chuckled without any humor. A horse this majestic no matter how wild was going for a fortune.

"How big of a discount?"

It was his turn to chuckle. "For people like you and me, not big enough. I heard he paid 5.2 million for him..."

I sucked in my breath... "Nossa! And to think I was going to try and purchase him."

We both shared a little laugh over that.

Over the last two months, I was a regular here at the Winston Stables. No...I couldn't afford any of the horses here, but this was a good place to be to keep abreast of what was going on in the world of horses.

When I came and found that Juan was still the stable master I was thrilled, because he still remembered me, and he let me fall back into helping him with the horses. He even came by my place and gave me some great suggestions for my own stable that I was trying to get up and running.

"Can I ride him?" My question was so low I didn't think he heard me.

"Do you think you can get a saddle on him?"

I nodded. "Yeah, why not?"

"Go right ahead, be my guest. I've always told you that you have an amazing way with the horses."

"What's his name?"

"He doesn't have one yet. His previous owner got so frustrated with his temperament he didn't bother to name him, knowing he was going to sell him."

Just like me, he wasn't good enough. As I carried the saddle out to the waiting beauty, I couldn't help but feel a kinship towards him. He and I were disposable. My mother, my father...Jo, Rome, the f***ing government.

I was nothing to them, my feelings, my heart, my life…it meant nothing to them.

I set the saddle down a good distance from the golden horse. His coat reminded me of a pair of eyes I once knew.

Although he didn't run, the stallion's nostrils flared as he began to paw the earth, attempting to intimidate me into backing off. I held my hand out straight in front of me.

"They told me you don't have a name."

He pawed at the earth a little more and began to step back and forward in an aggressive manner.

"F*** them, I'll give you a name…and if you like it, come to me so that I can rub your nose, and we can be friends."

He pawed at the earth some more…

"Your tan coat has little specks of gold in it that reflects in the sun, making you appear as if you'd been dipped in gold dust."

He stopped pawing the earth and blew loudly from his nose.

"As if God personally made you himself. The others may not know it, but your birth was special, you were meant to be here…just like me. And it really don't matter that nobody knows it…" Tears came to my eyes.

"I want to call you, Freedom, because you don't need the approval of others to be magnificent. Look at you, you are simply amazing."

His nose butted up against my hand and I giggled at him through my tears. I leaned my head against his.

"I'm in so much pain right now, Freedom." My words were just over a whisper. "I just want to be free too. I want to ride as fast as we can away from it, so fast, I feel close to God. Can you help me?"

He neighed as he gently pushed his head into my shoulder. Very carefully, I saddled him.

"You are a big beautiful boy, aren't you Freedom?"

I probably should have stopped by my house to change out of this dress... But I wasn't going to let it stop this show.

I hiked it up to my thighs and mounted Freedom's back. As if he knew and understood what I needed, he took off with just a gentle nudging from me toward the south gate. Juan hurried to it opening it for us.

"Good job, my girl!" He cried with a huge grin on his face as we raced past him.

Freedom flew across the plain towards the ravine. This had been the same journey that horses had taken me many years ago...the journey that made me feel free.

I held my head back as my hair whipped around my face... my tears ripped from my eyes and blew away as he flew.

"Yes, Freedom!" I cried as more tears fell.

Dear God, help me! Why was I the unloved?

My mother died hating me, my father refuses to acknowledge me...my man...

Well...my man can't trust me.

I needed to find the strength to carry on. I needed to find the strength to bounce back from this.

I needed to find that strength I had before.

Why was I breaking down now?

I let Freedom run until he got tired, and then we turned back to head toward the stables. Don't want old Winston sending his goons to look for me, thinking I'd run away with one of his prized horses.

And Freedom was a prized horse. If Winston paid 5.2 for him, he will easily get double back for his investment.

"I wish I could take you home with me," I told him as I stroked his beautiful mane that was the same golden color as his coat.

Yes, Freedom will fetch a pretty penny.

Juan helped me unsaddle him and left me to wipe and brush him down.

"You were magnificent, boy…"

"Why didn't I know how much you loved horses, *Minha Anjo*?"

The brush dropped from my hands as I whipped around. When my eyes connected with those honey gazers my mouth opened in shock.

There was no way he was here! I'd covered my tracks to the tee.

"Romeo!"

345

Chapter 18

Break Up-To Make Up...

Nakhti

"Hey, beautiful..." His deep voice floated around me shattering the doomed feeling that had settled on me like glass.

"How—" My words died off.

I could not believe he was standing here in front of me. I damn near moaned because he looked so damn good in that cream linen suit. My eyes thirstily drank him up.

Nossa!

I was tongue-tied because my senses were overloaded. The shock of him finding me, the fact that he looked good enough to eat, the knowledge that I was secretly thrilled to see him, but at the same time, my stupid pride was keeping me from throwing myself in his arms.

But still, ...he'd come for me.

"How did you find me?" I finally got out.

He took a step towards me; I took one back. The muscle flexed in his jaw as his nostrils flared.

"I told you, I will never let you go." He growled, clearly not liking the fact that I was prepped and ready to run from him.

Tough...

I held my head up high... "Well, you wasted your time. You might as well go back home."

Are you nuts?! Shut up already!

He chuckled shaking his head as if he could hear my inner dialogue.

"I don't have a home anymore."

I frowned. "What are you talking about? Your home is the loft in Chicago."

"It's gone...they blew it up."

"What!?" His words surprised me so much I took a step towards him. I will kill whoever did this.

"Look..." he exhaled. "So much has happened since the last time I saw you, everything is a mess. Have lunch with me and I'll fill you in."

I nodded as I handed Freedom's reins off to the stable boy whose job it is to take care of him.

"His name is Freedom," I told him before letting go of the reins.

He nodded. "Come on, Freedom, I have some nice toasted oats for you."

Longingly I watched him lead the golden beauty away. I know he was going to be taken care of, that was something the

Winston Stables excelled at. The horses here were treated better than royalty.

Rome took my hand startling me. There was something very primal and possessive in the way that he held it while looking down into my eyes. His look said... *I got you,* loud and clear. It also said *I'll never let you go...* just as clear.

I bit my lip as I gently tried to pull my hand away from his. His grip tightened. "Come, we can have lunch at the Ranch's Clubhouse." He said as if he didn't even notice I'd tried to pull my hand away.

I nodded... "Okay."

Without letting my hand go he turned and guided us in that direction. One of the servers who normally walked around the grounds getting drinks for the guests hurried toward him.

"Can I assist you with anything, senhor." He asked in Portuguese.

I opened my mouth to translate for him, but snapped it shut in surprise when Rome responded to him in full Portuguese.

"Yes, the lady and I would like to have lunch."

The server's eyes brightened. "Si, senhor. Right this way."

He showed us to the Ranch's Clubhouse where the very wealthy ate. I'd never been inside here. It was beautiful.

"Will this table be okay?" He asked Rome, tripping over himself to please him.

Rome chuckled. "Yes, this will do just fine."

"Your waitress will be with you shortly. Can I get you and the senhora another drink?"

Rome looked at his glass that was about a quarter of the way empty. "Sure, I'll have another…" He turned to look at me. "Would you care for anything?"

I shook my head. "No, thank you."

The server bowed to Rome before he hurried away.

"Nossa! You're his favorite person." I said as I eased down in the chair he held out for me.

He chuckled as he took his seat. "It's because I'm a good tipper."

Hmmmm… I bet he is.

"So tell me what's going on?"

He lifted his menu. "Let's order food first, I'm starving."

A beautiful young girl came over to take our order. She had to be no more than nineteen years old. Her eyes drank Rome up. In Brazil, the first thing a young girl learns how to do is spot money. She took in his watch, the diamond stud in his ear, his suit, his shoes…And to top it all off, he was drop-dead gorgeous.

She licked her lips… "How can I help you, senhor?" She purred.

I wonder if I'd get kicked out and banned if I punched her in the nose?

Without looking up from his menu, Rome held out his hand gesturing towards me… "What are you having, *Minha Anjo?*"

When the young twat heard what he'd called me, her insulted gaze came to me. I saw that Rome still looked at his menu and I just couldn't help myself, holding up my menu in front of me so that he couldn't see me, I turned to her and stuck my tongue out at her.

Take that, gold-digger.

She opened her mouth insulted and I pretended not to even notice.

"Ummm, I'll have the tuna steak salad," I said pleasantly before closing my menu and handing it to her.

"And I'll have the double chef burger, well-done with fries." He closed his menu and handed it to her.

However, I didn't notice any of that. I was still stuck on the fact that Rome had just ordered a double burger.

"What the hell has happened to you? Did aliens take over your body?"

He chuckled as he took the drink from the little server that aimed to please him. The little guy had even been nice enough to bring me a water.

"Naw, nothing like that. My woman left me and I lost the will to live."

Nossa!

He said that with a straight face. I blinked at him, waiting for him to say this is a joke. When he didn't and continued to look at me across the table with that intense honey gaze, I grinned.

"This is a joke, right?"

He shook his head. "Nothing funny about this, baby. I've been dying without you. What's the use of eating healthy when I have nothing to live for?"

"You have everything to live for. You do great work in your community. They need you?"

He exhaled. "Yeah well, I won't be doing much of anything since I'm dead."

"What are you talking about?"

He took out his phone and scrolled through it a bit before passing it to me. It was a news article speaking about the tragic death of the Warrens, their son, his future wife, their child that they shared...and his wife's two brothers and mother."

I looked up confused. "What did I miss?"

And then he began to tell me. Nossa! The sh*t had hit the fan when I left. He told me about the stuff he had found out about the Sarge, including the fact that Jo wasn't the only child like we all thought, but one of five siblings. And not only that...a triplet to boot.

The split personality that we all thought was just an undiagnosed mental condition had been done to Jo on purpose. Rome said some crazy doctor had done it to him in some kind of facility when he was a kid.

It was at that point in his story that the waitress had brought our food. Still not believing he was eating meat, I sat with my mouth open as he lifted the burger and took a massive bite.

Oh, Dear God! I broke him!

Pushing my salad to the side I began to eat his fries. I didn't want any of his burger because believe it or not, I haven't eaten any junk food since I left his place. Eating healthy had made me feel close to him.

"What are you doing? Why aren't you eating *your* food?" He asked with a grin on his face.

"I'm not eating that, she probably poisoned it." I didn't bother telling him I'd antagonized the waitress. Damn impulse control...I didn't think till after she'd left from taking our order that I should have waited until after she brought my food to show my a**.

"Do you want me to order you something else?"

I shook my head. "I'm not really that hungry. Anyway, go on...you were saying?"

And he continued to tell me what all had happened. Journey had been shot while she was carrying Ayana, and the Oldman kicked into gear and saved her and the baby.

I shook my head. The Oldman was deadly...many people didn't know that about him, because he came across as your typical lovable pop-pop...but he wasn't, he was a damn weapon, plain and simple.

When Rome found out Journey had been shot, he went to D.C. and he and the Politician linked up to take down Jo's fake parents and the company that was financing them.

"We had thought that was the end of our problems, little did we know that it was just the beginning. Jo's oldest brother...Judah found us." He paused for a minute shaking his head.

"Baby, I ain't never seen nothing like this dude. You know how Jo and his other siblings can mingle with regular humans?"

I nodded. However, I'd never met Jo's other siblings so I had no idea if they could mingle with *regular human,* as Rome said. But the Politician mingled just fine with people. So if they were anything like him, then yeah, I can see that.

"Yeah, well this dude can't. I don't know what they did to him, but he ain't right." He drained his drink and the little waiter that seemed to be at his beck and call had it replaced before he could even set the empty glass down.

"Anyway, he basically admonishes us for waking up a sleeping dragon that wasn't going to stop till us and everybody that knows about it is dead. Get this…While he's telling me this, I find out that my f***ing loft got bombed. It's gone…everything! My f***ing computer…everything!"

I reached across the table and took his hand that was balled in a fist. I know the loss of his computer hurt him. If ever there was a man who loved his tech, Rome is he.

He continued, telling me that nobody got hurt in the bombing, but that in order to keep him and his family safe, they all had to die, but he'd left shortly after that to come to find me and had no clue what was going on now, because he'd not talked to anyone in a while.

"What's going to happen to everything you've set up in Chicago? How will it run without you?"

He exhaled. "Before I flew here, I spent a few days hiding at Hitta's place while I made arrangements. He was the only one I could trust with the knowledge that I was still alive. Everybody else in my crew thinks I'm dead."

He squeezed my hand…this was tough for him. I wanted to get up and hug him…I had to force myself to remain sitting.

"With Hitta's help, I drew up a living will of sorts, giving everybody instructions on how to keep it running as smoothly as possible. Thanks to you…I don't have Saw Buck to worry about."

I blushed as I took a sip of water. I should have known he would have figured out it was me.

"The good thing is because I'd always figured I was going to end up dying early, I'd put people in place who were capable of carrying on what we started." He shrugged shaking his head. "I just pray they can keep it going."

"They will…I told you, you lit a fuse that can't be put out. The only being with the strength to put it out is God, and I doubt he's going to do that because he's the one who caused you to light it in the first place." He brought my hand to his lips and kissed the back of it.

"You have no idea how much I've missed you."

"I—" The words *I missed you too* almost slipped from my lips. I cleared my throat.

"Wow!" I told him instead. "Things have gone a bit haywire, huh?"

He didn't respond at first. The muscle ticked in his jaw as he held me prisoner in that gaze of his.

"Yeah, I guess it has." He finally muttered.

"So, what are you going to do now?" By this time, I was beginning to panic. I didn't know what to do. We'd reached that point in the conversation where he tells me he's come back for me…and I'm just not ready to hear that.

Honestly, I don't know what I want to hear. In a way, I'm thrilled he found me…But at the same time, I promised myself that I will never fall for this again. When I left Chicago, I'd been lost to who I am and who I've come to be.

And it took me a while to get back focused. However, I had not expected to come back here and actually develop a relationship with my mom. Even though it was a fake one since she only liked me because she'd forgotten who I was…Still, for a kid that grew up starved for her mother's affection, it was enough to draw me back in. Her death had hurt…and no matter how much I call myself a fool for caring, I cared.

And now Romeo was back…broken. And just like my mom, he was drawing me back in. I stood from the table, placing my napkin on my salad that still sat untouched. Not because I didn't like it, but because it probably had a wad of teenager spit on top.

"I'm sorry you had to go through all this. You do so much for so many people, you're the last person in the world that deserves this." I put my hand on his big shoulder. "I wish you the best of luck…thanks for lunch." And then I turned and walked away.

I could feel his honey gaze boring into my back as I headed for the door. When I got out of his view I ran for my truck. I needed to get home and I didn't want him following me.

Yeah, I'm sure he's going to find me, but I needed time to think about all the information he'd just given me. My emotions were not in the right place to make any decisions.

I laughed at my own bullsh*t. My emotions had never stood in the way of me making decisions before…that was a bunch of bull…

I ran because I was afraid, plain and simple.

I was afraid of what it meant now that Rome had found me. Before, I had worried that I was not going to be good for him with all the things he had going on, but now he had nothing...and he was here.

Jo and the Oldman were on the run as well; his parents weren't his parents and they were dead. Rome's loft had been bombed.

Nossa! He was right, everything is a mess.

As soon as I walked through the door, Giant ran up barking out his complaints. Poor fella had been at the mercy of Antonio and Pedro, the two guys that were helping me get my stable in order.

And I'm sure they didn't cater to him as I did. When I came home from jail, I had to rush right back out to make arrangements for my mom, giving him very little attention. And now he was letting me have it.

"Oh hush, Giant! I was the one who spent three nights in jail with a pervert..."

Hmmm...speaking of which, I still owed him a little visit. I was going to do the world a favor and exterminate his a**...I'm sure there will be plenty of women who'd fallen victim to his predatory ways that will thank me if they could.

I'd just changed out of the dress I wore into a tank top and cargo pants when I heard the vehicle come to a stop in front of my house.

I grinned down at Giant. "Daddy's home..." I whispered to him before I opened the door and walked out to the porch.

Okay…so you guys already knew I wasn't going to be able to resist him. I didn't have any place else to run. My mom had died, leaving me here all alone. And it's Rome…come on.

He hurt me, so I'm not going to make this easy for him. But in the same instance, I didn't want to die alone like my mom. And the fact that he'd tracked me down and found me meant that he cared for me, right?

I mean…My dad would have never done that for my mom. Hell, he probably wouldn't have even called.

I exhaled as I watched his beautiful form dressed in cream linen unfold from that truck. Maybe I was being a fool…But standing there over my mom's grave had shifted something in me. I didn't want to run from love anymore.

I thought of the words the Preacher had said. He'd said the young prince would find me, and for me to give love another try…

I smiled to myself…Yes, I was going to give it another try, but I wasn't going to let Rome know that. There had to be some kind of repercussions for him hurting my feelings. I wanted to see what he was willing to do for love.

I put my hand on my hip as he approached my porch. "How can I help you? I lost my mother today and I'm not in the mood for company."

He took off his hat and held it in his hands. "I'm so sorry to hear that. I wish I could have been here for you."

"I appreciate your condolences…how can I help you?" I repeated.

Not going to make this easy at all…

"Well, seeing that I am homeless and all. I was hoping you'll give me a job."

I held up an eyebrow. "A job? It doesn't look like you need a job. Plus, I doubt if a pretty boy like you can handle the workload around here. You don't look like the type that gets your hands dirty."

He was trying to hold back a grin. "Oh, I assure you, I can get the job done."

"Well, I'm not hiring."

He inhaled, that perfect mouth of his formed into a grin. "Do I look like the type that's going to beg you?"

I opened my mouth insulted before I turned to head back in the house…but he moved then grabbing me and whipping me around so that I faced him, and then holding me hypnotized with his golden gaze, very slowly went down to his knees on my dirty porch in front of me.

Nossa!

"Please baby, don't put me out. You are my home. I don't know where else to go. If you say that I can't stay here, then I will sleep outside your gate…if you say that I have to move away from your gate then I will sleep out on the road. I can't make it without you, *Minha Anjo* …Please, just…let me stay with you."

Mmm mmm mmm… Y'all don't even know what it's like to have a powerful man like this humble himself in front of me this way. I wanted to jump him and make love to him right here on my front porch. Instead, I folded my arms…

"Fine…You can sleep in the barn. Work starts at five a.m."

Then I turned and escaped behind my door before I did something silly, like give in to him too soon.

That night I tossed and turned in the bed as my body purred for him. He was too close, just a few yards away. I squeezed my thighs together as I thought about the last time he and I made love.

I don't know how many of you have even made love with a genius thug, but his mind doesn't work like regular folks, so I'm more than sure some of the things he'd done to my body was extraordinary.

By the time Giant and I made our way to the barn the next morning, I was cranky because I'd gotten zero sleep…and plus I was hot and bothered. I had a young man with a nice strong back sleeping in my barn, and my pride had kept me away.

Yeah…I don't need you guys to tell me I'm a fool…I already know.

Antonio and Pedro were cutting wood for the pen we were building on the side of the barn, their power tools were loud and annoying. I walked farther into the barn to find Romeo in one of the stalls sitting on a bundle of hay looking scrumptious in a pair of designer jeans, designer gym shoes, and no shirt busy typing away on his laptop.

I cleared my throat. "Is this your idea of hard work?"

He looked up at me with a smile on his handsome face. "Actually, it is."

"Yeah, but that's not what I hired you for." I gestured toward Antonio and Pedro. "That's how we work."

Rome looked over at the workers... "Oh...yeah." He closed his laptop and put on the t-shirt that was sitting on the hay next to him. The fact that his clothes were clean and pressed was amazing.

"Pedro...can you please show Rome here what real work looks like? I have to run into town for a few."

With a grin on his face, Pedro nodded. "Sure thing, senhorita."

"I'll have you know I can do *real work* in my sleep. Sh*t, it ain't rocket science." Rome said chuckling at his own joke.

I held up an eyebrow. Goodness, I've missed my thug. "We'll see...come on, Giant."

I went to walk away, but his arm shot out wrapping around my waist pulling me up against his hot body. I inhaled sharply at the sudden contact.

"Damn girl, give me a f***ing hug and stop tripping." He growled before he wrapped both arms around me nearly lifting me off my feet.

I couldn't deny his request if I tried. My arms as if they had a will of their own wrapped around his neck tightly as I buried my face in his thick beard. For just a moment he blocked out the whole world and encompassed me in a safe cocoon, where nothing can get to me and harm me.

I was in no rush to leave his arms and he was in no rush to release me.

"I missed you so much, shawty." He whispered in my ear before I felt his soft lips on my neck. The spasm that shot through my core right then stole my breath.

His kiss moved to my jaw…but before it could make its way to my lips I broke away, stepping out of his arms. If he kissed my lips it was over.

My face heated when I saw Antonio and Pedro looking at me with little smirks on their faces before turning away as if they were suddenly busy measuring wood.

My gaze went back to Rome's hungry one. "When I get back, I expect to see you hard at work," I told him trying to drive a bit of a wedge between us by reminding him that he was my employee.

A knowing grin came to his face. "You don't have to worry, *Minha Anjo,* I'm going to get the job done…that's a promise."

But it felt like a threat… I scooped Giant up in my arms and hurried to my car. I didn't know how long I was going to be able to hold out. My goal was not to give in too easily, to make him sweat…but it didn't look like I was going to make it. He'd almost got me with just a hug.

I knew what I was going to have to do…I was going to need to put some distance between us. For the next few days, I was going to have to stay away from the barn. That will keep me safe for a little while.

The first stop I made was to the nursing home to pick up all of my mom's belongings. They already had another patient waiting for the room. I thanked Sister Sousa for all her help and reimbursed her the money she'd used to bail me out of jail.

Then I decided to go and visit Mr. Olivera before I left and read to him for a bit. But when I got there the room was empty and the bed was neatly made.

"No…"

I turned to find a nurse… "Com licença…" or "Excuse me, where is Mr. Olivera?"

She took my hand patting it gently. "Oh sweetheart, he died a day before your mom."

I slowly shook my head. "Nossa!" What was happening? I had been so wrapped up in making funeral arrangements for my mom that I didn't even think to check in on Mr. Olivera. I felt like crap.

"I feel so bad…" I said to nobody in particular.

The nurse gave my hand a gentle squeeze. "You shouldn't, you made his last days very pleasant. It was good of you to read to him every day. He died happy. And it's all because of you. We can't control death…but we can try to do for people while they're alive. You made a difference in his world. Now go out there and help somebody else."

I felt numb as I left the nursing home. A reason, a season and a day. Mr. Olivera came in my life for a reason. I touched the small Bible that was in my cargo pants. But it seemed like I'd only had him for a day.

Goodness! It felt like my world was tilting on the edge. And if I'm being honest with myself, I was so glad Romeo was here with me. All this time, I'd convinced myself that I wanted to be alone secluded on my farm cut off from the world.

But that's not what I wanted at all. I didn't want to be alone. I didn't want to die and nobody comes to my funeral. Mr. Olivera, like my mom, had pretty much died alone. The only person they'd both had in their last days was me.

And although my mom still hated me in her right mind, I was glad I decided to come back to the nursing home and be with her these last few months. It almost felt like she'd waited for me before dying.

I inhaled... Now I needed to do something else. Rome was my season...he is the one that was made to be in my life. He had traveled a long way to find me. And he'd come back to me broken...and it was my fault.

Now I needed to fix him.

The first thing we needed to do was to get him back eating right. After I left Chicago I had not gone back to my horrible diet. I'd continued eating the way Rome had shown me. And now I needed to guide him back to the path.

I stopped by the market and bought some live foods. How many times had he given me the live food speech?

"Baby, eat foods that are alive and they will give you life. Eat foods that are dead and they will bring you death."

I'd gotten so tired of hearing him say that, I'd threatened to shoot him if he said it again. Of course, he did anyway.

Tonight, I will make him a feast of live foods...

When I finally got back to the house, I sat staring at it with my mouth open. There were several trucks parked around it and a whole crew of men in and out of the trucks. I picked Giant up in my arms so that he didn't get stepped on and made my way to the barn.

When I got there, I found Rome standing over a makeshift table looking over some blueprints with another man, who looked as if he was the boss of this crew.

"What the hell is going on here?!"

Rome looked up and smiled. "Baye, you were right. I didn't care for getting my hands dirty. However, my friend here doesn't mind at all. Meet Francisco, he and his crew are going to build you a brand-new barn.

Chapter 19

Tension...

Nakhti

With a perfect arch in my back, I bent over to pull the spinach lasagna I'd made for dinner out the oven right as Rome came in carrying his bags.

Had I timed it this way? Maybe...

"Dear God!" He called clutching his chest, I heard him stumble back in the door a bit. Biting my lip so that my smile didn't escape, I slowly stood placing the lasagna on the stove.

I had started going through me, my mom and my avozinha's things trying to clear out the house a bit. And I had found a bunch of my clothes from high school, including an old pair of my gym shorts. When I used to wear these things in gym, the boys and the gym teacher could barely focus on anything other than my hips.

"There you go wearing them little bitty a** shorts again!" Rome growled as he came farther into the house.

Making sure to keep that little arch in my back that causes my hips and butt to poke out just right...

Come on, ladies, y'all know the one...

I turned to look at him with feigned surprise on my face, now poking out my breasts that were braless under my tank top.

"I don't know what you're talking about. It's hot outside, I was just dressing for the weather."

What a load of bull...

He dropped his bags. "Nak...I swear to God, if you wear that outside, I will put you over my knee and spank yo' a**."

That he said while grabbing himself readjusting his erection in that vulgar way that he does.

Goodness, I've missed that.

I threw my head back and laughed. "Don't be jealous, Romeo."

The frown was still on his face. "Yeah, I got yo' don't be jealous...you gon' keep f***ing with me and get somebody killed. Where should I put my stuff?"

The sneaky bastard!

You should be putting your stuff in the barn. But thanks to the construction crew that had taken a wrecking ball to my barn, his sneaky a** was now a guest on my couch, which was why I was torturing him.

Two can play at this...

"You can use the hall closet," I told him pointing to the third door on the left before I turned back to the sink to rinse off the tomatoes for the salad...careful to keep that arch in my back.

I didn't hear him move for a good minute; I could feel his gaze raking over my butt as if it was a caress. I damn near closed my eyes and moaned thinking about his big strong hands palming my soft flesh.

When he finally did move, he mumbled something about me getting in trouble playing with grown men.

Screw him!

He thinks he's so damn slick. Let me tell you guys what he did…

My house only has two bedrooms, the one I slept in that used to belong to my mother and my avozinha before her and my old bedroom that was being used for storage. It was safe to say my place wasn't that big.

Which is why I told him if he was going to be staying here, he needed to sleep in the barn. Him being in the house was way too dangerous. But nooooo…. Guess who had found a way in anyway. And believe me, I'd put up a fuss, including telling the workers to stop because I couldn't afford them.

"We've already been paid for the job, senhorita. Excuse me." Francisco replied as he walked around me to start instructing his men on the destruction of my barn.

I turned angry eyes back to Rome's face and there lurking was a knowing grin.

"Romeo, what are you doing? I can't afford this!"

"Did you not hear the man say he's already been paid? Watch out…" He said taking my arm moving me to the side just as a man rode past me on a forklift.

It was all too much…I shook my head trying to find something to grab onto that will make this stop.

"What about Pedro and Antonio? I'd already hired them for the job. This is going to put them out of work and they have to feed their families."

Rome took my arm again moving me out the way of another forklift. "Already handled. I talked to Francisco and got the fellas on with him. They now work for him making triple of what you were paying them…" He turned those clever honey eyes of his to me.

"So, you see, you're helping them and their families out tremendously. In fact, they were so overcome with emotion, I believe Pedro actually shed a tear. He said something about now being able to send his daughter to music school." And then he smiled, knowing damn well he had me.

I wanted to call him a liar. However, Pedro constantly bragged on how talented his daughter was and how he and his wife were saving every penny to send her to music school so that she could learn her art. They believed she could go all the way.

My gaze went to Pedro, who sure enough had an extra pep in his step as he helped unload one of the trucks before it settled back on Rome's handsome smiling face.

The clever bastard had boxed me in. I didn't doubt he'd planned this to the tee. That's how his mind worked.

And so, you guys are saying, what's the big deal, Nak?

Well, the big deal is this… I was trying to hold out as long as I could and not give in to him too soon.

If I gave in to him now, he would think it was okay to break my heart whenever he feels like it. I had to hold out for a good while…I had to make him sweat, make him feel as if he wasn't going to get me back.

And I know some of y'all out there believe I am playing games, especially dressed the way that I am right now.

Maybe I am, but like I said earlier, there must be some repercussions for what he did. And since I don't have the strength to run away from him again, the least I can do is make him sweat a bit.

Something that would have been easily done if the sneaky bastard had not found a way to get into my house.

He wasn't playing fair.

Rome

Hell no, I wasn't playing fair. I was playing to win.

I was well aware of the little game she called herself playing by putting me in the mutha f***en' barn. What the f*** I look like? Nah, there will be no barriers between us. Yesterday when I'd found her, I'd accepted that sh*t because I was tired from searching for her nonstop. My mind needed a good night's rest, something I definitely blame on my diet. Before I started eating this crappy food, my mind never got tired. No...not ever.

Hell, most times I couldn't turn it off...

Anyway, I digress... the answer to my problem came to me as soon as I opened my eyes. How the hell could she make me sleep in the barn if there was no barn? When she'd found me this morning working on my computer, I was in the midst of making arrangements with Francisco. I'd even paid extra to get him to leave the project he was working on to get started on the barn himself.

I told him it was imperative for it to be demolished before nightfall…As you can guess, that came with a hefty price tag, but I didn't care. There was no price I was not willing to pay to be back between *Minha Anjo's* thighs. I was starved for the taste of her.

Now that I was in, it was only a matter of time. I stashed my bags in the hall closet as she said, but by week's end, I plan to have them moved to her bedroom closet.

When I came back into the kitchen, I paused for just a moment to take her in. She'd worn those little bitty shorts that hugged her lush a** perfectly on purpose. Knowing her, she probably called herself paying me back for getting her barn demolished.

I repositioned my erection for the second time because it was pressing painfully against my zipper.

Damn! She was finer than a mutha f***a. She'd partnered those little shorts with a white wife beater that she wore with no bra, so every time she moved, her pretty breasts jiggled in a way that made my mouth water.

Nak's body was banging. Because she was a warrior and was damn serious about her work out, it was beautifully muscled. But because she was all woman, she also had those curves that drove a man to distraction.

She stood barefoot at the sink cutting lettuce, her curly hair rolled up in a bun on the top of her head. A few soft tendrils escaped laying against her long graceful neck that my lips longed to kiss. She looked soft and sweet, till your gaze fell to her sleeve of art and the dog tags around her neck, and then you'll realize she was really a bad a**.

You know what she reminded me of? That character from Shrek…the pussy cat. I think his name was Puss in Boots or some sh*t like that. She was sweet as f*** at a distance, but as soon as you got within reach of those claws, it's been one, she was going to f*** you up.

Speaking of her f***ing some sh*t up…I may have left a few things out of our conversation yesterday, like the fact that she and I were now both employed by Joseph's older brother, Judah and some branch of the government that I have yet to figure out.

She was not going to like that; she'd told me a hundred times how much she was looking forward to retiring. At some point, I was going to have to tell her what the man with no shoes said about her.

She was born to be a warrior. She didn't know it, but that's why she always got in trouble. She wanted to live a civilian life, but it wasn't in her to do so. She just wasn't wired that way.

Silently, I approached as she stood at the sink and wrapped my arms around her waist pulling her back against me.

Dear God, that felt so good. As I searched for her, I'd been worried to death. Like I said, my little thug misses had a tendency to get into trouble. All kinds of scenarios went through my head about what could have happened to her.

She stiffened when she felt my arms around her and that sh*t hurt. She used to melt in my arms. I didn't like this…

I didn't like the fact that it didn't seem as if she needed me the way I needed her.

"Mmmm, something smells good," I told her before I moved her hair to the side and gently kissed her neck.

The way she sucked in her breath before a little moan escaped her throat told a different story. Maybe she *did* need me as much as I needed her and she was just playing hard to get.

Women…

Nahkti

Be strong, Nak!

Even though his soft lips on my neck felt so damn good and made other parts of me come awake wanting to feel his lips as well, I slid out of his arms. But as I did it, I made sure to rub my supple behind against his erection that he shamelessly pressed against me.

A groan left his lips.

"Uh oh…I'm sorry about that," I told him as I picked up the lasagna and took it to the table.

He chuckled with that knowing grin on his face as he sat at the table. "Yeah, I just bet you are."

Once I got the food situated on the table, I slid in the chair across from him and watched as he looked around for more food.

I had to bite my jaw not to laugh. "What's the matter? What are you looking for?"

"Where is the meat?"

I shook my head. "We don't eat meat, sweetheart, we're vegetarians."

His surprised gaze came back to me…

Damn! This man was fine…

"Since when were you a vegetarian? You just ordered tuna steak salad at the Ranch."

Hmmm… I did, didn't I?

I held my head up and shrugged… "Since today." Me going vegetarian was a small price to pay to get him eating healthy again.

He arched a doubting eyebrow at me and reached for the knife to cut the lasagna and for some reason, I embodied his mom and popped his hand.

"We say grace around these parts before we eat our food."

He chuckled. "Since when? You're a little savage heathen."

My mouth opened insulted. "I am not." I stood from the table and went to the room for my little Bible, then I came and plopped it on the table in front of him.

"You're not the only one that has been studying, Mr…" I opened it to show him my highlights and notes. "Look, I've even taken notes." I was very proud of myself.

He stared at it for a minute, the amusement left his face. "Nak…I have to tell you something."

I shook my head, I was on a roll. "Not before we pray."

Closing my eyes, I bowed my head. "Dear Heavenly Father," I said repeating after Rome's mom. "We come before you today to give thanks."

I spent a good while giving thanks in my prayer because although I thought my life was so bad, it wasn't. God has been good to me; I was just too blind to see it. I thanked him for bringing Rome, his family, Jo, and the Oldman out of that situation safely. I've seen enough carnage in the field to know that could have gone much different. They all could be dead right now and I wouldn't have known because I'd ran away to Brazil to have a pity party.

"And finally, Father, I'd like to thank you for allowing my life to settle down in peace…it feels good. All these things we pray in the name of your son, Yahusha HaMashiach …Selah."

Something else I got from Rome's mom.

When I opened my eyes, Rome was looking at me in wonder. "You spoke Hebrew."

With a huge grin on my face, because I felt like a million bucks, I nodded. Instead of telling him the truth, that I got that from his mom, I decided to nail the fact that I was not a heathen in his face.

"Yeah, well, that all comes with studying the Bible, right?" I said nonchalantly.

And then before he could ask any more questions that I surely didn't have the answers to, I cut the spinach lasagna.

"Oh…what did you have to tell me?"

He thought for a moment before he shook his head. "Nothing… just that it feels good to be eating healthy again. I'm really glad we're here."

I didn't know if *here* meant sitting at the dinner table or us being at this point in our relationship, but I was really glad we were here too.

After dinner, Rome helped me clean the kitchen and somehow managed to accidentally rub against me and bump into me so that he had to wrap his arm around my waist to catch me many times.

"Nossa! You've turned into a bit of a klutz since that last time I saw you." I admonished when I turned away from putting the lasagna into the fridge only to run into him from where he just so happened to be walking behind me for some strange reason.

Once again, he wrapped his strong arms around me, pulling me against his body. "Me a klutz? It's *you* that keep running into *me*."

He leaned down burying his face in my neck, putting me in the mind of that skunk on the Looney Tunes, who was always after that poor black cat that managed to get a white stripe on her back every episode. I wouldn't be surprised if Rome opened his mouth and started speaking French.

Be strong, Nak!

Before he could open his warm mouth on my flesh, I slid out of his arms turning to face him with my hand on my hip.

"Listen, brotha! The only reason you are here is because you refuse to leave. I don't like you anymore, so keep your damn hands to yourself!"

With a smirk on his face that said he wasn't buying my little speech, he put one of his big hands on his chest. "You don't like me no more?"

I had to bite my lip to keep from grinning when those honey gazers of his turned into puppy dog eyes as I shook my head.

"No, I don't…so stop touching me." I pointed at him. "Don't think I don't know what you're doing. You're trying to get me into bed with you…but that's not going to happen."

"It's not going to happen?" The tone in his voice said he didn't believe me.

I shook my head. "I can assure you, it's not going to happen."

He lifted an eyebrow. "Is that a challenge?"

Oh damn…

And although I knew he was going to make me eat my words, I said them anyway.

"Naw, bro…that's not a challenge. It's a promise."

Soooooo….

Yeah….

By the end of the week, he'd gotten me…

And just let me tell y'all, I put up a really good fight, but he played dirty.

That night after dinner, I'd given him some bed linen and a pillow and pointed to my avozinha's couch and told him good night.

He made a sound of protest as he stood frowning at the plastic covered antique looking like a little boy.

"How you gon' put me on the plastic couch? You know that sh*t is going to be all hot and sticky and then at some point, I'm going to probably slide off and hit my damn head on that antique gold spray painted metal table leg and knock myself unconscious."

I giggled… "Are you roasting my grandmother's furniture?"

"Come on, baye...what year did she buy this, the forties?"

I put my hand on my hip... "My avozinha was very proud of her furniture when she got it."

So much so, she'd left the plastic the couch came in from the manufacturer on it. My mom said my avozinha told her she did that so that no one would put stains on her new sofa. I don't know why, but after my avozinha died, my mom never removed the plastic that had long turned a brownish color in age.

And yeah, Rome was right, I used to hate sitting on that couch when I was little. The plastic always stuck to my leg and if you fell asleep on it, at some point, you did slide off it and wake up on the floor.

But since this was another form of punishment for hurting my feelings, I didn't feel bad.

"You'll be alright, I'll crank up the air conditioner for you."

After I turned up the window unit I'd bought for this room when I'd gotten back, I wished him good night and left him standing there frowning after me.

That night, I had to cover my mouth so that he wouldn't hear me laughing at him. That plastic crinkled all night as he tossed and turned...At some point, I heard him angrily get up and make himself a pallet on the floor while grumbling that he should come in here and kick me out of my comfortable bed and put me on this plastic mutha f***a. His words... Seconds later, I heard him typing away on his laptop.

However, the next night, it was *me* lying in the bed hot and bothered. That damn Rome had tortured me all day. That morning, he'd walked in the bathroom right as I'd gotten out of the shower in only a pair of boxers.

Had he timed it that way? Maybe…

I screeched and reached for the towel to cover myself…

"Oh! My fault, I didn't know you were in here." He lied as he stood there shamelessly staring at me. The bulge in his boxer shorts grew big right before my eyes. He grabbed it, only pretending to try and tame it.

"That's my fault too, my man hungry…" His sexy gaze slowly raked up my body, making me feel hot all over. "It's been a long time since he's eaten, he's f***ing starving."

Damn it!!!

I cleared my throat. "Are you talking about your private area in third person?"

Still standing there shamelessly holding himself, he slowly nodded with that sexy grin on his face.

I bit my lip…this joker was too fine for his own good.

Okay…so I managed to get out of that situation without giving in and feeding his "*Man*".

But then, he came upon me later to find me rubbing my lower back. Since the barn was being taken care of without me, I'd decided to continue going through all the junk that was stored in my old room.

Some stuff I will give away, some stuff needed to go right to the trash, and some stuff I was going to keep, like my avozinha's beautiful yellow dress that she called her happy dress. When I was a little girl, she used to tell me how she'd worn the dress when she was younger whenever she felt joyously happy.

She'd said back in those days her waist was very small, by the time I was born, she hadn't been able to wear it in years. But she refused to give it to my mother, who'd asked to wear the dress often. My grandmother said she couldn't have it because my mother was miserable, and she didn't want her spirit to drain the allure of the dress…My avozinha's words.

I didn't know why, but after my grandmother died, my mother never tried to wear the dress…it just hung in the back of my closet, where it's been for my whole life. Maybe she'd forgotten it was there.

Whatever the reason, I'm glad she didn't wear it either, because I would have never been able to look at it and see it how my grandmother saw it if she had…

Anyway, I'd been going through all that stuff and my back got stiff, so I was rubbing it when Rome came in to ask me something about the horse stalls in the barn. However, when he saw me rubbing my back, his attention shifted instantly.

"What's the matter, *Minha Anjo?* Do you have a sore back? Come here, let me help you with that…" He grabbed my hand and pulled me out of the storage room to my bedroom across the hall.

"I think I'll be alright," I told him, only half-heartily trying to pull away from him.

"Naw, baye…I don't want your back sore. I give really good massages."

I lifted an eyebrow. "Really?"

He chuckled… "Really…"

And then before I knew what was happening, he had my shirt up and over my head.

"What are you doing?" I cried crossing my arms over my bra covered breasts.

"I can't give you a good massage with that shirt in the way…here, lay down across the bed."

Everything in me said I should have protested…but my back was *really tense*. And come on, what girl doesn't like a good massage? So yeah, I laid across the bed.

He grabbed my body butter off my dresser before joining me…

Oh, my goodness!!!

He wasn't lying, he gave really good massages. At some point, he unsnapped my bra, but by that time he had me so languid, I didn't care.

"Your skin is so soft, shawty." His deep voice was drugging.

I moaned when he dug deep, forcing all the tension out of my back…Leave it to the genius to actually be good at this…

"I missed touching you," he whispered right before I felt his warm mouth on my back. I inhaled sharply as a spasm ripped through my center.

"I missed kissing you."

He took his time and adored me with his mouth… "But tasting you is what I missed the most."

I had to squeeze my thighs together to sooth the ache there.

At some point, I ended up on my back and his warm mouth was drawing the peak of my breast between his lips while his hands were busy caressing other parts of me that now hungered for him.

Closing my eyes, I lifted my arms above my head giving myself to him. I was lost, he'd successfully cast a spell on me. I didn't care that I was caving too soon, the only thing I wanted him to do was sooth away the pain that was building in my core…

I needed him to release the pressure…

But right before that happened, I mean, seconds before my world shattered, the screen door opened and closed.

"Senhor Rome, are you here?" Francisco's voice called from the living room.

I wanted to yell for him to get lost…but he'd cut through my desire enough for me to get a hold of myself and push Rome off me.

So okay…through no will of my own, I managed to escape that situation without giving him what he wanted, but it left me lying in bed that night miserable. It was *me* that tossed and turned, needing him to finish what he started.

Then the bastard had the nerve to stick his head in my bedroom door after he'd come out of the bathroom and tease me.

"You alright in here? You're doing a lot of tossing and turning…" His gaze raked up my legs to settle on my center. I'd long kicked the covers off and now just lay in bed in a tank top and a pair of panties.

And no, I didn't try and cover myself.

He slowly licked his lips as his eyes devoured the spot that ached for him the most…At the same time, he reached down and grabbed his growing erection through his boxer briefs.

Nossa! Give me strength…

"Is there something I can do for you?" He paused for just a moment. "You know, to help you sleep better?"

Yes, there is...you can come in here and finish what you started earlier! You can put out this fire you kindled, you young bastard!

But to him, although it almost killed me, I said...

"Naw, I'm good. The air-conditioning unit in here is not working that well. I need to get it replaced."

"You sure? Because I can help you cool down."

I just bet you can...

"Naw...I'm good. Night, night..." The last of that I said in a moan.

Needless to say, the rest of the week didn't get any better, but by Friday, my lady parts were no longer listening to me.

There was a strong, virile, young, robust male determined to devour her. And she needed to give him what he wanted.

Great! Now, I was talking about my private parts in third person...

Chapter 20

Nahkti Smiles...

The Real Power of a Man is in the Size of the Smile of the Woman
Next to Him...

--Sweety Text Messages

Nahkti

Alright y'all, listen close and I'll tell you how Mr. Man eased his way past my barriers and in between my thighs. As a matter of fact, no...I take that back.

Let me tell you how Mr. Man got me to jump him and rip his clothes off his body...after promising myself I was going to hold out as long as I possibly could. Yeah, that's more like what really happened.

That Friday morning, I had laid in bed thinking how Rome being here had taken my mind off my mom's death and the conflict that was going on within me about my grief and lack of grief...if that makes any sense. He had served as a beautiful distraction.

So, I'd gotten up that morning and made him a nice breakfast to say thank you. And since it looked like he was going to be staying here, I'd decided to give him my old bedroom now that it was cleaned out because, in just a short time, he'd turned my little living room into a full-blown computer lab.

He was back to not sleeping as well. I heard him up all night typing away on that computer. I came out of my room at about 3:00 in the morning to go to the bathroom and there he sat on the couch with his glasses on enthralled in whatever he was looking at on his computer. He was so enthralled that he didn't even look up when I passed.

Nossa!

I didn't even know where he was getting the equipment, it wasn't like Ribeirão da Ilha was full of Best Buys or something. Now granted it was nothing compared to his set up in Chicago…but still very impressive.

Anyway, I made buckwheat pancakes with spinach and cheese eggs for breakfast. He once told me that buckwheat pancakes were his favorite thing to eat in the morning. When he came in from his run, I was sitting at the table sipping coffee waiting for him.

"Mmm, that smells good. Give me a sec, let me jump in the shower really quick," he said as he came in and bent down kissing me on the cheek, something he'd taken to doing in the mornings.

In fact, if I was being honest with myself, I've begun to wait on that kiss to start my day, just like I had been doing sitting at that the table sipping my coffee…

Waiting on that kiss…

When he came out of the shower, he only wore a pair of black sweatpants…and nothing else.

And I do mean…NOTHING ELSE!!!

That should have been my first clue that there will be an all-out attack against my barriers today. Well…

That and for the first time all week, my place was empty and not swarmed with workers. Amazingly, they had finished the barn. When I had expressed my surprise to Francisco that they had done it so quickly, he had waved it away.

"A barn is nothing, senhorita…it's like a vacation for my crew. We are used to building skyscrapers."

As you all can guess, like Rome, Francisco didn't have a humble bone in his body. However, he was good at what he did. The barn was beautiful, way bigger and better than I expected. It looked like something you would find at the Winston Stables. I loved it! I mean I reaaallllyy loved it!

I spent all day yesterday looking around it and just staring at it amazed. Heck, I would have slept in it had Rome not picked me up and carried me to my bed.

He and I laid on a bale of hay looking up at the stars as I told him all about my plans of finding an affordable stallion and mare to try and breed them. I told him how in about ten years or so I'd hoped to produce a horse that was even a tenth as majestic as the Winston horses.

I talked to him so long that I'd nodded off on his big shoulder, only slightly coming awake as he carried me to my bed.

Another reason I made breakfast for Mr. Man. I love the way he takes care of things that I really don't know at first is stressing me out and just fixes it. He doesn't have to be told to do it…he just does it.

This whole week was so breezy. It was the first week since I've been home where I was practically worry-free. He took his rental car back and came back with a brand-new Ford Pick Up truck. It wasn't as nice as the King Rancher he'd left in Chicago, but it was a hell of a lot better than my truck.

For the last month, I've been trying to talk myself into getting something better, I was just too cheap to justify spending the extra money. Not Rome, he drove Big Red…what he'd taken to calling my truck, one time. And that was all it took; he went out and got us a better truck.

He got central air installed so that I didn't have to keep fighting with the window units. He got the old windows that he said was not energy sufficient replaced with new ones. He even set up Wi-Fi that I suspect was more a treat for him than me. But when I worried that it will put us back on the grid, he gave me a look that said…*Please! Have you forgotten who you're dealing with?*

LOL! As humbled as ever.

Anyhow…What was I saying at first?

Oh yes, so he came out of the bathroom with just those sweatpants on… and let me tell you, it took everything I had in me not to stare at the imprint of his *"Man"*.

"These are so good. How did you know buckwheat pancakes were my favorite?" He asked as he helped himself to seconds.

I grinned. "Because you told me."

He frowned… "When?"

"A long time ago…I just remembered."

For a moment he just stared at me, one side of his mouth lifted in a grin. Then he nodded approvingly. "That's cool, Nak."

I know…

After he'd eaten three helpings of pancakes, he sat back in his chair rubbing his belly, that was still nicely ripped...

"Damn... I'm so full I don't feel like getting up to feed the horses."

At the time I had been washing the last of the breakfast dishes. I frowned as I turned to him. I think the pancakes may have warped his brain.

"What horses, crazy man? We don't have any horses yet."

With a little devious smile on his face he shrugged...before he got up and without even putting shoes on headed out the door.

"Where are you going?" I yelled after him.

"To feed the horses!" He yelled back.

What the world...

Now more than curious, I picked up Giant and followed behind him. Since he didn't bother to put on shoes, I didn't either.

What was he talking about hors—

Right then, a loud neigh rent the air.

"Oh my God!" I cried putting Giant on the ground before I took off at a run. I heard him chuckle as I flew past him.

"Freedom!" I cried before I leaped the railing where he was being housed and threw my arms around his neck.

"Freedom...my golden boy, what are you doing here? I missed you so much!"

My hands shook as I vigorously rubbed his mane...He touched his big head to mine, telling me that he'd missed me too.

Without letting him go, I turned to look at Rome as he and Giant made their way into the barn. There was a huge smile on my face. I don't know how he got Juan to let Freedom come and visit me, but I was eternally grateful.

"How did you get Juan to let him out of his stables?"

He frowned. "I bought him."

My mouth hit the floor. I'm not joking...

I turned to face him completely and I know I was looking really special with my mouth hanging open like this, but I didn't care. Freedom, upset that he'd lost my attention that quickly, butted my shoulder with his head.

"What did you just say?" I asked when I could find my voice.

He chuckled... "I—bought—him..."

Freedom danced back out of the way when my scream filled the barn. I started jumping up and down like a little girl screaming my head off...

"Oh My God!!!!!" I yelled...

Another neigh came from one of the back stalls...

My scream died down as I whipped around to face that way... "What's that, Romeo?"

He chuckled again... "I don't know, baby. It sounds like another horse..."

"Oh My God! Oh My God!" I took off toward the back stalls and there right before my eyes were the most beautiful black mare I'd ever seen. I knew Winston horses... This mare was one of his top of the line...

This was one of his most expensive horses.

Nossa! I was going to faint!

"Her name is Luna. I told old Juan that my girl wanted to start breeding horses. So, I asked him what mare would be the best to breed with my buddy Freedom up there. And he asked me how much I was willing to spend. I told him, for my girl… price is not an issue—"

He didn't even get a chance to finish before I was in his arms, planting kisses all over his face. Now that act started off really innocent. Just a girl so very happy that she wanted to thank the person that made her happy with a few kisses.

But then…

His big hands cupped my soft butt and pressed my center against his…Now, remember what he was wearing and what he *was not* wearing. When my lips landed on his bearded cheek, he turned his head suddenly capturing my mouth with his. And well…

That turned my innocent little kisses to something not so innocent. I moaned as he ravished my mouth, the only thing I could do was wrap my arms around his neck and hold on. He was so hungry.

"Damn, baby…I missed you so much!" He whispered fervently as if to confirm my thoughts.

"I missed you too, Romeo…" I moaned completely giving myself to him. I was so ready for him my insides were vibrating.

I inhaled when my back touched the bale of hay that we laid on last night.

Nossa! I hadn't even noticed that he'd carried me back to the front of the barn, so urgent was our need for each other.

He and I both went to work on my clothes.

Dammit! Why did I have on so many? The one day I chose to wear jeans.

Once my heat was exposed to him, like a man possessed, he focused solely on it, going to his knees in front of me.

"You have no idea how many nights I craved your taste." He whispered as he lowered his head.

I closed my eyes as pleasure took over my body, it wasn't long before my moans echoed throughout the barn and wasn't long after that before my moans turned into screams as my world shattered.

He moved over me, but right then, I did a Jui Jitsu roll catching him off guard and flipping him so that he was on the bottom and I straddled him. He looked up at me with a startled grin on his handsome face.

I looked down at him with my lids lowered in desire.

"It's my turn…let me taste you." I whispered as I pushed him down to lie on the hay.

"Sh*t…your wish is my command." He muttered lifting his muscled arms to put his hands behind his head.

Mr. Man is so cool…

Mmmhhhmmm… let's see how long he keeps that pose.

I took my time and kissed my way down his body, showing him how much I adored him and appreciated him. By the time I'd gotten to his lower belly, his cool pose was shot.

He had his fists balled up in my hair and this time it was *his* moans that filled the stable. But it wasn't long before his moans turned into curse words as his fists tightened in my hair, my mouth bringing the thug out of him.

With eyes glazed over with passion, he pulled me up to straddle his lap. "I need to be inside you…"

As he filled me, our moans combined to make a melody so sweet to my ears I'll never forget it…

No…not ever.

****

"Baye, wake up…"

I moaned, snuggling deeper into Rome's side. He chuckled. "Nak, wake up…I still need to feed the horses."

"No…" I muttered as I buried my face in that spot between his chin and shoulder, burying it in his soft beard.

My whole body was deliciously sore. Rome and I had made love three times before I'd passed out in pure exhaustion. However, that was just an hour ago, not nearly enough time for me to have regained my energy.

"How about I feed the horses and you get dressed in something really pretty so that we can go to Rio for the weekend. It's Carniva—"

He didn't have to finish before I popped right up.

"We're going to Rio?!" I asked sounding like a little kid whose parents had just told them they were on their way to Disneyland.

But can you blame me? Carnival to Rio was like Mardi Gras to New Orleans. Yeah, Mardi Gras was probably kept in other parts of Louisiana, but it was nothing like Mardi Gras in New Orleans.

He grinned at me shaking his head. "If you're up to it…I have a place that I use whenever I'm there."

I lifted an eyebrow. "Do you go to Rio often?"

This would explain so many things, like why he could speak Portuguese like one of the locals.

He shrugged. "I'm a student at Gracie Barra."

"What?!"

Nossa! That's like the best Jiu-Jitsu school in the whole world. No wonder he beat me. Growing up, I'd dreamed of being a student at Gracie Barra.

"For how long?" I asked amazed.

He scratched his beard. "Sh*t…A little over ten years."

"Oh my God!" I screamed down at him punching him in the stomach.

He grunted as he balled up laughing at me. I folded my arms and pouted like a little girl.

"I am so freaking jealous of you right now."

He reached up wrapping his arm around my neck pulling me down in a gentle headlock.

"Damn, I missed yo' savage a**!"

I laughed before lifting my head to kiss his lips. "I missed my thug too."

He softly rubbed my cheek with his finger, his honey gaze holding me enthralled.

"Did you?"

I nodded. "Yeah…I did."

He lifted me so that our lips touched again. "Go on and get dressed. Put on something pretty, let's go to Carnival."

Excitedly, I jumped up from the bale of hay, the only time I ever went to Carnival had been when I was a small girl. My mom had gone because she'd heard my father would be stationed there during that time.

I vaguely remember her crying and yelling at my father. What stood out in my memory were the beautiful women in the colorful outfits. They looked like peacocks. I also remember the floats. I've always wanted to go back as an adult, but have just been too busy till now.

I bent down and scooped Giant up who was snoozing on my clothes. I slid my arms into my shirt not bothering to button it up before stepping into my panties. I turned to head into the house…but then a thought came to me. I turned back to face Rome with a frown on my face.

"We can't go to Rio for the weekend. Who's going to look after the horses?"

He still lay on the bale of hay with one arm behind his head, letting his hungry eyes roam down my body as if we had not just made love three times.

"There you go worrying about something you don't need to worry about. What did I tell you to do?"

He spoke in a lazy drawl, like a man who was well satisfied.

"You told me to go get dressed so that we can go to Rio."

"Simple...yet you are having trouble following those few orders. Now I understand what my man Jo went through."

I held my head back and laughed... "Oh, now he's your man? And for your information, I made the perfect soldier..."

"Sh*****t...you put that man through hell."

"Fine...Romeo! I'm going to go and get dressed..." I pointed at him. "But you better make sure nothing happens to my babies."

He held up his hands... "I got this..."

And I believed him...

Even though I was sore all over, I damned near skipped into the house. I was so happy...

I couldn't believe I was this happy. Just last week, I felt like my world was ending. What a difference a day can make.

After I showered, I went to my closet to look for something to wear. I really didn't have any nice clothes, I'd left damn near all the things Rome had bought me in Chicago, only taking a few items I couldn't do without, like my perfume.

Now I wish I had of at least grabbed a few things...

Hmmm...

An idea came to me and my feet were moving before it could even finish forming in my brain.

My avozinha's yellow dress.

Although old, it was the perfect dress for Carnival. It was too dressy to just wear to let's say, dinner...

But to Carnival...

It will fit right in. The top of the dress fell off both shoulders, so I wouldn't be able to wear a bra, but what I liked about the long bottom is although the dress would fall to lay sleekly on my body, there were several layers of soft material. The slightest breeze would cause it to float behind me like yellow smoke.

I pulled it from the back of the closet and removed the plastic. For once, my grandmother's habit of wrapping her valuables in plastic came in handy because the dress was spotless.

For a moment, I just took it in, seeing the allure of it. My avozinha thought the dress had magical powers or something. And you know...

I believed her.

I took my time and dressed, carefully arranging my hair in a messy bun on top of my head, letting several curls artfully escape.

I put on a pair of my avo's pearl earrings and wrapped her long pearl necklace twice around my neck.

Because it was Carnival, I will totally get away with strapping my superhero bat to my back. In fact, the sheath Rome had gotten made for me had a few specks of yellow in it, so that was perfect.

Since my dress was long and fell to the ground, I slid my feet in my combat boots…

Nobody will even notice, might as well be comfortable.

After I was dressed, I threw a few items in the bag Rome got for me in Chicago…making sure to pack my Bible and then I gave myself one last look in the mirror. I was ready!

By the time Giant and I made our way out of the house, Rome was dressed in another linen suit. This one tan…

Damn, he looked good in a suit…who knew?

It looked as if it had been made for him because it lay on his tall, athletic body perfectly, showing a physique that made Michelangelo's David pale in comparison. He was talking to a young fella that looked vaguely familiar.

I frowned…Was that the stable boy that took care of Freedom at Winston's?

The kid looked at me walking toward him and his eyes widened. Rome followed his gaze and looked away, but then his head whipped back to face me again.

I had to bite my lip to keep from grinning when both he and the kid stood staring at me as if I was a piece of meat. Rome got himself together first, when his gaze went back to the young fella and saw him still staring, he popped him upside his head.

"Hey! That's my lady you're slobbering over!" He told him in Portuguese.

The poor kid turned red in the face and tripped over himself apologizing. "Sorry, senhor! Please...I'm so sorry!"

"Yeah...don't let that sh*t happen again. Now, do you understand your instructions for the weekend?"

The kid nodded. "Yes, senhor..." He turned to face me, but Rome growled and he quickly turned away.

"Don't worry, senhorita...I took care of both Luna and Freedom at the Winston Stables. I will protect them with my life."

I chuckled... "Thank you...what is your name again?"

He took off his hat and it looked like he was going to look at me but thought about it and kept his gaze lowered.

"Carlos, senhorita."

"Okay, Carlos, take care of my babies while I'm gone."

"I will, senhorita...I will!"

"You stole Juan's stable boy?" I asked Rome as he helped me in the truck.

He chuckled. "That joker wasn't cheap either. Apparently, everybody who's anybody wants to work at Winston's place."

"How did you get him to leave?"

"I showed him that there were bigger fish in town..."

Chapter 21

The Mystery of Balance...

One of the Great Miracles of The Most High's Love is His Ability
to Grow Us from a Situation We Thought Would Surely Break
Us...

--Edwina Fort

Nakhti

That weekend in Rio was by far the most amazing time of
my whole entire life...and now looking back, I don't know if God in
his infinite wisdom granted me that time of pure bliss before
everything crashed down around me. Or if he's just a God of balance
and when one experiences such highs, they can bet their bottom
dollar that it will be followed by a great low.

No...I don't know. But I can tell you this, by the end of that
weekend, my life would be forever changed. Everything I knew to
be correct would be brought into question and the woman I used to
be would be dead...literally.

But before I tell you guys how I got that low, let me first tell
you about my high.

Rome chartered us a flight with one of the local pilots on the island. When he saw Rome coming, his face lit up and he called him his friend. Apparently, my lover was really good at making those.

We touched down in Rio just before nightfall. There was a really nice Jeep Wrangler waiting for us at the private airport. Because it was Carnival time, everywhere we drove was alive with activity. The top was taken off the Wrangler so that we could see everything. I felt like a little girl on my knees in my seat pointing at everything as he drove.

At one point when traffic forced us to a slow creep, I was standing in the seat to look at a group of Samba dancers that were preparing for their march, their band filled the street with music. Rome had to drive with one hand on the wheel and the other around my waist because he feared I was going to tip out the jeep, I was grooving so hard.

When we finally made it to his *little* place in *Rio*, I stood staring at it with my mouth open. First of all, it was a private villa on Leblon Beach and trust me, there was nothing little about this place. We drove through a beautiful iron gate that separated us from the world's biggest party.

The view from the top floor of the villa will be perfect in both directions. To the front of the Villa was the celebration in the streets, but to the back of the villa was the ocean in all its majestic glory.

Inside the gate was a well-manicured lawn and there was a beautiful fountain that was surrounded by romantic lighting. Oh...Did I mention the full wait staff waiting for us outside?

Nossa!

One of them was holding a golden tray with a glass of champagne and a rocks glass of amber liquid on the rocks.

My stunned gaze went to Rome…

"Whose house did you say this was?"

He chuckled as he took the glass of champagne off the tray and handed it to me. "An associate…" was all he said before he took a sip of his drink.

Hmmmm… an associate indeed. His *associate* was either a prince of some foreign country or a mob boss, but before I could ask him which, we were shown inside and all thoughts fled my mind.

This had to be what paradise looked like. Everything was lit in soft lighting casting a romantic glow on the open space. The whole back of the villa was a huge window with a perfect view of the beautiful pool that was also lit with warm lighting and the ocean behind it.

This part of the beach must be private because it was completely empty, except for the tiki-style torches that lined it casting that romantic glow on even the beach.

I turned to look at Rome who watched me take everything in. No way this was sporadic…He'd planned this.

"It's so beautiful…" I told him nearly breathless from taking it all in.

He smiled. "You like it?"

"I *love* it!"

He took my hand and led me out to the beach, it was so magnificent my eyes watered a bit. A gentle breeze drifted in from the ocean causing my dress to bellow around me. The sound of the waves drowned out the merriment taking place on the street.

There was a single lounger sitting there facing the water. He took a seat then pulled me down into his lap, my combat boot covered feet stretched out on the lounger in front of us.

"Before we go and get sh*t faced, I wanted to say a few things to you."

I rested my head back against his strong chest and nodded. I was so content staring out at the gentle waves of the ocean, I could sit here all night.

"I never apologized for what I did back at the loft in Chicago. For a man that is so smart, I sure missed the call on that one."

I silently agreed because I didn't want to interrupt him.

"I should have noticed all the signs of your loyalty. They were all there. I just—" He paused for a moment searching for the right words.

He exhaled. "Hell, I was just stupid…and for that, I am so sorry."

He gently kissed me on my bare shoulder. "Can you forgive me?"

I turned in his arms so that I was facing him a bit and leaned in to touch my lips to his.

"I already have."

He picked up my hand in his toying with it a bit, seeming lost in his thoughts. "You know, every time I think about how close I'd come to losing you…" he didn't finish that statement, he just shook his head.

"Damn, shorty, I almost f***ed up really bad. My life wouldn't be sh*t without you. When you left, I swear it felt like you took half of me with you. I was f***ed up."

I brought my other hand up to gently touch his perfect lips...

"Shhh... I shouldn't have left. I should have talked to you—" I shook my head. "I was stupid and insecure. I was embodying my mom's problem..." Laughing without any humor, I leaned in until our foreheads were touching.

"You're nothing like my father..."

"Your father's a b****!"

I chuckled... "Yeah, he is."

Pulling my left hand from his I brought it up to rub his beard, but I caught the reflection of something out the side of my eye and realized while he was playing with my hand, he'd slipped a ring on it.

"Romeo..." his name seeped from between my lips as I brought my shaking hand in front of me to see that he'd slipped a huge diamond ring on it. In the torch lighting, it reflected gold... for what seemed like the hundredth time today, my mouth dropped.

"This brings me to my next question." His voice was low as he concentrated on me with that honey gaze that also looked golden in the firelight casting his spell on me.

"I don't want to ever feel the feeling of losing you again. I want to live and die with you, shawty. When you go...I pray to be right next to you, 'cause I found out I can't live without you."

He took my hand with his ring on it and brought it to his lips kissing it gently.

"Will you marry me, Nak?"

Nossa!

I could have died right then and I would have been the happiest girl in the world. Through tears, I leaned in and kissed his lips again.

"Yes... *Mue Rei—*" But my words died off as a terrible thought came to me.

So terrible it caused my heart to freeze over and my eyes to fill with more tears.

He wanted to have children and I was barren.

When he saw the expression change on my face, panic crossed his as he sat up straighter on the settee, taking my bare shoulders in his big hands.

"What's the matter?" I could hear the urgency in his voice. I bit my lip as a tear escaped to run down my cheek.

He shook me... "What's wrong, Nak...Please don't tell me no, baby!" The agony in his voice broke my heart even more.

"I can't have children." My words came out just barely over a whisper. The knot that was in my throat was choking me.

A look of relief crossed his face as he wrapped me in his arms pulling me close.

"Dammit, girl, you scared the f*** out of me."

I remained stiff in his arms. "Did you hear me? I'm barren," I told him just to make sure.

He held me away from him a bit so that he could look down into my eyes. There was a smile of relief on his face.

"Let me tell you something, shawty...I don't give a f*** about none of that, just as long as you are mine. Sh*t, I'm fine with being an uncle, my sister pregnant with her second child. That horny bastard Jo will probably keep her pregnant."

I laughed at that...Wow! Who would have imagined Jo being the fathering type? But then my laughter disappeared as that sadness came back. I could imagine Rome being a father...He would be a good dad.

"No, don't frown, baby," He soothed lifting my chin so that he could kiss my lips.

"But I want to be a mommy too."

He chuckled down at me. "You are so sexy when you pout." He kissed my lips again. "Aren't you the same girl that plopped her little Bible down on the table in front of me and bragged about all the studying you've been doing?"

Still pouting I nodded my head.

"And have you not read about Abraham's wife Sarah and how she too was barren. But that the Most High touched her womb and she bore a child?"

I sat up on his lap and nodded as a spark of hope lit in my heart. I did read about Sarah and Abraham. Sarah was sad because she wanted to have a child for her husband like I wanted to give Rome a child.

"Baby, nothing is impossible for the Heavenly Father...and if it is his will, we will have a child. However, if it's not in his will, we have to be okay with that…Because there are two things I know for sure…" He held up one finger.

"One…Nothing in this world happens unless it's The Most High's will. Not anything from the smallest ant being born to the biggest mountain breaking off and falling into the sea. And two—" He held up another finger.

"If you don't finish saying yes to my proposal, I am going to go ape sh*t and start trashing this mutha f***a."

Laughter bubbled up in my throat as I circled my arms tightly around his neck…

This is my thug…and I loved him so much!

"Yes, baby! I'll marry you! A thousand times yes!"

He whooped coming to his feet bringing me with him…I held my head back and laughed as he turned around in a circle causing my dress to fly behind me.

"Damn, girl! You had a brotha sweating! Sh*t…" He put me on my feet taking my hand. "Come on, let's go and celebrate!"

And celebrate we did…We painted the town black.

His surprises did not end there. Do you guys know that he and I were married before that night was out? Somehow in the midst of all that celebrating, he found a judge that married us underneath a beautiful gazebo in the garden of a really nice restaurant.

It was magical…the celebrating around us paused for just a moment as we said our vows and then after the judge told Rome he could kiss his bride, it picked right back up…

When we signed our wedding certificate, I found out that my new last name was Law. He said that since Romeo Reevers had to die, he and the others had agreed to just take the last name Law. So now my name was Nahkti Law…

I loved it!

I drank and danced and ate wedding cake…

Yes, you guys heard correctly…Wedding cake.

Come to find out, Rome had set up everything. He'd actually rented out the restaurant we'd gotten married at and hired the Samba band and dancers… He allowed the people to come in and celebrate with us until the restaurant had reached its maximum.

Oh guys!!!! It was a night I'll never forget…

And so…

Now that I've told you the high, brace yourself because at this point, my story shifts drastically and it will be a long, long time before I feel such happiness again. The very next day and I do mean the very next day, everything changed.

He and I were kind of taking it easy because we'd partied so hard the night before that the both of us woke up hung over. We had a leisurely breakfast still basking in the fact that we were newlyweds. At some point, we decided to go for a little swim in the pool.

I don't know how it got started, but we ended up acting out that scene in Dirty Dancing…You know the one… *Nobody puts Baby in the corner.*

Yeah…it was goofy, but we were newlyweds.

"Okay, let's try it again. You have to stop laughing or you're going to drop me again," I told him.

"Alright, I'm ready." He held out his hands and I took off running toward him...When I got to him, I leaped up out of the water and he caught me holding me up in the air...

"Yes..." I cried making sure to hold my arms and legs straight out like Superman.

"You dripping water all over me, I can't see..." He complained before a deep rugged voice cut him off coming from somewhere over on the side of the pool.

"I wish I could un-see this."

"Oh sh*t!" Rome said before he quickly lowered me back down into the water behind him, using his big body to block mine. I didn't think to pack a swimming suit, so I'd gotten in the pool wearing one of his tee shirts and a pair of panties.

"Ay man, I can explain. This not what it looks like."

What the hell? I stood on my toes to look over his shoulder curious to see who my big tough husband suddenly felt the need to explain himself to and came up short at the sight that greeted me.

Standing on the side of the pool looking down at us was a grinning Jo and Albert...but it was the frowning man they were with that drew all the attention. And if my guess was correct, this was the man Rome felt the need to explain himself to.

If my guess was also correct, this was the one called Judah. I'm glad he warned me about him or else every fighting instinct in me would be on high alert right now. Everything about him was unrelenting, from the way he stood so powerful and sure, to the way his clothes fit on his big body. His long locs that appeared dark brown in the sun were pulled back in a ponytail that hung to his waist.

The whole bottom half of his face was covered in hair, but it did little to hide the sneer on his face. He looked like a wild man. Rome guided me out of the pool careful to keep my body blocked from the other men, then he quickly wrapped me in a fluffy white robe, closing it all the way up to my throat.

"Is that...The Unbreakable One?" I whispered.

"Yeah and he caught me playing damn Dirty Dancing with you." He whispered back before he turned to face them.

"Shall we talk inside over a cool drink?" Rome said once he'd made sure I was good and covered.

Nossa! I never thought there was anything out there as fierce as the Politician, but I was wrong, I could tell by the way the powerful men that I knew...Rome and Jo...hell even Albert held themselves around him.

He was clearly the boss.

Judah nodded once and then went inside and Albert followed him...But Jo stood there grinning at Rome. He held his lips in a way that said his laughter was going to burst through any minute.

Rome frowned at him. "What you got to say...chump?!"

"Dirty Dancing, kid? Is that what you do in your down time? Practice your dance moves..." He patted him on the shoulder none to gently. "You looked good out there, baby brother...I give you a perfect ten." And then he held his head back and barked with laughter.

"Man, shut yo' corny a** up!" Rome hissed shoving his hand off his shoulder.

"Hey Rome!" Jo called after. "Nobody puts Baby in the corner." And then he held his head back and barked with another round of laughter. He was laughing so hard he had to brace his hands on his knees to keep from tipping over.

I stood in front of him with my arms folded because his big body was blocking the door. When he saw that there was no laughter in my face his laughter died, and he stood opening his arms for me.

"Nak, baby...What up, girl?!"

I didn't bother to speak...I was still mad at him. I just shoved his arms out of the way and walked pass him like Rome had done.

"Hey! What's up with that?" He asked following me in.

"Not right now, Sarge..." I told him before I went into Albert's waiting arms and hugged him.

"You mad at me or something?" He asked when after I hugged the Old Man and still didn't talk to him.

Nossa! He figured that out all by himself. Okay, so I'm going to be honest, I didn't like seeing Jo and the Oldman. Seeing them meant they were going to try and pull me back into a lifestyle that I'm done with.

Jo never comes to just say hello or to check on me. If he was here, it meant I was going to have to kill somebody...and I was done with that.

"So, what brings you guys by?" Rome asked after the servers left from giving everyone lemonade.

Nobody had taken a seat, so I guess this wasn't a social visit.

"You ask that question, like you've forgotten you're now employed by me?"

Obviously, Judah was not one to mince words. I frowned at Rome...*What the hell was he talking about?*

"Why are you mad at me?" Jo whispered from my left. I turned my frown to him...

"Shhh!" I told him before turning back to once again give Rome and Judah my full attention.

"Yeah...about that—" Rome began, but Judah shook his head.

"I don't have time for your excuses...If I found you, the others can. You and Nak need to get packed and come back with us—"

I held up my hand... "Whoa! What do you mean him and Nak? I've ret—"

He cut me off. "You are wasting time that we don't have."

When I snapped my mouth shut insulted that he'd so rudely interrupted me, he turned to face me fully.

And let me tell you something, having his complete attention was intimidating as hell.

"What did you think was going to happen, Nahkti?" He didn't raise his voice. He didn't have to. His presence alone demanded your full attention.

"Did you think you were going to be able to turn the killer off inside of you and live happily ever after with the genius, on your f***ing horse ranch? How long did you think you were going to be able to suppress your urges? Tell me...did you kill the jailer that violated you?"

His question threw me…because first of all, how the hell did he know about that? And second of all, in all the excitement of Rome showing up, I'd forgotten to kill that bastard. Something I was going to amend as soon as I got back…

Just thinking about breast boy rekindled the anger inside of me…

"Don't bother…" Judah spoke as if he could hear my thoughts. "Rome already did the honors for you because he's a f***ing savage." He opened his arms. "That's what we are, baby, a band of f***ing savages."

I whipped my head around to look at my husband. He and Jo stood behind me looking like two little brothers in the presence of their older brother. It was strange seeing my old boss and my husband this way. They had always been the alpha males of their environment, but standing next to Judah, they came across as the little brothers.

When Rome noticed me looking, he gave a little shrug, one side of his mouth lifted in a smile.

Jo stepped forward clearing his throat. "About is *all* being savages. I can't speak for the others, but I'm no savage. In fact—"

"Shut up, Jo." Judah muttered not taking his piercing gaze away from me.

"Okay…" The Sarge said stepping back to his spot next to Rome.

Judah exhaled. "Look… you can't just turn off who you are. I know, I've tried a thousand times. Rome was so desperate to get you back, he didn't think about the fact that he was putting your life in danger. I've been watching you for a while…As long as you worked for my little brother, I let you be, he needed somebody like you watching his back. But now he and Rome work for me. I have a place for you on the team—"

I was shaking my head before he was done. "No, I'm finished with that life. I just want to be left alone."

He chuckled...It really was a horrible sound because it sounded like something he didn't do often.

"Unfortunately, that is no longer an option for you."

Anger ripped through me... I balled up my fists prepared to deck this big bastard if I had to.

"The hell it is! Let me tell you something—" Before I could get anything else out, Rome's hand came around my mouth cutting my words off completely.

"You will have to excuse her...she has a condition," he said calmly as if he was discussing the weather.

"Really, she does, it's been diagnosed," Jo finished.

Something like amusement entered Judah's eyes as he looked at me. He could see that I had been prepared to attack him...and the sick bastard liked it.

"I'm aware of her condition." He pointed to Rome. "Talk to yo' girl."

"Got it..." My husband said dutifully. I slammed my elbow back into his stomach mad as hell that he was speaking for me...but he knew me well and had it blocked before it connected.

"Won't you guys just give me a few days? I'll talk to her and get back with you," he told the fellas as he wrapped his other arm around me holding me so that I didn't take another swing at him.

"I don't know if you have a few days…I can tell you, y'all are definitely not safe here." His gaze came to mine.

"I hope you change your mind, we can really use you on the team."

My voice came out muffled behind Rome's hand…but what I said was…*So, f***ing what, I'm done! Dammit!*

"You know how to find us," he told Rome before heading out of the door.

"Baby girl, think about what the man said. I know you tired of this life and I'm sure we'll rest soon. Now just ain't the time." Albert said before he leaned in and kissed me on my forehead.

Old Al, always the calming voice in the storm. Feeling the tension leaving my body, Rome removed his hand from my mouth…but still held me close.

"How long you going to be mad at me?" Jo asked taking the Oldman's place in front of me.

The tension came back. "This is all your fault!" I growled…. He looked surprised at the venom in my words.

"My fault? How?"

"Hey…" Rome spoke up before I could say anything. "Just let me talk to her… okay?"

Jo's gaze came back to me before he exhaled. "Yeah…okay." He put his hand on Rome's shoulder and the grin came back to his face.

"Keep those dance moves sharp, kid." And then he followed his brother and the Oldman out the door laughing his head off.

"Man, I can't stand that mutha f***a..." Rome hissed.

I snatched away from him. "Forget Jo! When were you going to tell me you worked for the CIA?"

He held up a hand. "We don't know that he works for the CIA..."

I put my hand on my hip and gave him the, *really*? look.

He exhaled taking my hand off my hip and pulling me to the couch. "Sit down, baby, let me talk to you for a minute." I sat, but I folded my arms remaining hostile.

This was so messed up, I felt like he tricked me. He knew I was trying to get out of the business and now he'd pulled me right back in it.

I shook my head.

No! I was done, I'm not going back.

"Nak, what Judah said about you is true. Baby, you are a warrior, you were born to fight. You can't just turn that sh*t off."

I stood from the couch. "Watch me..." I told him as I marched toward the stairs.

"Where you going? You can't just leave me, we're married now!" He called after me holding up his hand with his wedding band on it.

I stopped at the bottom of the stairs turning to look at him... "Watch me..."

Okay, so, I didn't really leave him...I loved him, I don't care how mad I get, I can't walk away from him again. Plus, he followed me upstairs and tackled me to the bed, pleading for me to forgive him. I tried to stay mad and not laugh at him, but then he climbed on top of me burying his head in my neck tickling me with his beard, kissing me over and over again apologizing until I erupted in laughter.

And yeah, I forgave him, but I got a bad feeling in the pit of my belly and was ready to go home. I don't know who was after Rome and Jo, but Judah said it was only a matter of time before whoever it was found them. I wasn't lying to Saw Buck...I would kill whoever tries to destroy God's beautiful creation.

Rome's mind was worth killing to protect.

Being in a place like this was not safe, there were too many moving components to narrow down a target. Plus, I didn't like the fact that Freedom and Luna were back at home unprotected.

"Tell me everything you know," I told Rome on the plane ride home.

And oh my goodness! What he told me blew my mind.

"I've found an archive with a bunch of Father's notes..."

I held up my hand stopping him. "Father is?"

"The doctor that did this sick sh*t to them..."

I nodded... "Okay, got it."

"I found you in his notes."

I put my hand to my chest surprised. "Me?"

He nodded. "Remember I told you he was pairing Jo's real father up with women who had a certain X chromosome?"

"Yeah..."

"Well, I don't think it's the X chromosomes anymore…There is something else in the DNA he was after. I've studied your DNA and Jo's—"

"Wait, how and the hell did you get my DNA?"

He gave me the, *really?* look before he continued talking as if I'd never interrupted.

"It was not a coincidence that you and Jo ended up being recruited together at such a young age. They had hoped that you two would end up together and have a baby and then they were going to kidnap your child."

"Nossa!" I sat back in my seat floored.

"There is something in your DNA that makes you, Jo, and even Judah the way that y'all are. I call it a super-human gene. But get this…"

He sat up in his seat…getting closer to me as if he feared being overheard on the empty plane.

"I found it in my DNA too. I think it's what makes me smart like I am." He whispered.

"What is it?"

He shook his head. "I don't know, it's the answer I've been searching for. At first, I thought that maybe it was in all black people's DNA because it was in my mom's and Journey's and even Rob's, but it's not. I checked Hannibal's and he doesn't have it…However, it is in Hitta's." He paused for a minute lost in his head.

"Baby, it's so well hidden, it almost seems like there is a force keeping it from coming to the surface."

I stared at him as a chill raced down my back…He was really starting to freak me out. "When you say force…What exactly do you mean?"

He opened his mouth to tell me, but then thought better of it. Instead, he wrapped his arm around my shoulders pulling me back so that my head rested on his chest.

He gently kissed the top of my head. "Nothing yet, Minha Anjo. Nothing to worry about just yet."

When we finally landed back on the island, I exhaled. Ribeirão da Ilha still sat quiet and untouched.

However, as I carried Giant off the plane, a loud BOOM shook the ground. Several seconds later, it was followed by another BOOM!

Both Rome and I stared as two giant fireballs lit up the night sky. Something had just gotten blown up.

"Come on, baby!" Rome said grabbing my hand as he and I ran to the truck. He floored it down the street heading towards the house.

I got a sickening feeling in the pit of my stomach…

Dear God…Please don't let that be—

Rome slammed his fist down on the dashboard. "Mutha f***a! It's the barn!"

I closed my eyes for a split second as resolve washed over me. When I opened them again, the savage inside of me was back at the wheel.

Chapter 22

The Gathering...

Nakhti

I was out of the truck before Rome brought it to a complete stop. It wasn't just the barn that was burning, but my avo's house as well. A shattering cry ripped from my throat as I ran towards the burning barn.

"Nak, no!" Rome yelled from behind me before I felt his arm around my waist preventing me from going farther.

"Let me go—"

"Senhor! Senhorita!" Carlos cried running towards us, leading Luna by the reins. He was saying something while pointing towards the barn, but we couldn't hear him over the roar of the fires.

I was so relieved to see that he and Luna were safe, but my heart dropped when I didn't see Freedom.

"Where is Freedom?!"

Winded, Carlos shook his head. "I couldn't get him out! The beam collapsed on top of him—" A hole appeared in the center of his forehead before his eyes rolled to the back of his head and he collapsed at our feet.

Luna bolted out of the way as a barrage of bullets came at us. My body went into combat mode instantly as both Rome and I dove to the ground to avoid being hit. Rome came from behind his back with an M9 returning fire.

Sensing something like this was going to happen, I'd worn my Glock strapped to my thigh underneath my skirt. I grabbed it shooting toward the direction the bullets came from as I ran towards Luna. I grabbed her reins and quickly hauled myself onto her back.

The men who had killed Carlos were making their escape in two black SUVs.

"Hell no!" I yelled before I kneed Luna…she didn't need any more encouragement, as if she wanted them as much as I did, she took off across the plain.

Next to me, Rome revved the pick-up's engine, giving chase while firing at them. But the vehicles must have been bullet-proof because neither of our bullets made an impact. When the trucks got to the bend, they split, one going toward town and another going into the forest area.

I made eye contact with Rome for only a second, he nodded and veered to the right, following the truck that headed towards town and I followed the other truck into the forest…

"Good Job, Luna!" I complimented the beauty because she was moving as if she wanted them dead just as much as I did.

Knowing I was running low on ammo, I lifted my Glock and carefully aimed at the tires because even though Luna was a stellar horse, she would not be able to hang with the engine of the SUV for long. So, I had to make my last few bullets count.

My first shot missed…I calmed my breathing and did my best to steady my arm despite the galloping and then fired again.

My second shot took out the back right tire…The truck swerved left and then right before it hit a tree. Three men dressed in black military gear spilled out of the vehicle firing at me, one of them limped. My last bullet pierced his forehead in the same way they had shot Carlos.

One down…two to go.

I tossed my empty pistol and veered to the right avoiding their shots, disappearing into the trees. I'd grown up here, I knew this forest like the back of my hand. I brought Luna to a stop and listened.

Whoever these men are, they are highly trained. They moved without making a sound. But it didn't matter how good they were, the forest always protested the footprints of intruders. I quickly slid off Luna's back as the tempo of the crickets' song increased to my right.

After giving her a little pat on her butt that caused her to trot away, I quietly climbed the tree next to me. They were heading directly for me. And just like I figured, they heard the horse and hurried after the sound.

One man ran past with his gun aimed, I took a deep breath and dropped from the tree like smoke onto the back of the last man, the sound of his neck breaking did not alert the first man. However, the sound of his big body hitting the ground did.

I quickly drew my bat and by that time, the man had turned around to investigate the sound, I'd silently covered the space in between us and swung with all my might. He turned into my blow and it was the last thing he saw.

Rome brought his truck to a skidding halt.

"Is he still alive?" He asked jumping out of his truck.

Although I already knew that answer, I leaned down and checked the pulse of the body lying at my feet.

"He's gone...What about the guys you were after?"

Rome shook his head. "It was two of us racing around the bend. Only one of us made it out the turn." He pointed toward another blaze that lit the sky, opposite from my place before squatting down checking the pockets of the man whose neck I'd broken.

"Check his pockets for his cellphone or anything else that will tell us about him."

I squatted down and grabbed the man's phone at my feet and checked for a wallet. I was not surprised when I didn't find one. It was never wise to take anything that can identify you out into the field. Just like I'd said earlier, these men were professionals.

Rome

These men were the f***ing CIA...

*What the f***?!*

I kept a concerned eye on Nak, who was gathering Luna as I quickly dislodged the GPS from their SUV. One thing about the government, they were tracking all of their vehicles. Hopefully, this little device will lead me back to whoever the f*** sent them.

"Nak, baby, wait for me before you head back," I called to her as I shut the hood and ran to my truck. I didn't want her to go back to the house without me. I didn't think Freedom made it and I knew she was going to lose it when she found out.

I think there were only three fire stations on the entire island, and I doubted if any of them would make it here tonight, the fires will definitely have to burn themselves out. However, I was more than positive the local police were on their way and we needed to be gone before they got here.

Nak rode Luna back to the house and as soon as we reached the barn, she threw her leg over Luna's back and jumped to the ground.

"Freedom!" She cried racing toward the burning building.

Leaving the truck running I threw it in park and jumped out to grab her. Now was not the place or the time for her to mourn her loss. She would have plenty of time for it during our journey to Canada. The sound of the police sirens was getting closer.

She went wild in my arms; I tightened my grip on her.

"No, Rome! Let me go! I have to help Freedom!" The way her voice shook let me know she knew that he was gone.

"Baby! Listen to me..." I shook her a little to get her attention. "We need to get out of here before the police get here. I need you to get back on Luna and follow me. Do you understand?"

She looked up at me with grieving eyes. Although she was in pain, she nodded that she understood.

But then her grip tightened on my arm as she looked around desperately. "Where is Giant?!"

"He's in my truck waiting on us...Come on, baby we have to go."

I jumped back in the truck and threw it in drive. I didn't have to worry that she would not be behind me, she is a soldier, she was trained for this kind of sh*t.

By the time we made our way back to Carvalho's, the local pilot I'd paid to always be on call for me just in case anything like this happens, Luna was tired and very thirsty, so Nak took care of her while I made plans with Carvalho to get us to Canada.

There were several problems…Not unsolvable problems, but problems.

First of all, if we took his plane there, we would have to stop to refuel four times, turning a usually ten and a half hours trip into sixteen hours. However, his brother in Rio had a bigger plane that could hold triple the amount of fuel than his and was willing to let us use it, which meant we would only have to stop once at his cousin's place in Indiana to refuel.

Problem solved…

Now…and this was a big one. Carvalho's plane was not big enough to transport Luna, which meant he was going to have to bring her at a later date. Nak had not left her side. Like a lost little girl that had not just single-handedly killed a car full of men, she stood hugging Giant in one arm with her other wrapped around Luna's neck.

Although I thought it would, it didn't take me long to assure her that Luna was going to be okay and that Carvalho will be coming right back to get her and bring her to us in Canada. I introduced her to Carvalho's nephew, who was going to be taking care of her precious horse until Carvalho came back for her. And then promised the kid a small fortune in front of her if he could make sure not one hair on the horse's head is disturbed.

Only then did she let me guide her and Giant unto the plane securing them in their seat.

Another problem solved…

And now for the final issue. It was time to kill Nak…

To accomplish this, I enlisted the help of Carvalho's brother, the one that stayed here on the island with him and paid him to spread the word that Nak died in the fire, while I used my computer to do a little tweaking of the local morgue's roster.

The report now read that the police officers pulled a woman's body out of the fire, who was identified by her dental records as Nahkti Thomas. She had no living family and her remains will be cremated.

I closed my computer and boarded the plane. As soon as I sat, Nak climbed into my lap and wrapped her arms tightly around my neck, burying her face in my beard before she began to mourn her loss. I held her tight, letting her know that I was here for her.

 I loved that about my fierce warrior, she was tough as nails, but wasn't afraid to embrace her sensitive side and cry if she had to.

I would wait to tell her that she was officially dead. I figured that now was not the best time…Sometime after the plane lifted off the ground, she lifted her head and looked at me through the eyes of a savage.

"We are going to find who did this…and then we're going to f*** them up…" she growled.

I nodded… "Yeah, baby…their days are numbered."

Problem solved…

Nahkti

By the time our plane touched down in the Canadian Mountains, it was just after three in the morning. Rome had spent the last few hours of the flight telling me about my new home. So, when we stepped off the plane and saw Judah himself leaning against a black military issued Hummer waiting for us, I was surprised.

Rome said everybody had pretty much grown into one big family here, everybody except for Judah, who rarely communicated with anybody other than his team.

During Rome's short stay here, he said he saw him only twice, once when he'd explained to them that they would have to be retrained to work with him and when he showed Rome his new computer lab that my husband was itching to get to...especially now that his loft in Chicago was destroyed.

"I'm glad you two made it in safe," Judah said as he and Rome clasped hands and did that one arm hug that men did in greeting. `

"Did you get a chance to go over the intel I sent you?"

Judah nodded. "I did, which is why I met you guys here. Jump in, I'll give you a lift back to your place." His cold gaze fell on me and I shivered.

He felt like the Politician, cold and unfeeling. Jo was able to turn his alter off at will. Rome said Judah and his alter was one, so he was always on.

"How was your journey?"

It didn't feel like he really cared. It felt like he asked because it was something my future boss should do.

"A bit rough," I told him the truth.

He nodded. "I can imagine," was about all I was going to get from him as far as sympathy went.

"The two of you need to get a few hours rest and then meet me at headquarters in zero six-hundred hours. I may know where to find the ones responsible for this, but we need to move before they know we're coming. We have a small window, if we lose it, they'll be in the wind and then we'll be back at square one."

Well, damn...I didn't need his sympathy when he was presenting me with a chance to get revenge.

I'll take revenge over sympathy any day.

"You keep saying *they*. Once again, I ask you, who the f*** is *they*? I'll tell you who the *they* were back in Ribeirão da Ilha. *They* were the f***ing CIA!" Rome growled as he and Judah loaded our bags in his truck.

Judah exhaled before rubbing the bridge of his nose, for the first time showing a human emotion like tiredness.

"Get some rest, kid." His deep voice did in fact sound tired. "By the end of the day tomorrow, you will have the answer to your question."

And I guess that was the end of that topic because Rome let it drop. On the way to the house Judah talked to Rome about some of the intel he'd been sending him, and I wondered if that's how he knew about me being in jail and what happened to me there.

Nossa!

Had Rome been sending him updates this whole time? What else did he know?

I exhaled, too tired and broken-hearted to try and think about it now. I'd not only lost Freedom in that fire, I'd also lost the painting Rob had done of Rome and me asleep in the bed. I bit my lip to keep from crying all over again.

And poor Carlos, we had to leave without making sure he was taken care of. He'd said he would protect the horses with his life and that's exactly what he did.

Oh God help me! *I was going to cry again.*

I took deep calming breaths pushing my grief back down. Feeling Judah's gaze on me in the rear-view mirror, I looked up and was not surprised to see him watching me with disgust on his face. If what Rome said about him was true and he was like the Politician, then he would respect no weakness.

At this moment, I really could give a damn how he felt. Everybody was not like him, some of us were built with emotions, it wasn't my fault he was broken.

Anyway, I did feel a little better because Rome had assured me that he'd left enough money for Carlos's family to not only pay for his funeral but to keep them afloat for a while. He promised to send them more every few months. I knew he did that because he too felt guilty for the kid's death.

Both Carlos and Freedom… Just a waste.

Because it was dark, I couldn't see my surroundings very well, but when we pulled up to Rome's house, all three of us were surprised to see the lights on and people walking around in the living room.

"My little brother doesn't follow orders very well," Judah grumbled as his gaze narrowed on Jo's silhouette in the window.

Rome chuckled. "I could have told you that."

Right then Rob's head appeared in the window before it disappeared, the next second the front door opened and Rome's mom, sister, Rob, Jo, and Albert spilled out on the porch.

"Kick them out, the two of you, Jo and Albert need rest for tomorrow...I don't know what we are walking into." Judah grunted.

Rome turned to look at him with a disapproving look on his face. "What the hell is wrong with you? You just told me to kick my mother, who I haven't seen in months out my house. Damn, man, where is your heart?"

Judah was not offended in the least, his gaze, if it was possible turned colder.

"Sorry, kid, I don't suffer from weak things like feelings. I don't have a heart. I deal in facts and logic...not emotion. Don't ever confuse me with someone who does." He got out of the truck and went to the back removing our bags and sitting them on the gravel.

I clutched Giant to me, eyeballing him. You guys, this man was cold as ice. He was the type that would slit his mother's throat if the mission called for it.

He came to a stop in front of Rome, who stood with his hands balled into fists, the little muscle ticking in his cheek. He wanted to give Judah a piece of his mind. Judah stood in front of him as if he dared him.

"If I could have gotten my men without the nuisance of their families, I would have. They hinder you, make you weak. If you can look past your emotions, you know I speak the truth. Now kick them the f*** out, so that you two can get some rest…I won't have you tired on our first mission together."

Without saying another word, he turned and got back into the Hummer, pulling off without so much as a glance to the family on the porch.

Nossa!

"That sociopathic bastard better be lucky I'm tired," Rome muttered watching his vehicle disappear down the path that led back to the main road.

"Oh, yeah?" I asked coming to stand next to him. "What were you going to do about it?"

He turned to look at me with a grin on his face. "What was I going to do about it? Sh*t girl…what was *we* going to do about it." He used his finger to point between me and him.

Giggling I shook my head. I was getting ready to tell him that I didn't think so, but Rob made it to me right then lifting me and Giant in a huge bear hug.

"Sis, what's up girl?! I didn't think Rome was going to find you!"

I hugged him back as I thought about the beautiful painting he'd done of Rome and me… Anger anew welled up inside of me.

"Hey, little bro! I missed you."

"Man...unhand my wife!" Rome growled with a grin on his face before he opened his arms for his brother, who nearly took him off his feet when he hugged him.

"I missed you too, bruh! You had Ma worried to death."

"Yes, you did..." Mrs. Abby said when she and Al finally made it to us.

"Nakhti," she said opening her arms for me. "It's so good to see you again, sweetheart."

I handed Rob Giant and went into her arms, needing a mother's hug at the moment as much as I needed air. And it felt so good. She was warm and soft...she was a comfort. Those tears that I'd been fighting welled up in my eyes.

Folks out there listening to my tale, if you have a mom who loves you, never take her hugs for granted...Some of us were not allowed this.

However, I thank God for it now.

As if she knew I needed it, she squeezed me tighter and held me just a little longer.

"Come on, Ma, you hogging all the hugging, can't I hug my new sister too?"

I grinned at the beautiful, very pregnant Journey as she and Jo approached. She looked so cute waddling down the driveway.

"You must be Journey," I told her being very careful of her belly as I hugged her.

"And you must be the famous Wonder Woman who beat up my brother's friends and stole his heart."

That made me laugh. "Ummm…"

"Yep, that's her," Rob supplied.

Jo stood to the side of Journey looking unsure. Feeling sympathy for the nut I opened my arms for him.

"Come on, Sarge, I ain't mad at you no more."

He visibly exhaled as he walked toward me with a grin. "I am glad to hear that. I was one step away from ordering you a whole year's supply of red Kool-Aid."

I pointed at him. "Now that don't sound like a bad idea."

Rome chuckled. "It sounds like a horrible idea. I would hate to have to pollute the garbage cans with a year's supply of that poison. It can't be good for the environment."

Rob's, who still held Giant in his arms gaze came to mine before he tilted his head toward his brother. "See what I mean?"

Shaking his head, he turned to walk ahead with his mother and Albert. Excitingly, Journey wrapped her arm around mine.

"I'm so glad I finally have a big sister. We have so much to talk about. I can't wait to tell you all Rome's embarrassing stories, like the time he tricked Rob into drinking pee—"

"Hey, Journey…" Rome interrupted. "Does Jo know you used to be addicted to eating dirt?"

Jo's gaze flew to Journey's, whose mouth was now hanging open, her whole face had turned red with embarrassment.

"Did you have anything else you wanted to say, little sister?" Rome asked sweetly.

She shook her head. "Nope, that's it."

He smiled very evilly in only a way a big brother could. "I thought so…" He grumbled before he reached down for a few of our bags.

"So, Jo, speaking of brotherly love, I just had a heart-to-heart with your brother."

The Sarge shook his head as he leaned down and grabbed the rest of the bags. "Scary, isn't it?"

"Scary ain't the word, he just told me to kick all of your a**es out and get some rest for our first mission tomorrow."

Jo grunted as we began to follow the others back to the house. "Believe it or not, he was being nice. The other day Albert and I were at headquarters with him going over a few of the training programs he's planning to implement. I'd told Journey I was going to be home for dinner and that I would bring her one of the funnel cakes from town that she just has to have or she sits and pouts all night."

All of our gazes went to Journey. She shrugged. "I can't help it if the baby likes funnel cakes."

I rubbed her hand. "Of course not, little sister, you did nothing wrong."

She grinned. "Thank you."

"Well, Judah didn't see it that way," Jo continued. "I tell him I'm going to have to holler at him later, 'cause I'd promised my girl I'd bring her a funnel cake from town…Do you know that man looked at me and told me if I was going to continue to be a p***y, he might as well put a bullet in my head and put me out my misery now? I said bruh, my wife is seven months pregnant. Guess what he said."

"What?" Rome asked.

Jo chuckled. "That bastard looked at me dead serious…and was like, I don't give a f***."

Rome's eyes widened in shock. "And what did you do?"

Jo exhaled. "Not a damn thing…my kids need me around."

Rome chuckled. "Somebody needs to have a talk with that guy and let him know he's living amongst humans now."

Jo sat the bags down just inside the door before he patted Rome on the back. "You're the genius, I think the job should be yours."

"F*** that! You have the superhuman alternate personality, you should do it."

Jo shook his head. "Negative."

"Maybe we both should do it then," Rome suggested.

Jo shook his head again. "Negative."

Rome's amused gaze fell on me. "We can take Nak with us."

I damn near choked. "Oh, hell no you can't! Don't put me in it. I'm new on the job, I'd like to get in good with the boss."

"Well, we're not going to figure it out tonight and we do have an early start tomorrow. Come on, guys, we're going to let the newlyweds be for the evening." Jo called gathering everyone up.

After we all exchanged hugs, Rome and I stood by the door as everyone left.

"Ma, where you going?" He asked putting his hand on her arm as she passed with Albert.

Oh damn! For the first time, I just realized that there was tension between Rome and Albert. The Oldman tried to hug him back at the car and Rome had dodged it. He'd just tried to shake his hand again with still no response from Rome.

"Romeo, I don't have to tell you where I'm going," his mother said as she shook off his hand. He went to reach for her again, but I grabbed his hand.

"Good night, guys…" I called as I waved after them. When we closed the door, he turned and frowned down at me, but I wrapped my arms around his waist.

"Ohhh, stop frowning and show me around my new home."

That took his mind off of his mom. He took my hand and began the tour. The house was big. There was barely any furniture in it though. Rome had not stayed here long before he'd come to look for me, he thought his mother and brother would have decorated it in his absence, but apparently, Ms. Abby has not been here.

Rob had taken over the basement that was a pretty nice size apartment that came with its own bathroom and kitchen, so he didn't need to come upstairs for anything. And with his mom staying over at Albert's place, the upstairs was pretty much untouched.

There were four bedrooms upstairs, a huge living room, a huge den that I was sure will be a state-of-the-art computer lab in no time, and a huge kitchen. Rome took me out to the beautiful back porch.

"It's still dark, so it's hard to see, but we have about fifty acres back there that's all ours. Do you think that is enough space to build a nice barn and stable?"

"Fifty acres?" I asked because I couldn't believe this. It was too good to be true.

He nodded, taking a seat on the porch swing. "Yeah, fifty acres."

I eased down on the swing next to him. "This house is brand new; nobody has ever lived in it."

He didn't speak at first, he just gently swung us both on the swing. The rhythm was soothing.

"I think Judah prepared this place for us…"

I frowned. "But I thought you said this all just happened because you and Jo brought down Macon Tech."

He grunted. "I did until I talked with the man with no shoes."

"Your angel?"

He nodded.

"Do you really believe he's an angel?"

"I do."

He sounded so sure; I didn't dare question him. If what I was reading in the Bible was to be believed, then angels mingled with men all the time.

"What did the man with no shoes say?"

"He said—" his words died off. I knew he was trying to think of a way to tell me that wouldn't freak me out.

"He said that we were all going to come together… Us and Jo's siblings. And that we will all go on a journey. He told me that the next time I saw him, the world will be on fire."

His words made me think of what the Preacher told me. He'd said something very similar. At the time, I thought that maybe he was just a strange rambling man…but now…now I know differently. Hadn't he told me that the young prince would find me?

He also said that unrest was coming, but he did say that Rome and I will have a short time of normal.

I took his hand and brought it to my lips. "If the world is going to hell, there is nobody else I'd rather be with."

He smiled before gently kissing my lips. "Me either, *Minha Anjo.*"

Rome

The next morning, Nak and I barely made it to the headquarters on time. Headquarters was a two-story building located in the center of Judah's five hundred acres. No expense had been spared, which left me wondering who the hell was funding it.

When I'd first gotten here, I'd tried to hack my way into Judah's mainframe. Everything was squeaky clean like it was brand new.

Nak would freak out if I tell her this, but I'd discovered some years back that some computer code is not computer code, but rather spells made to look like computer code.

And I know you are all at home like…What-thee-f***? Rome just went there…

But listen to me for a minute and once I explain it to you, it won't seem farfetched. The box we call television teaches most of us how to live life. If ever someone wanted to get the masses to think a certain way or do a certain thing…all they have to do is put it on the box.

Unbeknownst to you…a spell has been cast.

Now, I could go deeper on that, but we just don't have the time. However, use your own observation skills. The next time you or your friends…maybe even your children are watching television and a commercial comes on, look around you to see how many of you are duplicating what you just saw on the box.

Abra ca damn dabra…you are under a spell. The sad part about it, I've been trying to fight this spell in my community for a long time. And I know Nak won't agree, but I haven't even made a dent. Most of my people are still falling prey to what they see on the box…and the box is leading them over the cliff…

Anyway, back to Judah's codes. His computer codes are a lot like the good doctors I've been chasing. They are protected with something that goes far beyond the 1's and 0's of the data world. But that's okay…Just because I haven't cracked it yet, doesn't mean I won't.

With me working this close to him, it is only a matter of time before one of my little burrowers find their way through. And when they do, I'm going to find out everything that he is hiding from us. Because I know he's hiding something…Something big.

Nak and I took a seat next to Jo and Albert. We were joined by thirteen of Judah's men. He came into the room dressed similar to us all, cargo pants, combat boots, and a black t-shirt.

"I don't have to tell you how the game is played. You all understand that as long as it appears to be unity on the surface level, many battles wage underneath." He picked up a pile of folders and handed each of us one.

"Included in the folders are several players that I suspect are involved with wanting us dead. Where we go today will catapult us into the game. They will know we're awakened and that we are united. There will be no turning back at this point. What we will see today will forever change us. Are we sure we're ready to take this step?"

He didn't look at his men when he asked that question, instead, his gaze rested on us. My gaze went to Jo...he lifted an eyebrow as if to ask me if I was sure. I looked at Nak, she gave me a little nod. I didn't bother to look at the Oldman, who gave a damn what his mama stealing a** thought? I gave Judah a little nod.

"Good, you can get briefed on the rest as we ride. We need to be in Virginia in zero eight-hundred hours." His gaze fell on his men. "Prepare the chopper."

All thirteen of them got up and hurried from the room. Judah pointed at me. "Just so you know...During the missions, you're in charge of the wild one. You need to make sure she behaves."

What the hell?! My gaze fell on Nak, who was looking at me with a little devious grin. Jo shook his head chuckling.

I loved my baby...I did, but she wasn't going to put me through the sh*t she put Jo through. Plus, I wasn't the leader here. This was Judah's show, she worked for him now.

I shot up from my seat. "Why I got to be in charge of her?"

Both he and Jo looked at me as if I was crazy. "Who else should be in charge of her, she's your wife."

"Yeah, I'm yo' wife." Nak agreed.

Damn it! I guess they had a point…but sh*t!

"Alright, team, let's roll out."

"Wait!" Nak called interrupting him.

Judah turned back not at all happy with the interruption.

See?!

See what the f*** I have to deal with?

She looked at the Oldman. "Lonesome Valley…"

"Oh yeah," Albert said as he made his way to the computer. "Is this hooked up to the speaker?" He asked Judah.

With a frown on his face, Judah nodded.

"Good…good." Albert told him before he went to work.

A few seconds later, what sounded like a negro spiritual from slavery times filled the speaker. The frown left Judah's face, he gently nodded as understanding fell over him.

I'm glad he understood because I was lost. I looked around amazed as the four soldiers in front of me…all dressed in fatigue pants, combat boots, black shirts, and dog tags, seemed to-- I don't know…center themselves.

It was as if each of them related to the song. I would later learn that this was something that soldiers that had seen combat did.

Nak said she and her team did it before each mission because they never knew if it was their last. And they needed to each take a moment to connect with their power and pray that He be with them.

Although, I didn't find all of that out till later…I did come to realize something else as I watched these soldiers automatically still themselves to reflect in such a way.

The man with no shoes was right. Nak, Jo, Albert, and Judah, are warriors of the Ancient of Days…even if they didn't know it yet.

I pulled out my computer and downloaded Lonesome Valley. From this day forward, I will make sure it plays before each mission.

Chapter 23

Unexpected...

"In that day יהוה shall shield the inhabitants of Yerushalayim. And the feeble among them in that day shall be like Dawiḏ, and the house of Dawiḏ like Alohim, like the Messenger of יהוה before them!

--Zechariah 12:8

Nakhti

"How you doing out there, Nak?"

I exhaled loudly and very ignorantly, Rome's a** was driving me crazy.

I could hear Jo and Albert chuckling on the line...hell, I even think I heard the rustic sounds of Judah's very dry chuckle.

"I'm doing just as I was ten minutes ago when you asked me and the time before that, and the time before that!" I hissed under my breath as I continued to pretend to read the book in front of me.

I was already irritated because I'd had these damn six-inch heels on since we touched down in D.C. two hours ago.

"So… does that mean you're doing good? You're not out there feeling impulsive or anything, are you?"

I stood from the library table and crossed the floor to the bathroom, making sure to switch my hips in a way that said come hither.

"You know what? Now that you mention it, I do feel impulsive. I have the sudden urge to pull you out of that damn cable truck and strangle you to death! Leave me the hell alone!"

All this I said while barely moving my lips, smiling at the group of college girls that left out the bathroom as I entered it.

I was past grouchy. We'd stopped in Virginia for supplies, one of which was the nice luxury cable van that his royal majesty was now reclined in. On the outside, it looked like your average everyday cable repair van.

On the inside was a portable computer lab fit for a king. Judah told Rome to get used to it because that van will become his home away from home. And guess what. The bastard sounded like he was right at home.

While the three of us have been stuck in our position to watch for the pervert, Rome's a** has been munching away on fruit, catching up on his Chess game…hell, I think we even heard him blending himself up a damned smoothie.

Yeah…the van was that nice.

"Hey, woman! Don't get mad at me for doing my job. I'm here to make sure you keep bat sh*t crazy locked up," his deep voice came out of the little device hidden in my ear.

I heard Jo chuckle over the line. Well…I was glad we could entertain everyone while we wait.

Not!

"Is that what you're trying to do?" I asked as I washed my hands. "Sounds to me like you're trying to wake bat sh*t crazy up."

"Heads up." Judah's voice cut in. "Our mark is heading toward you now…"

"How long?"

"Nine seconds…"

I quickly dried my hands off and then counted to four before I opened the door, colliding into the little nervous fella nearly knocking his glasses off his face. I made sure to really sell it, collapsing in his arms.

"Oh! I'm so sorry…" I cooed.

His grey eyes took their time looking over my body as he straightened his glasses. "No apologies necessary. Paul Howard…" He said holding out his hand to me.

"That's him…" Rome's voice came in my ear. I could hear him typing away on his computer. "Be careful, baye, he's a real f*** boy. He has several sexual harassment cases that have all managed to be thrown out. He has friends in very high places."

"Candy Parker…" I told him shaking his hand with a very loose grip.

His little weasel eyes brightened with interest. "Your name is Candy?"

I blew a huge bubble with my gum before licking my lips. "My mama named me right because I sure do like to eat candy." And then I giggled.

UGGGH! Disgusting…

So, I guess you guys are wondering why I'm here playing the bimbo.

I'll have to give you the quick version. Apparently, girls have been known to come up missing from this library. By this being one of the oldest libraries in D.C., their disappearances have been getting no media coverage and no real investigations.

It just so happened the girls that have come up missing all came from broken homes where no one will press the issue with the police because they were probably involved in illegal activities themselves. Judah believed these kidnappers are linked to the people that kidnapped them when they were babies and are the ones now trying to kill us.

Although Rome, who has set up a separate line for him and me to communicate without the others hearing, didn't think so. He said it was something altogether strange about this mission. He'd been looking into the place we'd gone first in Virginia to get our supplies for this job. Apparently, it was Judah's American headquarters. He found out that the same folks that found that place also found Judah's land back in Canada.

Rome has been telling me that something is not adding up with Judah and he is not to be trusted. He didn't think these people we were looking into today had anything to do with the mad doctor.

But hey…who was I to argue? The boss said this is where we are…so, this is where we are.

"Well, even though I do love candy, I think the real reason my mama named me that is 'cause she's a stripper." I laughed and patted his chest playfully, making sure to blow another ridiculously large bubble…when it popped some of it stuck to my lip.

"Oh…" I giggled and pulled the wad of gum out using it to remove the stuck-on gum from my lips. The little perve's eyes greedily watched. I saw when the fever fell over him; I'd seen it enough times to recognize the sign. He'd made his mind up…he had to have me.

"Damn, shawty, that's sexy as a mutha f***a…" Rome growled in my ear. I knew he'd switched the lines over and was talking to only me.

"Would you like to see George Washington's secret room?"

I opened my mouth surprised. "Like thee George Washington…the actor?"

If eyes could dance, they would look like his. "Yes…the famous actor."

"Will he be there; can I meet him?"

My stupidity only made him hungrier. "He should be…he's a really good friend of mine, I can call him to meet us there."

I clapped my hands together jumping up and down, his greedy eyes nearly bugged out of their sockets, which is crazy because I was fully dressed. When Judah's wardrobe person brought out my first outfit that was a little skirt and a halter top, Rome hit the roof.

"Hell naw, she not wearing that sh*t. Next!"

Of course, he made the little wardrobe guy extremely nervous. "But sir, she is supposed to lure our suspect out with sex appeal."

"Are you blind? She's already sexy as a mutha f***a." He stormed toward the clothes rack. "Are all these in her size?" He snapped at the guy.

The little man nodded... "Ye—Yes sir. These have all been ordered especially for her."

"Damn shame...I have to do everything around here." Rome muttered as he began to go through the clothing.

"I'm not impressed at all with your selections." He continued to berate the poor man. "You know what? I'll be ordering her costumes from now on...if you want something done right, you have to do it yourself."

Judah, Jo, the Oldman, and I stood back shaking our heads at him. It was clear Rome was definitely going to be the heartbeat of this budding team.

When he was done, I stood dressed in a pair of skinny jeans, a loose-fitting sweater that hung off one shoulder, and these damned heels.

Very proud of himself he held out his arms gesturing towards me. "What do y'all think?"

Judah nodded his head. "Not bad..." And that was that...

"Okay, fellas, heads up, they're moving," Rome told the crew.

The crew consisted of Jo, who was wearing a baseball cap pulled down low over his face and a cable repairman uniform, pretending to work on the library's Internet for the last two hours, but had only been installing what Rome calls his burrowers, Albert, who had been sitting at the computer researching natural remedies for arthritis, and Judah, who sat in another vehicle outside because he was too big and fierce looking to pass as anything other than a threat. He'd left his other men in Virginia.

The little fella led me down into the basement of the library. "Whe--where are we going?" I asked with a little quiver in my voice.

Quite naturally, I should be a little nervous at this point because not to be would only raise his suspicion.

"Did you know that there is a secret city built under this one?" he asked as he gently grabbed my arm, fearing that I may try to flee at this point.

Nervously, I shook my head as we went down another flight of stairs going deeper into the belly of the city.

"Do you still have eyes on her?" Judah's voice came in my ear.

"I do…" Rome told him.

"May—maybe I should come back another time, Paul," I told him as I looked around the long hall he was leading me down with wide eyes. There were no doors, just the one we'd entered and another way down at the end.

"But I thought you wanted to see George Washington. He's waiting to meet you and sign an autograph for you." His eyes brightened as a thought came to him.

"Have you ever thought about acting?"

"I sure have!" I told him, all the nervousness gone from my voice. "How did you know?"

He tapped his head. "I can tell. A girl as beautiful as you should be in the movies. Why I bet George will take one look at you and think so too. He has a lot of friends in the industry, he can pull some strings."

I clapped my hands together again. "Wow! Do you really think so?!"

This evil man's eyes nearly glazed over. "I know so…"

Once we exited the door at the end, the going got a little darker and a little rougher. We were now going deeper into the earth on steps that looked ancient. In fact, the walls were no longer walls, but stone. And I couldn't help but wonder how many young girls and boys too had ended up walking this route, never again to see the light of day.

"This tunnel was built in 1776…" He supplied as he continued to lead me deeper.

"They were built way before that…numbnuts…" Rome muttered.

Although I wasn't afraid, it was comforting to have his voice in my ear. For the first time, I didn't feel alone on a mission.

He walked to one of the torches that had been lit and pulled it…the stone opened to reveal a hidden door. When we entered it, everything brightened as once again, we were surrounded by pristine white walls…

"Wait a minute…something is wrong," Rome said in my ear…I could hear him typing away on his computer.

"What is it?" Jo asked.

"These codes…these codes aren't right."

"What's wrong with the codes?" Judah asked…

"They're not normal computer codes."

"Speak clearly, kid!" he barked at him. "What's wrong with the codes?"

"They're not codes at all...it's a *spell*! Get out of there, Nak, it's a setup!"

I didn't need to hear anymore...I slid the blade down my sleeve into my palm. When Paul turned to investigate why I'd slowed down I embedded the knife in his throat.

Before his body could even hit the ground, I was heading back towards the hidden door, but it was hard to tell exactly where it was because the bright white walls looked whole. Frantically I raked my hands over the smooth surface looking for some kind of latch.

"Rome, I can't find the latch."

"I'm working on it, baby! The space that you're in is completely covered in spells. It's preventing my burrowers from getting through! Give me a sec..."

I could hear his fingers attacking his keyboard. "Can you see the spells?" Judah asked. He was moving now.

"Yeah, I can see them...I've designed a program that can recognize them when it encounters them."

"Good kid...Hold on, Nak...we're almost there."

"Got it!" Rome cried as the hidden door slid open.

But I gasped...standing outside of it preventing me from going anywhere were several tall figures that were covered from head to toe in dark robes that hid their faces. They were way too tall to be humans and as if to confirm my thoughts, bright angry red eyes suddenly burned from the shadow of one of their hoods.

"What the f***?! Turn around and run, baby, I'm coming!" Rome called before the sound of him snatching off his headset and exiting the van could be heard.

He didn't have to tell me twice, I turned and hauled a** in the opposite direction.

Rome

*What the f*** is going on?!*

My heart was racing out of control as I forced myself to walk through the library so that I didn't draw any attention.

*What the f*** were those things standing outside of the door?!*

Once I got to the stairs that led down to the basement I was running again. I'd already looped the camera feed so the library's little security booth didn't see us. When I made it to the long hall that led to the tunnels, it was to see Jo, Albert, and Judah disappearing through the door.

By the time I made it to the secret door that led to the space that was covered by the spells, they were all gone.

"Dear Heavenly Father, be with your servant!" I prayed out loud as I ran in, but I didn't make it far before the Politician's arm shot out snatching me back. He put his finger on his lips signaling for me to be quiet.

He, Judah, and Albert stood with their backs pressed against the wall behind a tall stack of wooden crates. It looked as if we were in a factory, which was confusing as hell because I didn't pick any of this up on my signal intel.

Instantly, I searched for Nak. The Oldman held up a finger, getting my attention before pointing to a pile of crates across the huge space. Nak was there hunched down behind it. I exhaled when I saw that she was safe. When our gazes connected, she mouthed…

"What the f***?!" before she tilted her head toward what was taking place farther inside the factory.

Hell, I'd been so desperate to get to her that I hadn't even taken the time to look ins—

What the f***?!

I blinked, not believing what the f*** I was seeing.

There was a big rotating metal rack set up that had hundreds of human bodies hanging from it, like some sh*t you would see in a meat factory. Off to the side, two big ugly giants snatched one of the bodies down and threw it on the table. One of them lifted a huge meat cleaver and hacked off the leg at the thigh junction. It looked as if all the blood had already been drained.

He then proceeded to cut the leg into bloody chunks. The other giant carried a chunk of the leg and sat it on the desk next to a fat doctor in a dirty lab coat whose back was toward us. He stood typing something on a computer in front of him.

Without looking away from the computer screen, he picked up the chunk of flesh and scarfed it down like he was a dog.

A noise of surprise escaped the Oldman next to me. Nak's mouth opened as her frightened gaze shot across the room meeting mine. When the doctor turned in the direction facing us to type something on another computer behind him, we were able to see that he wasn't a human at all. He was something that looked as if he was part human, part animal…maybe a dog, or a wolf.

I turned my head and my stunned gaze met the Oldman's. Like me, this was blowing his mind. However, the Politician stood next to him with no expression at all, just a general frown that said he was ready to kill anything that threatened him. Obviously, he was no help.

Albert and I turned to look at Judah…desperately needing some answers. Nothing in his expression said that this was the first time he'd seen something like this. When he saw that we were looking at him and that we were f***ing tripping out…he stepped out from behind the box. The both of us reached out to grab him back before the beast man and his two ugly giants saw him, but he dodged our hands.

"End simulation…" He called and right before our eyes, everything just f***ing disappeared. But not really…it all seemed to be sucked up into a huge ball that turned into a bright light before becoming an older white gentleman in a suit.

This was some next level artificial intelligence. And trust me, I've seen some sick virtual reality, but nothing like this. The old man moved towards us…well, at least, I think he was old. His skin appeared young, but his hair was white as snow. I knew for certain that he wasn't really here with us, but he didn't appear to be a hologram, so he must be a part of the simulation.

We were no longer in the warehouse but in an underground cave. Standing surrounding us in a big circle were those tall hooded beings that had prevented Nak from leaving this space.

"What the f***?!" The words escaped my mouth as I turned taking them in. *This is some straight Eyes Wide Shut kind of sh*t.*

"You can say that again, kid." The Oldman said, his expression resembling mine as he too took in the strange beings surrounding us.

Nakhti

I stood on legs that felt numb and hurried to Rome making sure to give the man in the suit and the strange hooded things a lot of space. Rome wrapped his arm around pulling me close. I clung to him. I'm not going to lie, I was freaking out.

I'd never in my life seen anything like what I had just seen, and I've seen some horrible things in my life. I couldn't tell what was real or what was fake. I felt like Neo from The Matrix when Morpheus first brought him back into the simulation.

Judah went to stand next to the man in the suit as he studied us. He was taking in our response to what we'd just seen.

"Politician, bring back Joseph."

The Politician studied Judah for a moment. I knew him well and he didn't take too kindly to being ordered around, which was why I was surprised like hell when he nodded before his eyes started blinking rapidly as Jo came back to us.

The Sarge's stunned gaze fell on us before it took in the hooded beings. "What the f***!?"

"If you're wondering why we're surrounded by witches...the answer is quite simple. It's to protect me from you." The man in the suit finally spoke and I squeezed Rome's hand tighter. There was something wrong with this man. He was not good...He was evil.

Jo frowned. "That's ridiculous. Who are you?"

The man chuckled and for a moment, his eyes looked ancient. He touched his perfect tie straightening it because it was a habit, not because it was needed.

His gaze fell on me and Rome tightened his arm around me. "You are right, I am not a good man."

Nossa! How—

He shook his head. "And unfortunately, we don't have time for the hows...But I can tell you why." He paused for just a moment as his eyes rose to look at each of us.

"I am not a man whose expectation is in the Kingdom of the Ancient of Days...The four of you don't know it yet, but this makes me your natural born enemy." He chuckled.

"Every time I meet with your brother, I fear that it will be my last time before he kills me."

"Why do you do it then?" Jo asked dryly.

The man's head came up higher on his shoulder. "It's because I love my country. I am a patriot! I will do what needs to be done to protect it, even if it means putting my life at risk. And also because I understand this time here on earth is all that I have left. I don't have an expectation for anything else afterward except the suffering for the choices I've made."

"The Ancient of Day's wrath on the kingdoms before this great nation has been complete and utter destruction. There are many like me, who in their vanity, have gotten it in their heads to try and fight it." A look of sadness came into his eyes as he shook his head.

"Fools, the lot of them. They are doing nothing but bringing his wrath down on us sooner. However, there are a few of us…that are doing what we can to hold it off for as long as we can. Granted, none of them are foolish enough to work directly with a group of Slayers like me, but they are trying to do something. Maybe it's my vanity speaking, but I'd like to believe it's through our efforts that the brunt of his wrath hasn't fallen on us yet."

He shrugged. "And then there are others like us who say we are the fools because prophecy cannot be prevented. It was written that the young woman's stench shall reach His nose because the blood of his saints run in her streets. And when it does…when the stench of it reaches his nose, she shall fall."

"You keep saying us. Who are the us you speak of?" Rome asked.

The man's ancient gaze settled on him. "I'm surprised you don't already know. You meet with one of my brothers every week."

He's an angel… Now it all makes sense. But if he's an angel, why does he need witches to protect him?

He chuckled again. "I—used to be a melek. Now I am called the Fallen, biding my time before I have to pay for believing a lie. When the time comes, I will die the death of a man."

"Why have y'all brought us here and shown us that sick sh*t?" The Oldman hissed.

"Albert…" The man said turning to face him. "It's so good to see you again."

Al shook his head. "Man, I don't know you."

"Sure you do…but that clever little doctor erased your memories. Before Judah here came to me…You and his father did a good amount of work for me. However… Doctor Baxter did do a number on you."

His gaze fell on Jo. "It took us a while to realize it, but he's been working with Balaam. It was the wizard who showed him how to separate you from your Power and splinter you and your siblings like he's done."

He shook his head. "I cannot undo the spell he's cast on you, only the Ancient of Days can undo it…or Balaam himself, but I doubt if you'll get that old wizard to do anything for you…he hates your bloodline."

"My bloodline?" Albert asked putting his hand on his chest.

"Actually, all of your bloodline…believe it or not, you all have a few ancestors in common. But at last, I don't want to go further in that detail, it does not benefit me. I suspect it won't be long before the genius figures it out…just like he's discovered the difference between computer code and spells. Hell…thanks to the world wide web, wizards like Balaam can operate more freely. Isn't that right, kid?"

Rome shook his head. "The only Balaam I'd ever heard of is the one in the Bible…in the book of Numbers, chapter 22 through 24. And since you can't be talking about him…then I have no idea who he is…however, yeah…I have discovered a lot of spells hidden in computer coding."

With a greedy smile on his face, the man nodded. "Oh…that brain of yours, so much like your forefather you are. However…the Balaam that you read about in the Scrolls and the Balaam that walks the earth today…is one and the same, sweet boy. A spirit like that shall never rest until it meets its fate right along with the rest of us."

"So, if you're not an angel and you're not human…what are you?" I asked. I needed to know who he and the *us* he kept referring to was.

"Dear girl…" He opened his arms. "We are the gods of the planet earth."

Jo grunted as if he wasn't impressed. "If you a god, what do you need with us?"

The man's face lit in a smile. "And that is the question of the hour. Follow me, please…" He turned and walked farther into the cave.

Jo's gaze came to mine, mine shot to Rome's and Rome's settled on the Oldman. We all turned to look at Judah. He chuckled.

"It's cool, he is windy, but he'll eventually get to the point…follow him."

As soon as we started walking, the cave dissolved around us and a state-of-the-art board room appeared. It was so lifelike that even the smell changed from the musty mildew smell of the cave to that new office smell. I could even smell the leather of the chairs; I kid you not.

"Please take a seat…" the man in the suit called as he walked to the head of the table.

"Damn, what the hell is this? I can't wrap my mind around it." The Oldman muttered.

I looked at Judah… "What is this place?"

"This is neutral territory…this room rests on a ley line that can be openly used by any witch."

"What is a ley line?"

It was Rome that answered my question. "A crack in dimensions. A place where the spiritual and the physical co-exist."

I nodded, although I still was completely clueless as to what they were talking about. I would just have to ask Rome to explain it to me in layman's terms later.

You could tell we were all freaking out because the four of us slid down into chairs right next to each other, subconsciously scooting them closer. Judah sat at the other end of the table. None of this seemed to be bothering him at all.

He'd set all of this up. We thought we were coming to strike back at the ones who'd blown up my barn and killed Carlos and Freedom and he'd known the whole time that we weren't. I think Rome was right, Judah was not to be trusted.

"Would you guys care for anything to drink?" The man in the suit asked.

As if on cue, one of the cape figures came through the door carrying a tray with some kind of red liquid in rocks glasses.

Oh! Hell no!

All four of us shook our heads instantly. "Naw, we good, just had a few smoothies before we came," Rome told him. The being went to Judah and offered him a glass.

Judah's angry gaze shot up to it and it actually flinched before fleeing out the room.

"Play nice..." the man in the suit told Judah.

"Let's get this over with..." Judah growled.

The man stared at him for a little bit. "I won't have you much longer, will I?"

"That's where you're wrong, Patriot. You never had me to begin with."

So, his name was Patriot...

He inhaled before he nodded slightly, for a moment, there was sorrow in his eyes. "True...true indeed, for we all know there is only one who can tame the Lion of Judah..." When he blinked his eyes, his sorrow was gone and his gaze fell on Jo.

"Now to answer your question, I need you to do what you were created to do...slay demons."

Jo chuckled. "What?"

The man nodded. "It's true...I am so surprised the young prince has not told you. Surely his mentor talked to him about it."

We all looked at Rome. "Yeah... about that. I was going to tell you guys when the time was right."

"The time is right," I told him.

He took my hand bringing it to his lips. "Baby…You, Albert, Jo and his siblings…well, baby, y'all demon slayers."

I snatched my hand from his. "What?"

"It's true, Wild One…" Patriot said gaining our attention. "The Ancient of Day's created you to slay demons."

Jo frowned. "Demons? What? Like ghosts?" He looked at Albert and chuckled. "He wants us to search out and destroy the Bogeyman."

They both shared a good laugh at that.

"Naw, little brotha, not like ghosts." Judah's deep voice brought their laughter to a halt. "Before they became what we know as demons, they were the beloved children of him…"

His gaze went to the Patriot. "And those like him. They are called the Nephilim. It's the reason they fell…They lay with human women and bore children. But because that union was strictly forbidden…they bore giant monsters, monsters who hungered for human flesh and blood."

As he talked, he killed the rumor about him not being able to feel emotion. He was angry—No… I take that back, he was barely suppressing his rage.

"Because the Nephilim beings are so disgusting and foul, the Ancient of Days will not accept their souls after they die. So, their souls are stuck here to wander the earth looking for a host. It's their souls that are now called demons. All hate, all filth…all abhorrence can be attributed to them." His gaze centered on Jo.

"They are very real, little brother, the monsters that still walk this earth in the flesh…and the billions that prowl it in the spirit. Never doubt it."

"Although his words are a bit emphatic, they are true. The children of angels are allowed to walk in the flesh for five-hundred years before they die and become a demon. In the spirit form, they cannot touch or taste…they can't eat or drink. The only way they can experience these things is by taking over a body, whether human or cloned."

He held up one of his hands and the overhead lights dimmed before a bright light shone from the center of the table.

I gasped when a hologram image of a warehouse that looked like the one we'd just seen showed up in the light. There were racks with human bodies hanging from them and more of those ugly giant men standing around them.

"That's a real place?" I asked nobody in particular.

"Yeah, it's real. It's how they feed their children. It's a f***ing meat market for Nephilim!" Judah spat.

"There are thousands of these located all over the world." The Patriot said. "The problem is, eighty years ago, there used to be only three of them. Fifty years ago, twenty-four, which means the numbers are growing at a dangerous pace."

He stared off toward the corner of the office. "I have forty-two children that I love dearly. My children are monsters. When they walked the earth in their own flesh, they grew to a substantial size and had insatiable appetites for nearly everything. We found a way to grow food big enough to sustain them…" he shook his head.

"But they wanted meat. So, we allowed our servants to hunt animals for them. In a very short time, they'd depleted the livestock. It wasn't long before they started eating our servants. Daily sacrifices were made by the children of men to my children, but it wasn't enough. Soon, they began to consume mankind at an alarming rate. That's when we started cloning men, in hopes that the clones would appease them…"

"They didn't like the taste of the cloned flesh and continued to consume mankind. I and my brothers realized we'd made a mistake and we begged the Ancient of Days for forgiveness…But he told us that forgiveness was for man. And that we should have known better…and for our sins, we must pay. I watched all forty-two of my beloved children die in Noach's flood."

"So, if all of the Nephilim died in the flood, why are there meat shops popping up all over the place?" Rome asked.

The Patriot chuckled. "You would have thought we'd learned our lesson." He shook his head. "The children of men and the sons of Alohim are still having children to this very day. Through gene manipulation, most of the Nephilim are not grown to be giants anymore and can now blend in for the most part. The ones that can't are kept hidden underground." He pointed to the ugly giants that were working in the human meat market.

"However, the ones that can are so beautiful and so brilliant that mankind worships them, just like they did in days of old. But although they've managed to get them to appear more human-like, their appetites are still the same…and growing rapidly every day."

"So, what do you want us to do about it?" Albert asked with an unenthused frown on his face.

"I want you to allow Judah to train you to be able to kill the Nephilim and then I want you to search out and destroy as many as you can. For the most part, they stick very closely to their food supply. However, these meat markets are more than just a place where they obtain food, everything they need to function as a unit is there. They have scientists, and doctors, chefs…teachers to teach their young, trainers to train them in whatever field they're going to conquer… All located in the same spot. It's more like a nest. To bring down the nest is to bring down the hornets in the nest."

Jo shrugged. "How hard can they be to find? Can't be that easy to hide an underground city."

"I don't know, you tell me, Rome, how easy was it for you to find our mock factory?"

Rome shook his head. "I didn't see it at all until Nak actually walked inside."

"The spell that was cast over this room was a light one because I wanted you to find it. The Nephilim and their fathers will use all the weapons they have in their arsenal to keep you from finding their nest, including having it covered in some pretty nasty spells. These families have powerful human slaves, who are trained from birth to serve them. In most cases, they are being served by the same family that has attended to them for thousands of years. These slaves will stop at nothing to protect their masters."

Judah grunted. "Their *slaves* are some of the most powerful men in the world, whose masters keep them filthy rich in exchange for their unyielding loyalty."

Jo nodded… "Now I see…"

"You guys are not alone in fighting this evil… there are others in the field." The Patriot said before the hologram image changed in the center of the table. "Many of you may have seen this man before…"

A holograph image of the Preacher squatting down on a branch high up in a very tall tree appeared in front of us. His long black duster billowed around him making it look as if he had a pair of black wings.

"Rome, you speak of our spells that make your job as a hacker difficult. Well, our little spells have nothing on the Ancient of Days...his codes are unreadable by those whose eyes were not meant to see. You know what I speak is true, you've decided to decode your DNA and that of the others' in this room." He smiled as if to tell him...*yeah, good luck with that.*

"Anyhow, I can't tell you much about this man because he is made up of the Most High's most intricate coding and trying to solve it is impossible. The wisest of our kind have been trying for eons. But what I can tell you is that he is human...However, he is a human that has walked the earth for so long he can manipulate matter and time and space just like us."

"This is also one of the ancestors you all share in common." When our surprised gaze shot to his, he nodded. "Yes, he's so old that he can be the ancestor of all of you. He's also a Qoheleth, which makes him my enemy. I and those like me are trying to prevent the coming of the Ancient of Day's wrath...he is preparing for it. As far as we know, he is putting together an army. With any great army, there are rankings. I'll start at the top."

The hologram image changed to show a young man that for a moment, I thought could have been a younger version of Judah...But his long locs were a lighter brown as well as his skin...in fact, his eyes, hair, and skin were all the same color brown. It looked as if he'd just began to grow a beard and mustache...the kid was quite handsome.

"Young Dawid...the Lyon's Cub. From what we know, the Qoheleth is putting him and the wolf pup..." The hologram image changed to show another boy whose hair was pure white. I could tell right off that the boy was Hispanic or an islander.

Where the other kid was just handsome, this boy with his otherworldly looks was pure art. He was so beautiful that it was almost painful to look at him. The image changed again, it was a closer shot of his face and we were all able to see that there were white rings around each of his pupils… He too had started to grow a beard and mustache, but they grew in black unlike the hair on his head.

"Monroe…there is a wager going on, on whether or not this one will make it. There's a darkness in him that is showing promise. Nonetheless, we believe the Ooheleth is setting these two up to be the leaders of the army he is gathering together. However, they are still quite young and being trained by two of the deadliest men in the world…their fathers, Lyon and Gideon."

The hologram image changed to show two men that made Judah pale in comparison and that was saying a lot. He said they were the two deadliest men in the world…and I believed him. I could already tell who Dawid's father was because he looked like a miniature version of him. The image changed to show a huge lion standing next to Lyon. Like his son, his long locs, skin and eyes were all the same color…Hell…he resembled the lion standing next to him.

"Judah, you remember Lyon, don't you? I believe he is the reason you're not dead."

Our gaze went to Judah…He exhaled and began speaking. "When I was sixteen, Father had set me up so that I ended up in one of those meat markets…"

We all looked at him surprised.

Judah nodded. "It's so much I need to tell you guys…now is not the time. But I promise to fill you in on everything later. I know the kid doesn't trust me…" His gaze went to Rome. "But that's fine, he'll learn to trust me in battle. Anyway…Father had set me up and I ended up on one of those hooks, destined to become food for the Nephilim." He stood and snatched off his shirt, turning his back to us, moving his hair out the way so that we could see.

There was a big ugly scar at the top of his muscled back. I flinched…that must have been extremely painful. He put his shirt back on and sat. "It just so happened they had Lyon down a little deeper underground doing some kind of experiments on him. I know they took his DNA because I've seen clones of him…many. The demons like his clone because it's strong enough to hold their wretched spirits a lot longer than any of the other clones."

His seething rage was back, and I couldn't help but wonder about the woman that could make such a man feel love.

"Somehow, Lyon got free." He continued. "I was on that hook dying, my blood was draining from my body…their children drink the blood as well. The next thing I know, he was lifting me off the hook. His stronger than anything you can imagine. He told me we had to get out because the place was getting ready to blow. I didn't know who to trust, I was so afraid. So as soon as we made it out, I ran away from him as well. There was a car sitting out front waiting on him, I could tell he debated whether or not he wanted to come after me, but eventually, he jumped in. Seconds later, the whole nest went up in a blast."

They continued to tell us all they knew about the army the Preacher was putting together. When they were done, the four of us just sat there all lost in our own thoughts. This thing was huge, way bigger than some strange men blowing up my farm.

They were talking about a literal war between good and evil and they said that we were destined to fight in it.

"I know we've laid a lot on you, but as you can see, we are losing valuable time. We've already noticed the shift in the weather patterns. These are warnings...warnings that are growing more insistent. I was there when the windows of the heavens opened. I witnessed Him destroy all life in forty-days. I know what His wrath looks like when unleashed...and no matter what the others may think, there is nothing that we can do to fight against it." As he spoke, his eyes filled with unshed tears.

"Will you help me? Please?"

All four of us stared at him for a moment. I knew if the others were thinking like me, they wanted to tell him no. But then I remembered that weasel whose neck I had driven my knife in. He was no doubt one of their slaves, luring me into the pits of the earth to become food for the Nephilim. And I couldn't help but think about the others I'd seen on the hooks in the hologram pictures.

These are the missing persons whose faces were being flashed on the news above ground, asking...*if you've seen them.*

There were children on the hooks...babies.

I couldn't just do nothing. With resolve, I looked up at the Patriot.

"I'm in..."

Rome's gaze came to me. "Are you sure?"

I shook my head. "No...But I'm going to do it nonetheless."

He nodded before looking at the Patriot. "I'm in..."

The Oldman exhaled throwing up his hands. "What the hell? Got to play my part to keep the world as safe as I can for little Ayana and the rest of the little babies. I'm in..."

Our gazes fell to Jo, but he was looking at Judah. "I can't control the Politician."

"I'll teach you how..."

Jo nodded before he turned to look at the Patriot. "I'm in..."

"Good...I'll be in touch." And then he, the witches, and the state-of-the-art office all disappeared. When my eyes blinked again...we were all sitting in the musty cave on five crates.

"I don't think I will ever get used to that," The Oldman muttered as he looked around the now empty cave.

"I know you were looking forward to going after the people who'd destroyed your homes," Judah spoke to us all. "But you're not ready. If what you seen in the simulation today caused your hearts to fail, then..." He shook his head.

"The reality will devastate you. What you saw today was incredibly mild to the real thing. Trust me when I tell you, I brought you here because I needed you to see what we're really up against...and now we can prepare."

He stood from his crate. "The Patriot can only be trusted to a certain extent and not an ounce more. To preserve his life and the life of his children, he will kill you."

Jo raised his hand. "Wait, I thought his children were dead."

"Their physical bodies, yes. But their miserable souls still roam the earth just like the others."

"So, they're demons?" I asked.

He nodded. "Yeah, they are. The melekim love their own children. They can give a damn about the others, which is why it's so many battles between them. They f***ing hate each other. The

Patriot has agreed to fund us and use his authority to protect us…"
He paused for just a moment.

"Just as long as we agree not to kill any of his children."

Rome frowned. "What? How long do you think that is going
to work?"

Judah shook his head. "For as long as it has to…Come on,
let's get out of here."

On the chopper ride home, neither of us spoke. The way we
saw the world had been completed shifted in one day. There were
demons walking the earth… Demons that searched for human
bodies to take over, just so they can feel, touch and taste again.

I'd always believed in them, but in a way like Jo joked
about…bogeymen, ghosts, things of folklore. But they were very
real and now I'd become a demon slayer.

The Patriot thought that he could somehow delay God's
wrath, but I thought back to what the Preacher told me…

*"The young prince will find you and for a moment, you and
he will have normal. Cherish those days because they won't last.
Perilous times are coming and everything we once knew will be
destroyed in one hour."*

I reached over and took Rome's hand, he turned to look at
me and smiled reassuringly. And you know what? That smile
brought peace to my heart.

The young prince had found me… And he and I will have
our normal. I was going to make sure to enjoy it…

Because perilous times were coming…and life as we know
it will be destroyed in one hour.

The Epilogue

Nahkti

5 Months Later...

    I held Ayana in my arms and danced to one of the local band's renditions of *Happy*. As a matter of fact, she'd been my dance partner for the last few songs because my husband had disappeared shortly after Jo and Journey and Al and Abby said I do.

    Oh y'all...they'd had the most beautiful double wedding I'd ever witnessed. Actually, it was the only double wedding I'd witnessed, but I know the others couldn't hold a flame to theirs. Journey wanted to wait until she had the baby to get married so that she could look good in her dress.

    She'd given birth to a healthy baby boy named Ephrayim two months ago. We all spoiled him, especially me. Anyway, she'd wanted to wait and now she looked like a fairy princess in her white gown.

    Abby had decided to go with a more relaxed look. Her gown didn't billow around her like Journey's did, it lay on her beautiful body perfectly. Albert was beside himself when she walked down the aisle. I cried the whole time. Of course, Rome talked about me and called me a crybaby, but I couldn't help it.

    It was so romantic the way Albert and Jo looked at their brides. You could see their love for each other clearly in their eyes.

Yeah, I cried… I don't know, I've been doing a lot of crying lately.

"Have you seen my brother?" Rob asked as he nearly stuffed a whole piece of cake into his mouth.

Y'all already know the boy was high as a kite. I chuckled, I don't even know where he is getting his weed from, we lived in the Canadian Mountains. It was no telling, knowing him, he'd probably found some crazy mountain man who grew Canada weed with snowflakes on top.

"He disappeared shortly after they said I do. You know he's probably with Judah at headquarters. The two of them are practically attached at the hip."

It's true…

Surprisingly, the recluse has taken to Rome. The two of them always had their heads together frowning at something on one of Rome's computer monitors. Over the last five months, my husband has turned his computer lab at headquarters into his own space. It now resembled the setup he had in Chicago, including the plush computer chair made for a king.

I blushed thinking about what he did to me in that chair last night…

Mmmm…

"Good, if he with dude that mean that big nigga won't be all in my business," Rob grumbled as he loaded his plate up with the brisket sliders.

I laughed at him. "You better watch it, you can't run forever, he going to catch you one day."

The *he* we were talking about was Judah. Rob and his mischievous ways had become a thorn in his side. The other evening, just as the sun was setting, Rome and I were sitting on our back porch watching Luna graze in front of the new barn.

She'd been acting a little strange lately, so I had the local vet come out to give her a once over. Come to find out, Freedom had left us a little gift that will be introduced to the world in about another seven months.

Anyway, we were sitting out there making plans for the new colt when Rob bolted past us into the house. Neither Rome nor I batted an eye at that because it wasn't the first time. Shortly after he ran past us, Judah's Hummer came skidding to a halt in the driveway.

"What did he do this time?" Rome asked as Judah got out his truck.

"That little bastard is smoking his drugs in back of my house again!"

Judah's house sat on the peak of the mountain. The view from the back of his house was breathtaking. It called to the artist in Rob, it was one of his favorite places to paint and smoke apparently. He's driving Judah nuts because he just doesn't sit quietly and paint, he helps himself to Judah's things... Like the beer he keeps in the fridge in his garage.

And I'd like to say it stopped there, but I'd be lying. When Rob gets the munchies, he helps himself to Judah's snacks as well. Sometimes he even smuggled me some things because the healthy eating Nazi was back.

Y'all will never guess it, but our boss eats more trash than I used to. When I asked Rob why he was bugging Judah, knowing he likes to be left to himself, Rob's only response is…*Somebody needs to.*

Judah's been threatening to bring him on to the team, forcing him to clean himself up. I think Rob wants to be on the team, Rome has trained him to fight and shoot. However, he can't let go of the weed long enough to train with us.

And the training…

Nossa! The training…

It was tough, but nobody said being a demon slayer was going to be easy.

"Uh oh…y'all getting ready to get called away," Rob said bringing me back to the present.

I helped Ayana drink some punch from a plastic cup. "What are you talking about?"

He tilted his head toward the entrance to Jo and Journey's back yard where the reception was being held. Standing there talking to Jo, who looked so handsome in his tux, was one of Judah's men. And sure enough, a few seconds later, Jo was walking toward me.

"Come on, baby girl, your auntie have to go to work. Let's go get some more cake." Rob told Ayana before he took her out of my arms.

"She's had enough cake…She's going to be sick," I told him.

"You hear that, baby?" He asked her in a squeaky little voice. "Tee-Tee Nak hating. We gon' remember that next time she come downstairs begging me for red Kool-Aid."

"Bruh, why you trying to mess up a good thing," I called after him. He held his head back and laughed.

"We've been summoned," Jo muttered grabbing himself a cup of punch.

"What!? No...it's your wedding day!"

He chuckled as he turned to look at his beautiful bride who danced with the Oldman.

"You know he doesn't care."

"That's bullsh*t! You know what? Your brother needs a woman. He is all hard stone and tough leather. He needs some softness in his world."

"Well, until he gets it, he'll continue to be the tough leather across our backs. Get the Oldman... I'll drive."

Neither Journey nor Abby was happy with the fact that their husbands were leaving in the middle of their reception and I don't blame them. This was ridiculous!

I had made up my mind that I was getting ready to tell Judah about himself. Rob was right...somebody needed to.

However, as soon as we walked into the computer lab at headquarters, I knew something was wrong. Judah's frown was more fierce than usual and Rome was concentrating a little too hard on whatever he was looking at on his computer screen.

Jo exhaled and undid his bowtie...The Oldman followed suit. All three of us slid into a chair and waited.

Judah's angry gaze fell on Jo. "Your brother is in trouble."

"Let me guess...Naphtali?"

Judah nodded. "Yesterday, his adopted parents were murdered. The police report claims it was a boating accident, but of course, we know different."

"Do you think it's the same people that's after us?" Al asked.

Judah nodded. "They're trying to clean up all their loose ends. Naphtali doesn't know his parents purchased him. He believes he was adopted when he was a little baby."

"What's happened to him?" I asked.

Judah exhaled. "We believe he's been captured and taken to one of the nests. However, we don't believe it's the nest of the one that is after us. Either our enemy is testing us to see what we are capable of or they're setting up a rival family to fall."

"What happened to his alter? Why did the Bully allow him to be taken?" Jo asked.

"I believe he went willingly," Rome responded as his hands flew across the keyboard.

A very pretty brown-skinned woman, who wore a pair of red glasses appeared on the big monitor in front of him.

She wasn't supermodel pretty. There were no hard angles and sleek lines about her. She was soft and round like a baby doll... Don't get me wrong, she wasn't fat...not even close. She was a little thing really. She was just round and cuddly...cute.

Yeah, ...she was cute.

"Her name is Free Spirit Robinson."

We all stared at Rome, waiting for him to tell us he was joking.

"Are you serious?" I asked.

He chuckled. "Quite…" His hands went to work on the keyboard again and an older version of Free Spirit Robinson showed up on the smaller monitor next to the big one.

"May I introduce you to Flower Robinson…Free's mom and the only black hippie in Detroit. She died in 1993 of a drug overdose, leaving a twelve-year-old Free to go live with her estranged father and his wife, who had twin girls prior to her marriage to Free's father."

"Free came up missing from Vegas yesterday." Judah continued. "We believe the New York branch of the Cartel was responsible for that. However, when the enemy got wind of this, we believe they used it as an opportunity to capture Naphtali by making him believe they had her and getting him to walk willingly to his death, thinking he was coming to save her. With the death of his parents occurring on the same day, it's possible he's just not thinking straight."

"Why would the Cartel kidnap Free?" I asked.

"Sit back, my love and allow me to introduce you to the Bully," Rome said before a real grimy beat began to play from the speakers in the ceiling.

Judah folded his arms across his massive chest and shook his head. Jo exhaled. "Man, why do you have to be so extra all the time?"

Okay, on a side note, although Rome and Judah had grown quite close, Rome and Jo's relationship hadn't improved much. They still argued amongst each other every opportunity they got. And most times, it provided entertainment for us all.

A week before Journey had the baby, Rome and Jo had been arguing something fierce during training. I couldn't even remember what for, but they were going at each other. So of course, Jo started teasing Rome about his little Dirty Dancing routine that he'd caught us doing.

By the time we all got back to Abby and Al's place, who'd invited us over for dinner, Jo's teasing had worked my husband's nerves really good. Rome looked at Journey, who was helping her mom set the table.

"Hey lil sis…have you guys settled on a name for the baby yet?" To everyone on the outside looking in, his question seemed innocent enough.

But Jo, knowing how clever Rome was narrowed his eyes at him.

"We have a few names we're considering." Journey told him, not aware of the battle that was raging around her.

"Remember when you were little and you said if you ever had a boy, you were going to name him Velvet because most people didn't realize how masculine the word was?"

The look that came over Jo's face damn near made me choke on the water I was drinking.

"Yeahhhh…" Journey said remembering it. "Velvet is a very masculine name. Thanks for reminding me of that. It would be the perfect name for our son."

"What?! Wait!" Jo called after her as she walked back into the kitchen. His gaze flew back to Rome, who now wore a devious smile on his face.

"You little conniving mutha f---"

"What you say, Jo?" Abby called from the kitchen.

Jo's head popped up. "Huh? Oh…nothing, mom." He turned back to Rome with narrow eyes.

"This not over, you little bastard," he whispered before he hurried into the kitchen to find Journey and undo the damage Rome had done. Man, we laughed about that for weeks.

Rome spun around in his chair to face us… "Do I say anything about y'all having to go to church before each mission?" He snapped responding to Jo's comment about him being extra.

Jo opened his mouth to retort, but Judah signaled for Rome to get on with it.

"Thank you, fierce leader. Now…for your information, *Jo*, this is *Beanie Sigel's The Truth*. I put this song on because this grimy a** beat encompasses your brother. The man is a goon. He is the very definition of a Back-Yard Bully. If you all will be so kind as to look at the screen above, I've put together a little compilation for you."

The footage opened up with Jo…No…not Jo. He was dressed too street. It was Jo's look-alike chasing a man down the street. It looked like the footage came from someone's cellphone. Whoever it was provided some pretty vivid commentation.

"Yo, look at the big mutha f***a move. He finna catch Plank crackhead a**."

Yes…Naphtali was moving fast. There is no way a guy as big as he should be able to move like that. The guy he chased was crackhead fast and everybody knows you're not catching a crackhead. However, there was no doubt in my mind that one was as good as caught.

Without slowing down, Jo's look-alike snatched up a metal garbage can, held it over his head and hauled it at the man he chased with all his might. When the can came in contact with the man's back, we all flinched. Yeah…it hit him that hard. The impact caused him to fly off his feet.

The footage got really jumpy because the cameraman was going crazy at this point.

"Hey! Yo! Did y'all see that sh*t?!" He was surrounded by several men and they were all crazily excited by Naphtali's brutish behavior.

"That dude is a goon!" One of them yelled.

"Damn that! That nigga is a beast!" Another supplied.

"F*** that! The mutha f***a is a bully!" The cameraman cut in.

Naphtali went to the man and snatched him off the ground as if he weighed nothing and then slammed him into the brick wall knocking him out cold. However, that did little to assuage his anger because he picked the garbage can up and slammed it down on the unconscious man again.

Before he could repeat his actions, several more men with DEA written on the back of their shirts finally caught up to him grabbed him, stopping him. When they turned him around it was then I saw that he had a badge around his neck.

"He's a DEA officer? Are you kidding me?!" The words burst from my surprised lips. With the way that he was dressed and the way he acted, I thought he was a drug dealer.

Rome chuckled as he rocked back in his chair. "*Special Forces*…Keep watching."

The footage changed to Officer Bully sitting in an integration room looking bored.

"Goddammit, Tucker! You're killing me here! You're the only officer under my command that gets complaints from hardcore f***ing drug dealers. He's trying to sue!"

Tucker chuckled as he shook his head. "I don't know why. I didn't touch that guy."

Nossa! He even sounded like Jo. This was so strange…I felt like I was looking at the thug version of the Sarge. Everything about them except for their style of dress was the exact same. Same haircut, they wore their beards and mustaches the same…Same build. Even the way he chuckled was like the Sarge.

I turned my head to see how Jo was taking this and although his outward expression didn't show any signs of him being affected…the way he balled his hands up in his lap let me know he was bugging out at seeing this man who looked so much like him. If you changed him out of the jeans and t-shirt and into a suit, it could be him.

The man typed something on the computer before he turned it around so that Tucker could see the screen. It was a YouTube video of him beating the hell out of the crackhead with the garbage can. Tucker rubbed his hands down his handsome face trying to hide his laughter, but this only made his boss angrier.

The man's face got beet red and it looked as if he was going to burst a blood vessel in his head. He narrowed his gaze at Officer Tucker.

"Are you high on that sh*t?"

Tucker sat up a little straighter in his chair. "What sh*t, sir?"

His boss slammed his hand down on his desk in front of him. "You know what sh*t I'm talking about! Dope!"

Chuckling Tucker shook his head. Although his boss was good and worked up, he was as relaxed as a person getting a massage. Goodness, he reminded me of Rob.

"No sir, I don't do dope."

"So, you haven't been smoking weed?"

Tucker held up his finger. "You didn't say anything about weed...You said dope."

The man exploded from his chair. "That's it, you bastard! I'm enrolling you into a drug program..." That got to Tucker.

The smile left his face and he held up his hands. "For weed, captain?!" He frowned...

Wow! It was Jo's frown.

"Don't nobody go to rehab for weed!"

His captain exhaled. "I didn't say anything about rehab. I'm sending you to counseling."

"Say what?!"

"You heard me; you're taking a year off and you're going to see a shrink. It will be to your shrink's discretion whether you come back at the end of the year...." He paused for just a moment and it looked like it pained him to say his next words.

"Or not..."

Tucker sat up in his chair, he was not happy with this news...

"Why you doing this, Cap?"

485

The man shook his head and for a moment, sorrow came into his eyes. "I should have never let you talk me into bringing you back on so soon after coming out of deep cover like that. You were in too deep…You should have taken that year off then."

"What are you talking about? I'm fine…"

"Well, why haven't you stopped smoking the dope?"

"Cap…You keep saying dope. It's not dope, it's herb, there is a difference. Everybody smokes a little herb from time to time."

"You didn't…not before you went under."

Tucker sat back in his chair and exhaled.

"You see what I mean, kid? You need this time off. Go home, get your head straight. I set up something with a shrink in Michigan City, she was the only one the department will pay for. You know how cheap those bastards upstairs are. Anyway, she helps with people who have drug addictions."

"Cap…it's not—"

"Yeah…yeah, yeah. I know, it's herb. I don't give a f*** what it is! I want it out of your system. Meet with the doctor, do what she tells you…she gives me a good report and I get you reinstated. Easy peasy…"

"Easy peasy?!" I asked. "How does this guy still have a job."

"Ahhh!" Rome said sitting up in his chair going to work on his keyboard. When he was done, he sat back and pointed at the screen.

Picture after picture of Naphtali receiving medals of honor flashed across the monitor and one news article after another about how his team singlehandedly took down one drug ring after another.

"And this is the big one, the one where he picked up his little ganja habit."

A confidential report appeared on the screen that described how Officer Naphtali had gone undercover for nearly two years to bring down the New York branch of the Cartel. When it happened, he was labeled invaluable to the force.

"And this is why we believe the Cartel grabbed Free," Judah grumbled. "Suit up, Nak…You and Rome are going to Argentina to retrieve her. I, Jo and the Old Man are going to find Naphtali…We'll meet back here in two weeks. I will not accept failure." And then he turned and exited the room.

Jo exhaled. "Journey is going to be pissed when she finds out I've got to postpone our honeymoon for two weeks."

The Oldman shook his head. "Who you telling?"

The End…For Now

And so, our saga continues. This will not be the last time you hear from Rome and Nak, so don't pout. However, I'd like to present a question to you guys. What happens when the tormented becomes the tormenter? When the shoe ends up on the other foot and the opportunity to exact a little revenge is presented? Find out in…

Mean Tucker
The Bully

Connect With Us on Social Media!

Edwina's Place Chat With Me

Author Edwina Fort

Edwina Fort

BONUS CHAPTER!

Chapter 1

They Met...

I Knew from The First Moment We Met. It Was... Not Love at First Sight Exactly, but more...Familiarity. Like: Oh, Hello, Hey It's You...It's Going to Be You.

--Mhairi McFarlane (via 5000Letters)

Angel

For as long as I can remember, I've had nightmares. Not your average nightmares with monsters and such. No…

I dreamed about a world depleted of all life. A world on fire…

A world ravished…

These dreams I kept to myself. Coming up in the foster system you learn to keep a lot of things to yourself. I don't think I've ever had a good night's sleep. I am the only one with a case of sleep apnea that my teas cannot fix.

People came to my shop from all over the city to get teas that will help cure what ailment they suffer from naturally, and so far, I was the only one my teas did nothing for. I don't know if I'd become immune to the herbs because I've consumed so many of them, or if…and this is what I suspect it to really be, I'm meant to have these dreams.

For some reason, I think God wants me to see the world the way that I see it in my sleep. It does help me come up with tea recipes. LOL! I know that sounds strange, but it does…

However, I didn't start off my tale by telling you guys about my nightmares for no reason. I did it because although my nightmare's scare the heck out of me, it's nothing compared to the fear my foster brother's boss causes me to feel.

Westly, who is my foster brother, does maintenance work at the neighborhood gym, a job he's had for the past six months. It really is bittersweet. Sweet because for Westly having a job for six months is a huge improvement to his record. Over the last ten years,

I doubt if he'd held a job for longer than two weeks, let alone six months.

Westly has two major habits that keep him from being a reliable employee. One, he's a heroin addict and two, he often steals to support his heroin habit.

So the fact that he's held this job for six months is amazing. He's even for the most part been able to pay his half of the rent. Well…until recently, but I'll come back to that.

The bitter part about him having this job is that he works for a goon. There is no other word that can describe him.

Okay, maybe…Heathen, Thug, Savage, Animal, Bear, Lion…Brute!

Yes…Brute is a better word.

The man is a complete brute. When he walks down the street, people scramble to get out of his path. He's a bad man and his bad vibes go out ahead of him to clear the way.

I bet he kills people. He looks like the type. He's probably beat somebody to death with those huge, scarred monster paws he calls hands.

Anyway, the man is completely uncivilized.

But what makes things so much worse is the fact that he's attracted to me for some strange reason. I was nothing like the kind of woman that he should be attracted to. I wasn't a fancy dresser or a partier…I wasn't bold or even brave.

I am a boring tea maker. A boring tea maker that blends so well into the background that folks barely notice me. When people come to my shop, their eyes are drawn to the many jars of herbs and my tea displays that I have worked so hard on.

Although I'm standing there taking their order, very seldom do they stop and really take me in. My beautiful teas are truly the stars of the show.

This doesn't make me feel bad. It has always been that way for me. In fact, I love it that way. I didn't like drawing attention to myself, which is why I dressed in boring, loose-fitting clothes that took away from my looks rather than add to them.

It's an old trick I learned early from growing up in foster homes, you didn't want to attract the wrong kind of attention to yourself, things could get really nasty. So many times, I'd almost fallen prey…But thank God for Westly, who protected me in those days.

Anyway, I'll tell you more about that later as well… First, let me finish telling y'all about my amazing ability to go unnoticed.

Well…to everyone but Hitta.

The first time I came to the gym to pick up rent money from Westly, Hitta was standing at the front counter where the cash register was talking to the person that I assumed was his cashier.

When I came in, they both looked up, the cashier with a warm greeting smile and Hitta with a fierce scowl that almost made me turn around and run back out the door, but I didn't because our rent money was very late and the landlord was once again threatening to put us out.

So…I pressed on, but my eyes as if they had a mind of their own took in the monster of a man in front of me. His muscles were very hard and defined. I don't think he had an ounce of fat on him…anywhere.

This I was able to see because he wore a white wife beater that fell on him in a way that can be distracting to a weaker woman than I. He had several tattoos, but what really stood out were the two words that were angrily slashed up each of his forearms.

The right arm had the word Hard slashed up it, describing that forearm perfectly. And the left arm had the word Hitta slashed up it...not doubt describing those monster fists perfectly. There was another tattoo on his right bicep, but I wasn't close enough to see what it was. And it looked like another that began somewhere under his tank top and went all the way up to the left side of his thick neck.

Gracious!

In his ear, he wore a diamond earring that wasn't really big, but big enough to let the onlooker know it wasn't cheap. Around his neck, he wore a gold necklace that had a pair of diamond-encrusted boxing gloves hanging from it.

My gaze continued down his body. He wore a pair of brand name black sweat pants on his muscled legs that fell on his tampered hips as if he was modeling them and a pair of black Jordan's on his feet.

The fact that it looked as if he was fresh from the barber with the low-cut hair and full beard that was lined perfectly, did little to take away from his fierceness. In fact, if you could get past the frown that looked as if it may be a permanent fixer on his face, he was a really handsome man in a very rugged kind of way.

The closer I got to the giant the more I had to strain my neck to look up at him. And the closer I got to him, the more it felt as if he could just pick me up with one hand and snap me in half.

Gracious! The violence that was pouring off him was suffocating. You ever met someone and thought...this person is very dangerous? You look in their eyes and can tell they won't hesitate to hurt or kill…In Hitta's case… Smash!

I had to change my thoughts or else I was going to lose my nerve and go scurrying back out that door making a complete fool of myself. So I decided to do my best to ignore the big frowning giant to the right of me with the cold deadly eyes.

It wasn't easy though. First of all, he didn't move to the side like a normal, civilized human being would have done so that I could speak with the receptionist privately.

No… he just rudely stood there, forcing me to stand closer to him than I was comfortable with. He smelt like power. Instead of cologne, he smelt like whatever soap he'd used to wash his clothes and rage.

And I know you're saying, what the hell does rage smell like…?

And I'm telling y'all, it smells like Hitta.

Anyway, so I'm standing there trying to ask the receptionist if he'd get Westly for me and Hitta is staring at me as if I'm an ice cube and he's a man that had been lost in the desert for thirty days. I give him a look that says it's rude to stare…

And would y'all believe the heathen found that amusing? He even cracked those intimidating lips of his into a smile. I shivered because I didn't know what was more frightening, his smile or his scowl.

However, that wasn't the worst part. The receptionist then left to go and find Westly, leaving me alone with the brute.

Y'all, the gym was huge. Who knows where Westly was? So I take a few steps back and pretend to read the postings on the cork board that was there. The whole time he was watching me. He hadn't moved his big body from where he leaned on the counter.

And then he opened his mouth and spoke, the sound of his deep voice nearly caused me to jump out my shoes. I kid you not, a squeak of fear left my throat.

Don't shake y'all's heads at me, I told y'all I'm not that brave. I had a tragic childhood. I hate that I'm this way, but I am very squeamish.

Anyway, so he spoke.

"Why you dress that way?"

My mouth dropped open at his rudeness. "Excuse me?!"

"I don't like to repeat myself."

At that moment I was thanking God for my brown skin because if I had been a few shades lighter, I would be beet red right now.

Not only was he a rude brute…he was bossy and mean.

I held my head up as if he was nothing. "Dress what way?" I wanted to say heathen but changed my mind.

"Like a homeless person."

My mouth dropped open again.

Oh, my God! Did the man just tell me I dressed like a homeless person? I was so insulted that at that point, my fear of him faded for just a bit. I put my hand on my hip.

"For your information, this style is called Boho."

He lifted an eyebrow and I could tell by the little evil smirk on his face he was enjoying himself at my expense. "Hobo?"

"No! Boho…It's a difference." I nearly yelled. I started to begin that sentence with, *are you deaf!* But then thought better of it. This guy felt dangerous, like make you disappear dangerous.

He grunted, letting his intimidating gaze roam over my body.

Okay, so maybe I didn't wear the brightest of colors. That day I believed I had on my long maxi black skirt that fell to cover my feet completely and a grey oversized sweater that hung off one shoulder. I'd partnered that ensemble with my black hand beaded tasseled purse. I'll admit it wasn't the prettiest thing in my closet, but I didn't look homeless either.

His intense gaze was starting to unnerve me. He had yet to look away from me since I walked through those doors. He studied me so intensely it felt as if he could see under my shabby clothes to the figure I worked very hard to hide.

After his insulting words, he didn't say anything else, he just stood there watching me. And the way that he did it was so unnerving. People walked past and said goodbye to him, but he never looked away from me. He just nodded his head to whoever it was and mumbled something in a language that was purely his because I don't think it was English.

I know he was a brute and probably uneducated…but even he had to know that it was rude as hell to stare at somebody like that. It was almost as if he knew he was making me nervous and was enjoying it.

Although Westly and I were fairly new to this neighborhood, I'd heard enough from the girl who lived across the hall from me to know that he was something of a big shot around these parts. She said he used to be a professional boxer and was doing really good until an injury forced him to stop.

Of course, I was very curious as to what the injury was, there weren't many ailments my teas couldn't take care of. There were some...

But not many...

However, he was such a brute we will never find out. If he had been civilized, I would have tried to reach out to him. There was no way that was happening now.

I was so relieved when I looked up and saw Westly walking towards me that I nearly ran to him and threw myself into his arms. Although an addict, my brother has always protected me. The giant frowned when he saw this...

"Hey, Bo..." His deep voice seemed to rumble through the floor. "This yo' girl?"

He still hadn't moved from where he casually leaned against the counter.

Westly seemed shocked that his boss was actually talking to him. I would later find out that was the first time he'd ever said anything to him.

My brother chuckled in that way that let me know he was freshly high. In another few minutes, he would start the nodding.

"Naw, bossman, this here my little sista."

The giant grunted again as his gaze once again raked down my body. "This the sista that stay with you?"

Westly was now beaming like a small child whose hero had noticed them. "Yeah it is…I—I didn't think you knew anything 'bout me."

I rolled my eyes. I wanted to kick him for being so infatuated with the brute.

At one time y'all, my brother was so very strong and handsome. Girls used to line up at our foster parent's door to see him. Of course, I would get nervous whenever he went out because that meant I would be home with Kirk without Westly's protection.

Scary times…

Very scary times…

Anyway, back in those days, my brother was the man to know. Now, the heroin and whatever other drugs he liked had torn his body down. He was only a tenth of the man he used to be. Of late, he's been scratching big sores on his arms and face.

I pray he hadn't started doing meth, but I fear that he has. I have paid for him to go to rehab more times than I can count, but so far, nothing has worked. However, I can't turn my back on him. Had it not have been for him putting the fear of God in Kirk's heart, I would have been brutally raped many times.

No, I can't turn my back on him. I take comfort in the fact that although he steals like nobody's business…he's never stolen from me.

Not once…

"I know about everybody working for me." The giant spoke again, drawing my attention back to him. "Including the fact that you like to suck on that glass dick…" His intense gaze fell back to me.

But I was too busy trying to pick my mouth up off the ground for the third time. He'd just put my poor brother on blast and brought up his ailment in a most vile way. The guy at the register pretended to shuffle around some papers.

"You sure are rude..." I finally hissed. I'd had enough of his horrible personality.

"Baby, I don't shugga coat sh*t."

Westly gave a nervous laugh. "I'll be right back, boss, I just need to talk to my sista outside for a minute."

His hands shook as he led me away. I looked back over my shoulder at the animal man and I swear, what he did next nearly made me trip, had Westly not been holding my arm so tightly I would have.

He slowly licked his lips and then kissed toward me, but that wasn't the shocking part. The shocking part was my body's response to that scandalous gesture. I felt a spasm between my thighs that stole my breath.

That was the first time anything like that has ever happened to me. When I frowned at the brute's vulgarness, he had the nerve to wink at me with that evil grin on his face, as if he was very much aware of what his vulgar gesture had done to my body.

Needless to say, after that day, I did my very best to avoid going to the gym for anything, but then I started seeing him in the oddest of places.

Like the bus stop when I'm on my way to and from work. It isn't every day, but some days he'd be sitting there watching me in that big black Hummer with the tan leather seats that my brother thought was the best vehicle to have ever been created under the heavens.

He never said anything, just sat there and watched me get on the bus or get off. For my own sanity, I'd convinced myself that he wasn't sitting there for me. The gym was right across the street. He could be sitting waiting for someone to come out or just waiting to go in.

And then it was that time he'd shown up at the carnival that I'd taken my six-year-old niece to. She'd dragged me all over wanting this and that. And well, I was on a serious budget and could not afford to get any more tickets to get on any more rides.

My God, the tickets were nearly five dollars apiece, and you needed at least three to get on each ride, which meant every ride was costing a whopping fifteen dollars for four minutes. And of course, like any kid her age who didn't understand money, she started to have a fit on me.

I know I need to be firmer with her, but the truth is, I didn't have it in me...Both of her parents were drug addicts. The only time she got to be a kid free of worries is when she was with me.

So there I stood in the middle of the carnival checking my bank account with my phone trying to see which account I could get away with pulling a few more dollars from when suddenly she went quiet and started thanking someone like crazy.

I looked up to see her happily holding a hand full of tickets, so many tickets that it would take us the rest of the night of riding rides to use them all. My gaze rose to the crowd to try and see who the hell had just given her so many tickets when I saw Hitta's muscled back walking away from us. And just like always, the crowd just automatically parted for him.

Once again, I'd convinced myself that it was a coincidence and he was not following me. But I knew deep down that he was, which was confusing because he thought I dressed like a homeless person. Surely he wasn't attracted to me. So why else was he following me?

Anyway, I'd managed to avoid the gym and was doing a damn good job at it till today. Westly had been late on his half of the rent for the last three months and I'd had to pay the whole thing. Because of this, I'd fallen behind on a few things to do with my shop, like the insurance.

Well, actually I'd lapsed on my insurance policy a few times, but it had never been an issue till now. My shop is in a very old building, only God knows when the last time the electric wiring had been updated.

The fire started in the walls and did quite a bit of damage to my west wall. Because it happened during the time I'd let my insurance lapse, I was paying for the repairs out of pocket. With paying for that plus the rent on both the apartment and the shop, plus footing the bill for my niece's schooling, because neither of her parents could do it, and I didn't want her going to the school around her mother's house, because it was a death trap. Just last week, three kids had gotten shot standing in front of the school...

My money was extremely funny and for the life of me, I couldn't figure out why. The tea shop wasn't doing too badly. I was blocks away from a college campus, so I had a steady stream of customers... It was only me working there because I couldn't afford to hire anyone, so it wasn't like I was paying for labor...

And yet here I stood outside my brother's job broke and needing him to come through with some major funding.

It was bad...

Not only was my wall half repaired, but I was also behind on the rent for both the apartment and the shop…not to mention Jessie's tuition that will be due at the end of this month.

I paced back and forward in front of the gym, trying to work up enough nerves to go in. The members who went in and out looked at me as if something was wrong with me, but I didn't care, I was a nervous wreck.

What if he was in there?

What if he was standing right by the desk again?

After a group of three guys came out, I walked to the door and stood on my toes to try and look into the round window. I had to clutch the handle and try and hoist myself up because I was still too short to see.

As you guys may have guessed, I am vertically challenged in a world where everything was made for tall people. I think I stopped growing at twelve and a whopping 5'2.

My arms strained as I finally got myself up high enough to peep in the window and smiled when I saw he wasn't standing at the front desk. There was a pretty girl behind the cash register today.

A squeak left my throat when right then my arms gave out causing me to fall back. I braced myself for the impact with the ground, but it never happened.

I was caught by something hard, but it wasn't the ground. My eyes widened when I saw that the muscled arm that was wrapped around my waste shamelessly holding me against an equally muscled body, said Hard. The other arm slowly joined it securing me completely, said Hitta.

Dear God! I had fallen right into the brute's arms. For a moment I didn't move. He tightened his arms as he brought me even closer gently burying his face in my long braids at my neck. My lips parted in a gasp when I felt his mouth lightly brush my skin.

The caress was barely there, but because I was super sensitive in that moment, I'd felt it. His lips made their way up to my ear.

"Man, shawty…I want to f*** you so bad." He whispered.

His words that should have angered me caused an answering response in my center that surprised me.

The emotions that were racing around inside of me were all brand new and for just a moment, I paused to try and understand them.

Arousal I understood. Although it was true, I'd never felt it to this extent, it was a feeling I understood. It was the other thing he caused me to feel that stunned me.

It felt really good being held in his arms. The top of my feet rested on his bigger ones… For the first time in my life, I felt… safe.

I know I said earlier that Westly always protected me and he did, but his protection was as shaky as him. Even though he protected me from Kirk, I was still afraid. I was always afraid. The feeling that I felt now was different.

I felt safety in Hard Hitta's arms. That thought frightened me right out of the stupor I had fallen in and I scrambled away from him.

"I'm so sorry!" I told him staring at the ground because I was not brave enough to look into his face.

"You looking for somebody?" His voice was so very deep.

I nodded pushing the braid that had fallen in my face back behind my ear. "Yeah, my brother."

"Why?"

That made me look up at him startled. I can't believe how rude he is. I opened my mouth to tell him off but changed my mind. Instead, I cleared my throat.

"Nothing important, I just have to tell him something."

He took a step closer to me and I took another step back.

"This the only time I'm going to let you lie to me. Consider this a warning. You lie to me again and I will have to punish you. You hear?"

He growled those words at me. And I'm not going to lie, they scared the hell out of me. He'd just threatened to punish me. What the hell did that mean?

He is so freaking mean!

Not able to take his intense angry gaze any longer, I turned my head and nodded, looking at the cars that were passing. He was too intimidating. And to top it off, he was not moving to walk away, not getting the picture that I didn't want to talk to him about it. He just stood patiently waiting for me to tell him my business.

Tough Titty…I ain't telling him nothing. I may not be brave enough to tell him off to his face, but I can give the silent treatment like nobody's business.

I folded my arms and looked down at my foot that I was using to gently kick a rock around. He chuckled before his muscled arm came toward me. I jumped away from him as if he was holding hot coals, but exhaled in relief when I saw he was only opening the door. He held it open for me and gestured for me to proceed.

I did so quickly, practically running to the counter to ask the pretty girl if she could tell my brother I was here to see him, but she was only half listening to me. Her attention was on the big man that had followed me in.

He walked behind the counter and picked up a pile of mail and began to look through it. He must have just gotten here because he carried a gym bag on his arm. She walked over to him and began to tell him something with a big flirty smile on her face, but he stopped her.

"Get over there and help the lady standing there?" He grumbled in his truly rude fashion.

She turned red with embarrassment, for just a moment her mouth opened as if she couldn't believe he'd talked to her that way. There was no doubt in my mind they were sleeping together.

"I'm sorry, how can I help you?" She nearly snapped those words to me. She was not happy with me.

Great! Now she hated me because of him. I smiled kindly at her, hoping to extend an olive branch. I didn't want to make anything tough around here for Westly. He was doing so good.

"Yes, may I speak with Westly Baker, please?" I repeated for the second time.

She rolled her eyes and walked away to get him. This time I will not make the same mistake and stand here to be harassed by the mean guy. I turned and walked back out the door, Westly will know to look for me outside.

A few minutes later he came out. "What's going on, baby girl?"

I groaned because he was high. I really wished he was sober so that he can know the severity of my words.

"West, I need your rent money for the last three months. Ms. Armstrong came by the shop again today. She's threatening to put me out. Although the fire happened because of the wiring in her building, she still blaming me. She wants me gone! With me not having her rent money, this will be just the excuse she needs to put me out! West, you know I will go crazy if I lose my shop! Working with my teas is the only thing that brings me comf---"

"Whoa! Whoa! Whoa! Angel, Damn! Calm down!" He took my arm and pulled me away from the gym doors. "Just relax, I'm going to have the money for you tonight."

Y'all see what I mean? That was the drug talking.

I folded my arms across my chest. "Westly, I'm serious!"

He chuckled, his eyes blinked so slowly it looked as if he was going to nod off any second. "And I'm serious too, baby girl. I'm going to have the money tonight."

"Where you gon' get that kind of money from?"

"A patna of mine just got back into town. He owes me some money from a job he and I did a few years ago."

See what I'm saying? I was in no mood for his crap. My brother may not steal from me, but he had no problem lying to me.

"Westly, don't you understand what I'm saying?! I'm getting ready to lose my shop!"

"Hey! You ain't gon' lose nothing! Don't I always come through? Now I told ya, a patna of mine is going to drop off a package to me tonight. I'm going to bring it home, just relax. You'll be able to pay Ms. Armstrong worrisome a** in the morning."

I gave him a long look. He smiled at me with droopy eyes. "Relax…"

Note From Edwina Fort

Thank you guys so much for reading Falling For Rome. Please join my mailing list at https://authoredwinafort.com/ so that you can stay abreast of all the new and fun things we have going on...like The Love Chronicles.

The Love Chronicles are free love stories that are my gift to you for being so awesome! A new episode is added every week. You guys don't want to miss this!

The free stories in the Love Chronicles will also answer many questions some of you have about mysterious characters. Those who follow my work know that there are only 360 degrees of separation. Each story adds another piece to the puzzle.

Be the first to collect all the pieces and solve the riddle....

Happy Reading, family!!!!

P.S. If my stories make an impact on you and they leave you feeling good down on the inside...Please pay it forward. Go out there and make somebody else's day. It doesn't matter who or how much. You'd be amazed at how far a simple act of kindness can go and how much of an impact it can make on someone's life. Just sow love. We're in desperate need...

About the Author

Author Edwina Fort is a writer who writes with a passion and purpose. She was born and raised in Chicago, but now resides in the South. Although she is new to many, this author has been writing for many years and has given her unique style of writing away freely at no cost to those who would receive. Her passion for writing came about at an early age and developed into what it is today based on her experience and life lessons. With her stories, she wants to redefine all that we've been taught to believe and shed light on our truths and potential. Writing is her calling and she wants to share that gift with you through the pages of her work. Each book will take you on a memorable journey you will find hard to forget.